NO ROOM FOR GOOD MEN

First paperback edition November 2018

www.indiecrime.com
Facebook.com/ChrisCulverBooks

NO ROOM FOR GOOD MEN

An Ash Rashid novel

BY

CHRIS CULVER

ST. LOUIS, MO

Other books by Chris Culver

To my wife.

Prologue

May 28, 2006

According to our dispatcher, a homeless guy named Biscuits found the bodies while searching a park for cigarette butts with a little tobacco still left on the end. He puked, but he managed to do it out of the way, near the picnic tables. A lot of witnesses puked when they found mangled bodies, but very few were considerate enough to avoid doing it where people would walk. Even before I met him, I liked Biscuits.

Unfortunately, I didn't care too much for our first responders. By the time they arrived, rats had already begun nibbling on our victim's soft flesh, obscuring the full extent of their injuries and carrying parts of our crime scene to the far-flung corners of the neighborhood and sewage system. Our officers couldn't do anything to prevent that, so I didn't blame them, of course. One of them, though, decided to spit out his gum about two feet from our bodies. Not only did that contaminate our crime scene, it called our basic competence into question. If one of our officers contaminated the crime scene once, a defense attorney would argue, who's to say we didn't screw up a lot more? That one mistake would cost everyone working that case grief.

Olivia, my partner, got out of our cruiser first. She wore a tailored, light gray blazer, white silk shirt and a pair of jeans that hugged her very long legs. A tie held most of her blonde hair back from her face, but a few strands fell over her cheeks and blew in the morning breeze. She tucked the strays behind her ear and nodded in my direction, allowing me to see her strong cornflower blue eyes. When my colleagues first heard that I had been assigned to work with a female detective, many of them laughed and wished me luck, exhibiting the misogyny so common in police bullpens. Even I had felt nervous, but then I worked a couple of cases with her and found that my supervisor had done me a favor. Olivia was as driven, intelligent, and skilled as anyone with whom I had ever worked. I would have taken her over almost anyone in the building.

"You ever worked in this neighborhood?" she asked as I stepped out of my side of the car. We had parked in front of an abandoned firehouse. The mortar had begun to crumble near the foundation, loosening the brickwork and causing the building to sag in the center. Before time had pitted its stonework and vandals had broken its windows, I'd bet that firehouse looked grand, a point of pride in a neighborhood full of working class men and women. Now, like the neighborhood around it, time and circumstance had ravaged its exterior and left it a shell of what it once was.

"Unfortunately," I said. "Two drive-by homicides and a couple of domestic assaults. Last I heard, Gangster Disciples claimed the area."

Olivia nodded. "We'll bring Gang Intel in on this, then, and see if they've heard anything about a shooting."

We walked in unison toward the crime scene. Flashing blue and white police lights lit the park so brightly I could probably have read by them. If I closed my eyes, I could almost imagine them as carnival lights. In a better neighborhood, the kids who lived nearby might have seen those bright flashes through muslin draperies and fallen back asleep, dreaming of walking along the midway and eating funnel cakes or elephant ears. Here, though, the kids had no illusions about those lights. They knew what they'd find when they woke the next morning: a dead classmate; a dead sibling or parent; a dead neighbor if they were lucky; a future absence and ever-present reminder of the world in which they lived.

Though our killer had dumped the bodies amidst waist-high weeds near the jungle gym in the center of the park, the first officers on the scene had set up a makeshift command post beneath a covered awning and picnic area along the park's exterior.

"You working this case, Ash?"

A stocky officer about my age called out from a position to my left. I nodded a greeting to him but didn't stop walking toward the command post. He apparently interpreted that as an invitation to join me. The nameplate on his chest read Smith. He slowed as we walked and checked Olivia out from behind before raising his eyebrows at me and mouthing *nice*.

"I'm the primary detective," I said. "My partner, the woman you just checked out, is Detective Olivia Rhodes."

"Dude. . ." said my new friend, stopping and spreading his arms wide as if I had offended him. Olivia pretended not to hear, but I could see her smiling. I walked a couple of paces and then turned to him.

"Come on," I said, waving him forward. "At least tell me what's going on."

Officer Smith jogged to catch up. "We've got a bunch of bodies. I don't know what the dispatcher told you, but the guy who called this in is looney tunes. Called us out a couple of weeks ago because he thought aliens were abducting dogs from his neighborhood. Ten to one, he killed these four beaners because he thought they were from Mars or something."

I stopped walking again and tried to get a read on him. He gave me a blank, vapid stare.

"It's dark out, so you probably can't see me too well," I said, after some thought, "but I'm brown. Like our victims."

He narrowed his eyebrows. "You're an Arab, though,

aren't you? You're not Mexican, I mean."

I ignored him and started walking. Ignorance I could correct, but no amount of teaching could cure stupidity. The officer took the hint that I no longer wanted to talk to him and resumed his post along the crime scene's exterior. When I arrived at the picnic area, Olivia had begun talking to a middle-aged officer with dark—almost black—skin and sergeant stripes on his shoulders. His hair hugged his scalp so tightly that it almost looked as if someone had drawn it on, but he smiled as I neared, and it seemed genuine. At four in the morning, I appreciated a friendly face.

"Detective," he said, nodding to me. "I see you met our resident buffoon."

"Yeah," I said, glancing over my shoulder in the direction the officer had disappeared. "Good luck with him."

"Oh, as it turns out," said the sergeant, smiling, "you're the one who's in luck. Tim's uncle is on the city council, and he told me just today that he wants to become a homicide detective. You might have just talked to your new partner."

Having a powerful family member was one way to get a promotion. It also explained why so many of our administrators were complete assholes. I looked over my shoulder at the officer again before looking back to the sergeant.

"What's your name, by the way?" I asked. "So I know who to thank in case Detective Smith joins us."

The sergeant laughed again. "Art Rogers."

"Well, Art Rogers," I said, nodding toward the jungle gym and the bodies hidden beneath it. What have we got?"

Rogers reached to his utility belt and removed a legal notepad. As he spoke, the smile disappeared from his face, replaced by the stern countenance of a man accustomed to delivering somber news.

"Call to 911 came in about 3:00AM. Dispatcher said the caller slurred his words and sounded scared. He claimed he saw demons dump a couple of bodies out of a van in the park and then drive away."

I knew the time of the call before we came, but the demon comment gave me pause. Up until the early seventies, the government ran long-term mental care facilities for schizophrenics and others with serious mental illnesses. Now, with powerful and inexpensive antipsychotic drugs readily available and with budgets declining, the feds and the state had both gotten out of the mental health business, releasing a lot of men and women who would otherwise spend their lives in padded rooms. Most patients probably functioned well with a little freedom, but some couldn't handle it. The streets and our prisons had become the new dumping ground for the mentally ill. Unfortunately, if our 911 caller had a mental illness, we couldn't call him to testify in court even if he saw the murder from start to finish. I almost swore under my breath.

"Aside from the fact that he sees demons, what do we know about the caller?" asked Olivia, squinting in the harsh glare of the revolving blue and white lights.

Rogers sighed and then looked around for a moment. "Guy's real name is Jerome Patterson, but everybody calls him Biscuits. I see him every couple of days. Reminds me of my Uncle. He came back from Viet Nam kind of screwed up, too."

I wrote a few things down and then glanced up. "Biscuits is a vet?"

"Yeah," said Rogers. "Social worker from the VA comes by a couple of times a year, but Biscuits doesn't want help. Nothing you can do for a guy who thinks nothing's wrong with him. He lives in a boarded up house on 29th with a couple of other homeless men."

Olivia cleared her throat. "Think you can find him for us?"

Rogers looked over his shoulder and pointed toward the line of police cruisers parked on the curb up the street. "No need to find him because he's in the car with one of my officers. But, look, Biscuits is skittish. He's not going to talk to just anybody, and he's not going to talk at all until we get him some spaghetti."

"Spaghetti have significance for him?" I asked, confused.

"Guy's hungry," said Rogers, shrugging. "He asked for spaghetti as soon as we picked him up."

I nodded and smiled just a little. Olivia didn't look amused.

"What's your feeling on him?" she asked.

Rogers drew in a deep breath and then shook his head. "He's not good for this killing, if that's what you're asking. We've picked him up a couple of times for petty theft, but nothing violent. I've never even heard him raise his voice."

And presumably Rogers would have said something if he found blood on Biscuits' clothes.

"What do the neighbors say?" I asked.

Rogers panned his gaze to the nearby houses. "We knocked on the doors and handed out business cards, but nobody wanted to talk to us."

That was typical for the neighborhood. If the wrong person saw a resident talking to the police, bad things happened. Hopefully, somebody would give us a call and set up an appointment for a more private conversation.

"Biscuits wants spaghetti, huh?" I asked, reaching to my wallet. I pulled out a twenty and my business card. "How about you take him out for breakfast on my dime?"

Rogers took the money and my card and then raised

his eyebrows. "He really wants spaghetti."

"The Olive Garden is closed at four in the morning. He'll take bacon and eggs."

Rogers nodded and pocketed the money. "I'll see what we can do. Once he's done, you want us to bring him back here?"

"If he's sober and coherent. If he's not, arrest him for public intoxication and let him sober up in a box downtown. We'll see what he has to say once he's clean."

"You're the boss," said Rogers. "Have a good one, Detectives."

"Enjoy your breakfast," I said.

Sergeant Roberts left us, and I glanced toward the bodies.

"Let's go see some corpses," I said.

Olivia and I headed toward the jungle gym. Tall weeds crowded the base, preventing me from seeing the victims. But as the breeze shifted, I caught the fetid odor of blood and feces so common around the recently murdered. As we walked, an older heavyset man ducked beneath the yellow police tape demarcating the edge of the active crime scene from the rest of the park. Ringlets of white hair clung to his forehead with perspiration, while his black Coroner's office jumpsuit hung off his body like a second, loose skin.

"Detective Rashid," he said, looking to me and then to Olivia. "Detective Rhodes. You guys look well."

"Thanks, Doc," I said. "What have we got?"

"Body parts galore," he said, fanning himself with his hands. He looked at me. "How's the wife?"

He wanted to make small talk. I hated small talk.

"Still pregnant."

Dr. Garner started walking toward the bodies but looked over his shoulder at me. "You thought of names yet?"

"Megan Aliza Rashid," I said. Garner nodded, mulling

it over and seemingly approving. Olivia, meanwhile, put a hand on my forearm and furrowed her brow.

"Aliza?" she asked. "What happened to Megan Olivia?"

"Should have told you earlier. Sorry," I said, smiling apologetically. "When I told my brother-in-law we planned to name the baby after you, he assumed you and I were sleeping together and then told my mosque that I would very shortly be taking a second wife. Hannah and I thought it best to change it."

Olivia tilted her head to the side. "That's quite an assumption."

"Nassir's quite an ass," I said.

Garner turned to me. "Are second wives a common Muslim thing?"

"I'm pretty sure if I broached the subject of a second wife with my wife, she'd murder me in my sleep. So no. Let's try to focus on the bodies, please."

Garner nodded again and turned toward the jungle gym, but I overheard him mutter something about *crazy foreigners* as he walked. When we reached the bodies, I stopped immediately and closed my eyes to utter a quick *dua*, a prayer, for strength. The dispatcher warned me that we had a gruesome scene, but she left out an important fact.

"Nobody said they were kids," I said, opening my eyes.

"Old enough to pick up guns and shoot somebody," said Garner.

I glanced at him. "You found gunshot residue on their hands?"

"No," he admitted, shrugging. "But in this neighborhood? These kids have guns somewhere."

He may have been right, but I didn't plan to say that.

"What can you tell me about them without speculating?"

"We've got four victims, sixteen to twenty-four years old each, give or take. Light brown skin, likely Hispanic. Lividity and liver temp indicate time of death occurred five to seven hours ago. Didn't happen here, either."

Garner walked toward the bodies and knelt beside them. Then he wiped sweat from his forehead with the sleeve of his jumpsuit.

"As far as wounds, what you see is what you've got," he said, pointing to a jagged, red welt about three inches long across the leftmost victim's forehead. "Two of the victims have lacerations across their scalp lines or above their eyes. Could be caused by a closed first, could be caused by a club. We'll know more once I x-ray the skulls to see underlying damage."

He pointed lower to the nearest victim's cheek and nose. One eye had swollen shut, while the other had nearly popped out of his head. "This guy very likely has a broken orbital socket. Even if he had lived and received proper medical treatment, it's questionable that he'd be able to see again. Other victims have sustained similar injuries. There are indications that they occurred prior to death."

Garner pulled a pair of latex gloves from his pockets and snapped them on before reaching to the victim's lips and spreading them apart to reveal multiple gaping wounds in the gums.

"The teeth on all four victims have been pulled."

"Peri or postmortem?" asked Olivia.

Garner planted a foot on the ground and lumbered upright. "Before death, at least on John Doe number one. Others, I haven't examined that closely."

"Somebody tortured these guys," I said, looking at the bodies.

"I can't say that officially, but looks that way," said Garner, stepping beside the body and pointing toward a welt across the chest. "We have ligature marks across the chest, wrists, and ankles. Marks across the chest are rough and uneven, possibly the result of a braided rope. The wounds on the legs and ankles have a much cleaner edge, possibly indicative of a zip tie or handcuffs. Again, we'll know more when we can perform a closer examination in controlled conditions."

I took a breath. "Okay. Go on."

Garner walked toward the nearest victim's chest and then, once again, knelt down. He gently picked up the victim's arm by the elbow and forearm. A stump hung off the end where the hand should have been.

"As you can see," said Garner, "our killer removed the hands and feet. The wound isn't clean, so our cutting tool is likely pretty dull. Might even be a power tool like a reciprocating saw. I'll have a closer look at the bones when I can."

Whatever our victims did, they died in agony, taking their major identifying marks with them to the grave.

"Tattoos?" I asked.

"Two victims have ink," said Garner. "John Doe number two has a crucifix tattooed on his left scapula. John Doe number three has some kind of symbol on his right deltoid. I'm told it looks Aztec."

"Make sure you get pictures of those," said Olivia. "What happened to their genitals?"

"Removed," said Garner. "Twig and berries both. Can't say I've seen that too often."

As if pulling their teeth didn't send enough of a message. Sometimes I wondered what kind of world my wife and I intended to bring a child into. Olivia looked over her shoulder to the nearest uniformed officer. He jogged toward us.

"Did you guys find our victims' clothes anywhere?" she asked.

The officer shook his head. "Sergeant Rogers had us look around the park and neighborhood, but no."

"Did you go through the trash cans?" I asked.

The officer hesitated and then licked his lips. "Unless it's on the curb, don't I need a warrant for that?"

I glanced at my watch. "It's four in the morning. Nobody's out. Get a couple of guys and be quiet. You find anything, carry the can to the curb and take a picture of it."

"Okay," he said. He looked unsure, but he nodded anyway. "We'll do it quietly."

"Good," I said. Obviously, the officer didn't like the order, but he didn't question it. I didn't relish breaking the rules, but sometimes expediency trumped virtue. Once the officer disappeared, I looked at Dr. Garner. "You have an idea of when you can start cutting?"

The doctor hemmed and hawed. "We've got a couple of bodies on the slab. Might be a while."

I figured as much. Even as horrific as these murders looked, we had minority victims in a gang neighborhood, dead probably as the result of their own criminal activity. Nobody would fast track this case because nobody with any real power to make a difference in the world cared about our victims. To all the world, these guys didn't count.

Even though we came into the case at the end of a shift, Olivia and I worked for the next forty-eight hours straight, barely stopping to eat or sleep. After those first two days, we worked sixteen-hour shifts for the next week. We conducted over a hundred interviews, we held a press conference requesting the public's assistance, we visited every tattoo parlor in Indianapolis, and we called almost every tattoo artist in the state. We did our absolute best for those kids, but we never even ID'd them. When I wrote my final report on the eighth day of our investigation, temporarily closing it pending new developments, I had no idea that the case would haunt me for the next decade.

Or that I would see that murderer's handiwork again.

Chapter 1

Present Day

Aleksander didn't plan to wait long. Already, most of the neighbors had returned home from work. The few who hadn't arrived yet—doctors and lawyers, mostly—could stay away for hours more. He took a risk completing a job during the day, but everything worth doing required risk. Kristen Tanaka had to die. The others did, too. His family's life depended on that.

Aleksander drew a long, deep breath and adjusted himself on the leather seat. The Mercedes he had stolen for the job smelled like cigarettes, but no one would look at it askance in this neighborhood. If anyone saw him, they would see a white man in a sport coat in an expensive car in an upper middle-class neighborhood. He fit in well. No one would remember him.

His firearm, a Smith & Wesson .22-caliber revolver, weighed heavily in his pocket against his thigh. The young man he purchased it from had bought it new from a gun shop in upstate New York. He grew uncomfortable with it and decided to sell it when his toddler started showing an interest in it. Having children of his own, Aleksander understood the man's trepidation. He didn't feel comfortable with a firearm at home, either, and bought a new one for each job. Those that he had already used, he destroyed. It was better for everybody that way.

He took a deep breath and settled into the seat. Aleksander had worked in Indianapolis before, but only once. He had dumped the bodies of four young men in a park in a very public confirmation of punishment for prior misdeeds. The client had wanted them tortured. Aleksander didn't know why, and he didn't ask. In his world, reasons didn't matter. If someone wanted a job done a certain way and had the money to pay for it, Aleksander complied. It was business.

No one had paid him to kill Kristen Tanaka, though. In fact, he hadn't worked in years. He no longer needed the money. At forty-four, Aleksander had gone straight. He now owned one of the most successful carpet importing businesses on the east coast and acted as the exclusive distributor for carpet weavers in Turkey, Iran, Afghanistan and half a dozen other countries. Every Monday morning when he received new inventory, designers literally lined up outside his Brooklyn warehouse. Ms. Tanaka had become a threat to his new life. He didn't want to kill her, but he didn't have a choice.

From his vantage point on the street, he could just barely see her through the diaphanous white drapes covering her front window. She sat alone at her dining room table, very likely pouring over her fan mail. Left to her own devices, she'd eventually receive a job offer at CNN or one of the other major news networks and leave Indianapolis behind. She certainly had the ambition if not the talent. Unfortunately for her, that day would never come.

After ten more minutes of waiting, he spotted movement inside. Tanaka left the table and walked deeper into the house, possibly to the living room or the kitchen. Though he didn't intend to spend much time inside, Aleksander knew the layout. The first floor had a master bedroom suite, kitchen, dining room, office and family room. The second floor held three additional bedrooms and two full bathrooms, enough space for Aleksander's entire extended family. How one person used all that room, he couldn't say.

The street felt absolutely still and quiet. Aside from the wind, nothing and no one moved. Time to work. Aleksander opened his door and stepped out into the warm evening air. The cotton of his new, light blue Oxford shirt chaffed against his skin as he walked down Tanaka's driveway to her front door. In ideal circumstances, he would give his clothes to a homeless person once he finished with them—no sense in wasting a perfectly fine, warm garment—but that depended on him getting away cleanly. Any blood on the outfit meant he would burn it.

Aleksander had killed fourteen people in his career. Drug dealers, murderers, thieves, each one deserved the fate that befell him. As he walked to Kristen Tanaka's door, Aleksander felt something stir inside him, something he had never felt before a job. Kristin Tanaka had flaws, as everyone did, but she hadn't killed anyone or sold poison on the streets. Though she had sinned, she didn't deserve to die. This one would hurt. They all would hurt this time.

Kristen poured herself a glass of wine, sat at the dining room table, and organized her hate mail. Some weeks that took just a few minutes, enough time to read a handful of letters and assign them a score based on whether she knew the author personally, whether the letter included a threat, or whether the author seemed to know information about her personal life. Other weeks, especially when she broke a major story, the process could take hours.

This week's haul felt thin. Most people vented their rage through email, although some enterprising viewers chose to send physical letters to the station. Often times those came with little extras: bags of feces, crude drawings of penises, once even a dead gerbil. After the gerbil, the station started providing the interns latex gloves. That cut down on the complaints, but it didn't teach the interns the lesson they needed to learn: if you wanted to report the news, sometimes you had to get your hands dirty. Every time the mailroom received a new box of gloves, Kristen threw them away. The kids needed to learn.

She sipped her wine and picked up the first letter in the pile. One of the interns had printed it out for her and highlighted the pertinent parts. The writer called her a bitch and asked that she repent and give her life over to Jesus. Kristen didn't recognize the writer's name, and he made no allusions to knowing where she lived. Harmless crank, that letter went into the lowest threat category. The next several letters included similar language about various aggrievements she supposedly visited on the city. All scored a one on her scale, and all went into her filing cabinet, where they would likely gather dust for the next three years before she recycled them. Not a bad week.

Kristen's boyfriend thought she took the threats too lightly, but she didn't take them lightly at all. Though she put it in a drawer in an end table beside her bed when she came home, she carried a black Glock 19 firearm whenever she left her station. The textured grip fit her hand well, and she could slip it into a waistband holster behind her without anyone knowing she carried a firearm. Twice a month she put forty rounds through it at an indoor shooting range downtown. If she ever had the need, she could empty an entire magazine of nine-millimeter rounds into an assailant's chest at twenty paces in less than four seconds. Kristen didn't carry a weapon to show off; she carried it to eliminate threats should any arise.

At the moment, she sat in her dining room with her back to the entryway and front door. The afternoon sun had already gone down, leaving the room gloomy and dark. Days like today, she liked the gloom. It fit her mood.

She took another drink. The home's first owner had stenciled the word *EAT* on the wall in a curly script. Inspired, she purchased a stencil with a similar font and painted *CRAP* on the wall in her basement bathroom shortly after moving in. Her upwardly mobile friends would come over and wrinkle their nose when they saw her dining room, but they'd never say anything until she directed them to the basement downstairs. Then, once they closed the door and saw her hand-painted sign, they'd laugh uproariously, sharing in her joke on the provincial taste of Indianapolis's upper middle-class.

Kristen drained her wine glass and poured herself another. She shouldn't have to spend a Friday evening—her only night of the week off—alone. At thirty, she still had her figure, and she knew men found her attractive. For the past five years running, a men's lifestyle magazine had even named her to its list of ten hottest newscasters in the United States. Brad, her boyfriend, supposedly planned to come over when he finished work, but she suspected he'd call and make an excuse.

"Sorry, honey, but a patient went into labor. I had to stay with her."

Never mind that his hospital had nearly a dozen other obstetricians, not to mention their residents, who could deliver a baby. Never mind that Brad had cancelled their last two dates at the last minute because of work. Brad was a good man, and they loved each other, but lately she had found herself wondering if that was enough. Neither of them wanted children or a family, but she needed someone dependable in her life. She deserved someone who came home at the end of the day instead of sleeping in his office three nights out of five.

Resigned to spending the evening alone, Kristen took her wine to the living room, curled up on the couch, and turned on Netflix. Before she could get her show started, the front doorbell rang. Her disappointment disappeared, replaced by something very nearly approximating giddiness. She loosened her robe so that it exposed her belly and chest but still covered her breasts—barely. Brad may have spent the day looking at women, but he wouldn't mind one more, especially one who let him do much more than merely look.

"Coming, honey," she said, walking through the kitchen and the front hallway. Behind the front door's frosted glass, she could see her boyfriend's obscured form in the fading sunlight. He'd probably need a shower right after work, and she wouldn't mind joining him. After they worked up a sweat together, they'd order takeout Chinese. They both deserved a night like that.

Before opening the door, she stopped and considered how quickly she wanted the night to progress. On one side of her lived an elderly couple who spent winters in Florida. She hadn't seen them since Christmas several months ago. On the other side of her lived a couple with two young boys. The wife was a bitch who was having an affair with her personal trainer, but her husband seemed nice enough. She didn't care if either of them saw her, and the boys needed to learn the difference between men and women eventually anyway. She undid the knot on her robe, allowing the silk tie to brush against her knees and the silk to part and expose every bit of her to the afternoon air. Already, an excited chill traveled up her spine.

"Hello, sweetheart," she said, unbolting the lock and throwing open the door. She didn't see Brad staring back; instead, she saw a nightmare. Before she could scream, she heard a crack and felt a blow to her chest. She fell into the hallway behind her, her head tilted toward her dining room. Her lungs felt heavy as they filled with blood. Her vision began to swim and become blurry and then black. The last thing she saw was that damn sign.

EAT.

Why she hadn't painted over it yet, she couldn't say.

Chapter 2

The surveillance started a week ago. The men and women watching us could have passed for   accountants or grocery store clerks. They looked normal. That was the most surreal part of it. They came after a local politician called on the community to start monitoring Muslim families in the city for fear that we would start blowing things up. At the end of his speech, that politician held up his hands and said, "I swear to God, I don't want to hurt anybody if I don't have to, but we need to know who these people are so we can kill them before they kill us."

My parents came from Egypt, and my wife's parents came from Turkey and Iran. We didn't look like our neighbors. Nobody cared in the past, but now the world had changed. We hadn't seen anything like this before. My wife and kids were scared, and I was getting very tired of it.

"Can I do it now, *Baba*?" asked Kaden.

I took my eyes from the surveillance vehicle and looked at my son. He had straight black hair and my wife's big, brown eyes as well as her olive-colored skin. His nose, his thin lips and his ears that stuck out from his head just a little more than they ought, he had gotten from me. Kaden had just turned five, and I had given him a set of child-sized hand tools—a small finishing hammer, safety glasses, screwdriver, and a measuring tape —for his birthday. He could only use them with my supervision, and they stayed in the garage at all times, but he liked them and I liked spending time with him. We were in my garage with the door open, building his mother a picture frame.

"Of course," I said, handing him the frame and

smiling. "You hold onto this. I need to get something."

"When are we going to paint it?"

"Tomorrow," I said, grabbing a tube of wood glue. "We need to let the glue dry overnight."

The phone in the kitchen started ringing almost before the words left my mouth. I helped push the pieces of the frame together and then secured them with a clamp. As Kaden wiped away glue that had squeezed out of the joints, the phone rang a second time. Hannah and I rarely received calls on that line, but we kept it for emergencies. It was probably just a telemarketer, but my gut began to tighten anyway. As the lieutenant in charge of Indianapolis's Major Case Squad, I got calls when people died. I excused myself from my son and began to walk inside.

My wife must have gotten the phone because she met me in the laundry room that served as our mudroom. Wafting behind her from the kitchen, I could smell oregano, lemon, and some kind of roasting meat. Hannah smiled a half smile at me. Her olive-colored skin had a glow to it that matched the twinkle in her eyes. She wore hijab in public, but not at home. Her hair had just begun to come back in. She looked beautiful and alive.

Six months ago, doctors diagnosed Hannah with grade 2 invasive ductal carcinoma, a type of breast cancer. Hannah's mother died at forty-nine of breast cancer that metastasized to her lungs. We didn't know the particulars, but her grandmother had died of it before that. Though we caught Hannah's cancer early, it scared us. Thankfully, medicine had come a long way since she lost her mom.

Doctors performed a lumpectomy and then gave her three months of adjuvant chemotherapy after surgery to keep her cancer from recurring elsewhere in her body. The chemo made her hair fall out, but she was in remission.

When she handed me the phone, I reached out and

touched her elbow, grateful to still have her in my life. Prior to her illness, I never gave my wife's mortality any thought. She had always been there. I had never considered that I could lose her. After finding out she had cancer, work didn't seem as important, and my projects around the house stopped mattering. All that I cared about was spending as much time with her and the kids as I could. It should have been like that all along.

"It's Mike Bowers," she said. "He said it was important."

Captain Bowers was my commanding officer and the supervisor of the Indianapolis Metropolitan Police Department's Crimes against person's division. Though I had worked with Mike for years, I had only begun reporting directly to him a couple of months ago. He and I didn't agree on everything, but I liked working for him. He worked hard to get me the resources necessary to do my job, and then he stayed out of my way. Usually, I couldn't ask for more.

"Thanks, sweetheart," I said, taking the phone. "Dinner smells good."

She looked past me toward the garage. "What are you guys working on in there?"

"It's a secret," I said, winking.

She looked over my shoulder. "Kaden, honey, what are you working on?"

"A picture frame!" he shouted back.

Hannah focused on me again. "No one keeps secrets from *Ummi*. Let this be a lesson, grasshopper."

My wife had a gift for telling stories. On our first date, I laughed so hard that my sides hurt the next day. She was even better with our kids, telling them stories as good as anything they could find in the library. Now, she wrote humorous mystery novels for a living and made more money than I ever would as a civil servant. As much as I loved the stories she told, though, her taste in television and movies—the stories she loved to experience—were rarely in line with my own.

"You've been watching reruns of *Kung Fu* again, haven't you?"

She looked at me straight in the eye, her countenance serious. "In one lifetime, a man knows many pleasures: a mother's smile in waking hours; a young woman's intimate, searing touch; and the laughter of grandchildren in the twilight years. To deny these in ourselves is to deny that which makes us one with nature."

"You could have just said yes," I said.

Her lips parted and then curled into a full smile that filled me with warmth. "Dinner will be in twenty minutes. Make sure Kaden washes his hands." She turned and walked away but paused and then looked over her shoulder. "And if you can make it home early, I'll make it worth your while once the kids to go sleep."

That was one other nice thing about our marriage recently: not only did I appreciate time with my wife and kids more, Hannah and I took advantage of our time away from the kids a lot more often. Since she finished her chemo and began to feel better, we've put a whole lot more miles on our mattress. Some days, I almost feel like a newlywed again.

"I'll do what I can," I said. She smiled again and closed the mudroom's door as I put the phone to my ear.

"Mike, it's Ash. What's going on?"

"We've got a case for you, and it could be a big one. Female victim in her late twenties to early thirties, shot three times in the chest and then twice in the head at close range. She's going to get a lot of media attention."

I nodded and lowered my voice so Kaden wouldn't hear. "We know who she is?"

Mike hesitated. "Kristen Tanaka. You two have a history, but you're Major Case and I need you to work this one."

Tanaka was a reporter with a local television station. Though she covered big stories now, she had started like all reporters do with the crappiest assignments her station bosses could dole out. I still remember seeing a young Kristen Tanaka sent out in the middle of the night during severe weather with nothing but a rain slicker for protection. Her hair would fly in her face, the rain would soak her and smear her makeup, and her poncho would whip around like a sail that had come loose in the middle of a hurricane. It almost seemed like a recurring gag on a sketch comedy show.

Then, she must have gotten a promotion because she started covering more serious stories, including crimes. I had never liked Kristen. She held grudges, she colored her reporting with dubious interpretations of events, and, on one occasion, I caught her breaking into a crime scene to cover a story. Every time she showed up to a scene, she made my job that much harder. I hated to think it, but a lot of men and women in my department would welcome news of her demise with cheer.

"Where is she?" I asked.

"Her house on Washington Boulevard. I'll text you the address. Paul Murphy's already there. Emilia Rios is on her way."

Even though I led the Major Case Squad, I had to steal officers from other units every time I caught a case. Bowers and I had pushed the administration to assign me a permanent rotation of investigators, but we still had a lot of red tape to hack through and an entire ocean of office politics to swim across before that happened. In the meantime, I had Paul and Emilia on loan when I needed them.

"I'll be there as soon as I can."

Bowers wished me luck and then hung up. I looked up and saw my little boy hanging his head.

"You're leaving, aren't you?" he asked, stepping off

the stool in front of my workbench.

I knelt down so I could look him in the eye. "Yeah. I've got to work, but I'll be back. We'll finish in a couple of days. The glue will be nice and dry by then."

He kept his arms to the sides and wouldn't look at me. As sad as he looked now, he'd walk inside and see a race car on the floor or a bucket of Legos on the counter and forget everything. I wished I had that same ability. For me, the pains and disappointments of the past were a lot harder to forget.

I put my hand on Kaden's upper back and led him inside the house. As predicted, he saw something more fun than me in the living room and sprinted away, his arms extended from his sides like an out-of-control airplane. I walked from the linoleum tile of our laundry room and stepped onto the porcelain tile of our kitchen and stopped. Hannah was just pulling a chicken from the oven.

"Looks like I picked up a case," I said. "It might be a big one, so I don't know when I'll be back."

She put dinner on the stovetop and then went to a cabinet for aluminum foil. "Try not to blow anything up. Things blow up around you."

"I'll do my best," I said. "Maybe when I get back, we can talk about Spring Break. It's eight months away, but I know you like to plan these things. I was thinking DC. I think Kaden would like the Air & Space Museum."

She cut a piece of foil from the roll and created a tent over the chicken before walking toward me and putting her arms around my lower back. Hannah rarely wore perfume, but her shampoo had lavender in it, making me think of her every time I saw the plant in someone's yard. I took a deep whiff and felt contentment flood through my body. I didn't want to leave.

"I like not worrying about the future," she said. She put a hand flat on my chest and smiled. "And the kids want to go to Disney World."

I smiled and squeezed her tight before letting go. "We'll see. I'd kind of like something with a little educational value."

"And that's why I'm the cool parent," she said, winking before she kissed me. "Come home safely tonight."

I told her I would before going upstairs to change into a white button-down shirt and gray herringbone suit —appropriate attire for appearing on television. When I got back downstairs, Hannah had just begun mashing potatoes. The kids sat around the dining table. Megan did her homework, while Kaden drew. I hugged my son and daughter and then kissed my wife.

"You guys listen to *Ummi* tonight, okay?" I asked, looking to each of my kids in turn.

"I will, *Baba*," said Kaden. He immediately turned his attention back to his drawing. Megan's gaze, though, lingered on me.

"Are you going to my soccer game tomorrow, Dad?"

I smiled and hoped it masked my grimace. For years, Megan had called me *Baba,* just like her brother. I didn't realize how much that had meant to me until she started calling me *dad* instead. My father was murdered before I was born, so I never met him. My mom never missed an opportunity to tell me about him, though. In every story, he was always *baba*, never Ashraf, his actual name, or even *daddy*. It was a simple word, but it spoke to where my family came from.

It wouldn't have bothered me if Megan had taken to calling me *dad* on her own, but someone else made that choice for her. At the end of the last school year, kids in her class started calling her *camel jockey*. The kids didn't understand what they were saying, so I didn't blame them. The people who taught their children that name, though, knew exactly what it meant. At that moment, Arabic left my daughter's vocabulary. Hannah became *mom*, and I became *dad*. Prejudice and hate weren't crimes, but they hurt just the same. I wished people would think about that before they repeated stupid jokes around their children.

"I'll do my best to go to your game," I said. "You be good. I've got to go catch some bad guys. I love everybody."

Before leaving, I went upstairs to my bedroom once again and opened the safe secured to floor joists in my closet. A lot of my colleagues went hunting with their kids, they subscribed to gun magazines, and they went to the firing range for fun. I had never found firearms that fascinating. After over a decade carrying a badge and gun, I had come to learn a few things.

My gun didn't keep me safe, it didn't keep my family safe, it didn't keep anyone safe. I wished we had something that could provide that kind of security, but the world didn't. Contrary to the marketing slogans of the gun lobby, my gun's sole reason for existing was to kill people. It made me more dangerous then the men and women I arrested.

I hoped and prayed no one would make me prove that anytime soon.

Chapter 3

I backed my car out of the garage and checked my text messages to get Kristen Tanaka's address. She lived on Washington Boulevard. It was one of the premiere streets in the city, the kind of place wealthy doctors and lawyers called home. Evidently, Kristen's station had paid her well.

I left my neighborhood and took Keystone Avenue south, passing shopping centers, country clubs, and seemingly endless stretches of housing developments before hitting the city. When I got to Kristen's address, I slowed and parked on the street behind a row of marked police cruisers.

Outside my car, mature trees on both sides of the road swayed in the breeze. Something was in bloom because I could smell flowers. Kristen owned a craftsman-style bungalow. The front porch ran the entire length of the house and opened onto the carport on the left side. Two rocking chairs and a swing swayed lazily in the breeze.

On any other late summer night, it would have felt tranquil, like a piece of a 1950's television sitcom had somehow become real. The police cruisers parked in front of the house and the coroner's van in the driveway spoiled that image.

I walked on the sidewalk toward the front porch. Paul Murphy stood outside, smoking a cigarette and talking to a uniformed officer. I nodded a greeting toward him, and he nodded back. I didn't have a lot of friends, but Paul was one of them. He had sallow, gray skin and teeth like off-white breath mints. On those occasions he smiled, it reached his entire face. For the past year or so, his wife and doctor had put him on a diet and exercise regimen, and he had probably lost seventy pounds. If they could get him to stop smoking, he might be around to watch his granddaughter graduate high school in fifteen years. For his sake, I hoped that happened.

"What have we got?" I asked.

"Unless you've got Jesus in your basement, we got a dead lady," said Paul, taking a long drag on his cigarette. "You got Jesus in your basement?"

"Nope."

"Then we've got a dead lady," he said, tossing his cigarette to the front walkway and grinding it beneath his heel. The officer he had been talking to held out a log-sheet for me. I signed my name and rank and thanked him before returning his clipboard.

Paul walked toward the front door, where a group of uniformed officers had gathered to watch the coroner work. I followed a few steps back. Kristen Tanaka lay on her back about three feet from the entryway. She had long black hair splayed out around her head and light brown skin accentuated by a light pink lipstick and tasteful makeup around her eyes. She had a crooked half-smile on her lips. A silk robe hung on her shoulders, and a fleece blanket soaked through with blood covered her torso from her chest to her legs.

As much as she had rankled me when she was alive, Kristen didn't deserve to die like this.

"Okay," I said, looking to Paul. "Tell me about the scene. Who put the blanket on her?"

"Presumably our killer," said Paul, pulling a notepad from the inside pocket of his jacket. "We got the first phone call at 6:03 PM this evening. A neighbor two houses down heard gunshots, but she didn't see anything. We got a second call at 6:04 PM from a caller about a block away to say he heard gunshots. The dispatcher sent two officers out. Officer Stacey Prisco was the first person on scene here. When she saw Kristen's body, she walked through the house to make sure the shooter had left. Once she cleared the place, she called her supervisor. Prisco claims she didn't touch the body or anything inside the house."

I nodded and glanced toward the tech from the coroner's office. "Lift the blanket for me, would you?"

She did as I asked. A silk robe covered Kristen's shoulders but left the rest of her body nude and open to the night air. Blood obscured most of her chest, but she had three distinct entry wounds clustered within a two-inch square. Even at a short distance, it was very good shooting.

"So we're looking at three to the chest and one to the head?" I asked.

"It's probably two in the head," said the coroner's technician. She gently tilted Kristen's head to give me a better view, but I couldn't see anything through the mass of blood and hair. I stepped back to better see the entryway. The front door had a frosted glass insert. Kristen would have seen a figure though the glass, but the frosting would have hidden the details. She wouldn't have come to the door with her robe open for the mailman or a door-to-door salesman, though. She came expecting someone in particular.

"We find any shell casings?" I asked, looking to Paul. He shook his head. "How about the neighbors? Did anybody see the shooting?"

Again, Paul shook his head. "A couple said they looked out the window after hearing the shots. By then, everything was over."

I nodded, putting it together.

"So Kristen expected to spend a romantic night in. Sometime around six, someone came to the door. She opened her robe, probably to surprise him, and then opened the door. Instead of taking her to bed, he shot her in the chest and then in the head. Our shooter either used a revolver, or he collected the shell casings.

Afterwards, he felt guilty about leaving her nude body exposed, so he covered her with a blanket. Within seconds, he was back in his car. That sound plausible to you?"

Paul nodded. "That's my read on it, too."

If that was the case, that told us something important. Kristen didn't even have time to close her robe before she died. Most shooters needed time to build up the nerve before firing, like a dog growling and snarling, working itself up before a fight. Kristen's killer pulled the trigger the moment he saw her, though. I had investigated a lot of murderers, but few could kill a stranger without hesitation or remorse.

"We cleared Kristen's boyfriend yet?" I asked.

"How do you know she had a boyfriend?" asked Paul, smiling bemusedly.

"It could be a girlfriend, I guess," I said, shrugging. "But she's not wearing that robe for the pizza guy. In addition, she's not wearing a wedding ring. A spouse would have parked in the driveway and come in through the side door, anyway. Hence, boyfriend."

"He showed up about ten minutes after the first responder. He's pretty distraught. We checked his hands and shirt for gunshot residue but came up clean. He's not our shooter."

I nodded and knelt down to look at Kristen's body again. The Coroner's Office would give us a full report, but nothing to my eyes stood out.

"Our shooter went inside to get the blanket," I said, thinking aloud, "but he didn't touch anything else, he didn't leave shell casings, and he didn't leave tire tracks on the streets. If he had abducted her and killed her elsewhere, we'd never know she was dead. What does that tell us?"

"That our shooter is one bad mother fucker," said Paul.

"Yeah," I said, looking at that half-smile on Kristen's face. She didn't even have time to grimace. "She called me a week ago to ask about an old case I worked."

"Which case?" asked Paul.

"An old homicide. Four boys in the Franklin Young Park. Happened about nine years ago. They were castrated, had their teeth knocked out, their hands and feet removed, and their faces beaten so badly we couldn't even show their pictures on TV. We never got an ID on them."

Paul raised his eyebrows. "Sounds like an ugly case."

"It was," I said, nodding and standing. "Kristen said she had started investigating and had questions for me. I don't know if she found anything, but I wanted to put that on the record before you check her cell phone and see that she and I have spoken."

"Duly noted," said Paul, nodding.

"I'm going to walk through the house and see what there is to see," I said. I looked to the Coroner's technician. "Unless there's something else, I think we're done with the body. Any idea when the coroner will start cutting?"

The technician drew in a deep breath. "Tomorrow morning at the earliest. I'll have Dr. Rodriguez call you when we get her on the schedule."

"Do that, please," I said, nodding. The tech went back to her van for a partner and a gurney. I looked at Paul and then nodded through the front door to a crowd of neighbors across the street. "Think you can distract them while the coroner takes the body out?"

Paul followed my line of sight and then nodded. "I'm on it. We have anyone else working this with us?"

"Bowers called Emilia Rios. She's on her way."

"She's good," he said, nodding. I agreed. Paul got to work distracting the neighbors while I walked inside. Kristen had a dining room to the left of the entryway.

Letters lay scattered across her dining room table and in neat stacks on a set of file cabinets pushed against the wall. Most of the letters looked as if Kristen had printed them out, but some were clearly handwritten. Every letter I saw said something nasty about her. That gave us a lot of potential suspects.

I walked from room to room, giving myself an overview of Kristen's personal life. Unfortunately, I didn't find a whole lot. She had pictures of an older, Asian couple in the living room—probably her parents or grandparents—but very few other personal items. From all I could see, she liked modern art, leather sofas, and darkly stained wooden furniture. Or more likely, the designer she hired liked those things. The lack of personal items made the house feel like a corporate suite, the kind of place someone would sleep for an extended period of time but not one in which someone actually lived.

The second floor had a similar corporate feel to it. Then, I found the master suite, or at least the room the builder had likely intended the homeowner to use as the master suite. Kristen had lined the walls with corkboards and then positioned a table in front of each one. In addition to photographs on every corkboard, I counted a dozen empty coffee mugs strewn about and found notecards and stacks of documents on every table. I had seen a room just like that before in a private detective's office.

I walked around, looking from one corkboard to another. Each board looked as if it corresponded to a different story. A yellow legal notepad with Kristen's handwritten notes rested on each table. I stopped when I came across a board adorned with newspaper articles instead of surveillance pictures.

Four men slain.

The headline came from the *Indianapolis Star* the day

after a homeless man named Biscuits found four bodies in the Franklin Young Park. Beside that newspaper article, I found printouts of four missing person's reports from the Chicago Police Department's website. When Olivia Rhodes and I worked that case nine years ago, we never even ID'd our victims. Somehow, Kristen Tanaka had.

Mark and Cesar Cruz, Jeremy Estrada, and Joseph Gomez.

I took pictures of everything on that corkboard, hoping to add what she found to my old case file. Oddly, this was the only corkboard without a notepad in front. Maybe she had this one at work.

After taking a couple dozen more pictures of the room, I walked outside to find Emilia Rios on the front porch. Though she stayed pretty cool at work, Emilia had a smile that could light up a room and a temper that could clear it out. She was smart and ambitious without being aggressive or vicious. I liked her a lot and felt lucky to have her on my team. She smiled hello as Paul filled her in on the scene so far. When he finished speaking, they both looked at me.

"I'm not going to lie to you: this is going to be a hard one," I said. "By the looks of things, our shooter didn't leave much for us to go on. Paul, talk to the neighbors. Whatever they can tell us about this, I want to know. I'll call Captain Bowers and see if he can do the next-of-kin notification. He can question Kristen's parents, too, and see if they know anything.

"Emilia, Kristen has hate mail in piles on her dining room table. I want you to read through everything. Set aside letters from anyone who seems particularly crazy or who has detailed threats. We'll check those guys out. If needed, I can ask Captain Bowers for additional manpower.

"I'm going to start talking to her coworkers and see if anybody's been giving her grief at work. Questions?"

Nobody had any, so I drew in a deep breath.

"All right, then. You've both worked enough homicides that I don't need to remind you of this, but I will, anyway: our shooter executed an unarmed woman without hesitation. Be careful. If you feel threatened, take appropriate action. If one of you dies while on duty, I'll be stuck with a shit ton of paperwork. Nobody wants that."

They laughed, but I hoped they took the warning to heart. I had lost a partner before on the job many years ago. I didn't want to lose a friend, too.

Chapter 4

Charles Holden lived in an old farmhouse near Zionsville, roughly twenty-five miles north of the city. Given traffic in the city, his daily commute alone would waste two hours of his day.

Aleksander didn't know if he could have made that commute. He wouldn't have minded the drive, but the time would have eaten away at him. He had always like standing with his kids at the bus stop before school. When they saw the bus up the street, he'd kneel down and hug them one last time and then watch as they climbed aboard. They'd wave and smile from their seats, and he'd know he had done okay by them for one more day. If he had to spend two hours a day in a car, he would have missed that.

Holden got quite a house in exchange for the commute, though. With its brick facade and dark wooden trim, it looked like something from the English countryside. A white fence stretched from the street and off into the distance, demarcating the Holden's property from the farms to their left and right. Four horses grazed on top of the hill near a barn maybe a hundred yards to the home's west. Had that home and farm been even ten miles closer to the city, its price tag likely would have quadrupled. Out here in the middle of nowhere, though, a man with an upper-middle class income could live very, very well.

Kristen Tanaka had doomed Charles Holden the moment she told him about her investigation. According to her notepad, Kristen had talked to almost a dozen people about the murders. Unknown to her, she had even spoken to Alonzo Cruz, the man who ordered them. Why Alonzo had paid Aleksander to torture and murder his only sons and two of their friends nine years ago, he didn't know. He didn't need or want to know. Alonzo hired him for a job, and Aleksander had completed it exactly as requested.

Now, Aleksander had to clean up a mess before it spread, and Kristen Tanaka's journal had given him all he needed: a roadmap to her investigation and a list of people he had to silence.

He didn't feel good about what he had to do, but it didn't matter. Alonzo would hire men to kill Aleksander's family if he failed. Aleksander couldn't let that happen. The end justified whatever means he had to take.

He slowed as he drove past Holden's house, watching the windows and the neighboring farms for movement. He saw none, so he drove a few miles up the road and then pulled off onto the parking lot of a country church. He looked at his watch. It was almost time.

He turned the car off, slid the windows down, and breathed in the evening air. It reminded him of his family's home outside Belgrade. He hadn't been there since fleeing Yugoslavia's civil war in the early nineties. He wondered if his old house still stood. Even if it didn't, it didn't matter. He had everything he wanted here. He waited there, in the dark and the quiet, for a phone call. When his cell rang, he answered without looking at the Caller ID.

"*Dušo moja.*"

"I wish you wouldn't say that," said Vesna, his wife. "It makes us sound so foreign."

Literally, *dušo moja* meant *my soul*. And Vesna was his soul. She was everything good about him, and he had looked forward to hearing from her all day.

"You didn't use to mind when I called you that," he said, shifting on his seat and watching as a car rounded a bend in the road and drove past.

"Bah," said his wife, her voice light enough that he

knew she had smiled. "That was a long time ago. Save your declarations of love for those young enough to appreciate them. You've already swept me off my feet. Now I just want someone who comes home at night and makes me dinner. I wouldn't mind if you occasionally cleaned the toilets, either. You think you could do that?"

"For you, anything. I would even clean toilets. How are you?"

"Good, fine, the usual," she said. "I thought I'd call to keep up appearances. I'm on the patio. This should keep the neighbors from talking. It will make them think we still care about each other. How's your conference?"

Aleksander cleared his throat. Vesna didn't know how they survived their early years together in the United States. She thought they made it through hard work. And in a way, they had. Aleksander used the only skills he had, skills drilled into him by the Yugoslav People's Army, to survive. He didn't like the man he became, but it didn't matter.

Rich men could worry about morality. The poor cared about survival.

"My conference is good," he said, lying. "There are a lot of buyers here. I've talked to the managing partner of a design firm from Chicago. They're very interested. We'll be able to do some business."

"I'm so glad. I've always told you: good things come to good people, and you're the best man I know. I'm so proud of you."

Even from the start, Vesna had believed in the American dream. And maybe she was right to believe in it. Maybe some people did get ahead by working hard and dreaming big, but not in New York City, not for Aleksander. His hard work had only made him exhausted and impoverished. He and his family survived because Aleksander turned his back on his faith and everything he believed.

"You've always been my biggest fan," he said. "How's business?"

"Good. We sold four antique Turkish prayer rugs to a designer from the Upper East side who's probably never even met a Muslim. She though they would look good hanging on a wall."

Aleksander laughed. "They'll look nice even if the knees of the faithful never touch them."

"Her money spends the same either way," said Vesna. "A man stopped by and asked for you this morning. He worked for someone named Mr. Cruz. Mr. Cruz couldn't come himself, but he wanted you to know how much he appreciated what you've done for him."

Aleksander had expected Alonzo to send somebody eventually, but it still made his gut twist.

"He say anything else?" asked Aleksander.

"Just that he appreciated your hard work. I looked him up, but I didn't see a Cruz in our database."

"He worked for a law firm," said Aleksander, thinking quickly and looking around. Despite the open windows and the breeze, his rental car suddenly felt warm. "We sold him a rug for his conference room. I delivered it myself."

"That explains it, then," said Vesna. "Before you go, Sophia wanted to talk to you. She has something important to say."

He almost grunted. He loved his daughter more than he could put into words, but they didn't always get along. She had an older boyfriend. Aleksander tried to tell her time and again to watch herself around him, that he might try something with her. Aleksander had been a young man once, too, so he knew how young men thought. Sophia, though, thought she loved him. At her age, she didn't even know what love was. He feared that his daughter would give up too much for a schoolyard crush.

"Tell me she's not pregnant."

"She's your daughter," said Vesna. "Just talk to her."

Before he could say anything else, Vesna pulled the phone from her mouth and asked Sophia to tell him she wasn't pregnant. Sophia laughed a rich, throaty laugh.

"Don't worry, Daddy," she said, once Vesna handed her the phone. "I'm not pregnant. I got in at Brown. I know what you're going to say. It's expensive, but it's a really great school. They've got a good financial aid department, too, so-"

Aleksander's chest loosened some. His daughter's boyfriend went to a community college in the Bronx, almost two hundred miles away from Brown University.

"We'll make it work," he said, interrupting her and smiling. "I'm proud of you, *mischa*."

"I'm not a little girl anymore. You don't need to call me that."

He smiled even broader. "You will always be my little girl, my *mischa*. Remember that. Oh, and thank you for showing me how to set up that internet camera. It's come in handy already."

"It's a webcam, Daddy," she said. "If you call it an internet camera, people will think you're out of touch."

"I am out of touch, sweetheart."

She laughed again. He talked to his daughter for another few minutes and promised to sit down with her to discuss financial aid as soon as he arrived home in a few days. After that, he talked to his wife. It was a simple conversation, the kind that millions of men and women had every night, but it reminded him of all that he had in his life, all that he would lose if he didn't take care of things properly. After a few minutes, he hung up, but he knew he'd joyfully replay everything they said in his mind again that night in his hotel room.

As he sat in the stillness after that call, he felt stronger. When he died, God would judge him harshly for the things he had done, but it didn't matter. His family would have the lives they deserved because of his sacrifices. He would gladly give up everything he had for that.

Eventually, he turned on the car and drove to the Holden's home, wondering if he could call forth the meanness he needed to do this job properly. Kristen Tanaka had been on the news every night. Her death alone attracted the attention he needed. No one knew Charles Holden, though. Aleksander needed to make him famous. He hoped he wouldn't have to kill the man's family to accomplish that, but in the end, he'd do what he had to do. The lives of those he cared about most depended on it.

Chapter 5

I interviewed Kristen Tanaka's boyfriend, Brad Fairweather, in the back of a squad car. He told me about a driven, ambitious woman who loved her job and her community, and who felt she had an obligation to report the truth even when doing so hurt her career or relationships. She wasn't a perfect person, but that didn't matter anymore. She had died, and that wiped the slate clean.

I left Brad in the back of that police cruiser. Almost before my foot hit the pavement, he began crying softly. I wanted to say something to him, to tell him we'd get the guy who killed his girlfriend. That wouldn't bring her back, though, and that wouldn't make him feel any better. Some losses didn't have easy fixes.

Brad didn't know a lot about Kristen's work, but he knew someone who did: Charles Holden, her boss. According to my dispatcher, he lived in Zionsville, a middle class suburb north of the city. I put Holden's address in my phone's GPS and headed north on Meridian Street. This time of day, the interstates around Indianapolis turned into virtual parking lots with rush hour traffic. I stuck to surface roads and made decent time.

I hit the outskirts of Zionsville in about thirty-five minutes, and I reached Holden's address in forty-five. He lived in a country house set far off the street. A couple of horses grazed on a front lawn the size of two football fields. I opened my window and smelled fresh cut grass and a faint hint of manure. Somewhere in the distance, a dog barked, probably scaring off an animal that had the audacity to invade his family's farm without permission.

I slowed and turned onto a meandering gravel

driveway. The sun had just begun to sink low on the horizon, making the hills surrounding the Holden's house almost look as if they were on fire. It was pretty.

I pulled to a stop beside a silver Chevrolet sedan on the driveway beside the home. To the home's rear, the builder had poured an enormous concrete slab and installed a pair of basketball hoops as well as a four-car detected garage clad in the same cut stone as the house. Beyond the garage, I could see a garden and private sitting area for the family. The Holden family didn't expect me, so I made sure my badge was visible on my belt as I stepped out of my car.

The breeze blew from the direction of the house, carrying with it a chemical odor. Diesel. That made sense, though. The Holdens very likely had at least twenty acres of grass. It would have taken some pretty heavy equipment to take care of that much property, equipment that would require an on-site fuel source.

I wrinkled my nose and walked up a stamped concrete walkway toward the house. A pair of tricycles and a whiffle ball set lay on the lawn near the front porch. Holden had at least two children, then. Hopefully, I wouldn't walk in on the family during their bedtime routine. As a father of young children, I knew what a nightmare it could be to interrupt a toddler's sleep schedule. The sound of my footsteps carried on the breeze.

As I walked, the diesel smell became stronger. It didn't overpower me, but it got close. Something wasn't right here. Even if the family had a fuel tank with a leak, it shouldn't have smelled this strong this close to the house. I wouldn't have thought anything of it near the barn, but not here, not where their children played.

I hesitated and then unbuttoned the clasp that held my firearm inside my shoulder holster. As I walked the remaining fifteen feet to the front porch, I cast my eyes around the property. A car passed on the main road. The grass waved in the wind. Nothing else moved. In those moments when the wind hit a lull, though, the diesel smell grew even stronger. The source of the odor didn't come from the barn. It came from somewhere much closer than that. This was very wrong.

I pulled my weapon from the holster and climbed three concrete steps to the front porch. Then, I stopped and listened.

Nothing.

I pounded on the center of the door with my fist. It popped open, revealing a two-story entryway with a slate tile floor and carpeted stairs that led to a second-floor landing. Open archways led left, right and straight ahead to rooms deeper inside the house. The smell there was more than just diesel. There was gasoline, too. I covered my mouth with the sleeve of my shirt and stepped inside, my eyes burning from the fumes.

"I'm a police officer. Can anyone hear me? We need to get out of the house."

I coughed again and then heard a noise that sounded like a muzzled dog trying to bark. I followed it straight ahead to the kitchen. A man about my size sat on a tall backed wooden chair. He had a pillowcase covering his head and zip ties securing his extremities to the chair on which he sat. I didn't focus on him, though; I focused on the man with a gun behind him. He was older than me, but not by a lot. He was slight of build with graying brown hair and cold gray eyes. I dropped my left shoulder back, pivoting into a shooter's stance.

"Drop it now!"

My lungs and eyes burned from the fumes, but I held my ground. My stomach roiled, and I felt bile creeping into my throat. I slipped my finger to the trigger. There were two blue diesel fuel containers on the ground and one red one for gasoline. The diesel worried me, but the gasoline was the real problem.

The instant I squeezed the trigger on my weapon, a spring would propel my weapon's firing pin into the primer on a 40-caliber round, setting off a chain reaction that ended with my target getting an extra hole in his chest. Unfortunately, it would also send a hot shell casing from the chamber of my weapon to a ground covered in fuel. It didn't take much to ignite gasoline vapors.

As I looked at the man across from me, I realized something: he knew everything I did. He reached into his pocket and pulled out a zippo lighter.

"Oh, shit," I said.

With a flick of his wrist, the lighter ignited. He tossed it to the ground. Flames shot over the porcelain tile and pooled around the man in the chair before racing toward the adjoining living room and elsewhere in the house. The fire didn't quite reach me, but the heat made me stumble backwards. The man with the lighter ran out the back door. I wanted to chase after him, but I couldn't, not with the house on fire and a man tied to the chair. I held my breath and vaulted toward the hostage and threw off the pillowcase covering his head.

He was middle aged with a gray goatee and black hair. Packing tape covered his mouth. He shook his head violently and stamped his feet.

"I'm getting you out," I said, pulling his chair to the center of the floor, as far from the flames as I could. Then, I grabbed a knife from a block near the stove and began sawing away at his restraints. He stamped his feet so hard he nearly knocked the chair over. He had tears in his eyes, but not from pain. He was pleading. I ripped off the tape.

"My kids. Get my wife and kids."

I stopped sawing immediately. "Where?"

He nodded toward a hallway to my left. Already, flames covered the hardwood floor and had begun traveling upward on the walls.

"In the nursery," he said, his voice a deep growl.

All around us, the home's possessions began to smoke and burn. Though I carried a Lieutenant's badge, my department still considered me a first responder. I went through much of the same yearly training that our uniformed officers did, part of which included information on fire safety.

In the fifties, a house fire would top out at around fourteen-hundred degrees—as hot as a cremation chamber—but it would take ten to fifteen minutes to reach that. A fire in a modern home with furnishings built from particle board and walls constructed of half-inch drywall could reach two-thousand degrees in under three minutes.

Already, the couch in the living room had caught fire. Within moments, the fire leapt to the drapes, and the front windows shattered. Flames shot to the ceiling, gorging on their newfound oxygen source.

It would take me twenty seconds to cut Holden away from the chair. It would take me another ten seconds to carry him out of the house and dump him on the front lawn. Thirty seconds total. It didn't seem like much time, but as I looked left toward the hallway Holden had indicated, I found flames inching higher on the walls. If I didn't move now, I'd lose my chance to save anybody.

I looked in Holden's eyes. Something passed between us, some hidden bit of knowledge neither of us could have communicated verbally in that span of time. We both knew what he had asked me to do. I could save his family, or I could save him. I didn't have time to save both. Charles had made his choice, though. Now I had to follow through.

"I'm sorry," I said, leaving him there and sprinting down the hallway. Already, the building groaned and popped as nails and screws heated to their breaking point.

My skin felt hot and raw.

Then, the screaming started as the flames reached Holden. It was a nightmare made real, but I didn't have to hear it long. The fire's throbbing roar covered even the screams.

The nursery was a small room at the end of the hallway. To keep the flames out, I closed the door behind me after jumping inside. Three children—two toddlers and a baby—sat in the crib, all three crying. Their mother sat beside them, secured to a rocking chair with zip ties. Her arms and legs trembled as she tried to break herself free. Like her husband, a pillowcase covered her head. I tore the pillowcase off and then pulled the tape from her mouth.

"Get my kids," she said.

"I'm going to need your help for that," I said, already sawing away at the restraints on her wrists.

"Where's my husband?"

"He's fine," I said, more for the kids sake than her own. She knew the answer to her question before she asked it. If her husband could have helped, he would have been there with the knife instead of me.

Tears streamed down her face. Once I had her hands free, I handed her the knife and then grabbed the two toddlers. They wrapped their arms and legs tight around me, threatening to choke me. I didn't care. I just needed to get out of the house. When I stuck my head back in the hallway, I found Hell staring back. The fire roiled and twisted. We couldn't run through that. I kicked the door shut and put the kids on the ground before opening the nursery's only window. Cold air rushed in. I may have been hearing things, but it almost sounded like the fire roared harder around us.

The fit was tight for me, and the window was at least five feet off the ground, but we could do this. Mrs. Holden finished sawing away the last of her restraints.

The kids immediately jumped off me and latched onto her.

"You get out the window first," I said. "Once you're on the ground, I'll lower the kids to you."

She shook her head, pleading, crying. "I'm not leaving without them."

"I can't do this without you. Get through that window now. I'm not going to let anything happen to your children."

She looked toward the window but didn't move. Sweat beaded on my forehead. The heat was already making it hurt to breathe. If we stayed in there for too much longer, we'd die.

"Move, now," I shouted. She flinched. The kids cried harder, but she got moving. She wouldn't leave the baby, but that was okay. She stuck her legs out the window, one arm wrapped around her daughter, the other on the window sill. The moment her feet touched the ground, I handed her the first toddler. He squirmed and fought, but I got him through the window and into his mother's arms.

The house shuddered. A series of bangs erupted from the hallway as something crashed to the ground.

I reached for the second toddler, and he backed off, wedging himself between the crib and the wall. His entire body trembled. I straightened and then took a step back. My hip hit the doorknob. It burned me through my clothes like a branding iron. I swallowed hard to keep myself from screaming. We didn't have time for a fight. If I didn't get this kid outside now, we'd both die.

I knelt down. "I know you're scared, buddy, but we've got to get out of here. Your mommy's outside. I'm going to pick you up and hand you to her."

I held my arms out and stepped toward him. He pressed his back to the wall even harder, but he didn't have anywhere to go. I grabbed him, and he bit my forearm hard enough to draw blood through my shirt. It hurt, but I didn't let go. Instead, I pulled him tight against me so he couldn't draw his legs back and kick. As I held him out the window toward his mother, the fight left him, and he started wailing. I looked around the room, grabbed a pair of teddy bears from the crib and threw them out the window before diving out myself.

Once my feet hit the ground, I sucked down great gulps of air and then vomited on the grass. Once I had composed myself a little bit, I helped Mrs. Holden corral the children away from the house in case debris started falling.

In the back of my mind, I had hoped I could run through the front door and try to find Charles once I had the family safe. One look at the house told me I couldn't. Flames shot out the second story window. The front porch had collapsed. Charles Holden sacrificed himself for his kids.

I looked at Mrs. Holden. She held a hand over her mouth as she cried and watched her home burn.

"I'm sorry," I whispered.

The little boy who had fought me so violently in the nursery picked up one of the teddy bears I had thrown out. "Where's daddy?"

Mrs. Holden cried harder. I took a step away and then sat down on the grass, breathing hard. This had been a really bad night.

Chapter 6

The first police officers arrived on the scene within five minutes of my call, but the fire department took fifteen. As far out in the country as the Holden's lived, the firefighters had to truck in their own water. By the time they arrived, the house had collapsed in on itself. The fire department focused on preventing the fire from spreading to the nearby trees, which was a smart tactic given our drought. One spark on dry kindling, and the surrounding hundred acres would burn like tissue paper.

The first uniformed police officers at the scene asked me a few questions, but mostly they wanted to wait for a supervisory officer before doing anything. I appreciated that. I'd have to explain what happened, but I didn't have the patience or stomach to repeat the same story over and over again tonight.

I had done the right thing. Intellectually, the choice sounded easy. I saved four people—three of whom were children—by letting one man die. Not only that, the man who died had given himself up freely. He didn't have to tell me to save his family. He made the choice to sacrifice himself so his wife and children could live.

Most people probably imagined they'd make the heroic choice in that scenario, too, but I didn't know how many would go through with it with a building burning around them. Holden did.

Paramedics arrived shortly after the fire trucks. All three of the Holden children had inhaled significant amounts of smoke, and while they seemed to be recovering okay physically, the paramedics didn't want to chance more serious injuries. They drove the entire family to the Riley Hospital for Children in Indianapolis. It was one of the best children's hospitals in the country, so they'd get good care there. They'd also have counselors on staff who could talk to the kids about their father.

More than anything, they needed family now. Nothing would put their world right, but hopefully their mother and their aunts and uncles and grandparents and cousins and whoever else could make them feel safe.

Once the family left, I sat in my car and texted my wife to let her know I was okay. After that, I stared at the ceiling of my car as the first responders from Zionsville and Boone County worked around me. I felt more alone than I had in a long time, but that feeling didn't last long before my phone vibrated in my pocket. I put it to my ear and heard my wife's soft voice. The hard edge of my isolation lifted. I gave her the barest outlines of what had happened, after which she said she loved me and that she was thinking of me. I loved her for that, and I told her so.

Sometime after that conversation, I fell asleep and woke as a heavy hand shook my shoulder. My eyes fluttered open to see my supervisor, Mike Bowers, and Emilia Rios standing over me.

"You all right?" asked Bowers. I cleared my throat, nodded, and began to sit up. Before I could, my vision swam. I fell back to my seat.

"I'm a little dizzy."

Emilia flagged somebody over. An EMT appeared beside me in the door and put an oxygen meter on my finger. It beeped a few times. I didn't know what that meant, but he moved pretty quickly after that to help me sit up. Then, he put a respirator over my mouth, and I sucked down cold, clean oxygen. My dizziness faded, as did some of my fatigue.

"You get light headed again, let me know," he said. "Your oxygen saturation was down to about seventy-eight percent. You stay that low for too long, your heart might give out. Just sit here and breathe deeply for a few minutes."

I did as he asked. The oxygen cleared my head even if it didn't make the world easier to take. I wouldn't run a marathon anytime soon, but the dizziness left entirely after a few minutes, allowing me to sit up under my own power. The EMT checked my oxygen levels again and apparently found them satisfactory because he packed up his oxygen cylinder and left me to talk to my boss and partner.

"You want to tell us what happened inside that house?" asked Bowers.

"Not really," I said, "but you're probably going to make me anyway. Let's get the locals in on this. I don't want to repeat myself more than I have to."

Bowers nodded, so I swung my legs out of the car and stood. Holden's murder had happened well outside of IMPD's jurisdiction, so I told my story to a Captain from the Boone County sheriff's department and a Lieutenant from the Zionsville Police department. I didn't know how the two local organizations planned to divvy up the investigation, but they'd figure it out.

Everybody had questions for me, but I didn't have many answers. I didn't recognize the murderer, Holden didn't mention anything about him, I never had the chance to interview Mrs. Holden, and I hadn't gone there expecting to see anyone. Once they finished with me, I walked back to my car. Emilia followed.

"You sure you're okay, boss?" she asked along the way. "That was quite a thing you did tonight."

I sat on my VW's hood. She sat beside me.

"Yeah. The oxygen helped. The dizziness is gone."

We both knew she was more interested in my mental health than my physical well being, but she nodded anyway.

"The search in town didn't turn up a lot," she said. "Paul visited the neighbors. Three reported seeing a Caucasian male, approximately forty-five to fifty, walking through the neighborhood today. Two of them described him as being of slight build and standing approximately five feet six. The third said he was as big as an NFL lineman and stood at least six feet tall. I don't want to discount what she said, but she was elderly and had just gotten up from a nap. She didn't have her glasses on."

I nodded. The differing descriptions hurt. I didn't doubt that the older witness thought she saw someone hulking and brutish, but I put much more stock in the other witnesses.

"The guy I saw was middle aged and small. We'll put that description out and see what comes of it."

"We're already on it," she said. "I spent some time going through Ms. Tanaka's hate mail. Best I can tell, she's got archives going back at least three years. It's all neat and organized. The last serious threat she received came in six months ago. The writer was a woman named Tracy Lowry. She currently lives in San Diego and is sleeping off a hangover in the San Diego police department's drunk tank."

I nodded again. If we went to trial, we'd have to dig through all her files, but we needed to refocus right now. Our murderer had already taken out two people. He had a plan, goals, and a reason to act. I highly doubted he had finished by murdering two journalists. Unless we moved, we'd have more bodies and more families without loved ones.

"Did you drive here or get a ride with Captain Bowers?"

"I rode shotgun with the captain," she said. "In case you needed someone to drive your car home."

"Good," I said, reaching into my pocket for my keys. "You're going to drive us downtown. I need to make some calls."

She took the keys and climbed into the driver's seat. As we pulled away from the house, I glanced over at her.

"When we get to Indianapolis, I need you to interview Mrs. Holden. Paramedics took her kids to Riley Hospital for treatment, so she's probably still there. We need to know everything we can about tonight. After that, I need you to get in touch with Captain Bowers and make sure someone's done the next-of-kin notification with Kristen Tanaka's family. You need to interview them, too. Someone killed Kristen Tanaka for a reason. We need to find out why."

Emilia nodded and then drummed her fingers on the steering wheel.

"Are you sure you don't want to interview Holden's wife? You were at the house, so you'd have a better idea of the sort of things to ask."

My chest felt tight. I took a deep breath before speaking, hoping that would loosen it up.

"I left her husband to die. She doesn't need to talk to me. You'll be fine," I said. I took a deep breath. "Kristen Tanaka called me a couple of nights ago and told me she found something on a cold case I worked. I already told Paul, but you should know, too."

"What'd she say?" asked Emilia, glancing over at me.

I sighed. "Not a lot, but she ID'd my victims. That was more than we could do nine years ago. Did you see her home office?"

Emilia nodded. "Nice place she had."

"She had a notepad for each of her open investigations. Each corkboard had its own notepad except my old case."

Emilia looked at me quickly and then back to the road. "You think her killer took it?"

"Maybe. And maybe I'm crazy. Either way, we need to take it seriously. You and Paul are going to work the Tanaka and Holden murders just like you would any other case. I'm going to look at my cold case and see what I can find."

"If that's how you want to handle this," she said.

"That's how I want to handle this," I said, taking out my cell phone. As she drove, I called my department's Evidence Section and waited through thirteen rings before the night clerk picked up.

"Yeah?" he asked, sounding harried.

"Evening. This is Lieutenant Ash Rashid from Major Case. I need evidence boxes from a quadruple homicide in 2006."

The clerk grunted. "Cases from 2006 are in vault four in the Annex."

"Sure, great, so you know where they are. I don't remember the case number off the top of my head, but the victims are four John Does found May 28, 2006."

"Give me just a minute," he said. I waited for about five minutes and would have thought he had hung up on me except that I could hear the click of his keyboard as he typed. Then, he stopped typing and sighed. "We might have a problem. Can I call you back in a few minutes?"

"What kind of problem?" I asked.

"The big kind," he said. "I need a couple of minutes to figure this out. You going to be at this number for a while?"

He didn't need to elaborate; he couldn't find our evidence.

"Yeah, sure."

"Thanks."

He hung up without saying a goodbye. IMPD had a lot of good employees, but everybody made mistakes at times. Occasionally, an evidence technician might steal drugs or a firearm from the evidence locker, but my old investigation hadn't turned anything valuable up. If he couldn't find what I needed, it likely meant someone had accidentally marked the evidence boxes for destruction.

The clerk called me back a few minutes later. He wheezed like a lifetime smoker.

"Okay, Lieutenant, we've got a problem," he said, quickly. "Your evidence is gone."

"How'd it happen?"

"Supposedly, an officer came in nine years ago and requested it but he never returned it."

I blinked and stood straighter. "Who?"

"The form says it was David Toler, badge number 0001. You know who Toler was, right?"

Of course I knew. Everybody knew David Toler. He retired in 2006, but before that, the mayor appointed him as Chief during the merger of the Indianapolis Police Department and the Marion County Sheriff's department. He had to make a lot of very difficult personnel decisions during his short tenure in office, and he made a lot of enemies. Even ten years later, I still had colleagues who spit every time they heard his name. If Toler needed evidence from an old case, he would have sent his assistant.

"So everything's gone?" I asked.

"Yeah. I went to the vaults and checked. Since you were the primary on the case, you remember what was in the box?"

"Paperwork, mostly," I said.

The clerk paused. "So no drugs or anything valuable?"

"No," I said. "The case was a lot cause. We didn't have anything."

"Hmm," said the clerk. "Well, I'll call my supervisor and tell him what's going on. Since we're not dealing with missing weapons or drugs, our investigation might take a while. If your stuff turns up in the meantime, I'll give you a call."

"Yeah, sure," I said, not holding out much hope for that possibility. "Good luck."

He thanked me and hung up. I rubbed my eyes. The world was full of thieves stupid enough to steal boxes of worthless documents, but I didn't think we had that here.

"You know who David Toler is?" I asked, glancing at Emilia. She hesitated before answering.

"Name sounds vaguely familiar, but no."

"He was the Chief of Police for a couple of months in 2006. He retired shortly thereafter and died a few years after that. Paul still hates the guy. A lot of people do."

She tilted her head to the side. "That's a long time to hold a grudge, especially against a dead man."

"He gave a lot of people reason to hold grudges," I said. "Right before he retired, records say he checked out evidence from my cold case and never returned it."

"Why would the chief of police check out evidence from your case?" she asked.

"He wouldn't," I said. "My victims nine years ago had their hands and feet cut off and their teeth knocked out. Kristen Tanaka found them by searching missing person's reports from Chicago. If that's right, it means my killer drove them two-hundred miles south just so he could dump them in a park."

Emilia nodded, but I didn't know if she understood the importance of what I had said. Every city in the world had a dumping ground. Pelham Bay Park in the Bronx, the marshes around the Meadowlands in New Jersey, Leakin Park in Baltimore. I didn't know where people dumped bodies in Chicago—Lake Michigan, probably—but the city had a place. A normal person wouldn't drive three hours south with four bleeding, shit-stained corpses in the back of his car. My killer did. Then he stole evidence and proverbially gave me the middle finger by signing the name of David Toler, probably the most hated man in my department in the last decade.

"Why would he drive them that far?" she asked. "It doesn't make sense. Why not just get a hacksaw and a garbage disposal like that lady out in Geist last year?"

Indianapolis and the surrounding region rarely made

the national news except for sports, but occasionally our amoral residents did something so horrific the rest of the nation noticed. The woman Emilia referred to drugged her very wealthy husband with sleeping pills, chopped him to pieces with a reciprocating saw, and then, over the course of a week, fed his corpse through her garbage disposal. She claimed he left her for another woman. Supposedly unable to live in her huge house alone, the murdering wife immediately put it up for sale. Unknown to her, her husband's fat had congealed in a drainpipe beneath the kitchen. A realtor found the corpse when the pipes burst, causing a geyser of decaying, partially ground body parts to burst through the ceiling in the finished basement during a showing.

I never did find out if she sold the house.

"He drove them here because he wanted them found, but he didn't want us to get an ID on them. They were a message to somebody, just as my stolen evidence was a message to us."

Emilia blinked and nodded. "What are you thinking?"

"I don't know yet, but I don't like this."

Emilia nodded. The two of us didn't say anything for the rest of the drive. As we turned downtown, night had descended on the city. Pedestrians crowded the sidewalks as they walked to bars, restaurants, and movie theaters. Groups of teenagers hung out on street corners.

That normalcy ended as soon as we caught sight of the pedestrian mall in front of the City-County building. Trucks from every news station in town crowded the streets. More than that, people—families by the number of children running around—had begun pitching tents on the front lawn. I would have thought it was a protest of some sort, but people didn't usually bring their toddlers to political protests.

Emilia parked in the public employee's lot across the street, and we walked to the building. Almost the moment our feet touched the sidewalk, every reporter there rushed at me, shouting so many questions I couldn't even hear a single one clearly. Emilia and I pushed through the crowd as politely as we could and told them we didn't have anything to say. They followed us to the front doors and then, finally, stopped before going into the lobby. There, a man in a dark suit a little more expensive than most worn in that building waited for us. I rarely saw the Deputy Chief except at press conferences and meetings, but I doubted he would voluntarily work on a Friday night.

I looked over my shoulder at the reporters. "Are they all here for Kristen Tanaka?"

Chief Reddington looked to me, shook his head, and then looked to Emilia. "Do you have an assignment, Detective?"

Emilia looked at me and then to the Chief and nodded. "I do, sir."

"Get to it," he said, focusing entirely on me. "We need to have a conversation upstairs, Lieutenant. If you've got a lawyer, now's a good time to call him."

Chapter 7

Reddington and I took an elevator up to the executive floor. Neither of us said a word. I assumed he needed to see me because of the fire at Charles Holden's house. I did everything I could in Zionsville. Holden died, but I had saved four people.

If I could go back in time knowing then what I do now, I would have brought a dozen officers with me, and we would have stormed the house, blocked the exits, and taken our killer down right there. That might have saved Holden, but I had no reason to expend those kind of resources at the time. I had driven out there to talk to a man about his dead coworker. I had no idea what I would walk into.

When we reached the executive floor, Reddington led me down a wood-paneled hallway to a conference room larger than many studio apartments. A wall of windows overlooked Washington Street. Two men in suits watched the crowds outside, but even more people sat around a glass conference table. Most of them I recognized from briefings. In addition to the Deputy Chief, we had the Chief of Detectives, the prosecutor—Leonard Wilson—the deputy prosecutor—Susan Mercer—an attorney from the Office of Corporation Counsel, and a US Attorney.

The moment we walked inside, all eyes turned to Reddington and me. He directed me to sit at the head of the table and then walked around to an open seat on the side. The men at the windows sat down.

"Evening everybody," said Reddington. "Sorry to drag everybody out here on a Friday night, but, as most of you know, we've got a problem. For those of you who may not know him, sitting at the head of the table is Lieutenant Ashraf Rashid. He runs our Major Case squad."

Everyone around the table turned and looked at me then. Some people looked friendly, but most of their faces held neutral expressions.

"As some of you heard tonight, we activated Major Case tonight to investigate the death of Kristen Tanaka. We thought it was important to get as many hands on deck as we could. As part of that investigation, Lieutenant Rashid visited one of Ms. Tanaka's coworkers in Zionsville. Twenty minutes ago, we received word that several media outlets around town received an email with this video attached. I warn you that it's graphic."

Reddington grabbed a remote from the table and punched buttons. The lights dimmed, a screen lowered near the front of the room, a projector popped on. A static image appeared on the screen. It was a picture of the Holden's living room and kitchen prior to the fire. Holden was tied to a chair near the top of the screen. The top of my head was at the bottom. By the angle, I couldn't see the killer's face, but I could see his chest and hands. My best guess was that he had put the camera on a bookshelf in the living room.

Reddington hit a button, and the video played. I knew everything that would happen, but to see it again brought me right back to that room. I smelled the gasoline and diesel and felt the flames on my skin.

When the killer dropped the lighter, several people in the room gasped. The killer ran out the back door, and I ran into the kitchen for a knife. The video didn't have sound, but it clearly showed me sawing on Holden's restraints while talking to him, and it clearly showed the fire streaking towards us. Then it showed me leaving the frame to get his kids. The fire engulfed him within moments of my leaving.

I didn't need to see the man burn, so I looked away. Then I heard a mechanized voice and looked up. The screen had faded to black. Words to match the voice began to appear and then scroll by as they were read.

"The video you've just seen depicts events at the home of Charles Holden, executive news editor at the WIND television station. He died screaming. The police did not save him. The police did not save his colleague, Kristen Tanaka. They will not and cannot save you. Charles Holden and Kristen Tanaka were chosen. You are chosen as well. Your blood and flesh will sate my God's hunger. Your screams will be music unto His divine ears. My God demands your blood sacrifice. Prepare yourselves."

The screen went blank.

"Fuck."

I didn't recognize who said it, but anyone around that table could have echoed the sentiment. Reddington pressed another button on the remote, turning the lights on.

"The video was sent via email to at least twenty-seven reporters around the region," he said. "Each email listed the reporter's home address. Several included pictures of the reporter's home as well." Reddington looked at me. "Lieutenant Rashid, you've done good work for us, but we're going to be taking this from you. Given the events tonight, I think you need some time off. It's nothing personal."

He turned his attention to the rest of the room and started saying they needed to set up a task force, but I had tuned him out.

"Whoa, whoa, whoa," I said, raising my voice and standing so everyone in the room would see me. "Back up a minute. This is my case. My team's already out there working it. If you want to give me additional manpower, I'm all for that, but you can't just take it away from us."

I got a couple of distasteful looks for that. Reddington drew in a breath and force a smile to his mouth.

"Please sit down, Lieutenant. I've already made my decision. You're a good officer, but you're not the individual I want leading this investigation."

I didn't sit, but I did take a deep breath. At one point, I probably would have called him an asshole and stormed out of the room. That might have felt nice, but it wouldn't have accomplished anything. I had seen enough people die tonight. I didn't want to see more.

"You put me in charge of Major Case because I close high-profile, difficult cases. That's what I do. That's what my team does. We're very good at it. Let us do our jobs and prove it."

Reddington tilted his head to the side. "With all due respect, Lieutenant, has your team ever investigated a serial killer before?"

I shook my head. "No, but it doesn't matter. You don't have a serial killer. Until we've got more evidence, you've got a spree killer."

A couple of people scoffed. Reddington's expression hardened.

"That a joke, Ash? Because I've got two dead reporters already and a lot of scared people on the front lawn right now. That's highly inappropriate."

I took a deep breath and closed my eyes.

"I just let a man burn to death so I could save his wife and kids," I said, trying to keep my voice from shaking. "I'm not in the joking mood right now."

Before Reddington could say anything, one of the command officers spoke up. "If you don't think we've got a serial murderer, what's your theory?"

I looked at him and shrugged. "I don't have one, but think about the evidence. So far, we've got two bodies with two distinct causes of death. Kristen Tanaka died of gunshot wounds. Charles Holden died in a fire. Even still, our killer said they were chosen. He used the word sacrifice. Anybody here ever sacrificed an animal?"

Most of the people there gave me looks as if I was crazy. I took that as a no.

"When you sacrifice an animal, it's the act that counts, the ritual. The end result is just a dead body. That's just something to clean up. If our killer had said God wanted him to punish people, that's a goal-oriented activity. Our killer could punish his victims any way he wanted, but a sacrifice has to be done in the right way and with the right attitude. Our killer didn't care about how Charles and Kristen died. If he had, he would have taken his time."

Leonard Wilson, the prosecutor, laced his fingers together and shook his head. "You base that whole analysis on one word. That's a little hard to take."

"It's an important word," I said, pointing to the screen. "If the man on that video is enacting a religious ritual, this is his coming out party. He would have obsessed about this moment for years. He would have practiced that speech over and over. Every word would have meaning for him. He wouldn't have slipped and said sacrifice when he really meant punishment."

"Maybe he's just sloppy," said Reddington.

"Nobody's that sloppy. If this man genuinely believes he's enacting God's will, his entire life has led up to this moment. He's not going to screw it up because he got excited. Not only that, am I the only one who thinks this speech sounds familiar? It sounds like something out of a bad horror movie."

A couple of people looked incredulous, but I didn't back off. Though my wife was a New York Times bestselling mystery novelist now, she had started her writing career by maintaining a blog on which she rated and reviewed B-grade horror movies. I didn't even know how many bad movies she made me stay up and watch with her. I knew that speech. I had heard it before. The cadence was off but the words were nearly the same.

Susan Mercer, the deputy prosecutor, leaned forward. "Bottom line this for us, Lieutenant. What are you thinking?"

I looked at the screen and shook my head. "I don't have anything concrete yet, but we shouldn't buy into this guy's story immediately. He's blowing smoke up our ass to hide his real intention."

Leonard Wilson scoffed. "If Lieutenant Rashid wants to focus on movies because he refuses to take this case seriously, we need to find someone else."

I wanted to tell him off, but the room erupted before I could. Command staff members started throwing out names of who should sit on the task force. I recognized most of the names and couldn't say much good about their abilities. All of them, though, played office politics as well as Machiavelli incarnated. They wouldn't find our murderer, but they sure would get their faces on television. They could have all that. I intended to find this guy before he killed another family.

"I've got a job to do, so I'm going to head out," I said. "Good luck with your cluster fuck or witch hunt, whichever you turn this meeting into. And the movie was Splatter Master 3." I looked at Leonard. "The psychopath's first victim was an egomaniacal lawyer who cared for no one but himself."

I didn't wait to see the reaction to that before leaving. My department had a couple of good administrators, but more often than not, our bosses were venal jerks who achieved their lofty perches in virtue of their viciousness and contempt for everyone around them. The more I worked with them, the less I wanted to know them. I took the elevator to the homicide units' floor and met Paul Murphy in the office conference room. He looked up from some paperwork when I walked in.

"Captain Bowers told me what happened in Zionsville," he said, gesturing to the seat beside him.

"How you feeling?"

I sat down. "Pissed off. I need you to drive out to Zionsville to work with the Boone County Sheriff's department." I paused and took a breath. "Dan Reddington and the rest of our administration believe we've got a serial murderer targeting journalists. This is going to blow up and get ugly."

Paul crossed his arms. "Why would they think we've got a serial murderer?"

"It's a long story. They're going to start a task force full of dunces, but we're not backing off. Until they lock me up, I'm working these murders. Our killer is willing to kill an entire family to get his target. We need to take him out now. Call your wife and clear your schedule. We're working until this guy's in custody."

Paul nodded. "I'm on it. You going to be around here if I need you?"

"I'll be in my office, but I'll have my cell phone."

"All right, then," said Paul, standing. "You sure you're okay? Emilia and I can handle this if you need some time."

"I'm fine. Thank you."

"If you say so. You've got my number if you need me. We're going to get this guy."

I nodded, and he walked out of the room. I stayed still for a minute so I wouldn't have to share an elevator with him.

Paul was a good friend. If I rode down with him, he'd probably ask again if I was okay after what happened with Charles Holden. I wasn't. I hadn't been okay in a long time. I had seen so many horrible things in my career that they didn't hurt like they used to. When I first became a police officer, I'd go home at the end of a long, hard day feeling sick to my stomach. I'd have nightmares. I'd dream of flies crawling across the bloated body of a child we pulled from a drainage ditch, I'd dream of women so badly beaten by their abusive spouses that they'd never walk or have children again, I'd dream of the mangled bodies of accident victims.

For years, I had tried to escape my dark shadow by drowning it in alcohol. That worked for a few hours, but I always sobered up eventually and felt that darkness pulling at me again. When I gave up drinking, I tried to stay sober and fight. My daughter would draw me pictures, and I'd hang them in my office or tuck them away in the glove compartment in my car. I'd look at them when my world grew dark. Those drawings scared away the shadows for a while, but only a time. Sometimes, I'd call my wife and talk to her. Just hearing her voice again would bring light into my whole world, but eventually, that, too, would dim.

My colleagues didn't have the same problems I did. I had spent my entire life fighting that darkness. No matter what I did, it always found me again. Over the years of struggle, I had come to realize something important: it found me so easily because it knew me. It knew the hollow pit inside me, that blackened thing at the center of my being. As Nietzsche's aphorism warned, I had peered into that darkness and found it peering back. Over the years, I had grown tired of fighting it. Now I just let it in.

I had changed since I first became a police officer. I had grown colder, more cynical, meaner. More than any of that, though, I carried around this seething ball of rage in my gut. The world was not the place it should be, and every day, I grew more tired of it. Paul didn't need to hear that. No one did.

After waiting a few minutes, I took an elevator downstairs and walked a block to my office building. At one time, I had worked out of the City-County building alongside every other officer in the city, but I had recently received a promotion that required me to have a private office. Unfortunately, IMPD didn't have any free space, so they borrowed a room from the prosecutors, none of whom were in the building on a Friday night.

I took the elevator to my floor and fished my keys out of my pocket as I wound my way through the cubicle maze. The nameplate beside my door read STORAGE ROOM 1. I wish I could say the sign did my office a disservice, but it didn't. I worked out of a shit hole.

Despite my outburst in the meeting with Dan Reddington, I knew the department would conduct a competent if limited investigation. They'd talk to all of Charles Holden's friends and relatives, and they'd knock on a lot of doors.

My colleagues didn't always see things that seemed obvious to me, though. Kristen Tanaka's murder was almost clinical in its precision. Her killer didn't leave any chance that she'd survive. Charles Holden's murder, however, seemed sloppy in comparison. Even a gasoline and diesel mixture spread across the house didn't guarantee the house would catch fire. Had a breeze blown through the front door or had the family purchased flame-retardant drapes, Holden could have walked out of there unscathed.

Not only that, the killer hadn't left Holden's house with anything. From Kristen's, I felt pretty sure he had taken a souvenir, the notebook outlining her investigation into my four John Does nine years ago.

If the politicians in my department wanted to believe they had a serial murderer, they could. They'd contact a behavioral psychologist with the FBI, they'd start looking for people with a grudge against the media, and they'd milk the case for all the TV time they could get. Someone needed to actually work the case, though. If our killer stole Kristen Tanaka's investigative journal, he did it for a reason. I wanted to find out why.

Upon entering my office, I threw my keys on the desk, sat down, and called the night clerk at the Coroner's

Office. They had digitized their old records a couple of years ago, so it only took a few minutes to get the autopsy reports for my four John Does. I printed those out on the color laser printer in the break room and then called up the website of the Chicago Police Department back at my desk.

Indianapolis received thousands of missing person's reports every year. The vast majority solved themselves when the missing person returned from vacation or the runaway teenager called his or her parents. Those that didn't resolve themselves quickly, we put online for the world to see. Chicago, I found, did likewise. I printed the same missing person's reports Tanaka had and then started comparing them to the documents from the coroner's office.

Intellectually, I remembered someone had tortured my victims nine years ago, but seeing the autopsy photos again and reading about the details brought their deaths viscerally in front of me.

John Doe number one had a two-inch laceration above and along the medial aspect of his right eyebrow. The coroner called that a boxer's injury. In addition, he had abrasions on his lateral, mid-right forehead, a laceration on the tissue of his upper right eyelid, lacerations along the lateral aspect of both of his eyes, and purplish areas of abrasion on his right cheek and along his chin. His right ear and ear canal showed signs of significant trauma, including a perforated eardrum. The coroner found graphite in the ear canal, causing him to surmise that our killer had shoved a sharpened pencil into our victim's ear until his eardrum burst.

I wish the autopsy report ended on the first page, but it didn't. Every report went on for page after page like that, cataloging trauma all over each young man's body and annotating photographs of everything. This murderer wanted more than to merely dismember his victims; he wanted them to suffer, and every scrap of information I had said he accomplished his goal. More important than any of that, though, the reports verified Kristen Tanaka's finding: she had ID'd my victims.

Mark Cruz, according to the missing person's report, was twenty-two and had a tattoo on his shoulder of an Aztec sun. The coroner's report listed him as John Doe #1. Cesar, Mark's twin brother, had a tattoo of a crucifix on his back surrounded by tribal symbols, like John Doe #4. Jeremy Estrada and Joseph Gomez didn't have tattoos, but Jeremy had a pink birthmark to the right of his navel like John Doe #2 and Joseph had acne scars pockmarking his shoulders like John Doe #3.

Even with an active murder case going on, it mattered that we had identified these guys.

For nine years, their families had waited for word of their sons. In some part of their mind, they knew their sons had died years ago, but even still, some part of them, maybe even a big part, hoped otherwise.

Hope was a vicious thing. It caused us to cling to our false notions even well after we knew their falsity. If I called these boys' parents, I'd break their hearts anew. I didn't want to do that, but they deserved the truth. Not only that, I needed information they might have.

Since the missing person's reports had been filed in Chicago, I spent the next hour trying to get in touch with someone there who could help me. Eventually a tired-sounding watch captain suggested I fax in a formal request to the liaison's office so someone could see it tomorrow morning and get back to me.

I thanked him, hung up, and pushed back from my desk. As I sat there trying to think of what to do next, my night caught up with me. The scent of ash and gasoline and God only knew what else crept over me, making me nearly gag. My clothes reeked, my hair felt grimy, my skin felt chapped and raw from the heat at the Holden's house.

When I closed my eyes, I could even hear the roar of the fire.

My stomach began to churn. I needed to get out of my office before I puked, so I left the room and took the stairs to the building's ground floor. Outside, I took off my jacket and held it to my nose, making me gag once again. I threw it away, knowing I'd never get the stench out of it. After that, I sat down on a bench and took long, slow breaths.

Work became a distant thought. I could think of few worse ways to die than burning to death, and yet I had willingly condemned a man to that fate tonight. I hadn't lit the fire, and I hadn't tied him up, but I could have saved him. That was my choice to let him die. Intellectually, I knew I had done the right thing, but that didn't stop his screams from echoing in my head.

I licked my lips. I wanted a drink. A couple shots of bourbon wouldn't stop the nightmares from coming, but it'd make them fuzzier. I could practically feel my hands grip the shot glass. I even knew a couple of bars nearby that catered to police officers. I'd have drinking buddies, dozens of them if I wanted.

For years, I drank because I thought it made me stronger, that it made me a better spouse. I dealt with my problems so I didn't have to share them with my wife. I had a solution for my stress. If I saw a woman beaten to death by her husband, a couple of shots would make me feel better. If I saw an elderly woman locked in her basement and starved to death while her family cashed her social security check, I'd probably drink a pint of bourbon. My stress would disappear. If I picked up a hit-and-run homicide involving a toddler the same age as one of my children, I'd drink until I passed out.

For years, I didn't know any life but that one. Then, I started drinking every night after work instead of just the bad ones. It helped me unwind, so I didn't think anything of it. Then I started drinking at lunch. It helped me get through the day, so I didn't think it was too bad. Then, I started having shots of vodka alongside my Bloody Mary at breakfast.

I pretended Hannah didn't know I drank, but she did. Then, one day, I came to bed sober, and she thanked me. I had never felt more ashamed in my life. My entire world came crashing down on me that night. I'd like to say that I never had a drink again after that moment, but that'd be a lie. I had given in a few times, but I tried my best. Sometimes I succeeded and sometimes I failed. Tonight, I'd succeed, but not here, not alone. I needed help.

I pulled out my phone and texted my wife to see if she was awake. Instead of replying, she called me back.

"Hey," I said. "I'm coming home. I love you. I just wanted to let you know."

Chapter 8

As I turned onto my street, I slowed upon seeing the surveillance car watching my house. This time, it was a current-model luxury car, and I happened to recognize the driver. He was an attorney. I had gone to law school with him.

I probably should have just driven past, but I parked behind him and got out. The evening had cooled considerably from earlier that day, but not enough to make it feel comfortable. A warm breeze blew from the west, allowing me to smell the gasoline and ash that still clung to my clothes. Ash smudged my previously crisp, white shirt, while sweat and dirt matted my hair to my forehead. If I had seen a man who looked like me peering through the window of a vehicle at two in the morning, I might have gone for my gun.

I knocked on the car's safety glass and waited for at least thirty seconds for the window to roll down.

"Greg Becker," I said, holding out my hand and plastering a fake smile on my face. "It's nice to see you again. I'm Ash Rashid. I sat behind you in Professor Maloof's Torts class."

He didn't reach for my hand, but he didn't roll up the window, either. I smiled at him and then stood a little straighter, allowing my coat to part so he'd see the badge at my hip.

"I hear you do IP law now," I said. "You like it?"

"It's good," he said, his voice a little soft.

I put my hand on the top of his door and leaned forward. "I'm still a police officer, but I'm licensed to practice law, too. For me, I like keeping my options open. If I remember, I hear you got married and had kids. That right?"

"Twins. Two boys," he said, his voice stronger now. "They're good, too."

"I'm glad to hear that. I really am. My family means the world to me, and I'd do anything to protect them from someone I consider a threat. Are you a threat to my family right now?"

I couldn't see him well in the dim light, but he kept his hands on the steering wheel and his eyes straight ahead. I counted to ten in my mind.

"I asked you a question, Greg," I said. "Why the fuck are you watching my house?"

He kept his hands on the wheel but turned his head to look at me. "I'm not doing anything wrong. This is a public street, and I'm allowed to park here."

"Maybe so, but this isn't right and you know it. You're scaring my kids," I said, softening my voice as much as I could. "My son doesn't want to play outside anymore. My daughter wakes up with nightmares three nights out of five now.

"You're here because you're scared, and you think you need to watch us to make sure we're not dangerous. I get that. Assholes who happen to look like me and my family are blowing up buildings thousands of miles away, and you're afraid we'll start doing the same thing here. But here's the thing: we're not them. We've never done anything to hurt you or anyone else. We're a family, just like yours. Do us both a favor and go home. Hug your wife, and go to bed. Please."

He looked at my house again. "I think I'll stay right here."

I sighed and straightened. "That's your choice, and I can't stop you. I had hoped you'd be a better person than that."

He rolled up his window without saying another word, and I took a step back and took a picture of him and his car with my phone. After that, I sat in the driver's seat of my car for a few minutes as I posted the pictures to his firm's Facebook page and asked if they knew one of their senior associates spent his evenings watching a fellow attorney and police officer's house for fear that he, his wife, and his two children would become terrorists. Nothing would come of it, but it made me feel a little less impotent.

Then, I drove home, tiptoed inside the house, and stopped by each of my kid's rooms. For a moment, I just stood in their doorways, watching as their chests rose and fell. They probably didn't realize how much they brought to my life. I was lucky to have them. Hannah stirred as I walked into our bedroom. She wore one of my white t-shirts as a nightgown.

"You home for the night, or are you going back out?" she asked, yawning.

"I'm here for the night," I said, already unbuttoning my shirt. "I need to take a shower, though. I smell bad."

She nodded and then rolled over. "You've smelled worse. I love you. Try not to wake up the kids."

I showered as quietly as I could and then changed into some pajamas. Even as I lay beside my wife, I couldn't forget the rest of my night, the things I had seen. With her beside me, I could deal with them, though. I put my arm around her and felt her melt into me. I was out within moments.

Hannah awoke the next morning at 6:30 to take care of the kids. While she made breakfast, I showered, dressed for work, and then checked my messages and email.

Emilia had called me at about one in the morning to update me on her interview with Charles Holden's wife. Unfortunately, she didn't have much to say. Mrs. Holden didn't recognize the man who broke into the house, and he said very little in her presence. The intruder had an accent she couldn't recognize—Russian, maybe. He knocked on the front door, and Charles opened it. The intruder kicked him in the stomach, knocking him to the ground. Then he kicked him in the back and pulled a firearm. By then, the kids had started screaming. He forced Charles to tie his wife to a rocking chair in the nursery. She heard things after that—snippets of conversation. The killer was interested in Charles' work, but she couldn't hear what exactly.

I wrote down a few notes as I listened to the message. We'd talk through things later, but the interview partially confirmed my own thought process: this wasn't a serial murderer. Our killer came to the house with an agenda and a need for information.

In addition to the message from Emilia, I had a message from Mike Bowers asking me to give him a call. I planned to do that, but my kids were home, and my wife was making eggs. I had better things to do.

We had dawn prayer in our front room as a family and then ate breakfast as the sun rose. Megan told me about her week at school and the various projects she had worked on. It was amazing to see her grow up. When I looked at her, I still saw the four-year-old girl who would sprint toward me whenever I came home. But she was nine now and had just started third grade. I had missed so much of her life.

Kaden told me about the garbage trucks that had come by on Thursday morning. Apparently, they were awesome. After breakfast, I helped wash the dishes and then I drove into work. On the way, I called Captain Bowers.

"Mike, it's Ash. I got your message, so I'm calling you back."

Bowers grunted. "You probably know what this is about. Dan Reddington told me about your meeting with the administration last night. The department has decided that it's in the best interests of IMPD and the city if you discontinue your investigation into the murders of Kristen Tanaka and Charles Holden."

I had expected that, but it still stung a little. "Who do they have leading their task force?"

Bowers paused for just a minute. "Lieutenant Aleda Tovar."

Lieutenant Tovar had supervised me for a couple months when I worked for the department's public relations team. I didn't last long there, but I liked the assignment, and I liked my boss. She could lead a school assembly and convince kids to stay off drugs better than anyone I knew.

"Aleda's smart and well organized, but has she ever actually worked in the field?" I asked.

"She spent three years on patrol."

I merged onto the interstate, waiting for him to say something else. He didn't.

"That's it?" I asked. "She spent three years on patrol and then went into Public Relations?"

"She's good on TV, and she knows how to run a unit," said Bowers, sounding defeated even as he defended her. "In their infinite wisdom, that's who our administration decided on. Dan Reddington managed to get Paul Murphy put on the task force, so there will be some continuity at least."

Paul could work a case as well as anyone in our department given free reign to do his job. Unfortunately for him, Aleda liked to micromanage.

"They take Emilia, too?"

"No," said Bowers. "You've still got her."

"Good, then. While they're wasting their time looking for a serial killer, I'm going to find out why our killer stole a notebook from Tanaka's house."

Bowers sighed. "Try not to break anything while you're out there."

"I'll do my best."

He wished me luck and then hung up. I drove the rest of the way to my office in silence, knowing the task I had ahead of me and dreading it already. Aleda and her group would focus on Tanaka and Holden. Maybe they'd make some headway with that, but I doubted it.

These murders were about the past. Kristen found something about a cold case, and someone killed her for it. They wouldn't have taken her notebook otherwise. To solve her murder today, I need to look at the murder of four young men nine years ago.

I parked near my building, walked to my office, and then checked my mail. As I had hoped, I had a fax from the Chicago Police Department with the phone numbers of three families. I dialed the number of Mark and Cesar Cruz's mother, Anita, first.

"Hello?"

The voice sounded hesitant, likely because Mrs. Cruz didn't recognize my number.

"Yeah, hello, this is Lieutenant Ash Rashid with the Indianapolis Metropolitan Police Department. I'm looking for Mrs. Anita Cruz."

She hesitated. "I'm Anita Cruz. Can I ask what this is about?"

"About nine years ago, you filed two missing persons reports in Chicago for your sons, Cesar and Mark."

"Yes," she said, her voice growing almost a little high at the end, like she was asking a question. I leaned forward to rest my elbows on my desk.

"I'm sorry to report this," I said, speaking slowly and building speed as I went. "We believe we've found your sons in Indianapolis."

She drew in a quick breath. "Are they dead?"

"Before I say, I need to confirm a few things," I said. "Both of your sons had tattoos, right?"

She paused before speaking. "Mark had a cross on his back, and Cesar had *Tonatiuh* tattooed on his shoulder."

I pulled out a pencil and began writing details down. "*Tonatiuh*?"

"I'm sorry," she said. "He was the Aztec sun god. Cesar got it on vacation in *Cabo San Lucas* when he was in college."

That sounded like our boys, then. I gave Mrs. Cruz a moment to compose herself.

"I know this is difficult, but I need to ask you a couple more questions."

"I've been waiting a long time for this phone call," she said. "I knew it would come, but…"

Her voice trailed to nothing.

"If you'd like, I can give you a few minutes and call you back."

"No," she said almost immediately. "Just tell me what happened."

I thought back to the crime scene and what our killer had done to these boys.

"We need to have that conversation in person. As soon as possible, preferably. It would be best if you flew into town."

"I suppose I can do that. I'll arrange a flight in a few days."

Though she couldn't see me, I shook my head. "The sooner you get here, the sooner we can start working this case." I stopped speaking long enough to look at my watch. "It's 8:45 in Indianapolis. We've got a major airport in town. I bet you could get a flight this afternoon."

"I'll see what I can do."

"Good," I said. "When you come in, we're going to need a couple of things to help us legally identify your sons. Do you have any of their personal items still?"

"Why?"

I tilted my head to the side and hoped she wouldn't hear the half-truth in my voice. "This is an old case, so most of our means of victim identification are unavailable. We have to look at DNA. We can use a swab from your cheek to check for paternity, but we'd prefer to have something owned by the victim."

"This is just like TV, isn't it?"

She didn't sound excited to say that, and I couldn't blame her.

"It's a little like TV," I said, nodding. "I know this is a long shot, but anything you have would help. An old toothbrush, an old hairbrush, anything like that."

"My ex-husband and I kept everything they owned," she said. "In case they came back to visit. I'll bring you something."

I made a note on my pad to contact the Coroner's office and request that they start the process to exhume the bodies of our victims.

"That's great," I said. "My partner and I will pick you up at the airport, so give me a call on this number once you make arrangements. In the meantime, we need some information about your sons so we can start working. Is that okay?"

She inhaled a long, shaky breath. "Okay."

Mrs. Cruz answered my easy questions with little hesitation. Her sons had lived in Indianapolis for several years while one attended IU to the city's south and the other attended Purdue to the city's north. Apparently they had received full scholarships. They liked living hundreds of miles from their parents so much they actually managed to convince two of their friends from New Jersey to join them.

After college, all four boys started a web development firm in Indianapolis. According to Anita, they had quite a bit of success and ended up moving to Chicago to help grow the business. She claimed none of them had ever done drugs, none had ever gotten into fights in school, and none had ever been arrested. If I believed Mrs. Cruz, the boys had never done anything wrong in their lives. Given their manner of death, the fact that someone castrated and tortured them, I doubted that very much.

"Any of them ever have relationship problems?" I asked.

She hesitated. "You know how it is. My sons were good-looking boys, and they had money. Girls liked that. Sometimes, Cesar or Mark would have relations with a girl, and she'd think it was more serious than it was, so she'd get jealous when she saw him with another girl. It all comes out in the wash."

Reading between the lines, her sons slept around, and some of their girlfriends felt burned. That might earn them a slap, but they'd have to do a lot more than sleep around on the average girl to result in what happened to them.

"Any of these jealous young ladies threaten your sons?"

"I don't think so," she said. "Not that they told me. And they would have told me. They were good boys."

I pinched my phone to the side of my head with my shoulder and wrote a few notes down.

"Once your sons moved to Chicago, did they ever come back to Indianapolis?"

"Sure they did," she said. "They started their business in Indianapolis, so they had a lot of clients in the city still. Either Cesar or Mark came down every week."

I nodded and jotted notes. "How about their stuff? Did you keep any of that? Anything could help me."

She answered almost immediately. "We kept everything. We thought, you know, they'd come back and want their things. You probably think I sound naive. I wanted them to be alive."

"It's never naive to hope your kids are okay," I said. "Is their stuff with you in New Jersey?"

"No, we rented a storage unit in Chicago. It's still

there. We pay every year."

I glanced at my watch again. Nine in the morning. I could get to Chicago by one, pick Mrs. Cruz up at the airport, and see the storage unit that afternoon. Depending on the time of Mrs. Cruz's flight, I could even get back to Indianapolis to tuck my kids in. It'd be tight, but it could work.

"Let's try this," I said. "Chicago has two good airports, and I bet they've got flights all day. If you fly into there, I'll pick you up and we can go straight to this storage unit."

Her voice seemed to brighten a little. "I think that would work out well."

"Great. Make some flight arrangements and give me a call back at this number when you've got them."

Before hanging up, I promised that I would do everything I could to find out what happened to her sons. She thanked me and said she'd call about a flight shortly. I couldn't ask for more. After that phone call, I stood and resumed pacing around the office.

Indianapolis had some violent men and women, but rarely did we see cases involving victims whose limbs and genitals were hacked off. When I picked up the case, I recognized that my victims' injuries matched injuries described in FBI bulletins coming out of southern Texas and Arizona. It looked almost like a cartel hit, one the hitters wanted made public.

At the time, the cartels didn't work the streets and stayed mostly in Chicago. Indianapolis's drug wholesalers would drive to Chicago and buy direct, only to then repackage and dilute the drugs for distribution to mid-level dealers. The mid-level dealers would then dilute further and repackage for distribution to street-level dealers. The level of risk increased with every step down the ladder, but everybody made money.

When I caught the case nine years ago, I theorized

that my victims had somehow disturbed this happy hierarchy. Maybe they ripped off the wrong guy, maybe they made a payment late, maybe they moved in on somebody else's territory. I assumed from the very start that they played some role in the drug trade, or that they had disturbed that drug trade. Now, though, I had no idea. These guys had good jobs and college degrees. Men like that rarely showed up dead in tiny parks in gang neighborhoods.

I sat down at my desk and called the remaining two families. Both Jeremy Estrada's mother and Joseph Gomez's father knew the Cruz family well and agreed that Mrs. Cruz could act as their representative in Indianapolis. They also agreed to give her whatever personal effects they could find that might have their sons' DNA on them. While I appreciated their help, they, unfortunately, provided little extra insight into their sons or why someone would want their sons dead.

After those phone calls, I spent some time on the FBI's National Criminal Information Center Database. As far as I could tell, none of these kids had ever seen the inside of a squad car. Maybe these kids slept around and treated women badly, but they didn't sound like criminals.

I drank my coffee, thinking. I had seen jilted lovers shoot their former partners, stab them, kill their pets, burn their houses down, and destroy their cars, so if we didn't have a drug killing, we needed to start looking closer to home. I had never worked a castration before, but I had known plenty of men and women with the requisite rage to castrate their former partner. I don't know that I had ever met one angry enough to castrate her former partner's roommates, too, but I needed a theory and this one fit the little information I had.

As I scribbled some notes, someone tapped on my door.

"Come on in," I said, looking up. Emilia Rios stepped

inside. She wore a pair of dark jeans, a pink V-neck shirt, and a charcoal gray blazer. Even in the dim light in my office, her eyes had a light in them I didn't see very often. I hoped I never saw that snuffed out. "I'm glad you're here."

"I interviewed Amber Holden last night like you asked. I left you a message."

"I got it. Our situation's changed. We're still working Kristen Tanaka and Charles Holden's murders, but we're doing it indirectly. I'll brief you on the way, but we've got a long drive ahead of us. You probably want to go to the restroom."

"Thanks, Dad," she said, smiling just a little before looking toward my door. "Where we going?"

"Chicago."

Chapter 9

Lieutenant Rashid had a two-story home on a quiet cul-de-sac in a middle-class neighborhood northeast of Indianapolis. A large weeping willow cast shade over parts of the back yard, while hydrangeas near the house brought a pop of pink against the gray of the home's siding. Birds chirped nearby. A red scooter leaned against the railing on the back deck. Lieutenant Rashid had children. Aleksander could use that.

He had found the home easily enough. As usual when he needed to find someone, he started by looking through public records and newspapers. The Rashid family had sold a historic home in the city about nine months ago for a little under three-hundred thousand dollars. Unfortunately, neither the Marion County assessor nor the tax collectors in the counties surrounding Indianapolis had a record of the Rashid family buying a new home, which forced Aleksander to broaden his search and dig a little deeper.

He found what he needed on the Indianapolis Metropolitan Police Department's own website. As a command officer, the department had conveniently placed Rashid's biography online for the world to see, and in that biography, Rashid mentioned he had a bachelor's degree from Purdue University. One ten minute phone call to the Purdue Alumni Association, and he had the address of the home in front of him.

Interestingly, Aleksander wasn't the only person interested in the Rashid household. While he had parked two blocks away and watched from the rear of the home with a pair of binoculars, a four-door sedan had parked maybe two hundred yards from the front door. The man inside the car watched from a distance and occasionally fiddled with something to his side. That man could make things difficult if Aleksander had to kill Rashid later on. It was a problem for another day, though.

Like he had for every job he worked, Aleksander had closely followed Lieutenant Rashid's investigation nine years ago. Rashid and his partner at the time, Olivia Rhodes, had done their best, but in the end, they had gotten nowhere. Not that Aleksander expected them to. Removing the identifying marks from the bodies was gruesome work, but highly effective. Killing them hundreds of miles from Chicago, their homes, made it even harder to begin. Lieutenant Rashid didn't have a chance. Aleksander hadn't given him one.

Now, nine years later, Kristen Tanaka had done what the police couldn't: she had given four murdered young men names. Knowledge spread like a virus, and Tanaka's discovery had made her patient zero.

By killing her and Charles Holden, Aleksander should have averted a catastrophe. Rashid, like the rest of his department, should have begun a fruitless search for a serial murderer. In the mad scramble, the real evidence would have grown cold and memories would have faded. After a couple of days, IMPD would have become hopelessly lost. He had seen it before. Aleksander would have returned to his life in New York, secure in the knowledge that he had taken care of one of the last strands of his prior self.

Instead of joining the search, Rashid had come home at seven in the evening. Why? Aleksander didn't have an answer to that question, and it left him worried.

He held his binoculars to his face and watched. A young boy and a strikingly attractive woman wearing hijab came out the back door. A wife and a child.

Aleksander understood all too well the depths a family man could stoop in order to protect his own. When he and his wife escaped the Republic of Yugoslavia in the midst of a civil war, they first went to Greece, but neither of them spoke Greek, and the local population made it clear that they weren't wanted. From there, the couple went to Rome and then London, always seeking a permanent home but never finding it.

Then they came to the US. They had sold everything they owned to get there, but it was worth it. An immigration lawyer helped them with the paperwork that allowed them to claim political asylum. For the first time in a long time, they felt safe, surrounded by good-hearted people, many of whom had experienced lives very similar to their own. A charity even helped them rent an apartment in a neighborhood in Brooklyn.

True, their apartment had bars on the windows, and they occasionally heard gunfire at night, but they had both grown accustomed to that over the years. He and Vesna got jobs—lousy jobs, but jobs just the same—and they enrolled in community college at night. They saw their American dream just around the corner.

And then Vesna became pregnant.

It was a wonderful thing at first, but then she started getting tired. She worked the front desk at a dry cleaner, but she couldn't keep up with the other girls. She lost her job and, without her salary, the bills began piling up. She tried to find a job in an office, but no one wanted to hire a pregnant woman who spoke stilted, broken English.

After two months in which they couldn't pay their rent, their landlord knocked on their door. Aleksander didn't know his full name, but people called him Roscoe. Though he didn't show up often, everyone in the neighborhood knew him. He owned half a dozen apartment buildings, most of which rented by the week. For those tenants down on their luck, he offered loan services, and for those flush with cash, he ran a poker game in the basement of one of his buildings. People around the neighborhood speculated that he had connections to organized crime, but then everyone in that part of Brooklyn did.

The day he knocked on the door, Roscoe wore a green overcoat, a pair of jeans and an orange shirt. It was sprinkling, and the light in the hallway glinted off his wet, olive-colored skin. Vesna answered. When Roscoe saw her and her belly distended with child, he smiled the cold, unfeeling grin of a man who knew quite well the position of power he had over the people before him.

"Mrs. Popovic," he said, nodding to her and sliding his eyes up and down her frame. He chewed the end of a toothpick like some gangster from a bad movie. "Did your husband say I was coming by?"

She nodded, her back straight as she swept her arm toward the living room. Aleksander sat on the couch.

"Come in," she said. "My husband is there. I'll make coffee."

"Make sure it's the good stuff," said Roscoe, his eyes passing over pictures and bookcases full of the few items they still possessed from their lives overseas. "I don't drink that decaf shit."

"Of course," she said, turning and going to the kitchen. Aleksander hated the man in front of him. He hated his swagger, he hated the power he wielded over others, he hated the comfort with which he walked into a stranger's room and catalogued his possessions. One day, he'd be rid of men like Roscoe. But not yet. For now, he had to sit and listen while an imbecile lectured him on the importance of financial responsibility.

"Please sit down," said Aleksander, standing and gesturing toward the armchair kitty-corner to the sofa. He had carried that chair for almost two miles on the sidewalks of New York after finding it with the trash on a middle-class family's stoop on his way home from work. The fabric over the arms had worn so thin he could see the batting beneath, and the seat sunk so low his pregnant wife needed help to stand after sitting in it, but still, it was his. He didn't consider it a prized possession, but it mattered to him. He had worked hard for that chair, sweating and enduring the stares and insults of the people he passed. Roscoe looked at it with barely held contempt and then shook his head.

"Next time, you ask a man to sit, you better give him something worth sitting on. You understand me?"

Aleksander hadn't meant to insult him, but it didn't matter. He had known men like Roscoe before, had fought beside them in the Yugoslav Army, had even killed one. Men like that heard what they wanted to hear. The world, in their view, should accommodate them rather than the other way around.

"I'll do better next time."

Roscoe smoothed the front of his coat. "That's all right. I know you ain't from around here. You do things different wherever you're from. Here, we do things my way. And here, you owe me. Big. Five grand. We need to start a repayment plan, or we're going to have a problem."

Aleksander owed him money, but not nearly that much. He and Roscoe both knew that, but Aleksander didn't have a lot of negotiating room.

"I thought I owed you two months rent," he said. "That's sixteen-hundred. I can pay you that in a week. I'm going to help a friend rebuild his deck. He's going to give me a loan."

Roscoe wagged his finger and shook his head. "You're forgetting the fines for not paying. And then you've got to pay for my time coming out here. That comes to five large. You pay me that today, I'll leave and we'll be good. You don't, you and that pregnant coffeemaker can get out of my building."

Aleksander swallowed. The room felt hot, and he could feel himself losing the grip on his temper.

"We don't have anywhere to go."

Roscoe tilted his head to the side. "Then I sincerely hope you've got a stack of cash for me."

Aleksander clenched his fists to keep his hands from trembling. "I can give you three-hundred dollars today. It's our grocery money for the month. It's all we have."

"Afraid that ain't enough. Time to get going."

Aleksander had never begged in his life. It wasn't that he was too proud; he simply never had the need.

"Please," he said. "Vesna is pregnant. You can't put us on the street. Tell me what I can do. I can fix things. I'm good at that. And I can clean. I clean at an elementary school already. I can clean your buildings, too."

Roscoe crossed his arms. "I've already got people who fix things and clean my shit. What else can you do?"

"I can repair appliances. I fix dishwashers and refrigerators."

Roscoe exhaled a long, slow breath. "I already said I've got people who can fix things. If that's all you got, you better get going before I get mad."

"I was in the Army," said Aleksander. "I was a medic. I can…" His voice trailed off. "I can do something for you. I don't know."

Roscoe went silent for fifteen or twenty seconds. Aleksander held his breath.

"You ever kill anybody?"

Aleksander hesitated and looked at the ground. "Yes."

Roscoe didn't respond verbally, but he nodded almost imperceptibly. "Maybe I can use you then. I'll think about it. Meantime, the bitch in 4A has been complaining about her sink backing up. Fix it. I'll see you tomorrow."

Aleksander fixed the woman's sink and then came home. Roscoe didn't ask him to kill anyone the next day. Instead, he gave Aleksander a list of people who owed him money. If Aleksander didn't come back with at least two-thousand dollars, he and his wife wouldn't have a place to sleep.

Looking back, Aleksander had options. Roscoe couldn't just kick them out in the middle of the night. There were procedures to follow, paperwork to fill out, notices to be given. It would take months, long enough for Vesna to have her baby. And then, if they did lose their home, there were people who would have given them shelter.

Aleksander didn't know that, though. He was a foreigner in a world he didn't understand. In his mind, a list of seven people stood in the way of his family surviving one more night. He needed almost three-hundred dollars a person. Surely people could afford that to keep his family from the streets.

The first apartment he visited, the guy who answered the door told him he didn't have any money to give. By his ratty clothes, Aleksander believed him. He didn't beg the man or tell him his story. It wouldn't have helped. People didn't go to men like Roscoe for a loan if they had anywhere else to turn. The second man on the list cried when he saw Aleksander at the door. He begged Aleksander not to hurt him. Aleksander left without a thing. Two more times it went like that. With each name crossed off the list, he felt his heart beat faster. His wife couldn't sleep on the street. Not at seven months pregnant. Not in the dead of a New York winter.

He knocked on the door of the fifth house, and a man in a blue sweater and a pair of jeans answered. He had big hands and an inch-long scar on his brow. His skin had the perpetual glow of a man who spent time in tanning booths. The scent of cigarettes wafted over him. Even from the hallway of the apartment building, Aleksander could see furniture a little nicer than anything in the homes he had previously visited. A hockey stick rested on top of a credenza beside the front door. A man who could afford a hobby like hockey could afford to pay his debts.

"Roscoe gave me your name," said Aleksander. "I'm here for his money."

For a moment, the hockey player just looked at him as if he didn't comprehend what Aleksander had said. Then, he raised his eyebrows and a smile lit his face.

"Get out of here," he said. "I'll pretend you didn't just wake me up from a nap."

Aleksander put his hands in his pockets and felt the pocket knife he had brought along for protection. He hadn't pulled it out yet today. He hadn't needed it.

"I can't leave until I have his money. If I don't get it, I lose my home. My wife is pregnant. Do you understand? We don't have anywhere to go. Please. You don't have to pay me everything. Just what you've got. This is the only way. Please."

The smile faltered for just a moment. Aleksander thought he might give in, that he'd have his first success of the day, but that hope died in an instant.

"I've got a sleeping bag if you want it. Might do your old lady good. Twenty bucks."

In that moment, something, some further bit of his humanity, broke. This new world into which he had brought his wife was no different than the old. The villains spoke a different language, but they were just as vile as the men he had left behind. As a medic, Aleksander knew enough about anatomy and modern medicine to patch up the men in his unit for many common battlefield injuries. He also knew how to hurt people.

Before the hockey player could react, Aleksander allowed his anger, his rage, his frustration to overcome him. Life shouldn't have been like this. He worked hard every day to protect and take care of his wife. They prayed together and lived good, decent lives. And yet, wicked men hurt them with impunity. He had known that even before he and Vesna left Belgrade, but it took this moment for the last facade of his idealism to crash to the ground.

The world didn't care about him or his values. If he wanted to survive, he needed to become as mean as the men oppressing him.

He slipped the knife out of his pocket and stepped forward. His arm swung without conscious thought. He stabbed the hockey player in the gut and felt the blood cascade down over his hand. The bigger man groaned, his eyes wide.

"I was a medic in the Army, and I've stabbed you in your hypogastric region. Don't move," said Aleksander, forcing his voice to a whisper so the neighbors couldn't hear. "If I slide my knife to the left or the right, I will cut your bowels open and spill your intestines on the floor. You'll die. Do you understand what I'm saying?"

The hockey player nodded. Beads of sweat began to form on his forehead as he trembled. "Yeah."

"Do you have any loved ones? A wife? Children? Girlfriend?"

"I've got a girlfriend."

Aleksander nodded. "Then get my money, or I'll do this to her as well. I want five-thousand dollars. You have one hour."

Aleksander pulled the knife out. The hockey player fell to his knees, gasping. Aleksander wiped the blade on the man's shirt.

"Put some tape on your wound to temporarily close it. If you want to avoid contracting septicemia, you need to get to an emergency room and receive antibiotics. If you don't, you'll die. But get my money first."

He nodded, and Aleksander left. His hands trembled, and his breath came out in spurts. He had blood on his clothes, his arms, and everywhere else. Outside the hockey player's presence, the gravity of what he had just done crashed over him. He tossed his knife into a storm drain and raced home. He was lucky he didn't run into a police officer. Vesna met him at the door, her eyes wide.

"Are you hurt?"

"No," he said, pushing past her to the bathroom. "Get your things. We need to get out of here. I did something stupid."

Vesna's chest rose and fell with her breath. "Did you kill Roscoe?"

"I should have," said Aleksander, scrubbing his hands to get the blood from beneath his fingernails. "It's not important what I did. I need to burn my clothes. Get me something to wear."

Vesna left and went to their bedroom. Aleksander could hear her crying, but she did as he asked. For the second time, she would have to leave a life behind. He had failed her, and he hated himself for it.

"I'm sorry," he said. "I'm sorry for everything. You deserve better than this."

"I deserve the man I love," she said, bringing a pair of brown corduroy slacks, a white t-shirt and a green sweater to the bathroom. "Give me your clothes. I'll take them."

He stripped and then stepped into the shower to wash the blood from his arms. Ten minutes after stepping into his shower, he heard the knock on his door. It started softly, a normal knock. Could have been a neighbor. Could have been a friend. Then it turned into a heavy thump when he didn't answer.

"Hey, Aleksander. Open up. It's me."

Me being Roscoe. Aleksander turned off the water and dressed quickly. Vesna hadn't returned yet. Aleksander suddenly wished he hadn't disposed of his knife. He couldn't solve their problems, but maybe he could take Roscoe out with him. He grabbed a fillet knife, the largest knife he and Vesna happened to own, from the kitchen and then opened the door. Roscoe stepped inside, grinning and wagging a finger at him.

"Jesus, my man, I didn't think you had it in you," he said. "Gives me chills what you did."

"My wife isn't here," said Aleksander, hiding the blade against his forearm and hoping he wouldn't have to stab a second person in a day. "Just please let her go. I lost my temper. She had nothing to do with it. We'll clear the apartment."

Roscoe cocked his head to the side. "You think I'm going to kick you out now? Are you kidding me? I could use two of you. Tony Barnes just called me from a payphone outside the hospital to tell me he's got five-grand for me. He only owed me two grand. That was brilliant, stabbing him like that. I think you might have found your calling, my friend. I have work for you."

And that was how Aleksander earned his first permanent American home. Roscoe moved them to a new apartment in a better building, and Aleksander became his debt collector full time. The first few weeks left him feeling empty and angry at the end of the day, but he and Vesna no longer had to worry about sleeping on the street. His wife was safe. They had a beautiful, healthy daughter two months later. That gave him purpose.

Aleksander had no illusions about what he had sacrificed by working for Roscoe. The moment he plunged a knife into a man's gut, he had stopped being the good, kind man he had always strived to be. In the end, though, it didn't matter. Aleksander's world didn't have room for good men.

Now, as he sat on the street two blocks from Lieutenant Rashid's back door, watching a woman and her son play, he wondered if he still had that meanness inside him. Could he kill a family now if he had to? He had almost killed Charles Holden's family. He wouldn't feel good about killing the Rashids, but he could do it. He hoped it wouldn't come down to that, though. His soul didn't need another black mark against it.

He watched for another few minutes and then reached to the seat beside him for the notebook he had taken from Kristen Tanaka's house.

Unknown to her, she had marked herself for death by tracking down Alonzo Cruz, Aleksander's employer, in prison. The moment she left their meeting, Alonzo had called Aleksander on a cell phone his lawyer had smuggled to him and said they had a problem.

Tanaka got lucky in her investigation. That much was obvious after reading just a few pages of the notebook. She found Cesar, Mark, Joseph and Jeremy by searching missing person's databases at random. Then, once she had their names, she began interviewing everyone connected to the case that she could. Indianapolis's cold case unit probably would have done the same thing had they opened the case again.

From what he could tell, Tanaka had started off well, but she didn't get anywhere. She believed the boys had become involved with drug trafficking. Aleksander didn't know what sin they committed, but he doubted that very much. Alonzo knew enough not to order a hit on a cartel member, his blood or not. Aleksander was in the dark about the precise nature of his job, but that didn't matter, either. He knew what he needed to do.

He looked up a final time as Lieutenant Rashid's wife and son ran around their backyard. They looked happy. For their sakes, he hoped Lieutenant Rashid fell into line soon. If Charles Holden hadn't convinced Rashid they had a serial murderer attacking reporters, he'd simply add another piece of evidence for him to ponder. This one would push IMPD and the media into a frenzy.

It was time to kill a journalist.

Chapter 10

I began briefing Emilia on the case as we walked out of the building and to my car. Clouds partially obscured the sun, leaving most of the streets covered by shadow, while a patchwork of dirt, weeds, and dormant grass covered what should have been a healthy stretch of lawn around us. It hadn't rained in what felt like months, and even Indianapolis's normally humid air felt dry on my throat. I didn't like driving in the rain, but we needed it at the moment. Judging by the clouds in the sky, maybe we'd finally get it.

Emilia listened to my recitation and nodded where appropriate, at least until we hit the second row of the parking lot and I clicked the button to unlock my car, a Volkswagen Golf R. To most people, my car looked like just another economy hatchback in a parking lot full of similar vehicles. But those who knew cars recognized I drove something a little special. My car had almost three hundred horsepower, could hit sixty miles an hour from a dead stop in under five seconds, and had a top speed of 155. When we reached it, Emilia began walking her fingers down the hood the same way my wife walked her fingers across my back when she wanted me to take her to bed.

"Given what happened last night, I didn't think it was appropriate say anything," she said, "but I love your new car."

Having seen Emilia drive, I probably should have expected her interest.

"I'm a fan myself."

She took her eyes off the car long enough to look at me. She had an exuberant look on her face that reminded me of my fourteen-year-old self after learning a friend of mine had intercepted his father's latest issue of Playboy Magazine before the old man knew it arrived.

"You thought about remapping the ECU?" she asked. "With just a little work, I bet you could get your quarter-mile time down to the low eleven-second range."

"I'm not exactly sure what that means, but it sounds like it would void my warranty."

She chuckled a little. "Oh, yeah. Think of how much fun it would be until the engine exploded, though." She took a step back from the vehicle, shook her head admiringly, and then said something almost beneath her breath. "The things I could do with you."

She once again walked her fingers across my car's hood, this time leaving me little doubt about her interest.

"My wife preferred my Audi before those crazy assholes in Bloomington wrecked it," I said.

"Hannah is wonderful, but she doesn't know cars," said Emilia, finally taking her eyes off my car long enough to look at me. "I do. Just so you know, if your car were a man, I'd rip his clothes off right now and go to town on him until neither of us could walk for days. What'd you name her?"

I took a moment to think through my answer. Every year, my department has required training seminars for all supervisory officers to ensure we understand how to create an inclusive work environment. Based on what I had learned, I felt pretty sure Emilia had just sexually harassed ....someone. Who or what, though, I couldn't say.

"As much as I like the car, I haven't given it one yet."

"She deserves a name. If you let me drive her to Chicago, I'll think of one for you."

I didn't drive with Emilia often, but those few occasions she had driven me somewhere had left me terrified. Before working with her, I had never seen a police cruiser hit 130. I hoped to God I never had to see it again.

"Maybe next time," I said, my speech still halting and slow. "I'll take this one."

She begrudgingly climbed into the passenger seat. Since I didn't know how long we'd stay in Chicago, we stopped by Emilia's apartment so she could pack an overnight bag. That only took a few minutes. It took considerably longer at my house because Kaden saw me and then clung to my side as if he would never see me again. Eventually, Hannah peeled him away so I could pack a bag. I hugged him and then held my wife tight before leaving.

After that, I joined my partner in the car, and we passed through the city without saying a word. Once we hit the interstate north of Indianapolis, flat farmland extended for miles around us. After maybe half an hour of driving, I glanced at my partner out of the corner of my eye. She fiddled with something on her cell phone.

"You know what the difference between an ice berg and a lint roller is?" I asked, forcing my voice to sound chipper.

She popped her head up from her phone. "Excuse me?"

"The difference between an ice berg and a lint roller. One crushes boats, and the other brushes coats." She looked confused, so I tilted my head to the side. "My daughter told me the same joke when we drove this road last. She had just learned that glaciers covered most of this part of Indiana during the ice age and flattened the landscape."

"I see," she said, a little smile on the corner of her lips.

"My next joke will be funnier," I said. "I swear."

Emilia didn't respond beyond smiling. We drove the rest of the way to Chicago in relative silence, interrupted only by a phone call from Mrs. Cruz to let us know she had booked a flight and would arrive at Midway Airport at three in the afternoon. I had hoped she could get there earlier, but we'd take what we could get.

After arriving in the city, we drove straight to the Chicago Police Department's headquarters on South Michigan Avenue to tell them what we were up to. Once we finished that, we drove to Midway Airport where we waited for Mrs. Cruz. Before we even realized her plane landed, a very attractive woman with black hair and small, hairline wrinkles around her eyes came toward us. She could have passed for forty-five, though I knew she was probably closer to sixty. She carried a purse half the size of a pillow over one shoulder, and she wheeled a red, rolling suitcase behind her. She grimaced when she saw us.

"Anita Cruz?" I asked, standing. She nodded, so I shook her hand. "I'm Lieutenant Ash Rashid. We spoke on the phone." I then gestured to Emilia, who had stood beside me. "This is Detective Emilia Rios."

"It's nice to meet you both," she said, shaking both our hands before turning to face me. "I recognize you from your pictures. You're in the newspaper a lot."

"More often than I'd like to be," I said, already turning and gesturing toward the exits. "If you don't mind, let's head out. The sooner we get going, the sooner Detective Rios and I can get to work."

"Of course," said Mrs. Cruz, nodding. "I'd like to talk about my sons, too. I need to find out what happened to them."

I glanced at Emilia. She didn't have children, but she understood what we'd have to do today, at least intellectually. Almost ten years had passed since this woman had lost her sons. A lot of old wounds could scab over and heal in that time. Time had likely blunted some of the pain Mrs. Cruz felt for her sons, but very shortly, we'd bring it all back.

When we got to my car, Emilia sat in back, while Mrs. Cruz took the front passenger seat. I spent the next fifteen minutes telling her what I knew and how her sons had died. She took it better than I expected, but her face paled noticeably about halfway through, and she asked me to turn on the air. After I finished speaking, she thanked me and then sat in silence for a few minutes.

"There's more going on here than just your sons," I said. "I believe that the person who murdered them also murdered two journalists from Indianapolis who started investigating your sons' deaths. It's very likely that he will murder more people unless we stop him. You can help us. You know your sons. Can you think of anyone who would try to hurt them?"

She looked to the window and shook her head. I couldn't see her face well through the reflection on the glass, but I heard her cry.

"My sons were good…I mean, they owned a business. They didn't hurt anyone."

"Did your sons ever experiment with drugs, Mrs. Cruz?" asked Emilia, leaning forward on the backseat.

Mrs. Cruz looked back at her and wiped a tear from her eye.

"Every kid experiments. That's part of being a kid."

Emilia took a notepad from her jacket pocket. I wish she hadn't done that because Mrs. Cruz immediately stared at it. A notepad could play a surprising strategic role during an interview or interrogation. In the past, I had shown suspects irrefutable evidence that they had participated in a crime only to have them lie to my face about it and produce elaborate stories to explain away my findings. When I got that notepad out, though, they realized they had to speak carefully or risk having their lies used against them. Sometimes, that notepad alone scared them into speaking the truth. Other times, though, it stopped an interview cold.

"How did your boys experiment?" I asked. "We're not here to get anybody in trouble, especially for being a kid. I remember the things I did in college, and I'm sure Detective Rios has similar stories. Unless they added more hours to the day, I guarantee your boys didn't do more drugs than me."

That seemed to loosen Mrs. Cruz up a little bit. I had actually only smoked marijuana once—and even then I did it accidentally, believing my buddy's bong was a hookah with tobacco inside—but I heard one of my philosophy professors from college say something similar in an argument about the legalization of marijuana.

"I caught them with some dope once," she said, looking from me and then to Emilia. "I didn't think it was a big deal. Cesar had a joint in his pocket. I was doing the laundry and found it when I started washing his jeans."

"They ever do anything other than marijuana?" asked Emilia. Mrs. Cruz eyed her warily, but then shook her head.

"No. They were good boys."

Before Emilia could ask a follow up question, I cleared my throat.

"When we spoke on the phone," I said, nodding to Mrs. Cruz, "you mentioned a storage space you rented for your sons' things. Detective Rios and I would very much like to see that."

Mrs. Cruz stared at me with dark, implacable eyes. Then, she blinked and took a breath.

"It's in Wrigleyville by their old apartment." She began digging through her purse. "I've got the address on my cell phone."

Once she gave us the address, we headed out. With traffic, it took us about an hour to reach that part of town. The storage facility had green awnings over the windows out front, neat landscaping, and an indoor loading dock for trucks. I turned into the lot and parked.

Nobody loitered on the street nearby, and nobody seemed to take notice of the red VW in the parking lot. Mrs. Cruz led us inside. At roughly five feet wide, the storage units near the front of the building could probably hold about a room's worth of household furnishings, but we kept walking until the units increased to the size of a two-car garage.

Without saying a word to us, Mrs. Cruz stopped in front of unit 98-c and used a key from her keychain to open the padlock. Before she could open the door, I gently put a hand on her shoulder until she looked at me.

"Thank you for leading us here, but I need you to wait in the lobby for us at this point."

"Excuse me?" she asked, lowering her chin. "This is my sons' property. You have no right to tell me to leave."

Actually, Emilia and I had every right. In Indiana, I could have had a search warrant within half an hour for the storage unit with or without Mrs. Cruz's approval. Here, we would have needed to call the Chicago Police and work with them, but we could still get in the unit within a few hours. I didn't want to do that, but I didn't want someone looking over my shoulder as I investigated a sensitive case, either.

"I understand your concern. I'm a father myself, and I can't imagine what you're going through," I said, hoping to make my voice sound comforting. "Detective Rios and I will treat your sons' property with all due care and respect, but this is how it has to be. I need you to trust that Detective Rios and I will do everything within our power to find the individuals who killed your sons. Sometimes that means we have to speak very bluntly with each other. We can't properly investigate your sons' case if that means guarding what we say so we don't offend you."

She stared right through me, but then she took a step back and then another. She left without saying a word.

Once she disappeared around a bend, Emilia stepped close.

"I don't think she's going to put you on her Christmas card mailing list."

"I get that same feeling," I said, kneeling down to pull open the rolling door. Both Emilia and I groaned as soon as I did. The unit had enough boxes and furniture haphazardly stacked inside to furnish a four-bedroom house. It would take us hours to catalog everything and even longer to separate the significant pieces from the insignificant.

"Any idea what we're looking for?" asked Emilia.

"Preferably, boxes that say things like 'contains secret list of people who want to kill us.'"

Emilia smirked. "Barring that, anything else?"

I took a quick breath and surveyed the room. Nothing stood out to me.

"Anything unusual, anything that would give us a glimpse into their lives."

She nodded, pulled a pair of blue polypropylene gloves from her pockets, and then snapped them onto her hands. I did likewise beside her and stepped into the room. The air smelled stale, and a thin layer of dust covered the tops of dressers and tables. Emilia started on the right side of the room, while I started with the boxes on the left. The first few boxes I opened contained small kitchen appliances and utensils. Nothing helpful there. The next few I opened held clothes. I didn't recognize all the brands, but judging by those I did know—Ralph Lauren, Valentino, and Versace—these boys had money to spend.

As I looked through the boys' clothes, Emilia opened a wooden chest on the other side of the room and laughed.

"What'd you find?" I asked, glancing up.

"Porno," she said, holding up a few DVD cases and

looking at the backs. "Our victims liked large-breasted, flexible women. Think we should add that to the profile?"

I smiled genuinely for the first time in several hours.

"If we knew which of the boys the porn belonged to, we could take it and bag it for DNA."

Emilia stood up straighter and looked at me. "That's really gross, Ash."

"Just be glad you're wearing gloves."

She went back to her search, but not with the same gusto she had displayed a few minutes earlier. I made my way through the boxes until I found one with four identical clamshell cell phones, each about the size of two decks of cards glued together. They probably only stored twenty or thirty numbers, but if we could find a charger for these, they might tell us who our boys talked to before they died.

"I've got cell phones," I said. "We'll take these with us."

"And I've got computers," said Emilia, almost immediately. "They're in some kind of shelving system."

I put the phones on top of a pile of boxes and weaved through piles of furniture to Emilia's side of the room. The computers she found looked like rack-mounted servers, the kind that ran corporate IT networks behind the scenes. I only recognized them because I had noon and afternoon prayers with a member of the city's IT department in their break room. I pointed to a plaque screwed into the side of the rack.

"Property of TNT Enterprises," I said. "Must be our boy's company."

She nodded and took a step back and then put her hands on her hips. "I bet you want to take these home with us and have our techs look at them."

"Yeah. We'll call down and get a van and some bodies to help us move everything. We're going to have to stay in Chicago for the night."

She looked over the room and nodded. "I'll call my mom so she can feed my dog."

We continued our search in relative silence, but very little else stood out. Our victims had money and expensive taste, but we didn't find drug paraphernalia, guns, or cash. Even after several hours of searching, I had no idea why someone would want them dead. I straightened after opening the last box and finding about a dozen, carefully folded T-shirts.

"What do you think?" I asked, looking toward Emilia. She wiped a bead of perspiration from her forehead with the back of her forearm and then shrugged.

"It's looking like a bust," she said. Then she nodded toward a row of utilitarian gray file cabinets near the back of the room. "We should check those before we leave."

With our luck so far, they'd probably contain long-expired coupons, but I nodded anyway and crossed toward the cabinets. Each of them had a lock, but I had gotten fairly adept at picking simple locks in the last few months.

I picked the first one and found row after row of what looked like freelance employment contracts. The boys did own a business, so that made sense. As I pulled one of the folders, out, though, a photograph of an attractive and nude young woman slipped out. I put the picture back in that folder and picked up the next file. It, too, contained a picture of a nude young woman.

"Hey, Emilia, I need you to see something," I said, pulling out a file at random. This one had several pictures of a nude girl, but it also had a document that claimed it provided information pursuant to 18 USC section 2257. Even though I had taken multiple courses in employment law when I was in school, I didn't recognize the section. As Emilia walked over to me, I took out my cell phone to look it up. She picked up a file and leafed through it.

"These pictures look homemade," she said, raising

her eyebrows. "You think she's underage?"

Before answering, I looked down at my phone and read the first search result.

"No, she's 18," I said, looking up from my phone. "Our victims made porn."

Chapter 11

"Well, well, well," said Emilia, rubbing her hands together. "The plot thickens."

"Something like that," I said, slipping my phone into my pocket. "We'll take the filing cabinets with us tomorrow. Meantime, I want to grab the cell phones and a couple of files from the cabinet. We can work on those tonight. You didn't see anything that looked like a cell charger, did you?"

"No, but I'll look again."

Emilia and I spent another twenty minutes in the unit until we found a box full of cables and chargers of various sorts. I grabbed that, stuffed the phones inside, and went to the file cabinets.

Most of the girls whose files were in the cabinets lived in Indiana, but I found five that listed their addresses as Chicago. A lot of time had passed, but hopefully a few still lived in town. I doubted they could tell us much about our case, but they knew our victims. We needed an honest assessment of them, one not filtered through a mom's rose-colored glasses.

Before leaving, I took almost forty pictures with my cell phone to document the room. Then, I locked the door with a padlock, and Emilia and I met Mrs. Cruz in the lobby.

"Did you find anything?" she asked.

"A few things of interest," I said, nodding. "We'd like to come back with a moving van tomorrow and pick some of the larger things up. We also found some cell phones, which we'll look at tonight." I paused for just a second. "How much did you know about your sons' business?"

Mrs. Cruz blinked a few times and then tilted her

head to the side. "I barely know how to use a computer, so they didn't tell me much. They were an internet startup, but they were doing well. It was a tough business with a lot of competition."

Probably tougher than she realized. The porn industry had every legal right to exist, but it attracted a more unsavory class of businessman than a traditional web development firm. I had even read an FBI bulletin once that said at least two of the major crime families in New York had ties to porn. Our victims had ample opportunity to get into things way over their head. We were getting somewhere.

"We padlocked the unit, so that should be good to go until tomorrow," I said. "Do you have somewhere to stay tonight? A hotel, maybe?"

Mrs. Cruz looked to the receptionist's desk and pointed to the woman behind the counter. "That young lady said there's a rental car place up the street. If you'll drive me there, I'll rent a car and find a hotel. There are a few things I need to do while I'm in town."

I agreed and then got directions from the salesperson. Hertz was a couple of miles straight east, directly across from Wrigley Stadium. We dropped off Mrs. Cruz and found the nearest budget hotel, where we rented two rooms. Normally, the department put us up in dumps, but my room had a king sized bed, a clean bathroom and even a small, round table and two chairs. I couldn't ask for more for less than seventy bucks a night in a major city. After getting settled into her own room, Emilia sat on one of the chairs in mine and called Captain Bowers to arrange for a moving van tomorrow. While she did that, I called home. My daughter picked up the phone.

"Hi, sweetheart," I said, in the quiet singsong voice I reserved for only my children. "How are you?"

"I'm really mad at you, dad," said Megan, her voice almost shaking.

It took me a moment, but then I remembered. "Because I missed your soccer game. I'm sorry."

"Yes," she said. "Mr. Abaza came, and he's really important."

David Abaza, her friend Lelia's father, owned the only *halal* grocery store in town. I didn't know if that made him important, but it did make him a prominent member of our rather insular community.

"I'm sorry, pumpkin, but I had to work," I said, glancing up at Emilia. She pretended not to hear, but I caught her smiling nonetheless. "You knew I might not be able to make it."

"But it's different, now. You've been home."

In years past, she treated my absences like just another part of her life. They didn't upset her because she didn't expect me to show up. Since my promotion to Lieutenant, I had spent a lot more time at home and had started earning back some of the faith she had lost in me over the years. I didn't have a choice about coming to Chicago, but she wouldn't understand that. And nor should she. She deserved a father who kept his promises.

"I'm sorry, honey. You have every right to be mad at me."

"You told me you would come. I told my friends."

"I'll do better next time," I said, hoping I'd hear some the anger leave her voice. "I promise."

"You'll just break it."

"Honey, I'm-"

My wife's voice cut me off before I could apologize again. Hannah explained that Megan had stormed outside and thrown the phone on the couch. I couldn't blame her. I had an amazing mother who did her best for me, but she worked two jobs, and I barely saw her. My older sister helped me get ready for school and made us both dinner. For a long time, I blamed my mom for not being there at my baseball games or my soccer games. Only after having kids of my own did I realize how much she sacrificed for me. She gave up her entire life so her kids could have decent educations and a safe place to live.

I didn't have an absent mom; I had the best mom I could ever ask for. I hoped one day Megan would say something similar about her father.

"Can you tell Megan I'm sorry?" I asked.

"She knows you're sorry," said Hannah.

Before hanging up, she mentioned that the surveillance car out front had moved even further from the home, but now they came with binoculars. Very subtle. I told her I loved her and reminded her to call the police if she felt threatened—not that she needed the warning.

After Hannah hung up, I held the phone to my head, pretending to be on a call still, when in actuality I said a prayer asking God to watch over them all while I was away. When I looked up again after slipping my phone in my pocket, I caught Emilia looking at me and smiling.

"Megan loves you," she said. "I could hear it in her voice. You should also turn down your cell phone. It's practically on speaker."

She wasn't the first to tell me that about my phone. Ear protection or not, I think I had spent too much time at the firing range over the years.

"Probably good advice," I said. "What do you say we get to work?"

Emilia nodded, and we turned our attention to the items we took from the storage unit. We could only find one of the cell phone chargers, so we had to charge the phones in a rotating schedule. Next, we turned to the employment files we had taken and started by simply calling the phone numbers listed. Two were out of service, one went to a Chinese restaurant, and two others were answered by individuals who had never heard of the young women we had hoped to call. Next, we started looking people up on Facebook and found three of our young women within ten minutes. Two of the three had moved out of town, but the third, Jean Whitfield, had become a lawyer and now worked for a very large law firm with offices in Chicago, Indianapolis, St. Louis, New York, and Washington DC. She had fifty-eight friends and had adjusted her privacy settings so that we couldn't see much of her page except her picture. Evidently, she valued her privacy. If we had to, we could probably use that.

"She looks normal," said Emilia. "All three women look normal."

"What do you mean?" I asked, looking up from my phone.

"They've got kids and husbands and careers. I just thought a thirty-year old porn star would look different. You know, more strung-out heroin user than suburban housewife or big shot lawyer."

I knew what she meant, but I didn't know if I agreed. A couple of years back, two of our vice detectives arrested a female escort from Washington DC who had a master's degree in economics and a head for numbers that could have landed her a job with any number of Wall Street firms. Her client, an Indianapolis businessman, flew her into Indianapolis first class and paid her fifteen-thousand dollars to spend the weekend with him, to stay on his arm at a business party, and to sound intelligent when his guests asked questions. She slept with him, sure, but this guy could have gone local if he merely wanted sex. He needed something more.

"Sex work is changing," I said. "Wouldn't surprise me at all to find prostitutes with law degrees."

Emilia raised her eyebrows. I didn't know what she wanted, but then she rolled her hands as if she wanted me to continue.

"What?" I asked.

"You can't talk about lawyers who hook on the side without making a joke. It's practically a rule. I'll give you an example." She lowered her voice to mimic me. "I met a prostitute with a law degree last night. For the first time in my life, I got screwed by my lawyer, and I got a happy ending."

I closed the Facebook app on my phone and then opened a browser so I could find the website of Jean's firm.

"Normally, I make the wisecracks when I work with somebody. I didn't realize I had given up that responsibility."

She nodded, her expression serious. "Women are funny now. I saw a documentary on it."

I didn't know if she meant that as a joke, too, so I nodded and clicked over to Jean's page on her firm's website. According to her bio, she had joined the firm five years ago with a specialty in anti-trust litigation after graduating Order of the Coif from Northwestern University Law School. Oddly enough, it didn't mention anything about her early work in pornography.

"Now that we know who she is," said Emilia, "you want to go by her office tomorrow?"

"No, we're not going to ambush her like that," I said, shaking my head. "I bet we can find her office phone number."

Emilia looked at her phone and then to me, her eyebrows furrowed. "It's after seven. You think she's really going to be in?"

"She will be if she wants to make partner," I said, navigating to the firm's directory. I couldn't find Jean's direct office line, but I did find an emergency number for non-clients who needed to talk to an attorney. I dialed and settled into my chair. When the receptionist answered, I didn't give details, but I introduced myself and said that I needed to speak to Jean Whitfield. She transferred me straight away. That was nice.

"Ms. Whitfield, my name is Ashraf Rashid, and I'm a lieutenant with the Indianapolis Metropolitan Police Department. Your name has come up in a murder investigation, and we very much need to talk to you right away."

Jean paused for what seemed at least a minute. "Is this a joke?"

"It's not a joke. I'm working the murder of Mark and Cesar Cruz, Jeremy Estrada, and Joseph Gomez. Those names sound familiar?"

The phone went silent, but she hadn't hung up.

"Say those names again," she said.

So I did, speaking slowly and clearly enunciating every syllable.

"I'm sure you remember these men," I said. "And I know what you did for them. That's why my partner and I didn't want to come by your office. You deserve some privacy."

"You son of a bitch," she said, her voice barely audible.

I softened my voice. "I know how unnerving it is to receive calls like this, but please understand that we are not trying to hurt you in any way. This is an active and very serious investigation. We need to talk to you."

"I can't believe you're calling me now," she said.

"Lieutenant Rashid is one of the most respectful and respected men in our department. He's telling you the truth," said Emilia, her voice also soft. "We need to talk to you. Just tell us the place, and we'll be there."

It took her several moments to respond, and when she did, she had regained her composure.

"Millennium Park by the Park Grill. One hour."

"We'll be there," said Emilia.

Jean hung up, and I slipped my phone back in my pocket and nodded to my partner.

"Thanks for the save," I said.

She hesitated before speaking, but then she gave me a small, tight smile. "I meant it. You are one of the most respected detectives in our department, just not by the people in charge."

I had always felt awkward when people said nice things to me, probably because most compliments directed to me carried derision as well.

Growing up, people would remark that I spoke well for my age, especially considering my circumstances. I hated that. I hated it even more when people said similar things to my mother. Though she had a strong Arabic accent, my mother spoke three languages fluently and had a PhD in literature. Even still, people spoke to her like they might have spoken to a toddler. She claimed that didn't bother her, but I knew otherwise. My mother wanted nothing more than for her family to fit into our community, but our neighbors reminded us at every opportunity that we didn't.

I looked at Emilia and tried to find a smirk or sneer. None met my gaze, and I had to turn away, almost embarrassed.

"Thanks," I said. "We should get going if we're going to make it to the park on time."

She agreed, so we hailed a cab outside our hotel rather than drive. By the time we arrived at Millennium Park, the black of night blanketed the sky from horizon to horizon. Crowds of tourists walked past, their cameras in hands and their eyes wide. Ms. Whitfield certainly had picked a public place.

"You see Ms. Whitfield anywhere?" I asked, scanning the crowd. Men, women, and children of all ages and in all manners of dress thronged the park. Emilia nodded, drew a breath, and pointed toward a lone figure sitting at a bench away from the crowd. She had blonde hair, just as she had in the picture on her firm's website, and she wore a black pencil skirt, white shirt and black suit jacket. She watched the street, probably waiting for us.

I unclipped my badge from my belt and held it upright so Jean would see that first thing. Emilia did likewise. As we approached, Ms. Whitfield turned and watched us, never blinking and never shrinking away. She had found whatever confidence our phone call had taken from her, evidently.

"I'm Lieutenant Ash Rashid," I said, clipping my badge to my belt again as we drew closer. I held out my hand for her to shake, but she made no move to reach for it. I dropped it to my side and gestured to Emilia. "This is Detective Emilia Rios."

"Well, I'm here," said Ms. Whitfield. "What do you want?"

I looked around us for a coffee shop or at least a semi-private alcove but found nothing.

"Is there somewhere a little more private we can talk?" I asked.

Ms. Whitfield blinked several times and then frowned. "No one's listening to us. This is fine."

I looked to the bench. "Do you mind if we sit down?"

"I'm not queen of the park, so you can do whatever you want."

Emilia and I sat down, but Ms. Whitfield remained standing. In an interrogation booth, I wanted control over the temperature, over what my suspects drank and ate, over who he saw and interacted with, everything about his life. More than that, I wanted him to know I controlled everything. Out here in public, I felt exposed and powerless. I didn't like either feeling, but I had no reason to suspect Ms. Whitfield of involvement in my murders. As long as she talked, we could go wherever she wanted.

"Okay, so, we're here to talk about Cesar, Mark, Joseph and Jeremy," I said, reaching into my jacket pocket for a notepad and pen. "I believe you knew them."

"I did," she said, reaching for a briefcase beside her. She opened it and pulled out a stack of forms. "If we're going to talk, I need you to sign a non-disclosure agreement."

I interviewed dozens of lawyers a year, but never had one asked me to sign an NDA. I didn't even know if a court would enforce it, but if it did, I couldn't testify against her, I couldn't arrest her, I couldn't submit a report about our interview, I couldn't even tell anybody about the interview without violating the agreement.

"I'm sorry," I said, shaking my head, "but that's not going to happen."

She bent down again and started to close her briefcase. "Then this meeting is over. Thanks for wasting my time."

I stood up quickly before she could leave. "I've seen your CV. You're smart enough to know that I wouldn't sign your agreement, and you're smart enough to know why. But you still came. That tells me you want to talk to me."

She pursed her lips but didn't say anything.

"We'll keep everything you tell us as private as possible," I said.

"But you'll still use it in your investigation," she said, lowering he chin. "If you need to, you'll put my name on a search warrant affidavit and file it in open court."

I nodded. "Yes, we will."

"Then I'm leaving."

Despite what she said, she didn't turn to leave. She had something to say, but she knew it would hurt her if it came out. She had planned this moment, probably from the instant I called. I could see it past the defiance in her eyes. She wanted to talk, but she needed someone to push her. More than that, she needed an object to direct her anger at. I didn't mind giving that to her.

"Sit down, Ms. Whitfield," I said. She promptly sat on the seat I had vacated and glowered at me. "I'm a police officer. I will try to protect your privacy as much as I can, but that's not my first priority. I'm trying to find someone who committed a very serious crime. I believe you have information that can help me do that. So here's what I'm going to do: if you don't talk to me now, I'll visit you at work. I'll talk to your coworkers, your friends, and your boss. Then, I'll go to your house and talk to your spouse. I might even show him the employment file I picked up from our victims. It had a nude picture of you in it. Is he into that sort of thing?"

Her face turned so red I thought she'd hit me. Emilia shot me the dirtiest look I've ever seen her give.

"What the hell?" she mouthed to me. I held up a hand, hoping to keep her from saying anything. Ms. Whitfield swallowed and then, with a shaking hand, rubbed a tear from her right eye.

"If you're here about those assholes, I hope it's because they're dead, and I hope somebody cut their dicks off."

Every muscle in my upper body seemed to slump at once.

"I really wish you hadn't said that," I said, feeling a dull melancholy wash over me. "Before we continue, I need to read you your rights."

"Why?" asked Jean, genuinely confused.

"Because they are dead," said Emilia, looking at me with a very confused look, "and somebody did cut their genitals off."

Jean's face went slack, and then something strange happened: she smiled, a little at first, but then it stretched across her face. Then, she laughed. When she regained her composure, she looked at me with a crooked grin.

"Seems I owe somebody a drink."

Chapter 12

Marion County had four men named David Parker, but only one of them worked for the *Indianapolis Star*. Last year, he made the short list for the Pulitzer Prize for a series of articles he wrote on the influence of business lobbyists on state legislation supposedly enacted to preserve religious liberties. Aleksander had only seen pictures of him, but he had hair as black as the night sky, and he wore it cropped short against his skull. He shouldn't be hard to spot.

Aleksander had parked across the street from the *Star*'s building on Meridian Street at four in the afternoon and watched and waited. He didn't have a lot of time to put a plan together, but he knew where Parker lived and the most direct routes to his house in Greenwood. Assuming the man drove straight home, Aleksander could pull this off without too much difficulty.

By five, people began emerging from the building under the watchful eye of a uniformed police officer. Evidently, the city had taken his ruse seriously. Aleksander looked at each person, but he didn't see his target, so he slumped in his car and waited.

By six, the flow of office workers turned to a trickle, and the officer left his post. Aleksander hadn't planned to take Parker anywhere near the downtown area, so that didn't affect his plan at all. Nearly two hours after the rest of the newsroom's departure, Parker exited the building. He wore gray slacks, black shoes, and a white, Oxford shirt that he left open at his collar. The moment he crossed the street and climbed into his BMW in the parking lot, Aleksander turned the keys in his ignition. Normally, he liked to plan a job down to the smallest detail, but here, he didn't have that luxury. He'd do his best. One way or another, Parker would die tonight.

Aleksander followed for several miles, always staying a few car lengths back. Quickly, they left the forty-story buildings of downtown behind them. As they drove south, they passed grocery stores and movie theaters at first and then anonymous warehouses and then finally expansive, grassy fields. Power lines extended beyond the horizon.

Eventually traffic thinned and the road narrowed to two lanes. As they drove, the area began to feel more and more remote from the city ten miles north of them. Thickets of trees so dense he couldn't see beyond their first layer lay on either side of the road. The only light came from their headlights. Though he hadn't driven by Parker's house yet, he knew it's general location and features. Parker lived in a new development outside Greenwood. Few other houses had yet been built. It was well off the main road. He still had time.

Aleksander let Parker get ahead of him as they drove through Greenwood, but he began feeling the urgency build in his gut. He caught up with his quarry just a few blocks from the Parker's house. He needed to move. He pressed his foot down on the accelerator.

No streetlights illuminated the pavement this far from town, and no other cars met them on the road. As Parker turned toward his neighborhood, Aleksander slowed his own car, but not enough. He needed to hit Parker hard enough to cause some damage, but not so hard as set off the airbags in his own car.

At the last second, he pounded on his brakes and felt the tires bite into the pavement. Rubber chirped, and Aleksander's heavy car slipped on the asphalt. It struck Parker's BMW with a clang. The seatbelt ripped into Aleksander's shoulder. He gritted his teeth and grimaced, expecting the airbag to hit him in the face next. Thankfully, it didn't.

The impact had driven Aleksander's car to the left and forced Parker's BMW into a ditch. Aleksander took off his belt and shook his head to clear it of any grogginess before reaching into his glove box for a syringe containing a pre-mixed, fast-acting sedative. If he did this right, Parker wouldn't see him coming. He stepped out of his car. It was evening. Crickets chirped in fields nearby. Lightning danced in distant clouds.

Parker got out of his car and stood by the door. Aleksander waved.

"I'm sorry. Are you all right?" he asked, intentionally slurring his words and making his accent thicker than it really was. He needed Parker to drop his guard. The drunk routine usually worked well.

Parker walked toward him. "Yeah, you?"

Aleksander looked around. "I'm fine. Where are we?"

Parker shook his head and walked to the rear of his car to peer at the damage. His rear bumper hung loose. Then he sighed and looked at Aleksander.

"You're going to pay for this."

"I will," said Aleksander. He swallowed. "I have good American insurance."

Parker straightened and peered him at. "Are you drunk?"

Aleksander reached down to his car with his left hand and pretended to fall.

"No. I'm fine. I had a few drinks after work, but I'm not drunk."

"Jesus Christ," said Parker, raking his fingers through his hair. "You're drunk off your ass."

"I've got insurance," said Aleksander, tottering toward his car. He grabbed brochures—the first papers he could find—from the glove box and held them up. "I'll make this right."

"You sure as hell will," said Parker, walking toward him. He snatched the brochures from Aleksander's hands and held them for a moment before closing his eyes and clenching his jaw. "You've got to be-"

Aleksander didn't give him a chance to finish the thought before stabbing him in the neck with the syringe. Parker immediately stepped away, but not before Aleksander depressed the plunger.

"What the hell?" asked Parker, ripping the syringe from his neck. He threw it to the ground and then dove toward his car. He got about three steps before falling drunkenly to the ground. His eyes stayed open. Aleksander had jabbed him with a very powerful paralytic. It wouldn't kill him or even knock him unconscious, but it rendered Parker unable to control his muscles. He crawled forward for about a foot before the drug spread through his system completely.

Aleksander walked to Parker's car, turned it off, and then threw the keys into some nearby woods. Then, he popped his own trunk open and dragged Parker toward it, his feet dangling behind him. It took some work, but he muscled Parker into the trunk, and then felt his pockets for his cell phone. The man stared at him, his eyes wide and scared. Aleksander glanced through the previous texts Parker had made.

"I'm sorry for this," he said, looking at his captive before tapping a text into the phone.

Breaking story at work. Will be late. Sorry, honey.

He sent it to Parker's wife and then took the battery out of the phone to disable it and prevent the authorities from tracing it. He slipped both into his pocket and shut the trunk. Aleksander didn't relish the thought of hurting him, but the man needed to scream for this to work. Last night, Charles Holden had given the city a spectacle in flames. Tonight, the spotlight belonged to David Parker. Aleksander hoped he had the stomach to go through with it.

Chapter 13

Ms. Whitfield's admission outburst about our victims changed our interview to an interrogation, so Emilia took a card from her wallet and read Jean her Miranda rights. I had heard a lot of people say things they later regretted during an interview. This didn't feel like an admission of wrongdoing, though. This felt like a release. I hadn't expected that.

"What'd these guys do to you?" I asked.

She looked right at me, and the smile disappeared slowly. "They tried to ruin my life."

"What'd they do?" I asked again.

Jean looked from me to Emilia and then back. "You two seriously don't know?"

"No," I said. "Until yesterday, we didn't even know their identities."

"Okay, then," she said, raising her eyebrows. "They made me sleep with them."

I took a step back and nodded to Emilia. I had never worked sex crimes, and I hoped no one would ever ask me to. The investigative work, I could handle, but the victims, I didn't know. Homicide victims bothered me enough, but I took solace in knowing that they couldn't feel pain anymore. A little boy or little girl molested by a family friend, or a woman assaulted by someone she trusted, though, would carry that pain forever. I didn't know if I could see that day after day.

"Did these men rape you?" asked Emilia. "If they did, you did nothing wrong. There's nothing to be ashamed of."

"No, they didn't rape me," said Jean, her voice sharper than it had been just a moment earlier. "Not forcibly, at least."

Emilia glanced up at me, and I took another small step back to let her know I needed her to take charge of the interview. She nodded almost imperceptibly and returned her focus to Jean.

"Let's start over," she said. "How'd you meet these four men?"

Jean started to answer, but then her voice faltered and her face contorted so that her angry facade could no longer mask the pain she tried to hold in. A tear rolled down her cheek.

"They emailed me. I was a senior at Northwestern, and I had just finished applying to law school. I didn't know who they were, but they said they needed to talk to me about my applications. I thought it was a scam, so I ignored them."

I slowly and cautiously started jotting down quick notes while Emilia continued the interview.

"You did eventually contact them, though," said Emilia. Jean nodded.

"They emailed me again, but this time they said they wanted to talk about the work experience I listed on my applications and my criminal history."

Emilia waited for Jean to say something further.

"What was significant about that?" she asked after a moment of silence.

Jean's voice faltered, so she coughed to clear her throat. "I said I worked at the Walt Disney Company as a junior creative director, but it was just an internship for a summer. It was stupid, but I said it."

An exaggeration would have hurt, but it wouldn't have ruined her career. Had she come clean about it, her law school would have put a note in her file, but I doubt they would have rescinded her offer of admission. I had the feeling she had a much bigger secret.

"Why did they want to know about your criminal history, Ms. Whitfield?" I asked, having a feeling where this was going.

She looked to me and then closed her eyes, sighing. "I was arrested for driving while under the influence in Florida. I told the cop he could search my car for liquor, and he found a bag of marijuana wedged under the front seat. It was stupid, but it was Spring Break and I was nineteen. I made a mistake, so I plead guilty to the DUI. The prosecutor dropped the possession charges, so I paid a fine and did fifty hours of community service back home."

In and of itself, that wouldn't have hurt her too much. Her problem ran deeper than that, though.

"Did you mention the arrest on your law school application?" I asked.

Jean slowly shook her head. Every law school application specifically asked whether a prospective student had ever been convicted of a crime. It didn't matter if a court had expunged an applicant's record or sealed it permanently. A lot of lawyers considered a lie of omission on a law school application a serious offense and believed it raised questions about a person's fitness to practice law. I didn't think the Illinois Bar Association would strip her license for that, but they could definitely sanction her. Theoretically, her law school might even have the power to rescind her degree. No matter what happened, it would damage her career.

"I don't understand," said Emilia, looking from Ms. Whitfield and then back to me. "You made a mistake when you were a kid. Everybody makes mistakes. Why'd you lie about it?"

"I was on the bubble. I did well in school and on my LSAT, but so did thousands of other people. If I told the truth, Northwestern would have picked somebody else. I couldn't risk my spot."

I knew how nerve-wracking a law school application could seem, and I knew how unfair and opaque the process felt. It was a lot of pressure for a twenty-two year old kid.

"Your application isn't our concern here," I said. "As far as we're concerned, that's your private life. We won't bring it up unless we absolutely have to."

"Thank you for your generosity," she said, glaring at me. "I appreciate it."

"What happened next?" asked Emilia, stepping in. "Did you reply to this second email?"

"Yes," she said, nodding. "We set up a time to talk at a coffee shop in Evanston a couple of blocks from campus."

That was both smart and manipulative. The boys knew Jean wanted to go to school at Northwestern, so they met her in the school's shadow, knowing they could crush that dream with just an email.

"Did all four men show up to the meeting?" I asked.

"No," she said, looking to me. "Just Cesar. I don't know how he got them, but he had a stack of my emails half an inch thick. They had a lot of private stuff in them."

For the moment, we didn't need to concern ourselves with how Cesar got those emails, nor did we need to pry into Jean's private affairs. I nodded and spoke before Jean could say anything else she didn't need to say.

"What'd Cesar want?"

She looked at me, her eyes glassy and wet. "He said he and his partners were businessmen. I thought they wanted money, so I offered them a couple thousand dollars, everything I had. My boyfriend and I planned to go to Europe after we graduated college, so I offered them that money. He said they didn't want money."

"They wanted sex," said Emilia. Jean shook her head and then tilted it to the side.

"Not at first. He said they saw my picture in the campus directory and thought I was perfect for their website. He said if I took a couple of pictures in my underwear for their website, he would delete everything he had on me."

I almost grimaced. Giving in to blackmailers rarely worked out. Despite their assurances, the blackmailers always wanted more, and their schemes usually worked out very badly for everyone involved.

"And you agreed," said Emilia, prodding her.

Jean nodded, and a tear rolled down her cheek. "I was stupid. I went to this apartment a couple of days later, and all four of them were there. I took my clothes off, and they took pictures of me. Then, they told me they deserved more."

"Did they physically coerce you to do anything against your will?" asked Emilia.

She slowly shook her head. "Not physically, but they said if I didn't sleep with them, they'd make sure everyone knew I had lied. They filmed me doing things with them I had never done. It was awful. It's probably still on the internet."

When she finished speaking, the silence felt heavy and profound. The story turned my stomach for more ways than one. Every single woman with a picture in those filing cabinets had now become a suspect. They had also become victims. Dozens and dozens of victims. If one of them had killed our pornographers, I didn't know if I'd want to arrest her or thank her for taking predators off the streets before my daughter came of age.

"Thank you for talking to us," I said. "I'm very sorry for what happened to you. For what it's worth, those boys aren't going to hurt anyone again."

"Is that all you need from me?" asked Jean, any trace of the strong attorney who had greeted us gone, replaced by a meek and damaged person.

I nodded, so she turned and walked away, not saying another word. Once I was sure she was out of earshot, I turned to Emilia, who looked stunned.

"What do you think?" I asked.

"I can see why somebody would want to cut their dicks off."

"Me, too," I said, nodding.

We took a cab back to our hotel, after which Emilia went to a bar nearby for dinner and a drink. I would have joined her for the dinner, but I didn't feel up to sitting in a bar. Instead, I took a walk and headed east until I hit the north end of Lincoln Park.

I liked being a detective, but I joined IMPD after college because I didn't think a guy with a philosophy degree could get a job with better benefits or pay right after college. Over time, though, the job became part of my identity, something I cherished and felt proud of. On good days, I helped people put their lives back together after a tragedy. I helped make the world a better place. On bad days, I saw things that make me wonder if the world would be better off without human beings in it.

Today felt like a bad day.

I found a park bench and pulled out my phone. Hannah's cell phone was the first number in my address book, the number I called more than any other. Though she didn't go into an office, she worked just as much as I did—if not substantially more. Even after an exhausting day with the kids and hours at a keyboard writing, she always wanted to talk to me. We could talk for hours. We didn't even have anything important to say—we simply needed to hear each other's voices. Those conversations gave me hope; they reminded me that the world still had some life left in it.

I called her number and waited three rings for her to

answer. The moment I heard her voice, my entire body felt lighter. We didn't talk long, but for those few minutes, I let the rest of the world go. For the first time in hours, I could be myself, not Lieutenant Rashid, not the Muslim man everyone feared on the airplane, not the angry man who just interviewed a rape survivor so he could find her rapists' murderer. When I hung up, I stayed on that bench, not wanting the moment to end.

As I stared up at the grayish black sky, I felt my phone vibrate in my pocket. I hoped it was Hannah calling to say she had forgotten to tell me something, but when I pulled it out and looked at the caller ID, I saw Paul Murphy's name staring back. I swiped my thumb to answer and then put the phone to my ear.

"Yeah?" I asked, looking around to make sure no one walking by had taken an interest in me.

"He took another one."

I didn't comprehend what he had said, so I shook my head. "What do you mean?"

"Our killer took another journalist. You were wrong, buddy. I'm sorry. About half an hour ago, he sent us an email with a link to a video and a message. He said his God demanded another blood sacrifice. It's a goddamn live feed." He paused. "He's drowning this guy in front of us."

Paul had spent well over two decades in the department, and he had seen a lot of stuff. Despite all that, I had never heard the catch in his voice that I just had. My heart started beating faster, and I leaned forward.

"Tell me what's going on."

"A reporter who works for the *Indianapolis Star* didn't make it home tonight. His wife heard about Holden, so she got upset and called 911. Officers from Greenwood drove out to her house and found his car on the side of the road. Somebody rammed it from behind. They found a syringe on the road."

He paused to take a few breaths.

"About half an hour after that, we started getting calls from reporters around town. One of them sent me the link and message. Our killer's got David Parker tied to a wooden chair. Arms, legs, chest, everything. He can't move anything but his head. He has tape on his mouth so he can't even scream. He's in some kind of concrete structure. The city engineer saw the video, and he says he's in a catch basin. When it rains, water from the streets pass to storm drains. From there, they flow into these catch basins. The water's up to his waist now, and we've got storms moving in. We don't find him soon, he's gone."

I leaned back and lowered my voice. "Shit."

"If you found anything on this guy, now's the time to share it or we're going to watch a guy drown on live television."

I leaned forward and ran my hand across my brow. "Emilia and I are working, but we don't have anything. What about Public Works? Can't they go out and check the storm drains?"

"They've pulled in every crew they've got, but there are hundreds of thousands of these kinds of storm basins within the county," said Paul, his voice sharp. "And that's just Marion County. This guy could be anywhere."

I thought to everything Emilia and I had found. It was nothing. I didn't even know how our cases were connected yet.

"I'm sorry, Paul, but I don't have anything."

"Yeah. You're sorry, I'ms sorry, we're all sorry. I've got to go."

He hung up, and I felt a heavy pit grow in my stomach. I stayed on the bench and called up an app to check the weather in Indianapolis. The city had a severe storm warning. It wouldn't hit my house for another forty-five minutes, but it would hit the outskirts of the west side of town in fifteen minutes. I got up and started pacing, checking my phone every minute or two to see if I had received a text message.

After fifteen minutes, I checked the weather app again to see if, by some miracle, the storm had dissipated or moved north or south. If anything, the squall line had intensified. A hook echo had developed near Mooresville, southwest of the city. As anyone who had spent time in the midwest during tornado season could attest, that kind of radar signature did not bode well. Torrential rain, high winds, lightning, hail, possibly a tornado. I felt ill.

I kept an eye on my phone but started heading back toward my hotel. After half an hour, the line of thunder storms had begun lashing downtown Indianapolis. Meanwhile, a calm, cool breeze blew through nearby trees in Chicago. A couple strolled by, holding hands, not a care in the world. It felt surreal knowing what I did. I walked to my hotel and then crashed on the bed. I didn't want to put on the TV. I just stared at my phone, waiting, hoping for some word. Paul sent me a text message about five minutes after I lay down.

Parker's gone.

I read the text message five or six times, half hoping it would change or that I had read one of two words wrong. It didn't change, of course, so I tossed my phone to the nightstand and rubbed my eyes. Even if I had fought to stay on the case, I wouldn't have changed anything. Our killer still would have taken David Parker, a storm would have rolled in, and he would have died. Knowing that didn't stop me from feeling complicit, though.

That was a real bad way to die.

Chapter 14

The next day, Emilia knocked on my door at eight carrying two cups of coffee and wearing a pressed white blouse, black blazer, and dark jeans. She wore little makeup, but she didn't need much. She knew she looked nice, and it showed in the confident look in her eyes. My wife told me that was what makeup was about, making the wearer feel good about herself. We needed more things like that in the world. I took a cup of coffee from her hand and thanked her before inviting her in. I had already gotten up and dressed, but I hadn't yet brushed my teeth.

"I'll be right out," I said, walking into the bathroom. "You talk to anybody from home since yesterday?"

Emilia hesitated. "Like my mom?"

I put toothpaste on my brush and stuck my head out. Emilia had sat down on the foot of my bed. "I didn't say that well. Did anybody at work tell you about David Parker?"

She shook her head. "No. Who's David Parker?"

"Tell you in a minute," I said. I brushed my teeth and packed up my toothbrush before drying my hands and joining my partner in the room. I didn't have many details about Parker's death, but I told her what I could. Afterwards, she took a long breath and exhaled slowly.

"What does that change?" she asked.

"Not a lot for this investigation, but I thought you should know," I said, walking toward the table on which I had put the boy's cell phones. "Bowers tell you when to expect a truck?"

"We're not getting a truck," she said, shaking her head. "But we're getting a big van. They're bringing an appliance dolly in case we need to move anything heavy.

They're going to leave Indianapolis at eight, so they should get here by noon."

I nodded and turned my attention to the phones. Since I only had one charger, I had been switching them on and off overnight. Two of phones hadn't worked at all —not surprising after all these years—while the third looked as if someone had erased its memory. The fourth, I had charged most of the night in the hope that it might give us something. I flipped it open, and lo and behold, the backlit screen came to life.

"Works," said Emilia.

"Let's hope it's more helpful than the others."

I hadn't used such an old phone in a long time, so it took me a moment to reacquaint myself with the technology. Eventually, I found the list of the last twenty outgoing calls and started writing down the information. None of the phone numbers had names attached to them, but one belonged to the block of numbers assigned to IMPD detectives. I didn't know which of our victims owned the phone, but he had called that detective at least four times.

"Our victims might have been somebody's CI," I said, writing the number down and putting a star beside it. I showed the pad to Emilia. "This is an IMPD number."

"You know who it belongs to?"

"Nope," I said, crossing the room to grab my phone from the nightstand beside my bed. "But I'm going to find out."

I dialed the number and waited through six rings before it took me to the voice mailbox of Denise Smith, a forensic accountant in our financial crimes section. I only knew her because she helped seize the assets of a drug smuggling ring I busted a couple of months ago. She had a master's degree in accounting and had spent twenty years at the IRS before joining IMPD. Our victims couldn't have called her because she didn't work for us nine years ago.

I hung up and slipped my phone back in my pocket before looking at Emilia. "Call went to voicemail, but I know the owner. She's only worked with us for a few years," I said, rubbing my eyes with the palms of my hands and then yawning. "They didn't call her. You packed and ready to go?"

"Just got to grab my bag and check out. What do you want to do?"

I picked up my phone and flicked through the pictures until I found the ones I had taken of the rack-mounted servers we found in our victim's storage unit. Screwed directly into the rack, I had found a steel plaque that claimed the servers were the property of TNT Enterprises. It even listed a phone number.

"We're going to find out what we can about these boy's company," I said, dialing the company's number. Somebody answered almost before it finished ringing once. I spoke quickly.

"Morning. My name is Ash Rashid. Is this TNT Enterprises?"

"Yeah. What do you want?"

Didn't sound like the friendly type, which meant I doubted he'd answer a police officer's questions without a better reason than I could provide. I decided to play dumb and held a finger to my lips to keep Emilia from saying anything.

"Well, I'm calling because I bought a storage unit out in Wrigleyville at an auction. You know, like on that TV show? Somebody stops paying, and you get to buy the unit without seeing it. It's in the rental contract."

"Yeah, I know the show," snapped the man from TNT.

"I found some old computers in my unit, and they had your name on them. I wondered if you'd want to buy them from me."

He paused for a moment, and I heard what I guessed was a chair rolling across a solid surface. His voice had a hard edge to it when he spoke. "What's the serial number on these computers?"

"Well, I don't know. Let me see."

I opened the pictures on my phone and zoomed in as closely as I could. The plaque did have a long serial number, but I could only read the first four characters.

"I can't read the whole thing, but it starts Z78T and then keeps going."

He typed something and then came onto the phone quickly. "You said your name was Ash Rashid?"

"Yes," I said, hoping he hadn't just looked me up.

"I'll have to talk to my partners, but we would be interested in buying that old equipment from you. Can you come by our office today with the servers? We'll pay cash."

I didn't want to sound too eager to meet him, so I hesitated.

"How much cash? Because I paid a lot for that locker."

"I'll give you three hundred per server. They're twelve years old, so you're not going to do better if you take them to a pawn shop. Do you have all ten from that rack?"

"I do," I said.

"Good. Bring them all to our office immediately."

He hung up before I could agree or try to bargain for more money. At twelve years old, those servers had less computing power than my cell phone. His willingness to buy them told me they had something important—or maybe incriminating—on them. Maybe that storage unit would help us more than I realized.

I looked at Emilia. "It'll take me a few minutes to get my stuff together, but how about you meet me in the lobby? We're going to visit TNT Enterprises."

"You're the boss," she said, turning to leave my room. It was only as she stepped out that I realized I didn't even know where TNT's offices were. I Googled the company and started packing everything up while my phone searched. According to the internet, we were headed to Rosemont, just east of the Chicago O'Hare airport. When I got to the lobby, Emilia had already checked out, so I handed her the keys to my car so she could put her bags away while I settled my bill. When I got to my car a few minutes later, Emilia sat behind the wheel with a hopeful expression on her face. I put my bag in the back and then sat in the passenger seat.

"Can I drive, Dad?" she asked, smiling broadly.

I looked around us. It was still early on a Saturday, so few cars passed.

"If you get a speeding ticket, you pay for it."

She grinned and turned the car on.

"I guess that means I'll have to make it count, then."

I thought she'd floor it out of the hotel, but she took it easy and looked almost thoughtful as we pulled onto the interstate a few minutes later.

"Something on your mind?" I asked.

"This case," she said. "So nine years ago, you found four bodies. As it turns out, those four bodies belonged to four shit bags who blackmailed women into having sex with them. Not only that, they've been talking to somebody from IMPD. You never ID'd them, but Kristen Tanaka did. Now Tanaka and two other journalists are dead."

I crossed my arms and nodded. "Right so far."

"What's the connection between your old case and the present one?" she asked.

I shrugged and looked out the window at the passing traffic. "I don't know if there is one. I thought the guy who killed my original four victims had killed Tanaka to stop her from investigating, but evidently I was wrong."

"It's still a pretty big coincidence," said Emilia, glancing at me. "Tanaka starts investigating, she finds out something major about your old case, and then boom, somebody just happens to kill her and the man with whom she might have shared her findings."

"Somebody killed David Parker, too," I said. "He didn't have anything to do with her investigation into my old case."

She nodded and kept driving. After a few minutes, she began tapping the steering wheel. "It doesn't feel right to me. I don't know what it is, but this doesn't feel right."

I didn't say it, but I agreed with her. "We'll just work the case and see what we can find."

Neither of us said anything else until we arrived at TNT's offices. They rented the eighth floor of a thoroughly modern concrete and steel office building in the middle of a nondescript office park. Every few minutes, a plane would seem to float overhead as it landed at the nearby Chicago O'Hare airport. A row of fir trees separated the office park from the surrounding streets, blocking most of the road noise and the view of the airport's economy parking lot across the street, but did absolutely nothing for the roar of the massive jet engines.

We followed signs to the correct building and then met a security guard in the lobby. He said we were expected and directed us to a bank of elevators, one of which had our floor preselected. A sign inside warned us that CCTV cameras monitored us at all times. When the door popped open on the eighth floor, a man in a black suit with gray pinstripes glared at us from TNT's lobby. A thick layer of gel slicked his black hair from his face, and a nickel-plated firearm, only partially concealed by the folds of his jacket, weighed down his right hip. He looked like a character from a bad detective show on TV.

His eyes passed over me, but he didn't seem to notice

I had a gun strapped to my chest. Instead, he focused on Emilia, openly leering at her. I couldn't smell booze on him, but his pupils were constricted to the size of pinholes. That happened to cocaine users a lot. When they got high on the weekends, their pupils expanded to the size of dimes. When they came down from their high on Sunday morning, their pupils shrank. I didn't know the causal mechanisms, but I recognized it when I saw it.

"I'm Ash Rashid," I said, holding out my hand. "We spoke on the phone earlier."

He crossed his arms.

"I don't see my servers."

I looked around the lobby. Though TNT had a large receptionist's desk near the elevator and a waiting room, we were alone. A partition blocked me from looking deeper into the office.

"We can get them. Don't worry. I thought we could talk about price. What's so valuable about these old computers?"

He pointed to his chest. "They're mine. That's what's so valuable about them. You're in possession of stolen property. That's a felony. I can arrest you right now. I'm a cop."

I had known a lot of bullies in law enforcement, but somehow I doubted this guy carried a badge. I held up my hands and took a step back anyway. He matched my movements but failed to notice that Emilia had unclipped the buckle on her firearm's holster.

"No need to get pissed, man," I said. "I'm just wondering why you want them is all. I can get them. They're here. I just wondered what you were going to do with them. I didn't mean anything."

"My interest in my own property should be obvious," he said, leaning in so closely that I could smell his mint toothpaste. I'm sure his dentist would appreciate knowing he brushed. "As for what I want to do with them, that's my concern." He considered me for a moment and then shook his head. "You know, screw you and your little friend. Both of you. Put your hands on the wall. I'm arresting you right here."

"What agency are you with?" I asked.

He pointed to the wall beside the elevator and pushed back his jacket to expose the firearm on his hip. Emilia slipped her weapon out of its holster but keep it at her side. If he made a move, he would have a really bad day.

"Put your hands on the wall now," he said again.

"They carry badges in your agency?" I asked.

He stared directly into my eyes. "You think you're some kind of tough guy? Is that it? Because we can see how tough you are after a night in jail."

He stared in my eyes so intently that he didn't notice as I reached to my belt for my badge. I unclipped it and held it in front of me.

"This is my badge. Would you mind showing me yours? The detective behind you, by the way, has a loaded firearm."

He drew in a breath and then looked at me and then to my badge, his posture softening. "That says Indianapolis."

"Yes, it does."

He looked over his shoulder at Emilia and then sneered at me. "You two are out of your jurisdiction."

"True," I said, tilting my head to the side. "But we can hold you until CPD arrives and arrests you for impersonating a police officer. Or, maybe we can forget this whole thing happened and have a conversation like adults. How's that sound?"

He didn't say anything, but a voice boomed out from near the partition that led into the office.

"That sounds more than fair." A tall man in a gray, tailored suit stepped forward. He had dimples on his cheeks, cold blue eyes, and a chip in one of his front, lower teeth. The tips of his otherwise black sideburns had begun turning gray, the only sign that the man in front of me was anywhere near middle aged.

As he neared us, he ignored Emilia completely despite the firearm in her hand and nudged his partner aside so he could shake my hand.

"Please forgive James. He's our chief of security, and he gets a little jumpy when strangers show up at the office."

I looked at the first man and plastered a fake smile to my lips.

"Chief of security is an important job. Consider it water under the bridge."

"Excellent," said the newcomer. "I'm Evan Kelly, and I'm the director of the company. Let's all go to the conference room. We'll talk about these servers of yours."

I glanced at Emilia long enough to see that she had kept her firearm in her hand. I liked her instincts; they might keep me from getting shot one day.

"Let's do that," I said. "We've got some questions."

Chapter 15

TNT Enterprises had evidently furnished its offices with a mind to practicality and frugality rather than aesthetics. The first door we passed contained an employee break room with a fridge, old tube-style television, and a foosball table with so much flaking paint and damage that it looked as if it had been stolen from a fraternity house attic. The desk and chairs in other offices as well looked cheap and flimsy.

They did like their art, though. Of course, an art historian would probably cry foul if she heard me refer to the prints on TNT's walls as art. They looked like the posters from major Hollywood movies except that few of the women wore clothing. Emilia stopped at one in particular and stared with unabashed disgust at a nude woman atop a pile of books. *Hairless Potter and the Sorcerer's Scrotum.* I had the feeling J.K. Rowling wouldn't approve.

"Hairless Potter a big seller here?" I asked, glancing at Evan.

"She's earned her spot on the wall."

I took that as a yes. Emilia simply shook her head in disgust and kept walking. After passing two or three dozen posters, we came to a glass walled conference room. A woman, probably in her early thirties, waited inside with her arms at her sides. She smiled at us. Her posture was straight, and she held her head high, but she brought her hands together in front of her, working her fingers together. She was nervous. Emilia and I walked into the room and took seats around the conference table without invitation. The staff of TNT sat on the other side.

"Before we go any further," I said, looking at James, the security chief. "I need your firearm."

"I'm not giving you shit," said James. "This is my office, pal. You don't get to call the shots."

I looked at Evan. "I've got two sides. One side is nice, but the other's a dick. Which side you get is up to you. Do you want to see my dick?"

Emilia tittered and covered her nose with a hand, pretending to have coughed. Considering the company, I probably should have chosen my words better.

"Piss off," said James, not taking the bait I dangled in front of him.

I pushed my chair back and stood up, already thinking back to some of the research I had conducted earlier into pornographic law.

"If this is how you want to play it, this is how we'll play it. I'm going to contact CPD, and we're going to get a warrant for every piece of computer equipment you've got in the building. We'll also need to see 2257 papers for every actor you've ever cast. I'd hate to find out you had any underage performers."

James muttered something under his breath but Evan remained cool.

"Would you consider a compromise? James has a safe in his office. Would it satisfy you if he stows his firearm inside for the duration of your visit?"

"That'd work."

He looked at James. "Then do it."

"But-" began James.

"Just do it," said Evan. He stared unblinking at his subordinate until James walked off. Then he looked to me and plastered that fake smile across his lips. "If you'll have a seat again, we can get this meeting going. Jessica, our general counsel, can answer any question you have."

I sat down again and looked around the room. Windows overlooked a parking garage to the outside, and a video screen hung on the west wall. A projector dangled from the ceiling. Given the products TNT produced, I imagined Powerpoint presentations given in that room were a lot more lively than the ones I typically saw at IMPD. I reached into my jacket for a notepad and tossed it to the table.

"Now that we have those unpleasantries out of the way," said the female TNT employee, "I'm Jessica Warren, general counsel for TNT Enterprises. Can we get you anything? Coffee, water, soda?"

"We're fine," I said, looking from her to Evan. "For the record, I'm Lieutenant Ashraf Rashid. My partner is Detective Emilia Rios. We're here because we're working a quadruple homicide in Indianapolis, and we believe our victims had a connection to your company."

Jessica swallowed hard, but the smile didn't leave her face. "I'm sorry to hear that. We're obviously happy to answer any questions you have. I've heard you found some of our equipment. We'd like to claim that if possible. If there's a fee involved, we'd be happy to pay."

"We'll give you your computers back, but not any time soon. It's evidence in our investigation," I said. "And by the way, you should look into getting some Xanax for your security chief. He's wound a little tight."

"We'll bear your suggestion in mind. Can I ask now about your investigation?" she asked. "Who are your victims?"

"Mark and Cesar Cruz, Jeremy Estrada and Joseph Gomez," said Emilia. "Recognize the names?"

Jessica blinked rapidly but said nothing. Evan nodded.

"What happened to them?" he asked.

I outlined the facts pertinent to them. Once I finished speaking, Jessica looked to Evan knowingly.

"We assumed they were in an accident," she said, nodding. "They traveled together often. It was out of character that they would disappear without contacting us first."

"I think I can guess what your company does by the

wall art, but tell me about it anyway," I said.

"We're a diverse media and technology company that produces some of the finest adult entertainment in the industry," said Evan. "Our website division runs twenty-two of the most highly trafficked websites in the world, our production facilities in Los Angeles are among the best in the country, and our software development section has developed apps that have revolutionized the consumption of adult entertainment."

"How do you know our victims?" asked Emilia.

Evan looked at her and then blinked several times. "Has anyone ever told you that you could make a fine living as an actress? We have a full line of videos featuring more…mature women."

"I'm twenty-nine," said Emilia, quickly. "I hardly think I qualify as mature."

Evan looked down to Emilia's chest and then back to her face. "I didn't realize you were that old."

Emilia sat up straighter and looked as if she were going to say something else, but I stepped in and spoke before she could.

"Let's get back to our victims. How do you know them?"

"They ran a very successful website for us," said Evan. "They specialized in introducing fresh faces to the business. It was one of the first sites we developed."

He failed to mention that his partners had blackmailed those fresh-faced young women into doing the things they did, but we all had faults.

"Whose idea was the site?" I asked.

Evan leaned back and blinked. "I'm not sure if you're familiar with our products, but the concept is very simple. Willing adults engage in various sexual activities on film. There's not much of an idea beyond catering to the tastes of our audience."

"Okay," I said, nodding. "How involved were you

with the production of the site, then?"

"We oversaw everything," said Evan.

"Let me rephrase," I said. "Did you help recruit the actresses? Were you or representatives from your company there during shoots? How involved were you, specifically, with this company?"

Evan started to fumble through another answer that expressed little more than he had already stated when Jessica stepped into the conversation.

"Primarily, we provided resources, both monetary and technical. We provided little in the way of day-to-day supervision. Whatever Misters Cruz, Estrada, and Gomez did, they acted of their own accord without prompting or interference from us."

Jessica evidently had the brains. Evan had, well, whatever else was needed to run a porno company.

"Who owns the intellectual property they produced?" I asked.

Jessica hesitated and then took in a deep breath.

"For all content produced after our contract began, TNT Productions. We owned most of the website."

Which meant they also owned the liabilities. Maybe we couldn't prosecute TNT for what our four victims did, but the young women they extorted sex from might have the option of suing in civil court. The legal wrangling would get complicated because of the amount of time that had passed, but they could make life difficult around TNT for a long time.

I wrote a few notes down and then looked up.

"So you provided technical expertise, and our victims provided content. How did payment work?"

Evan started to respond, but Jessica cut him off. "I'm curious as to the relevancy of your questions. Why do you need the details of our agreement?"

I glanced up. "Normally, I ask questions during an investigation."

She perked up and smiled. "Then I'm afraid you've run into the limit of our cooperation. We'll get somebody to escort you out of the building."

Jessica stood up and gestured toward the door. James stepped in, this time sans his firearm.

"Did you know your contractors coerced the young women on their website into having sex with them on film?" I asked.

Evan crossed his arms but stayed seated. Jessica slowly sat, her head cocked to the side and her brow furrowed.

"Lieutenant Rashid, we've extended to you every courtesy," said Evan, "and we've cooperated with your investigation to the best of our abilities, but I'm not going to let you sit there and lie to us."

Ultimately, my goal as a detective was to uncover truth and bring it to light. To do that, I had a wide range of tools, very few of which an honest man would wield in his personal life. I didn't want to lie or cheat to get the job done, but sometimes I had to use the tools at my disposal.

"Believe what you want," I said, "but I'm not lying. So far, we've reached out to eight young women, and all of them have told us similar stories. Your partners dug into their personal lives and then blackmailed them into performing sexual acts on camera. They stayed quiet for the last nine years because they feared to have their secrets outed in public."

The confused look left Jessica's face, and she shook her head. "We must have had some sort of miscommunication. The actors we cast are here of their own volition. They're paid quite well for their time."

I nodded and flipped pages in my notepad until I came to something Evan had said earlier. "Our victims, according to you, specialized in fresh faces. You've never wondered how they convinced so many young women to have sex with them on film? We're talking dozens and dozens of women."

Jessica looked down at the table. She almost looked a little embarrassed. "Finding fresh talent is not the challenge in our industry that it is in others."

I started to ask her to clarify, but James, the security chief, cut me off.

"She means that if we put an ad on Craigslist offering hot girls five-hundred bucks an hour, we'll have more responses in ten minutes than we know what to do with. Our customers want new snatch every week, and it's not hard to find. Our *actors*," he said, making air quotes, "are interchangeable. All they need are two tits and one twat and a willingness to screw a stranger on camera."

I didn't know anything about the porn business, but the assuredness with which they spoke made me believe them. At the same time, I also believed Jean Whitfield, the attorney we interviewed the night before. I thought my victims couldn't disgust me any more than they already had, but they had somehow managed it: if their partners at TNT were right, my victims didn't need to coerce women into having sex on film with them. They did it because they could and because doing so probably saved them money. Given everything I had found out, I was starting to think my murderer did the world a service.

I cleared my throat and wrote a few pertinent notes down.

"Did you know your partners were in contact with a detective from Indianapolis?" I asked.

Jessica and Evan looked at each other.

"I didn't," said Jessica. "Did you?"

Evan hesitated for just a split second. If I hadn't been watching closely, I wouldn't have seen it. Then he shook his head.

"No. It's news to me. Who were they talking to?"

"We don't know yet," I said. "The records are old, but we're working on it. Can you guys think of anyone who would want to harm your partners?"

"Other than the women you allege they assaulted?" asked Jessica, raising her eyebrows.

"Including them," I said. "Did any of them contact your company to complain?"

Jessica looked at Evan. He shook his head.

"I've not heard of any," said Jessica, turning to face me. Emilia opened her mouth to ask a follow up question, but Jessica held up a hand to stop her. "Before you ask, bear in mind that we are a large studio, and we work with hundreds of actors, male and female, every year. We have over a dozen producers on contract and nearly three dozen photographers and videographers. We have procedures to deal with complaints before they become a problem. We will double check our records, but I don't recall any complaints."

I looked at Emilia. "You got anything?"

She nodded and looked to Jessica. "Yeah. Our victims made a lot of money for you, right?"

Evan nodded. "Both parties profited by our arrangement."

"When communication stopped with them, what'd you do to find them?"

This time, Evan didn't bother looking to his lawyer for confirmation before answering. "We made the appropriate inquiries."

"And what does that mean?" asked Emilia. "Did you go by their house? Did you contact their neighbors? Did you call the police? Did your security chief pretend to be a cop and bust down doors looking for them? What'd you do?"

"We made the appropriate inquiries," said Evan again.

"I see," said Emilia, her face flat and disbelieving. I leaned forward. She had asked a couple of good questions, the kind I should have asked. We needed answers.

"My partner may understand, but call me dense because I don't get it," I said. "These guys were your partners. If Detective Rios went missing, I'd do a whole lot more than simply make appropriate inquiries, whatever the hell that means. Maybe that's just me, though."

"You think these four deadbeats were our partners?" asked Evan. Jessica put a hand on his shoulder to stop him from speaking, but he shrugged her off. "These guys weren't our partners. At best, they were our employees, and they stole from us. They walked into our datacenter in Dallas and ripped off over a hundred thousand dollars worth of computer equipment. That's a hundred grand we lost. Gone. Poof. We agreed to write it off as an expense because it'd cost us more than the equipment is worth to get the lawyers involved, but it's hard to forget that. Then these little shits had the gall to try to recruit some of our people and start their own company.

"So you want to know what I did when they disappeared? I went home, nailed a couple of actresses, and had a celebratory drink. That's all those little shits deserved."

Jessica covered her face with her hands.

"Okay," I said, nodding. "That's one way to react. Presumably, your company has outside investors. Think any of them would become so pissed that they'd torture and murder people who ripped them off?"

Jessica dropped her hands from her face, stood, and pointed toward the door. "You two need to leave right now."

I stayed seated for a moment, but then reached for my wallet and pulled out two business cards. I put them on the table and pushed one toward Jessica and one toward Evan.

"If either of you change your minds about anything you've said, here's my card. Depending on what you have to say, I'd be happy to bring in the US Attorney's office as well."

Evan simply looked out the window as if he were alone in the room, while Jessica stayed motionless, still pointing at the door. Emilia and I walked out, passing James in the hallway. It looked like he wanted to stop and say something to us, but Jessica called him into the conference room before he could. As Emilia and I took the elevator down, she cocked her head at me.

"How much do you think they're hiding?" she asked.

"They're hip deep in shit, but I don't know who's," I said. "We'll make some calls and see what we can find out about them. Meantime, we've got to move some furniture at the storage unit."

Emilia groaned but didn't say anything. We left the building, and as I drove to the storage unit a few minutes later, Emilia called Captain Bowers to confirm that our moving van was on the way. It had left right on schedule, so we had an hour to choose what we wanted to take and what we wanted to leave. When we arrived at the storage place, we parked on the side of the building, walked through a long interior hallway lined with green commercial rolling doors, and then stopped in front of the unit rented by Mrs. Cruz. Emilia took a step back and exhaled slowly, and I swore under my breath.

The padlock on our unit was gone.

I swore again, this time aloud, and then balled my hands into fists in my pocket, mostly to keep myself from punching the unit next door. Without that pad lock, we had lost custody of the unit and its contents. For all we knew, a dozen people could have gone in and out, removing some items and adding others. Even if we found our murder weapon in there, we couldn't introduce it in court.

"I checked twice," said Emilia. "You locked this. I know you did."

"Yeah," I said, reaching down for the door handle and pulling up. Neither Emilia nor I spoke for a moment as we surveyed the unit's contents. Or lack of contents. It was completely empty. I exhaled slowly and then took a step back, feeling my face and neck grow hot.

"We shouldn't panic yet," said Emilia. "Maybe the storage company moved things."

"Yeah, maybe," I said, already walking down the hallway toward the front office. By the time we arrived at the receptionist's desk, I had to grit my teeth to prevent myself from saying something rude that the kid behind the counter probably didn't deserve.

"Can I help you, sir?" he asked, his voice halting. I reached to my belt for my badge.

"One of your storage units contained evidence pertinent to a homicide investigation. It's empty today."

The clerk drew in a breath and looked at my badge before holding up his hands and taking a step back from the counter. "I just got on shift an hour ago. I don't know what's going on. This is my third day working here."

"It's okay," said Emilia, her voice much softer than mine. "You're not in trouble, but we need to find out what happened. We were just here yesterday with the unit's renter. Today, it's empty. Did anyone from your company move things?"

"No," he said, shaking his head immediately. "We don't touch a rented unit unless someone stops paying. That's in the contracts."

I took out my cell phone and called Mrs. Cruz. While I did that, Emilia continued her conversation with the clerk.

"Do you have video cameras here?" she asked. He nodded. "If possible, we'd like video of whoever emptied out our unit. It was a huge unit with a lot of stuff in it. They'd have needed a truck."

The guy went to work on a nearby computer terminal.

Mrs. Cruz's phone went to voicemail immediately, so I left a message and tried to keep my anger from my voice.

"Hi, this is Lieutenant Ash Rashid. Give me a call as soon as you can."

I hung up but kept my phone in my hand, waiting and hoping she'd call back immediately. She didn't, so I rejoined Emilia and the clerk at the desk.

"Our system's a little slow," said the clerk, looking up. "I've only gone through the footage from midnight to three in the morning so far."

"Then keep going," I said. The clerk focused on the screen again for the next ten minutes before finally looking up.

"I may have something. A U-haul came by at a little before nine this morning."

He flipped the screen around and showed me a static image taken from one of the cameras in the lobby. Two men stood near the front desk. If I had to guess their age, I'd put them in their mid-fifties. One had black hair streaked through with gray, while the other had shaved his head completely. One kept an eye on the clerk at all times, while the other watched the entrances and exits. Had they come a few hours later, I would have suspected they worked for TNT, but given the little I knew, I couldn't even guess who sent them now.

"Do you have any shots of their truck?" I asked.

"Sure," he said. He twisted the monitor around and then worked at his computer. After another minute, he showed us an interior shot of one of the garage bays. A U-haul moving truck backed slowly into the bay, directed by the bald man I had seen earlier. For a while, the bald man blocked my view of the license plate. Then he stepped aside, and I swore again.

"They covered the plate," said Emilia.

"Yeah. Looks like cardboard," I said, feeling frustration and confusion in my gut build as the video kept playing. A moment after the truck stopped, two new figures entered the frame. The first was the man with the silvery black hair, but the second was Mrs. Cruz. She pointed to the nearest hallway, while the bald man rolled up the door of his truck.

"What the hell is she doing?" asked Emilia.

I took out my phone again and started dialing the liaison officer for the Chicago Police Department.

"We'll ask once she's in custody."

Chapter 16

Though I didn't know Mrs. Cruz well, she seemed intelligent. We weren't going to find her in Chicago after this. I walked to the storage unit for privacy and then searched through my phone's address book until I found the number for the Transportation Security Administration's law enforcement helpline. After two rings a cheerful voice wished me good morning and asked what she could do for me.

"Hi, this is Lieutenant Ashraf Rashid with the Indianapolis Metropolitan Police Department. I'm looking for a suspect in a murder investigation, and I've got the feeling she might have flown out of Chicago this morning."

The woman typed for a few moments. "All right. Before I can fulfill your request, I'm going to need some information."

We spent the next few minutes going through a form that would document the request. Thankfully, that's all I needed for the information I wanted.

"And who is your suspect?"

"Anita Cruz," I said, beginning to pace. "Very likely she's headed to somewhere in New Jersey or possibly New York."

She typed again for a moment. "Looks like Mrs. Cruz boarded a nonstop United Airlines flight from Chicago O'Hare to Newark Liberty International Airport and will arrive at 1:45 PM local time."

"I'm guessing the chances of having that flight turned around are pretty low."

The operator's voice turned a little tight. "Does Mrs. Cruz present a threat to the flight?"

"No, not at all," I said.

She breathed just a little easier. "Good. Mrs. Cruz's flight does not have an air marshal on it, but the Newark airport police should be able to take her into custody upon landing."

I shook my head. "Don't worry about that. She's going home. I know where to pick her up. Thank you, though."

So now I was pissed off. Mrs. Cruz lost her sons. That sucked, but it didn't give her a right to steal evidence from my case, even if that evidence proved her sons were shit bags. I thumbed through my recently made calls until I found her number. As before, her phone went to voicemail immediately.

"This is Lieutenant Ash Rashid again," I said, trying to sound calmer than I felt. "When your flight lands, please give me a call."

I wanted to tell her that if she didn't call me immediately, I'd have her arrested. I didn't, though. I needed to solve this diplomatically. That gave me the best shot of getting my evidence back. Once I had that back, then I'd haul her ass into jail.

With the phone calls made, I went back to the lobby, where I found Emilia and the clerk still watching footage from the security cameras. Emilia thought she could identify the men who helped Mrs. Cruz if she saw them, but the truck was a lost cause. They never removed the cardboard over the license plate, and it didn't have any other identifying marks.

"Mrs. Cruz is on a flight to New Jersey," I said. "We'll deal with her when she lands."

The clerk behind the counter listened to us with rapt attention. Emilia noticed and stepped away so he couldn't hear us.

"What do we want to do in the meantime?"

I sighed and shook my head, feeling my frustration rise to the surface. "I don't know. This is looking more and more like a cold case. It's not going anywhere, and I'm exhausted. I say we head home. We'll take the rest of the day off and come back at it tomorrow morning."

Emilia smiled at the corners of her mouth. "You know, if you're too tired, I could drive and you could nap."

Instead of answering, I reached into my pocket for my keys. "The car's yours until we get home."

She took the keys and raised her eyebrows. "This is going to be fun."

We took Lakeshore Drive south before hitting I-94 and then finally merging onto I-65 for the rest of the drive to Indianapolis. I settled into my seat and closed my eyes.

Somewhere along the way, I slipped into a dream but woke up when I felt Emilia rap hard on my shoulder. Perfectly flat fields stretched for miles around us, broken only by the occasional copse of trees. Despite being a Saturday—or maybe because of it—cars surrounded us.

"What's going on?" I asked, sitting upright.

"We've got a tail," said Emilia, glancing in her rearview mirror. "I spotted him in Chicago, but I didn't think anything of it there. He's still here, though."

"And where is here?" I asked.

"I have no idea." She looked in her rearview mirror. "It's the white Ford Focus two cars back."

I wiped sleep out of my eyes and yawned while adjusting myself on my seat so I could see the car in my sideview mirror.

"You sure he's following us?"

"Not positive, but I've varied my speed for the past hour. He keeps matching, but he always keeps at least one car between us."

It was hard to tail somebody with only one car. Ideally, a person following a car would have at least two or three friends within radio contact who could switch roles as the chase vehicle at random intervals. If the cars behind you kept changing, you wouldn't notice that someone was after you. Best case scenario, you would have additional vehicles placed at on-ramps along the way so the chase vehicles could get on and off the highway.

"Pull into the next rest area or gas station. We'll park and see what he does."

She glanced over to me and then back to the road. "You want to call ISP?"

The Indiana State Police. They had highway patrol officers on most every major roadway in the state.

"Not until we're sure he's following us."

"If that's how you want to do it," she said, nodding. We drove for another fifteen miles before seeing a sign for a rest stop near Walcott, a small town about two hours north of Indianapolis. Trees dotted the landscape, but open sky stretched as far as I could see. We had very little to block our view of our fellow drivers. It'd do nicely.

Emilia put her blinker light on and turned, just as she would if this were a regular stop. The Wallcott rest area had restrooms, vending machines and picnic tables on a grassy lawn—everything an average traveler would need —but no swings or playground. At least we wouldn't have to worry about children if this asshole pulled a gun. Emilia parked near the welcome center, and we both watched the highway entrance. Sure enough, a white Ford Focus turned in. He drove past us without even glancing in the direction of our car. Then he parked near the exit.

"You were right," I said. "Stay parked. I'm going to use the restroom. You stay here and see what he does."

She nodded, and I got out of the car. I didn't stare at the white Focus as I walked, but I watched him out of the corner of my eye. The driver, the only person in the vehicle, never exited his car, and he never seemed to take his eyes from his cell phone, which he held in front of him. From the distance, I couldn't see him well, but he could have passed for the gray-haired man who had cleaned out Mrs. Cruz's storage area.

After using the restroom, I climbed back in the car and put on my seatbelt. "Get out of here in a hurry and see if he follows."

"How much of a hurry are you in?"

I looked around me to make sure I couldn't see any children who might run into the road unexpectedly.

"Don't light the tires on fire, but get a move on. Then slow to seventy on the interstate. Let's see what he does."

Without saying another word, she put the car in reverse and backed out of our spot so quickly my face almost hit the dashboard. Then, she spun the wheel, threw the car into first gear, and floored it. My forward momentum shifted almost instantly, pinning me to the back of my seat. We left the rest area going at least seventy-five. Emilia giggled furiously beside me.

"That was so much more fun than in one of our cruisers," she said.

"You've never done that with your own car?"

"Oh, no," she said, shaking her head and glancing at the rearview mirror. "I drive a twelve-year old Oldsmobile. I'd probably break an axle if I tried that."

I looked in the sideview mirror. The Focus rocketed out of the rest area just as we had, but then settled into traffic two vehicles behind us.

"He's back," I said.

"You want me to try to lose him?" she asked.

"No. Unless he threatens us somehow, I want you going an even pace," I said, taking out my phone. I called the State Police to tell them about our situation. They had troopers stationed beneath a bridge about twenty miles ahead of us as well as troopers behind us approximately fifteen miles. We'd use them both to box the Focus and force him to the side of the road. I had never done anything like it, but a highway trooper would have. Now we just had to wait.

About a mile later, Emilia glanced into her rearview mirror and then actually turned her head to look behind her.

"He's onto us," she said. "He's sped up."

Before I could register what she said, a white blur passed us on the left. Emilia immediately downshifted and then floored it. The engine roared, and the acceleration pressed me back into my seat. It surprised the hell out of the car in front of us, too. He swerved to the shoulder while Emilia moved to the left, chasing the Focus.

"Slow down and back off," I said, gripping the door handle beside me.

"We can get him," said Emilia. "Our car's faster than his."

I glanced at the speedometer. We had accelerated past a hundred and were closing in on one-ten.

"It is, but I'd rather not die in it."

"We're catching up to him." And we were. Though he was still a good quarter mile ahead of us, we'd overtake him shortly. "I passed the department's tactical driving course. I know what I'm doing."

"Yeah, but the other drivers around here don't know what you're doing. Slow down before a semi changes lanes and we plow into his backside at a hundred miles an hour. I'm not kidding. Slow down, or we're done right now."

We kept rocketing forward, but then she sighed, and the car decelerated. The white Focus grew smaller as it continued its reckless pace.

"We could have had him," she said.

"Or we could have killed somebody—or ourselves. Your first and most important goal is to make it home at the end of your shift alive."

"I don't need the lecture," she said.

"I'm not lecturing," I said, my face flat. "I'm reminding you of something you already know. We can't put anybody in jail if we're dead."

"I got it."

I called the State Police to apprise them of the situation. They said they'd call me when they picked him up. After that, Emilia settled into an easy, slow pace for the next sixty miles. The more time that passed, the more anxious I became. ISP should have had the car within fifteen minutes. We should have found him on the side of the road by now.

I took out my phone and called my contact at ISP. He said our driver disappeared somewhere near Lafayette. They had officers on every exit in his direction of travel, so they knew he hadn't pulled off. He hadn't pulled over to the side of the road, either, or we would have seen him. They thought he had either turned around on a service road and went back north or that he had gone off road to one of the farm roads that ran parallel to the interstate. Either way, they hadn't found him yet, and I doubted they would. They had too much ground to cover.

I hung up and sighed.

"We get him?" asked Emilia.

"No," I said. "He's in the wind."

Neither of us had anything else to say, so we drove the rest of the way to Indianapolis in silence. Emilia parked in the employee lot beside the City-County building and then drummed her fingers on the steering wheel.

"We've got a lot of daylight left," she said. "Are you sure you want to call it quits?"

I ran a hand across my face and rubbed my eyes. "Yeah. This is a cold case now. You just earned a ton of overtime, so go home and relax. I'll see you tomorrow morning."

She sat up straighter. "This isn't about what happened

on the drive, is it? Because I agree with you. I probably shouldn't have taken off after the car. I just got excited."

"No. This is because I'm tired, and I want to go home. The case isn't going anywhere. We'll talk to Mrs. Cruz, find out where our evidence is, and go from there tomorrow."

She squinted at me and then looked around the parking lot. "Are you sure you're okay?"

"Just tired."

Although, maybe tired was the wrong word. I felt something deeper than that, something empty where I had previously felt strength. I could deal with feeling under appreciated or burned out, but this was different.

I didn't want to work this case anymore. That bothered me. As a police officer, I wasn't supposed to care who my victims were because everybody deserved the same protection under the law. I believed that intellectually, but it was so much harder to fight for a dirt bag than for an innocent person. On top of the vicious departmental politics, it didn't feel worth it anymore.

Emilia handed me the keys, grabbed her bag of clothes from the backseat, and left. I took the evidence we still had remaining from the storage unit—namely, the cell phones—and took those to the offices of our technical support staff. One of the techs promised to see if he could restore the phone so he could view any text messages the boys might have sent. I didn't know how much that would help us, but it was better than nothing.

After that, I drove home. The kids and Hannah had gone somewhere, hopefully somewhere fun, so I crashed on the bed for a late-morning nap.

Kaden woke me up at about 1:00 in the afternoon. Some of the tension I had felt in my gut that morning left, and I breathed easier. Without saying a word, he jumped on the bed and gave me a hug before jumping off and then somersaulting on the floor.

"Did you see that?" he asked, smiling as he got back to his feet.

"Yes," I said, nodding. "It was awesome. Where's *Ummi* and Megan?"

"In the kitchen. *Ummi* said to get you for lunch."

I sat up, yawned, and then stretched my arms above my head, inadvertently untucking my shirt in the process.

"I'll meet you down there," I said, yawning.

"Okay," he said, spreading his arms like the wings on a plane and making engine noises as he rushed out of the room. Once I woke up enough to go downstairs and face the world, my family and I had lunch and then spent an afternoon together at the Children's Museum. Kaden and I spent some of the time looking at exhibits about dinosaurs, while Megan and Hannah rode the carousel. Afterwards, we caught a show at the planetarium. The afternoon didn't go perfectly, but it went well, and we left the museum with smiles on our faces.

That night, after we washed the dishes, tucked the kids into bed, and brushed our teeth, I stopped Hannah before she could turn off the light to go to sleep.

"Yes?" she asked. She wore a black nightgown. She looked beautiful, but she always looked beautiful.

"I missed you last night," I said. "I just thought you should know that."

She scooted closer to me. "I missed you, too, sweetheart."

I felt her against me and breathed her in and felt contented.

"I've had a rough couple of days."

"We can talk about it," she said.

And she meant that. It was one of the amazing things about her. She would sit there and listen to me as long as I needed someone to listen to me. I loved that about her.

Hannah knew me better than anyone in the world. She was proud of the man she fell in love with, the father who wrestled with his kids on the bed, who built picture frames in the garage with his son, the man who smiled and pretended to enjoy her terrible coffee. More than anything in the world, I wanted to be that man, the guy who could smile, who didn't need a drink just to feel normal. I was happy as that man, but I knew deep down he was an act.

The real me was one bad day away from taking my gun, driving through a bad neighborhood, and shooting every drug dealer I saw in the hope that maybe some of the kids in that neighborhood could have a normal childhood for at least a few weeks. Because that was the world I lived in. If I arrested a dozen drug dealers, rapists, or murderers a day, two dozen would pop up the next day to ruin even more lives.

I had been a detective long enough to know how the world actually worked. I didn't help people. I wished I could, but that wasn't my job. I lived and worked in a broken world, and I sent the worst people imaginable to prison, a crucible of suffering that burnt away the soft edges of anyone who passed. Nine times out of ten, the men who emerged were worse than the ones we sent in. And then they just went outside to ruin the lives of the next generation.

I wished I knew how to put a stop to that, but I didn't. I didn't stop my four victims from assaulting Jean Whitfield—and who knew how many other women—and I didn't stop someone from killing them later. All I could do was sweep up the pieces of broken lives and pretend that was enough.

Hannah didn't need to hear that. I preferred the husband she thought she knew.

"It's just a bad day," I said. "I'd rather talk about something else."

She nodded and looked directly in my eyes. "I know you think you're alone, but you're not. You're stronger than you think."

"I know I'm not alone. And it's not strength. I'm just stubborn."

She started to say something, but then she caught herself and tilted her head to the side. "How are you feeling now?"

"A little tired."

She smiled, an almost mischievous grin. "If you aren't interested in talking, you want to fool around?"

I put my arm across her back and pulled her into me. "I think I could fit that into my schedule."

I kissed her, and she kissed me. Within a few minutes, her nightgown hit the floor and my evening had started looking a whole lot better.

Chapter 17

Mrs. Cruz called several hours after I had turned my phone off. She left a voicemail saying she had received my message and expected a call at my next earliest convince. Unfortunately for her, that opportunity arrived just after six in the morning when my kids woke up. While Hannah fed the munchkins, I took over our first-floor home office. Mrs. Cruz's cell phone went to voicemail immediately, so I tried her landline and then kept calling once that went to voicemail. She picked up on the first ring of my fourth call.

"What?"

"Morning," I said. "This is Lieutenant Ashraf Rashid from IMPD. I'm glad you got in touch."

She didn't answer for a five count. "I couldn't stay in Chicago anymore. I'm sorry."

"I wouldn't want to stay either. Why did you empty the storage unit?"

"I don't know what you're talking about," she said, her voice high and a little petulant.

"We've got it on video. You and two men arrived with a truck. They backed the truck inside, emptied your unit, and then you all left. Where did you put my evidence?"

She drew in a breath. "What's wrong with you? Those men were detectives from your department. I lost my sons. I'm sorry if you're so disorganized you can't keep track of your own men, but that's not my fault."

I took a moment in case she wanted to say anything else. She didn't, so I asked the obvious question.

"They were IMPD detectives?"

"Yes. That's what I said. They called me and asked me to meet them at the storage unit. When they showed up, they showed me their badges. I'm not stupid, Mr. Rashid.

I'd appreciate it if you didn't treat me as if I were."

I reached to Hannah's printer for a piece of paper and pinned the phone between my ear and shoulder to free up my hands.

"What did their badges look like?" I asked.

"It was a badge like you see on TV," she said. "It had a star in the center and some kind of tower near the bottom."

The tower sounded like the Soldiers and Sailors monument in Monument Circle. I didn't recognize the guys on film, but it sounded like they carried the right badge at least.

"What color were the badges?" I asked.

"Does that matter?" she asked, clearly growing exasperated. I didn't say anything, mostly because I had started focusing on the computer. "Detective?"

I rubbed my face to get my composure back. "Yeah, it tells me their rank. Were the badges silver or gold?"

She sighed. "Silver. Okay?"

I didn't have to sort through the supervisory officers, then. That narrowed my search down to detectives, patrolmen, and a few other groups. Well over a thousand individuals carried those silver badges, but none of them should have showed up in Chicago without calling me first.

"How did they contact you?" I asked, pushing back from the desk.

"I didn't do anything wrong," she said.

"I understand that, but these men were not detectives assigned to this case," I said. "I need to find out what's going on, and to do that, I need your cooperation. How did they contact you?"

She paused for a few seconds. When she spoke, her voice sounded sharp. "They called my cell phone. They said you gave them my number."

That told me more than she probably realized. Very

few people knew I had started working this case, and even fewer would have known about Mrs. Cruz. We had a leak somewhere, one willing to help cover up a murder of some very bad young men.

"What number did they call you from?"

"It was blocked. My phone doesn't say."

I'd have to call her cell provider, then.

"Did you know what kind of websites your sons developed?" I asked.

She hesitated for just a moment too long. "Not really. Just that they were websites."

"You never heard rumors? Never had someone send you a link, never checked out their portfolio?"

Once again, she hesitated. "No. That was always their thing. I wasn't interested in it."

Though I wasn't always proud of this aspect of the job, I lied to suspects for a living, and I was fairly good at it. I knew how to manipulate people and how to spot when others tried to manipulate me.

"They ran pornographic websites," I said. "From what I'm told, they were quite successful. Who handled their estate?"

"The lawyers," she said, her voice soft and meek. "They send us a royalty check every month."

Whether she knew it or not, I had her then. If somebody sent the estate a check every month, the lawyers who oversaw it would damn well make sure the beneficiary knew where the money came from. I could call her on the lie if I wanted, but sometimes it was better to hold on to leverage than to use it right away.

"Did young women ever contact you about the website?"

She didn't hesitate to answer. "My sons had lots of girlfriends. They weren't ready to settle down."

It didn't take a lot to read through the lines. Women had called, and they were pissed.

"Did these women contact you directly, or through your lawyers?"

"I didn't say-" She stopped herself mid sentence and took a deep breath. "They contacted me through the lawyers."

"Good," I said, nodding. "I'm going to assume these women were angry. Any of them sue?"

"Three threatened lawsuits. The lawyers said we should pay them off to protect my sons' reputations."

I waited for her to continue, but she said nothing. "Did you know your sons coerced these women into having sex with them on film?"

"I don't care what those little sluts said," she said. "My sons wouldn't force anyone to do anything. They didn't need to. Women wanted them."

I put my thumb over my phone's microphone and took a deep breath, hoping to flush the revulsion from my voice.

"I'll need the names of these women."

"I don't know them. I'll tell our lawyers to contact you."

Mrs. Cruz and I spoke for another few minutes, but I couldn't get her to change her story materially. That didn't mean she had told me the truth, but it made me lean in that direction. She knew more about her sons and their activities than she had let on, but how much, I couldn't say.

I hung up the phone and joined my family in our eat-in kitchen. The kids had toast and eggs at the table. Hannah handed me a mug of coffee and put a hand on my shoulder as she passed. When the kids weren't looking, she winked and dropped her hand to squeeze my butt. I smiled at her and then focused on the kids.

"So what are you guys doing today?"

Megan started to answer, but my wife cut her off. She smiled, but I couldn't hear it in her voice. "Mrs. Griffen from Child Protective Services is coming by to ensure that we have a safe living environment. That means we're staying here and playing in the house until she leaves."

Until the moment, I had been having a good morning. My hands started shaking, so I had to put the coffee mug on the table to avoid spilling it.

The call to Child Protective Services happened two weeks ago in the middle of the afternoon. Because of the work I did, I knew a lot of social workers both in Indianapolis and the suburbs surrounding it, and they had kept me informed of what had happened. The call originally came into the state of Indiana's tip line, which routed it to the local CPS office in Hamilton County.

I'm calling to report an instance of child negligence. I'm in front of a man's house, and his son is running around the front yard without clothes or shoes. It's not the first time, either. I don't know if that's a Muslim thing or what, but I just thought you should know. His parents aren't around, either.

Then he gave his name and phone number. I matched them to the license plate on a black Chevrolet that had stopped in front of my house. The call lasted twenty seconds at most, but it threatened some of the things I held most dear.

The caller, of course, hadn't mentioned Kaden was wearing a bathing suit at the time and playing with a sprinkler with the neighbor's two boys in front of their house under the supervision of their mom. The moment we heard about the complaint, Hannah and I talked to our neighbors to tell them what had happened. They understood the situation and agreed to talk to the social worker when she showed up.

We wouldn't lose our kids because of a frivolous complaint, but it burned me up that someone we didn't even know would try to hurt us like that. That was personal. Unfortunately, I couldn't do much about it.

"If you guys are going to play inside anyway, I need

some new pictures in my office," I said, smiling and taking a sip of Hannah's truly awful coffee and trying not to wince. I coughed to clear my throat afterwards. "My budget for artwork is lower than I expected this year."

Megan looked up at me and nodded sagaciously. "I think I know what you want."

I didn't even know what I wanted, but I nodded anyway. "I appreciate that, sweetheart."

For a moment, Megan returned her attention to her breakfast, but then she cocked her head at me. "Did you work yesterday?"

"A little," I said. "I would have rather spent the day with you."

She shook her head disapprovingly. "Sunday is the Lord's day. You shouldn't work on Sundays."

I smiled at her. "Uncle Jack tell you that?"

She nodded seriously. "Yes."

"Christians go to church on Sunday," I said. "But we go to prayer on Fridays, and Jewish people go to temple on Friday night or Saturday morning. That's what God wants."

She screwed up her face, as she often did when asking me theological questions.

"Why?"

"Well," I said, tilting my head to the side. "I don't know, but would you want that many people talking to you at once? Maybe God just likes the days spread out so He can hear everybody."

"Oh," she said, nodding. "That makes sense. Sometimes, when the teacher talks in class and Sydney talks to Elizabeth, and Michael talks to Andre, I can't understand a thing."

"I'm glad you understand," I said, nodding and making a mental note to talk to Megan's teacher about extra-curricular conversations in class. I looked at the uneaten eggs on the plate in front of her. "Eat your breakfast before it gets cold."

She started eating again, so I left my coffee on the table and went upstairs to get dressed for the day. At just a little before eight, I came back downstairs and noticed a to-go coffee mug sitting on the counter. With Hannah standing just a few feet from it, I didn't think I could pretend that I hadn't seen it. Hopefully she wouldn't ask me to drink it in front of her.

Prior to meeting me, my wife didn't drink or make coffee, but when she found out I liked it, she bought her first coffee maker and made me a pot. It was the most awful drink I've ever had. I read an article that said smoking a cigarette took an average of fourteen minutes from the smoker's life. Though I wasn't a smoker and didn't plan to become one, I had tried cigarettes when I was young. They didn't make my eyebrows twitch involuntarily for hours, and they didn't make me feel as if I had just had a stroke. The steaming, ink-black liquid my wife served me every morning did. Still, I drank it because she loved me enough to make it for me every morning, even if I felt a little part of myself die each time.

I picked up the mug, kissed my wife, hugged my kids, and then got in my car. Before going into work, I stopped by a coffee shop and poured my mug of coffee down a storm drain in the parking lot, half-expecting to hear it sizzle as it ate its way through the steel grate. It didn't, of course, but it did leave a black stain on the metal. Inside, I purchased two cups of coffee, one straight back and the second full of cream and sugar. I replaced Hannah's black death roast with something earthy and wonderful and then drove to the City-County building, where I parked in the employee lot across the street.

Emilia had a desk in the homicide unit's bullpen, and as I took the elevator to her floor, I realized how much I missed that place. I liked most of the men and women who worked in the prosecutor's office, but my building didn't have the same sort of frenzied energy I found in an office surrounded by other detectives. Walking onto her floor and seeing men and women I had known for years felt a little like going home.

I weaved through the desks until I came to Emilia's, where she sat checking her email. She glanced up at me.

"Morning, partner."

"I got you a coffee," I said, putting her cup on her desk. "It's got a ton of sugar in it."

"Thanks, but give me just a minute," she said, again glancing up from her monitor long enough to smile at me before returning to whatever she had been reading when I walked up. She took a sip of her drink without looking at me. "That's good. Did you break something?"

"Is that how you thank all your partners when they bring you coffee?"

She shook her head. "No, but when men bring me gifts at eight in the morning, I assume they broke something. Or that they had cheated on me. You're not working with other detectives behind my back, are you?"

"You're it," I said, sitting at the unoccupied desk beside hers. "I talked to Anita Cruz this morning."

Emilia pushed back from her desk and crossed her arms. "She explain why she stole evidence from the murder investigation of her sons?"

I filled her in on the conversation. She listened to everything and then exhaled hard.

"So you think we've got some dirty cops?" she asked.

"Possibly," I said. "It would explain a few things," I said, nodding. "I need you to do some work. We know one of our victims had regular phone calls with somebody from IMPD. I need you to find out who. Human resources should have the directory from back then."

She looked at me and nodded. "I'm on it."

I stood up. "Give me a call when you've got

something. I'll be in my office filling out paperwork justifying all the money we spent in Chicago."

She picked up her coffee and smiled. "You enjoy yourself. Thanks for the coffee, and don't forget yours."

I walked back to her desk for my cup and then began the one block walk to my office building. Along the way, I felt my phone buzz, signaling an incoming call. I answered without looking at the caller ID.

"Yeah, this is Ash Rashid."

"Lieutenant Rashid," said a high-pitched male voice from the other end. "This is Travis from Tech services. I've been working on the cell phones you brought by."

"You find anything?"

"Not yet, but I'm still working. I wanted to call and let you know, though, that I pulled a working SIM card from each phone. We should have everything on them shortly."

"That's great, I think. What does it give us?"

I stopped walking and sat on a nearby bench overlooking Alabama Street. Birds chirped from trees nearby. A couple of people leaned against the building behind me smoking. A woman waited for the bus up ahead. Nobody stood close enough to me to overhear my conversation.

"Text messages, address books, subscriber information, list of incoming and outgoing calls, maybe even pictures if these old phones have cameras. At this point, the technology is archaic, so it's taking me a while to process it into a format I can use."

I sipped my coffee and leaned forward, resting my elbows on my knees.

"That's excellent. You have an estimate for when you'll have data I can actually use?"

Travis paused for a few seconds. "Too many variables to say. Best case scenario, this afternoon or tomorrow. Worst case, a couple of days."

"That's great," I said. "Thanks for calling. I always like

good news."

I gave him my email address just in case he needed to get in touch with me via email and then hung up. I didn't know what the phones contained, but it couldn't hurt our case. I pocketed my phone and took another sip of coffee. We had a real shot of closing this nine year-old case soon. Once Emilia identified the police officer our victims talked to, we could check his photo against the men who cleaned out the storage locker. If we had a match, we very well might have had our killer. If we could put him in Indianapolis on the night Kristen Tanaka and Charles Holden died, we might have their killer, too.

I stood and threw my now lukewarm coffee in the nearest trashcan. This might actually turn out to be a good day.

Chapter 18

For the second time in four days, Aleksander found himself near the Rashid home. Unlike his previous trip, this wasn't about surveillance or planning. Someone would die today.

Killing David Parker should have taken Lieutenant Rashid off the board. He should have joined the rest of his department and focused on the serial murder in their midst. Instead, he had driven to Chicago. Aleksander didn't know what the Lieutenant did in Chicago, but he never should have gotten that far.

Rashid was making headway, just as Kristen Tanaka had. Inside his car, Aleksander's hands shook. When Alonzo Cruz hired him nine years ago to eliminate four young men, he thought it would be a simple job for a wealthy businessman. And for almost ten years, everything had worked out. He couldn't run from the devil forever, though. Aleksander's past sins had resurfaced. He needed to gain control of the situation and curtail the investigation before it ended up on his family's doorstep.

He would have killed Detective Rashid, but that would only raise new questions. He needed a better option. Thankfully, fate had given him one.

The minivan he had stolen for the job had a much higher center of gravity than he had grown accustomed to, so every gust of wind blew him nearly out of his lane. It probably wouldn't do well around a sharp curve at speed, but then its designers hadn't made it for that. This was a people carrier. He and Vesna could have used a similar vehicle when their kids were younger. Lieutenant Rashid and his wife very likely got a lot of use out of their identical vehicle.

He pulled into the neighborhood, noting the red light cameras suspended on the traffic light outside. That would help. Beside him, he had a subcompact Glock 27, the perfect weapon for fitting in a purse, and a red silk shawl purchased at a second hand store. He drove through the winding network of roads to Rashid's cul-de-sac but slowed before turning inside. This time, a dark red SUV sat at the curb.

Aleksander couldn't see the occupant well through the tinted rear windows, so he pulled his van onto the street and then around the cul-de-sac and back. A woman occupied the driver's seat of the SUV. She had a pair of binoculars pressed against her face, and as he slowed to a stop near her car, she pointed her binoculars to a nearby tree.

Aleksander rolled down his window and motioned for her to do likewise. She acted surprised, but then her lips grew into a tight, nervous smile.

"Can I help you?" she asked. She was younger than he expected, maybe thirty. She had delicate hands with alabaster skin stretched taut across her knuckles. A plain gold band adorned her left ring finger, and a heart-shaped locket hung on a chain around her neck. She had an attractive if unremarkable face.

On another day, he would have imagined her as a school teacher. Today, he didn't want to imagine her as anything but the woman in a car. He didn't want to think of her as having a husband or children given what he had to do.

Aleksander pointed behind him toward the Rashid's house. "I noticed you watching his house."

"I'm watching the birds, actually," she said, flashing that fake smile again. She pointed out her window to a tree looming over Aleksander's minivan. "There's a white breasted Nuthatch nest in that tree. I love birds."

"I'm sure they're lovely," said Aleksander, not taking

his eyes from hers. "But I've been here before. I've seen people watching the house. You're one of them."

"One of who?" she asked, tittering nervously and shaking her head.

"Someone who understands," said Aleksander. "You're watching Ashraf Rashid and his family. You don't need to deny it. I've been watching, too."

She looked to him and then to the minivan in which he sat. Her back was straight. "I almost thought you were her in that car. The tinted windows make it hard to see."

"I assure you I'm not Mrs. Rashid," he said, smiling. "I've been here a few times. I see different people watch each time, but they always park in that spot."

"This was my shift," she said. She licked her lips. "I don't know if I'm comfortable talking to you. How do I know you're not one of them?"

Aleskander didn't even know who *they* were, but he nodded anyway. "Do I look like one of them?"

She hesitated and then shook her head. "No. I guess not. But look, we're not supposed to talk to anybody when we're out here. If you're interested, you can go to our website. We're the Indiana Citizen Watch Network. Google the name, and you'll find the site. You can fill out an application so one of our leaders can talk to you."

That made sense now. Similar groups had formed in the past to watch the US-Mexico border. Now, after a series of terrorist bombings in Europe, groups had turned their focus inward to watch for Islamic-terrorist sleeper agents already embedded in American society.

More than most, Aleksander understood how scary the world could be. Monitoring those they feared probably made the men and women from the watch networks feel empowered. He wondered if their leaders had considered simply knocking on the door and saying hello instead. That seemed like a better use of everyone's time.

"Do the Rashids know you watch them?"

"Yeah," she said. "That's part of our job. Unlike these Muslims, we don't hide. We're here to protect people."

"Have they ever come after you?"

She drew in a breath and then nodded. "Hannah Rashid tried to bring me something to drink once, but I threw it on the ground. I know what she's really like. She can't tell me she wants to be friends."

"Have they come after anyone else?"

"Oh, yeah," she said, leaning forward. "That Ashraf guy came after one of our watchers once. He had a gun. The police came out and told him we had every legal right to park on a public road."

Better and better. This would work well. Aleksander smiled and then reached to his side for his hand gun.

"I'm sorry for this," he said, slipping his finger inside the trigger guard of his pistol.

She furrowed her brow and cocked her head to the side. Aleksander raised his weapon, and her face twisted with fear. She held up her hands and opened her mouth to scream. Before she could, Aleksander squeezed the trigger of his weapon twice, striking her in the face and forehead. The report of the shots echoed off the nearby houses like fireworks on the Fourth of July. Blood and brain matter splattered across the passenger side seat of the woman's SUV. Someone should have told her there are better things to fear than law-abiding families.

Aleksander tossed his gun to the seat beside him, closed his tinted window to obscure his features, and hurriedly wrapped the shawl around his head.

Anyone who saw him now would see the van identical to Hannah Rashid's and the shawl similar to the hijab she wore, and their minds would make the obvious connection. With the dark windows, they couldn't see his face to contradict their judgment.

Then, he floored his accelerator. The nose of the

minivan lifted as the tires bit into the asphalt, propelling him forward. The van didn't accelerate like a smaller sports car, but it could move when needed. As he neared the entrance to the neighborhood, he purposely slowed when he saw a green light.

"Come on, come on, come on," he said, imploring the traffic light to change. He needed a picture to complete the job.

As the light shifted to yellow and then red, Aleksander floored his accelerator again and pressed the horn in a long, continual beep. He blew through the intersection at roughly fifty miles an hour. Several cars slammed on their brakes to avoid hitting him. More important than that, he saw the flash of a traffic camera as it took his picture.

He had seen images from those cameras before. They didn't show detail well, but they captured a driver's profile in general. In this case, they captured the picture of a red minivan driven by someone wearing hijab barreling through the intersection after a murder three blocks away. The Rashid household would have a very bad day very shortly.

Chapter 19

I walked the rest of the way to my office and settled in front of my keyboard, but before I could get started on anything, Emilia called. She didn't give me time to say a thing before she spoke.

"Chris Buchanan."

I said the name a couple of times, hoping it would spark a memory. It didn't.

"Who is he?" I asked.

"He's the IMPD detective who called our victims. I couldn't find much on him. He retired in 2009, but before that, he worked narcotics and vice. I googled him but couldn't find him on Facebook, Twitter or any of the other usual sites. The news mentioned his name a couple of times, but not many."

If people looked me up, they would find dozens of articles about the cases I had worked and even two Facebook pages created after a recent shooting to glorify or excoriate me. But then, I had spent most of my career working homicide, and few cases garnered more media attention than horrific homicides. A search for most officers would turn up results that looked just like the results for Buchanan's name. Considering he made it to retirement, Buchanan likely had a stable and productive if unremarkable career. That wasn't a bad life to live.

"He still around?" I asked.

"I didn't find an obituary for him if that's what you're asking."

I didn't mean to ask that, but we should probably answer it, too.

"Go to the county health department's website and look him up on the death certificate database. If you can't find him there, look him up on the county assessor's website. We need to find him."

She paused for a moment, presumably as she wrote down my request.

"How's your paperwork going?" she asked.

I grunted. "Haven't started, but I'm sure it will drain my will to live. I'm going to call Captain Bowers. He's been around for a while and knows everybody. Hopefully, that includes Buchanan."

"All right," she said. "You want me to call you if I find anything?"

"That or stop by the office. I need you to sign a few reports."

"Fun times," she said.

I wished her luck and then hung up before calling Mike. We talked only long enough for him to tell me he hadn't heard of Buchanan. He suggested I contact Susan Mercer, the deputy prosecutor. If nothing else, she could look up the cases he brought in.

I thanked him and then hung up and called Susan's assistant to make sure the boss was in. She was, so I jogged to the stairwell, knowing that would be quicker than waiting for the elevator.

I made it up two flights of steps before coming to an abrupt halt on the landing before Susan's floor as the door to the office flew open. A man in a well-cut, black suit with gray pinstripes jogged out. He had neatly trimmed blonde hair and calculating blue eyes.

From our very first meeting when he ogled my old partner, I had never liked Sergeant Smith. He was a competent officer when he wanted to be, but he also was a bully. Every department had men like him, people who enjoyed exploiting the power their position gave them over others. I tried to avoid him wherever possible.

"Move, Rashid," he said, barreling past me and down the steps. I stepped aside and then leaned over the handrail to watch as he ran down the steps to the building's first floor. Sergeant Smith was the senior-most officer among the contingent of detectives assigned to the Prosecutor's Office. I had once held the same post and enjoyed the job. I couldn't ever recall running out of a building like that for work, though. As much as I disliked the guy, I hoped he was okay.

Once Smith disappeared through the door that led to the building's parking garage, I left the stairwell and walked into the prosecutor's office. The Prosecutor's office didn't put many attorneys on Susan's floor, but those who worked up there usually had their own assistant and offices large enough to hold entire conference tables. Susan was the exception, at least for the office. Where she once worked out of an office the size of my living room, she had moved to a much smaller space after being on the losing end of some political maneuvering. I nodded hello to the office assistants I knew on my way to Susan's corner of the floor.

"Hey, Pam," I said, nodding to Susan's assistant as I walked up. Pam looked up from her computer and smiled. "How's Sarah liking college?"

The smile dimmed a little but didn't disappear. "More than she should. She got picked up for public intoxication on Saturday. Raymond and I had to bail her out of jail."

"Children are truly a joy forever," I said. "You guys get everything sorted out?"

Pam shook her head. "We're not letting our friends help. Sarah got into this mess, so she'll do the community service and pay her fine just like her friends."

I had only met Pam's daughter once, but she seemed as if she had a decent head on her shoulders. As long as she stayed out of trouble for the rest of her time in school, one mistake a couple of weeks into her freshman year of college wouldn't ruin her life. Everybody made mistakes. Even law enforcement hiring boards would overlook something like that.

"I don't envy you, but good luck," I said. I nodded toward Susan's door. "She mind if I go back?"

Pam looked at her computer and clicked a few buttons, probably messaging her boss. Within moments she looked at me again. "Go right on back."

"Thanks," I said, already walking toward my former supervisor's door. I knocked and then turned the doorknob. The office had a desk, two chairs in front, and filing cabinets beside the door. Stacks of file boxes leaned against the east and west wall, while a bank of windows on the wall opposite the door allowed in natural light.

By almost all standards, it was a very nice office, but it was also totally inadequate for my former boss's needs. As the deputy prosecutor, she met with defense attorneys, prosecutors, detectives and accountants all day, and she needed an office that accommodated more than two or three people at a time. Moving her from an office that actually fit her work requirements to this one was an intentional slap in the face by a career politician. It pissed me off that anyone would treat a friend of mine like that, but it wasn't my fight. Besides that, Susan could handle herself.

She looked up as I stepped inside.

"Ashraf," she said, nodding toward the chairs in front of her desk. "Have a seat."

"I ran into Tim Smith in the stairwell," I said, picking up a white cardboard banker's box from a chair so I could sit down. "Just about knocked me over."

"Probably off to kiss some politician's ass. As far as I can tell, that's all he and the rest of his lackeys do around here. What do you need?"

I shifted on the seat to make myself a little more comfortable. "Mike Bowers suggested I visit. You know a cop named Chris Buchanan? We think he worked vice, and we're pretty sure he was in contact with the victims in a case I'm investigating."

Susan slowly nodded. "I've met Sergeant Buchanan. He brought us a couple of cases."

I waited for her to continue, but she said nothing. That in and of itself should have told me something, but I couldn't figure out what. Susan rarely held back when asked what she thought of someone.

"Okay," I said, drawing the syllables out slowly, hoping it would coax her into continuing the conversation. I blinked several times and when she still hadn't spoken, I stood up and closed her door. "Why don't you want to talk about him?"

She shrugged and sighed. "I don't know what there is to say about the guy. He was a decent cop, I guess. Not terribly bright, not terribly stupid."

"Just like a lot of people. What's different with Buchanan?"

She turned her head and looked out the window. "I can't prove anything. You understand that?"

I nodded. "Yeah. Tell me what you're thinking."

"He was too smooth. Whenever you asked him a question, he always had the perfect answer waiting for you, and that answer never reflected badly on him. He never screwed up, he never violated procedure, he never got careless with paperwork. By all accounts, he was the perfect officer."

I crossed my arms. "What's the catch?"

"No one ever filed a complaint against him. He worked vice."

I shook my head. "I don't know what you're getting it."

Susan leaned forward and rested her elbows on the table. "Every single cop who works vice receives formal complaints. A detective picks up a hooker one day, and the next day her lawyer's banging on my door claiming that cop asked for a freebie in exchange for overlooking her evening escapades. That's how it is. IA investigates, but almost every time, they can't prove a thing."

Of course that was a big step from claiming the event didn't happen. I loosened the arms across my chest and then leaned back, relaxing.

"But nobody ever complained about Buchanan?"

"Never. It wasn't just the lack of complaints, though. He made me feel uncomfortable, and I'm not the only one."

That actually said a lot. As the Deputy Prosecutor, Susan saw rapists, murderers, and child molesters on a weekly basis. She knew how to spot a predator.

"You know anything else about him?"

Susan immediately shook her head. "No. All I know is that he gave me the creeps."

"You remember if Buchanan ever had a partner?"

She furrowed her brow and then leaned back. Her chair creaked. "Yeah. Quiet guy. Bill Smith or Bill Baker or something like that. His last name was an occupation."

I ran the list of men named Bill who worked in the department. "How about Taylor?"

She knocked on her desk and nodded. "That's the guy. Bill Taylor. In ten years, I think he said five words to me."

I had only met him once or twice myself at a holiday party, but her description sounded right. He worked an odd detail for the burglary squad, if I recalled. Whenever somebody brought a high-ticket item to a pawn shop, the proprietor filled out a yellow card with the customer's information in case the item was stolen. Bill traveled from pawn shop to pawn shop collecting those cards and occasionally arresting idiots who tried to pawn tools they stole out of their neighbors' garages. The assignment sucked, but he still had a badge. I could find him.

Susan and I talked for another few minutes, mostly to catch up. I would have stayed longer, but she got a pressing phone call, and I had to get back to work. As I walked back toward the stairwell, I called Emilia Rios.

"You getting anywhere?"

"No. Apparently, Buchanan just up and disappeared," she said. "The Department of Health doesn't have any records for him, so he's probably not dead. Unfortunately, he doesn't have a driver's license in Indiana or any of the surrounding states, he has no cars registered in his name, nor does he own any property in Marion County, Boone County, Hendricks County, or Morgan County. I got his social security number from HR and ran a credit check on him. Wherever he lives, he has no mortgage or credit cards. He's not declared bankruptcy in Indiana, and nor has he gotten married or divorced. I thought about requesting a tax transcript from the IRS, but I need his home address to do that."

I nodded and drew in a breath. Wherever Buchanan lived now, he had gone to a lot of work to hide himself. Not many people would do that without reason, which made me think he was hiding from somebody—maybe even us.

"All right. Plan B, then. Buchanan had a partner when he worked vice. His name was Bill Taylor. You want to pay him a visit?"

"Does that mean I don't have to do paperwork?"

I stopped outside the stairwell, Emilia said something, but I couldn't hear her because I noticed a commotion coming from the other end of the floor. Susan Mercer was jogging towards me, holding a cardigan over her shoulders.

"Ash," she said. "Hold up."

I furrowed my brow. "Emilia, I'm going to call you back."

Again, Emilia said something, but I didn't hear. Susan didn't overreact often, and never did she come running out of her office. Something wasn't right.

"Hey," I said once she was in speaking distance.

"What's going on?"

"You need to go home," she said. "Right now."

"What's going on?"

"I don't have details, but there was a shooting near your house. You need to get there right now."

I felt a sudden cold stab of dread. "How near my house?"

"I don't know, but Hannah's name was mentioned…"

The cold spread from my chest to my extremities. Men have been watching my house, men with weapons. My fingers trembled. Before Susan could say another word, I threw open the door to the stairwell and ran.

Chapter 20

I didn't run into anyone as I sprinted downstairs, but even if I had, I didn't know if I would have noticed. My mind focused only one thing: my wife. She had to be okay. We had gone through too much together for her to be hurt now.

When I reached the first floor, I ran outside to find streets already becoming clogged with traffic. Due to budget cuts, I no longer had an unmarked cruiser with lights and sirens; I only had my own VW, and in this traffic, it'd take me an hour to get home.

Instead, I sprinted toward the City-County building a block away and flagged down the first marked patrol cruiser I could. I didn't know the driver, but he rolled his window down as I flashed him my badge.

"We've got an emergency. You're driving me to Carmel. I'll call your supervisor on the way and tell him what's up."

The officer must have heard the urgency in my voice because he leaned over and popped open the passenger door.

"Get in, sir."

The moment I had my door shut, the officer flicked on the lights and siren and took off. I could barely think straight, but I called my driver's commanding officer to tell her I had commandeered her officer for an hour to deal with an emergency.

I was abusing my position, but I didn't care at that point. If my wife was hurt—or worse—I needed to be beside her. The buildings around us blurred as we drove. As we pulled onto my street, I felt my heart start pounding. There were half a dozen marked police cars parked nearby. My wife's minivan was parked on the street half a block away. I couldn't see her, but I did see a familiar face in the crowd. Sergeant Tim Smith. My driver pulled the cruiser to the side of the road.

"Thank you so much," I said. "You can head back to work. I'll get a ride from here."

"Any time, sir," he said. "If you need anything, you've got my boss's number."

I stepped out of the car and waved as the officer drove off. I didn't have enough information to make any sort of conclusion, so I approached the yellow crime scene tape, behind which stood several officers including Sergeant Smith. I unclipped my badge from my belt and showed it to the uniformed officer nearest the edge of the crime scene.

"I'm Lieutenant Ashraf Rashid with IMPD," I said, nodding down the street toward my house. "I live at the end of the cul-de-sac. Who's the victim?"

"A woman named Gloria Johnson."

Not Hannah. My shoulders slumped.

"Thank you very much," I said, taking a step back and reaching into my pocket. The officer went back to manning the log book, and I called my wife. Somewhere nearby, I heard her phone ring. I looked toward the sound but couldn't see her. I did, however, see one of the detectives beyond the crime scene tape answer a phone. The sinking sensation reappeared in my gut.

"Why do you have my wife's phone?" I asked.

"Who is this?" asked the detective. I walked toward the crime scene tape and flagged down the same officer I had spoken to a second ago.

"This is Hannah Rashid's husband. I'm standing beside your uniformed officer on the edge of the crime scene. You'll know me because I'm the one with the IMPD lieutenant's badge."

The detective looked up, hung up my wife's phone, and then walked toward the crime scene tape. Sergeant

Smith walked a few steps behind him. I slipped my own phone in my pocket, expecting him to beckon me over. He didn't.

The detective had brown hair cropped short, and he wore a suit that looked as if it would have fit a man twenty pounds lighter than the one in front of me. Acne scars pockmarked his face.

"Lieutenant Rashid," he said, nodding. "I'm Detective Lane Carter. I'm with the Carmel Police Department."

"It's nice to meet you, Detective. Why do you have my wife's phone?"

Carter looked around the crowd and then pursed his lips. "I'll be happy to answer your questions if you answer some of mine first. Can I ask you where you were this afternoon at noon?"

My mouth popped open before I could stop it. Sergeant Smith snickered, but Detective Carter ignored it.

"I was at work," I said. "You can talk to half a dozen sworn officers to verify that. Now where's my wife?"

"We've taken her into custody," said Carter. "Did you know there were people watching your home?"

I blinked several times, sure that I had misheard him. "Why do you have my wife in custody?"

"We have reason to believe she shot a woman outside your home this afternoon. Let me ask again: did you know people were watching your home? We'll be searching your home this afternoon once we secure a search warrant. I don't need to tell you that this whole thing will go easier if you cooperate with my investigation."

"Does my wife have an attorney with her?" I asked.

"Did you know people were watching your house?" asked Carter again.

"Answer my question, and I'll answer yours. Does my wife have an attorney advising her?"

Detective Carter crossed his arms. "Not that I know

of."

I nodded and reached for my wallet. All around me, officers tensed and put their hands over their firearms. I put my hands up slowly.

"I'm getting something out of my wallet. Can I do that?"

Detective Carter looked at my waist. "Slowly."

I reached behind me once more and grabbed my wallet.

"Hannah Rashid is my wife. I will be acting as her attorney until such time as she can acquire more appropriate counsel," I said, pulling out my laminated Indiana Bar Association membership card. I held it in front of me. "Call your commanding officer and tell him that the questioning needs to stop right now."

Detective Carter looked over his shoulder at Tim Smith and then back to me. "Given some of the things I've heard from your colleagues, I'm not sure that I'm comfortable with that."

"I don't care what you're comfortable with. Call your CO and tell him Mrs. Rashid has an attorney. He's not to ask her any more questions. If he—or anyone else—asks her another question, we're all going to court. Nobody wins then."

He pulled out his cell phone and reluctantly stepped away from the police line. Tim Smith smirked at me. Now I knew why he had run out of the building. He wanted to beat me to the crime scene.

I wanted to punch the guy, but that would only end up with me placed under arrest. I'd deal with him later. In the meantime, I took out my phone and looked up the office number of John Meyers and Associates. Meyers was the most gifted trial attorney I had ever met, a fact reflected on the fees he charged. We'd have to sell some stock to pay his retainer, but if Hamilton County charged my wife with a crime, she'd have the best criminal defense team in the midwest behind her.

Meyers wasn't available, so I left him a message asking for a call back. As I waited for that call, Detective Carter hung up and joined me at the crime scene tape.

"Your wife is in our station. You can meet her there."

I nodded and took a breath and looked around. "And where are my kids?"

Detective Carter blinked and then drew in a breath. "Your kids are safe. Don't worry about them."

A cold feeling began to spread in me. My fingers began to tremble. "What have you done with my children?"

"They're safe," said Carter, his voice calm. "They're in the custody of the Hamilton County Department of Child Services."

I balled my hands into fists. My kids were well adjusted, but they knew someone was watching the house. They didn't understand, but they knew they weren't supposed to talk to strangers. And now, strangers had come into my house, arrested their mother, and taken them away, probably by force. This was wrong on every level.

"You stupid asshole."

"Excuse me?" asked Carter.

I ignored him and took out my phone to call our family attorney. When we hired her to represent us in the family court system, she had outlined what we all thought was the worst case scenario, but it didn't even come close to this.

She answered on the second ring, and I stepped away from the crime scene tape, barely able to contain my voice. I told her what had happened, and she promised to get on it and do what she could. The court system wouldn't give my kids back to me without a lot more work, but maybe we could convince them to give my sister-in-law and her husband temporary custody.

That phone call made, I turned my attention back to Detective Carter.

"You guys are searching my wife's car," I said. "I need a ride to your station."

Detective Carter didn't blink. "You probably should have thought of that before calling me an asshole. I'm sure you can get a cab."

I looked to Sergeant Smith. He smiled and then shook his head. "Don't even bother asking."

"You're a tool," I said, shaking my head as I walked away. I knocked on a friendly neighbor's door and explained the situation. Her sixteen-year-old son drove me to the station in a car that smelled like weed. I didn't care about the drugs. I just appreciated the ride.

Carmel's government center looked more like a bucolic college campus than anywhere public servants worked. Green lawns as thick and soft as any carpet I've ever stood upon stretched from the front of the planting beds at the base of the buildings to the street. The architecture was Georgian and reminded me of Colonial Williamsburg. When Hannah and I lived in the city, I oftentimes wondered where my taxes went; here, I knew without a doubt. The entire place smelled like money.

My neighbor dropped me off in front of the police station, and I walked inside. Quite easily, it was the nicest, most orderly police station in which I've ever stepped foot. Gray marble tile ran from the front to the back and white dentil molding adorned the ceiling. I almost felt surprised that I didn't hear soft music in the background. If I hadn't seen the armed police officers milling about, I might have thought I had stepped into the lobby of a hotel or private hospital. I told the receptionist my name, and she called somebody and told me to have a seat. Instead, I paced, feeling my worry build.

A few moments later, a man in a black suit came toward me. He had thick salt-and-pepper hair parted on the right side, and a bushy, unkempt gray mustache. He wore square, rimless glasses perched on a nose too large for his round face. He looked like somebody's crotchety grandfather. When he stepped toward me, he extended his hand, allowing me to see the weapon in the holster at his waist and the gold badge on his belt.

"I'm Captain Donald Greer. You must be Lieutenant Rashid."

I ignored his hand and nodded to the door through which he had come. "Is my wife back there?"

Greer dropped his hand to his side and straightened. "She is. I understand you're here as her legal counsel."

"You understand correctly. I want to see my client right now."

Greer's eyes traced the contours of my chest and then rested upon the weapon in my shoulder holster. "If you're here as Ms. Rashid's legal counsel, I'm going to have to ask you to check your firearm at the desk."

I didn't bother fighting the request. This was their station, their rules, and my IMPD badge carried no authority here beyond what the locals gave me. If I were just Hannah's husband, or if I were just a police officer, they could have kept me out of there. As her attorney, though, I had every right to see her. I left my firearm in a locked box at the front desk, but I kept my badge on my hip. That should at least afford me some common courtesy.

After that, they led me to an interrogation room. Like most modern interrogation rooms, a camera hung in the corner. I couldn't see microphones, but they likely had several hidden about the room. Gray carpet covered the floor, the walls, and the ceiling. IMPD did the same thing. The carpet cut down on the echo, but more than that, it muffled noises from nearby rooms. A detective could raise his voice without fear of disturbing a delicate interrogation in another room.

Hannah sat on a folding chair beside a solid steel table. Hand cuffs secured her wrists to an O-ring welded to the wall. She looked at me, her eyes red with tears. I wanted to throw my arms around her and whisper that things would be okay. That's what a good husband would have done. I hadn't come as her husband, though, so I stopped in the doorway and looked at Greer.

"Has Mrs. Rashid threatened you in any way?" I asked.

Greer considered and then shook his head. "No."

"Did she resist arrest?"

Again, Greer considered and then shook his head. "No."

"Then do you think it's necessary to hand cuff her?"

He drew in a deep breath and then exhaled slowly. "I'll get somebody to take them off."

"Don't bother. I'll do it," I said, stepping inside the room and reaching to my pocket. Police-issue handcuffs used a standard key in every station because it made it easier to transport prisoners. I carried one with me on my keychain. I unhooked my wife and held my hand on her wrist. "Can I have some time with my client?"

"You've got five minutes, but that's it. I'd like to get this started."

Greer shut the door behind him. Almost immediately, Hannah shot upright and gave me a hug. Her breath sounded ragged, labored. After a few moments, she calmed down and took a step back.

"I'm going to get you out of here," I said, doing my best to smile at her. "As best I can tell, somebody shot one of those crazy people watching our house. They think it was you."

Hannah drew in a breath. "Where are the kids?"

I tried to make my voice sound calmer than I truly felt. "They're with CPS. I've already called Linda Baker. She's working on a brief. She thinks there's a good chance

CPS will release the kids to your sister's custody."

Hannah blinked, trying to clear her vision. A tear fell down her cheek.

"Have you talked to them?" she asked, her voice catching in her throat. "The police just came in on us. It was awful."

"I haven't yet," I said, "but I'm going to try. We need to focus on you. What happened?"

"I don't know," she said, sitting down again. "We were in the living room watching TV, and then we heard a bang in front of the house. We ran to the basement."

"Did you call 911?"

"No," she said, shaking her head. "I didn't even think about it. I just wanted to get the kids somewhere safe."

I drew in a breath. The police would wonder why she hadn't done that, but any parent would understand her reasoning. I probably would have done the same thing.

"Have you told the police anything?"

She swallowed and then shook her head. "Not really. We started talking, and then somebody came in and started talking to Captain Greer. He left for a while and came back with you."

"Did anyone wipe a swab on your hands or clothes?"

She shook her head. "No."

"And you haven't fired a weapon lately, have you?"

"No," she said again.

That stoked my already burning temper. The moment the police showed up, they should have swabbed her hands and clothes for gunshot residue. Not only would it have exonerated her, it would have saved them a lot of hassle down the road. Somebody screwed up.

"We're going to get you out of here. I've already called a very good defense attorney. In the meantime, we don't gain anything by talking to the police. They'll lie to you about evidence, they'll pretend to be friendly, they'll pretend they just want to clear this up so you can go on with your life. It's all a lie. They brought you in because they, for some asinine reason, think you committed a crime."

"I didn't," she said, her voice low. "I didn't do anything."

I reached across the table and put a hand over hers. "I know. We're going to get you out of here, and then we're going to get the kids. Everything will work out."

"I feel like I'm on TV," she said, meeting my gaze and giving me a half-baked smile. "Maybe this could make it into my next book."

"Maybe," I said, trying to smile back. As much as she thought this looked like TV, it wasn't. I knew interrogations, and they weren't pleasant. I had sat in an interrogation booth for four hours straight, whittling away at a suspect, trying to convince him to tell me something. When I got up, a colleague came in and continued to do the same thing for another few hours. We could go for eight, ten, twelve hours straight and pepper a subject with so many questions, so many scenarios, he wouldn't even be able to keep his own thoughts straight. By the end of a long interrogation, many suspects would say anything I wanted them to say just to make it stop.

Hannah didn't need to hear my concerns. As long as she remained silent, we'd be fine. Captain Greer returned, as he said, five minutes later. This time, he carried a folding metal chair and a file folder. He set the chair up for me beside Hannah and then sat across from us.

"Now that we're set up here, we'll get this going. I'm Captain Greer, and we're in the Carmel Police station in Carmel, Indiana." He looked at his watch. "It's approximately 1:15 in the afternoon, and I'm talking to Hannah Rashid. Her attorney, her husband, Ashraf Rashid is beside her. As I'm sure Mr. Rashid has told you, you are under arrest right now. You have the right to remain silent. Anything that you do say, we can use against you in court. You have the right to an attorney. If you can't afford one, the court can appoint one for you. Do you understand your rights?"

Hannah nodded. I prompted her to respond verbally for the cameras.

"Yes, I understand," she said.

"Do you still wish to talk to me?"

She looked at me, and I shook my head.

"I didn't do anything," she said, looking to Captain Greer again. "My husband said I shouldn't talk to you, but I wanted you to know that. I didn't shoot that person."

I could think of worse things to say, but even that statement opened the door to a conversation she didn't need to have.

"My client has said what she needed to say. Beyond that, we're not answering questions, and we're not going to give any more statements."

Greer looked at me. "Are you in the least bit interested in why we arrested your wife?"

"Not because of evidence, I can tell you that," I said. "You didn't even swab her hands for GSR. That's just sloppy work."

"The gunshot residue isn't going anywhere," he said, licking his thumb and then opening his folder. "Since you're talking, maybe you'd care to comment."

He pulled out a series of grainy, black and white photos that looked as if they had come from the traffic camera near our neighborhood's entrance. The first picture showed a minivan barreling through the intersection and causing an accident. The driver looked as if she wore a hijab, but it was hard to see in the low-resolution photo.

"This was taken about three minutes after residents of your neighborhood first heard gunshots. Mrs. Rashid has a minivan registered in her name, and she wears a head scarf just as the driver did."

"Do you have a question?" I asked.

"Not just yet," said Greer, taking the picture and putting it in his folder again. Hannah shifted on the seat but didn't say anything. "We talked to your neighbors. Seems a group of people have been giving you trouble lately."

I looked at Hannah and then to Greer. "My client has nothing to say."

"One of the neighbors said she heard Mrs. Rashid get into a shouting match with a member of this group." Greer looked to me. "We also heard you had an encounter with a gentleman named Greg Becker. He said you threatened him."

I didn't need to look at Hannah. "Again, my client has nothing to say. I hope you didn't arrest my wife on evidence this flimsy."

"Three people said they saw Mrs. Rashid driving away. They recognized her head scarf and her minivan. One person saw the murder. He said Mrs. Rashid pulled to a stop beside the victim's SUV, talked to the victim, extended her arm, and fired two shots. He already picked her picture from a lineup."

Greer could lie about evidence during an interrogation and make his case seem stronger than it actually was, but this didn't feel like a lie. Someone really had said that.

"My client has no comment."

"I didn't do this," said Hannah. "I was with my kids."

"Do you own any firearms?" asked Greer.

Hannah started to open her mouth, but I put a hand over hers, stopping her. "If you believe Mrs. Rashid shot someone, swab her hands for GSR."

Greer looked to me. "You carry a firearm, don't you, Lieutenant?"

I shut my eyes. "Yes, of course."

"And you practice with that weapon on a regular basis?"

"Again, yes," I said. "Now if you have a question for my client, I'd be happy to tell you she has no comment."

Greer tilted his head to the side and sighed. "GSR stays around almost indefinitely, and it easily transfers from one person to another with physical contact. Did you have any physical contact with your wife upon seeing her today?"

I sat up straighter. "That is absolutely none of your business."

"I believe it is my business. If you hugged your wife today, what do you think the chances of her testing positive for GSR are?"

Given the environment in which I worked, a virtual certainty.

"You still need to swab her hands for a particulate count. Once you do that, you'll find she doesn't have near the concentration to have shot a firearm recently."

"But the initial swab will come back positive," said Greer. "That's why we haven't done it yet. When we book her, we'll take her clothing into evidence. We didn't do it earlier because we wanted to do it in a clean environment to avoid cross-contamination."

I put my hand to my forehead. Hannah may not have understood the implications of what Greer had said, but I did. My hands started trembling again.

"My wife didn't do this. She had absolutely no reason to shoot that woman."

"She had all the reason in the world," said Greer, reaching into his folder again. He pulled out a form and began reading. "'I believe the men and women parked outside my house represent a tangible and immediate threat to my family's safety. As such, I request the courts immediately institute a restraining order against them, barring them from coming within five hundred feet of my home.' Those are your wife's own words when requesting a restraining order a week ago, counselor. She believed the woman in front of her house presented a real danger."

And that would become their case. They would say Hannah felt threatened, so she shot the woman. She then drove off, probably to dispose of the murder weapon. Several people saw her fleeing the crime scene, and then traffic cameras caught her car. Not only that, she would have gunshot residue on her hands. Motive, means, and opportunity, all in one neat package.

Only, she didn't do it.

"This interrogation is over," I said, running my hand through my hair.

"Are you sure?" asked Greer, looking at Hannah. "Because this is your opportunity to set the record straight. If you tell me why you killed this woman, I'll do everything I can to protect you. I've got a wife and children of my own. I understand. I'd do everything I could to protect them, too."

"I didn't kill anyone," said Hannah, shaking her head in disbelief. She wasn't crying, but I knew her well enough to know she had tears just beneath the surface. She looked at me. "What's going on?"

I looked at Greer. "Can I get another few minutes with my wife?"

He exhaled through his nose. "Sure, but we need to get her processed. I'll be back in about five minutes."

I waited for him to leave the room before taking Hannah's hands in my own. Tears, first one and then a torrent, began falling down her cheeks. I felt almost numb.

"What's going on?" she asked.

"They're going to take you back and fingerprint you and give you a uniform to wear," I said, my voice low and weak. "Don't talk to anybody. Don't say anything to anyone except your lawyer. You'll be okay."

"I'm not going home, am I?" she asked.

"No," I said. "This is more serious than I thought."

She started crying freely then, and I put my arms around her and held her until two female officers and a female forensic technician came into the room. She clung to me, but I needed to go. The detectives separated us, and I left the room to the sound of my wife sobbing. Greer met me in the hallway and put a hand on my elbow.

"Let's get your weapon and get you on the way."

I didn't know what else to do, so I let the captain lead me to the lobby and then out the door. Sergeant Smith stood in front of the building, smoking a cigarette. When he saw me, he raised his eyebrows and took a long drag.

"Wow, man," he said. "I saw that interrogation. Just wow."

"Good for you," I said, stepping past him toward the street as if I had somewhere else to go.

"I didn't see that coming. I hope your wife likes 'em butch, because I have seen some of the women we arrest. This is not going to be a good time for her."

I stopped moving but didn't turn to look at him. I wanted to ram his head through the door, but I stayed still and took a couple of deep breaths.

"This isn't the time, Sergeant."

"They took your kids, too, didn't they?" he asked. "That's really got to hurt."

I wanted to punch him. I wanted him to hurt as badly as I hurt. If I did anything, though, I'd only end up beside my wife in jail. My family needed someone to fight for them. I felt dizzy. Dozens of things popped into my mind. Threats, promises, curses. They didn't really matter. I leaned close to him, my voice low and wavering.

"I hope what just happens to me never happens to you."

He opened his mouth to say something, but then

quickly closed it and gave me a confused look. I didn't care. I left him there, slack jawed and silent, and walked outside to a parking lot that didn't hold my car in a suburb that no longer felt like home. In the span of ten minutes, my world had gone from comfortable familiarity to something else entirely. I had never felt so lost in my life.

Chapter 21

The sun beat down on the back of my neck. I had dozens of things to do, but I needed a moment to compose myself. So I sat on a bench in front of the City Hall, watching as two boys—probably eight or nine years old each—threw a frisbee to their Golden retriever. The city probably had an ordinance against allowing a dog to run around a public space without a leash, but nobody stopped them. The carefree sight didn't make me feel better, but it put things in prospective.

This was a temporary disaster. Hannah was safe. My kids were safe. I'd get everybody back, and we'd move on with our lives. In the meantime, though, I had a lot of stuff to do.

I started by calling John Meyers and Associates again. Meyers was in court, so the receptionist transferred me to one of the other attorneys in the office. I had a pretty high profile in the community, and the firm had offered me a job once, so most of the attorneys in the office knew me by name and reputation. When I told this guy what had happened, he agreed to drive out to the Carmel Police Department immediately. I didn't know what he could do for Hannah, but it gave me at least a little comfort knowing we had legal representation.

That done, I called Linda Baker, the attorney we hired to help us deal with Child Protective Services. She was already in conversation with a juvenile court judge, but she didn't have news yet except to say that my kids were safe. She said she'd call back when she had something.

That left me with nothing. I didn't know what the hell to do with myself, so I stayed in the sun until my phone rang. It was almost three in the afternoon. I ran my hand across my hair and to my face and answered.

"Ash, it's Emilia. Where are you?"

I looked around me. "I'm in Carmel. I had an emergency at home to take care of."

"Everything okay?" she asked.

"No," I said, "but what do you need?"

She hesitated for a moment. "I don't have anything special, but you got off the phone quickly earlier. We still on to pay a visit to Bill Taylor?"

I had so many names floating through my head that it took me a moment to remember the name. Bill Taylor. He was the partner of the IMPD detective whose number we found on the cell phone we confiscated in Chicago. I couldn't do anything to help my kids or my wife, but if I stayed still, I'd just worry myself into a heart attack. I needed this distraction.

"Yeah, we'll visit him," I said. I took a deep breath. "You mind picking me up? My car's downtown."

"Sure. Where are you?"

I gave her directions and then hung up and started walking while I waited for Emilia. Carmel had a Japanese garden just south of City Hall. It had a pond and benches, and as I walked through it, I felt some of the tension leave me. My shoulders never relaxed, and my gut never stopped twisting, but it let me focus on something other than Hannah or the kids.

After about fifteen minutes in the garden, I walked back to City Hall to wait for my partner. She showed up in an unmarked police cruiser, and when I opened the door, she gestured to a paper cup of coffee in the cup holder.

"I got you something on the way. Sounded like you needed some coffee."

I needed a drink, but I guess I could settle for coffee.

"Thank you. I appreciate that," I said, settling into the passenger seat. "How is...uh..."

My voice trailed off as I lost my train of thought.

"How's the case?" asked Emilia. I nodded and sipped my coffee. "It's coming along. I've got Bill Taylor's address, and I called his commanding officer. He's not at work. Hopefully he'll know why his partner knew a bunch of now deceased pornographers from Chicago."

"I'll cross my fingers."

Emilia pulled away from the curb and started heading toward the interstate. After nearly an hour of driving, we arrived at Detective Taylor's single-story brown brick ranch. A row of gnarled oak trees, likely planted by a farmer a hundred years ago as a windbreak for his corn fields, separated Taylor's house from the nearest road, giving him some privacy. Emilia turned onto his gravel driveway and parked behind a gray Ford Crown Victoria with police lights in the back window.

"Detective Taylor gets a take-home car?" asked Emilia.

"Apparently," I said, nodding and unbuckling my seatbelt. Emilia did likewise and then chambered a round in her firearm.

"You know anything about this guy?"

I shook my head. "Not much. I've met him a couple of times. He never impressed me as being too bright, but he's still IMPD. We'll knock on the door and see how the conversation goes. I don't think he's going to do anything stupid."

"Of course, he's probably not going to talk to us, either," said Emilia, quickly.

"There is that," I said, opening my door. Almost immediately I caught a whiff of acrid smoke on the breeze. Somebody had a campfire, evidently, and it smelled as if they had used some old, molding wood. The gravel crunched under my feet as I walked to the front door.

Before knocking, I unclipped my badge from my belt and then glanced back at Emilia. She had unbuttoned the strap that usually kept her firearm firmly seated in the holster at her belt, allowing her to reach her firearm quickly without seeming aggressive. Smart.

I knocked hard on the front door and rang the bell twice.

"This is Lieutenant Ashraf Rashid with IMPD," I said, holding my badge to the peephole embedded in the door. "If anyone's home, I need you to open up."

I waited for a moment and listened for footsteps inside. Nothing. I pounded on the door with my fist and announced myself again. Like before, I heard nothing.

"What do you want to do?" asked Emilia.

I stepped back and peered through the nearest window. Nothing moved inside, so I looked at Emilia.

"You mind taking a walk around the house and making sure the back door isn't hanging open? Be kind of embarrassing if he's sitting on his back deck reading a book and we didn't look. I'll hang out here and make sure nobody runs out the front."

She nodded and started walking. I waited near the front door for one minute and then a second and finally a third. Taylor didn't have a big house. It shouldn't have taken Emilia that long to walk around it. I counted to sixty, expecting to see her round a corner at any moment. That made me start to get a little nervous.

I followed in her footsteps around back. The smell of burning wood grew stronger as I walked. I couldn't hear Emilia.

"I'm coming around," I shouted. "You found anything?"

"Everything. I found everything."

She didn't sound stressed, but I hurried around the corner of the house to the backyard anyway. Taylor had a nice place, the kind of home and yard very few police officers could afford in the city. His garden had an Asian feel to it with a stone pagoda beside a koi pond. Raised flower beds constructed of redwood timbers held two Japanese red maples, while meandering stone pathways led to the creek that demarcated the edge of the formal garden from the woods behind his house.

I saw all of that, processed it in a moment, and then ignored it. Emilia stood near the patio, beside a fire pit. She stirred embers, still red and hot, with a wrought iron fireplace poker.

"What have you got?" I asked, passing flower beds gone empty for the season.

"The files stolen from Chicago," she said, nodding to the pit. "Taylor burned them."

"How do you know they're our files?" I asked, stopping beside her to look into the fire.

She nodded toward the house. "There are bits and pieces of pictures remaining, and the filing cabinets are just inside the back door. You can see them through the glass."

I turned and looked. A sliding glass door led into the kitchen and dining room. Right there on red oak hardwood sat three institutional green filing cabinets. I recognized them just as Emilia had.

"Son of a bitch," I said.

"Computers are in the garage," said Emilia, turning and then pointing to the side of the house I hadn't come down. "You can see them though the back window. Looks like he took a sledge hammer to them."

I inhaled deeply and slowly, hoping the cold air would calm my temper some. It didn't, but it gave me a moment to think.

"Something spooked him. Our victims must have had something on him."

Emilia put her hands on her hips. "What do we do?"

"We call it in," I said, pulling out my cell phone to call Captain Bowers. While his phone rang, I looked at Emilia. "If anybody asks, you conducted a safety check after we were unable to get in touch with Bill Taylor. You went to the backyard after seeing it had neither gate nor fence. While there, you saw our filing cabinets and computers in plain sight. You then noticed a familiar looking photograph in the fire pit. That should give us a search warrant."

She nodded as Captain Bowers picked up. As soon as I filled him in, he agreed to get things rolling. He also said he'd call the Center Grove police to get them involved. Officially, that left us to secure the scene until additional officers could arrive. In actuality, that meant Emilia and I had to sit and wait while Bowers applied for the warrant and got a team together.

Emilia put the radio on, and we settled into her cruiser. The Center Groves officers arrived in a convoy of three vehicles, the only three vehicles owned by the department, I would later discover, about ten minutes after our call. We didn't have a warrant yet, so we couldn't go into the house. Still, Emilia and I got out and told the other officers what we had going on. The next hour and a half passed as a slow blur.

Captain Bowers arrived with the search warrant, and I picked the home's deadbolt. The Center Groves officers went inside first, their weapons drawn. They cleared each of the rooms, and then we walked in. Taylor had a locked gun safe in one of the bedroom closets and a loaded .38-caliber pistol in a drawer in an end table in the master bedroom. As expected, the filing cabinets in his living room were empty. He hadn't saved a thing. The computers in the garage were toast as well. It looked as if someone had taken a hammer to their cases, cracking them open like a walnut. From there, he took out the hard drives and drilled through each of them multiple times. Even if we had access to the best data recovery specialists in the country, we wouldn't have been able to pull anything from them.

Aside from the computers and the files, it didn't appear that Taylor had anything else from the storage unit. We'd probably find everything else somewhere on the property, not that it had much evidentiary value. Mostly, the search was a bust, but at least we now had someone to arrest and question.

We were about to close the place up when a pickup turned into the driveway. The police had searched my house a couple of times in the last few years, and I had walked in on them twice. Neither time left a good taste in the back of my mind. If this was Bill Taylor coming home, things would get really ugly.

Chapter 22

Captain Bowers and I met the pickup in the driveway. The man in the driver's seat stepped out and slammed his door shut. The sun wouldn't set for another few hours, but already it had begun to slide toward the horizon, elongating shadows on the lawn.

Bill Taylor was probably in his early to mid fifties. A thick, black and gray goatee adorned his chin, but his head was completely bald. His eyes were narrow slits, forced nearly shut by the evening sun. Had a whistle hung around his neck, I might have mistaken him for a high school football coach.

"The hell is going on, Bowers?"

"Calm down, Bill," said Bowers, holding his hands in front of him. "I tried to find you to inform you, but you didn't answer your phone. We have a search warrant for your house."

"Bullshit," he said, looking at me. "Who the hell are you?"

I unclipped my badge from my belt and held it toward him. "Lieutenant Ashraf Rashid. Major Case. I picked the lock, so you don't have any damage to your door or frame. Inside, we did our best to keep the place clean."

"Well, gee golly, thanks," said Taylor. "You picked my lock. You're a true friend."

Normally, I did everything I could to remain polite and calm while on the job, but I had just enjoyed one of the worst days of my adult life. My grip on my temper wasn't at its best.

"Next time, I'll kick your goddamn door down and gut your couch with a utility knife to look for hiding places. Fair enough?"

Taylor opened his eyes wide. "You know who you're

217

talking to, buddy?"

"Yeah, I do. I'm talking to a piece of shit who helped four assholes blackmail dozens if not hundreds of girls into having sex against their will. That sound about right?"

Taylor took a step toward me, and I slipped my hand toward my firearm. I didn't plan to shoot him, but I carried a pretty heavy weapon. Two pounds of steel to the side of Taylor's head would make me feel a whole lot better. Before I could pull my weapon out, Bowers stepped between us and shoved Taylor back.

"Bill, back off. Ash, take your partner's car and drive downtown. She'll ride home with me."

I let my hands fall to my waist. "There's no need. I'm fine. I spoke without thinking."

"We've got this, Lieutenant," said Bowers. "Get out of here."

Part of me wanted to stay and argue, but Bowers was right. In my mood, I didn't need to be around people. I walked toward the house but didn't have to go inside before Emilia stepped outside. She handed me her keys and then took a step back.

"You need anything, give me a call," she said. "Maybe it's none of my business, but we're partners. Right? You need anything at all, I'm a phone call away."

"Thank you," I said, holding up her keys. "I'll see you at the office."

She nodded. As I walked toward her cruiser, I felt half a dozen pairs of eyes on my back. I didn't care. Everybody had bad days. I'd be just fine.

I backed the cruiser out of the driveway and headed north toward the city, losing myself in the monotony of the drive. For an hour, it felt good to let my mind go blank. When I got to the office, I sat down and started filling the copious amounts of paperwork that came with the job. That, too, was a welcome distraction.

At six, Emilia called.

"Hey," I said before she could say anything. "I'm in the office. Sorry I had to borrow your car. I'll turn the keys into the motor pool if you want."

"Sure. I'd appreciate that," she said. "You doing okay?"

"I will be," I said. "I've got some stuff going on at home. It's nothing to worry about."

"Good," she said. "Listen, though, I'm calling because Captain Bowers and I are downtown with Bill Taylor. He's still pretty pissed off."

"He say anything?" I asked.

"He's curious why we burned pictures in his backyard and dumped broken computers in his garage."

I nodded. "So he's denying involvement."

"It's worse than that," said Emilia. "He's been on vacation in the Bahamas for the past week. He came back last night."

I closed my eyes and swore under my breath. "Where are you?"

"In Captain Bowers' office, but you don't-"

"I'm on my way," I said, interrupting her before she could tell me to stay away. I saved the document I was typing, took the elevator to the ground floor, and then jogged a block to the City-County building. Though the news vans had left, there were still probably fifty tents pitched on the grass beside East Washington street. The children of journalists and reporters ran around and played, reminding me to call Paul Murphy to ask how his task force had fared tracking down the psychopath who murdered Tanaka, Holden and now Charles Parker. That was for another day, though; I had work to do.

I went inside the building and took the elevator straight to IMPD's executive level. Wood paneling lined the walls, and gray carpet lined the floors. It felt more subdued than most floors in the building, but that might have been because very few people had offices up there.

I introduced myself to the uniformed lieutenant manning the front desk, and she led me back to the glass-walled conference room. Bill Taylor sat with his back to a row of windows overlooking Market Street. Beside him sat Randy Prather, an attorney who specialized in representing police officers. Our union kept him on permanent retainer. He had represented me in a complaint a couple of month ago and did an admirable job. Knowing him, I highly doubted he'd let Taylor say a damn thing to us. At the head of the table sat two men in gray suits. Both worked for the professional standards division, internal affairs. I didn't know their names, but they had questioned me about a shooting a few months ago and tried to convince me to lie on the record so their reports would look better. That didn't work out well for them.

I had expected to see those kinds of officers, but I didn't expect to see Sylvia Lombardo, the city's Director of Public Safety, storming toward me the moment she saw me. Captain Mike Bowers and Emilia Rios followed a few steps behind but stayed in the doorway.

"What the hell is going on, Lieutenant?" asked Lombardo. Evidently, she considered her question rhetorical because she spoke before I could. "I've got a detective and his lawyer here who says you're investigating a fellow IMPD officer for murder without so much as contacting the Professional Standards division or my office. Do you understand what's going on in the city right now? I've got seventy-four people camped out on the building's front lawn because they are terrified the man who killed their colleague will come after them. I don't have time to deal with this shit right now, too."

I didn't think she had asked a question, so I didn't say anything. The more I stood there in silence, though, the redder Sylvia's face became and the more ragged her breath sounded. After a few moments, I decided I needed to say something if only to prevent her from having a heart attack.

"First, I want to make it very clear that Detective Rios has acted under my orders this entire case."

Sylvia looked at Emilia dismissively and then narrowed her gaze at me once more.

"Sure. The kid's out."

"Good. Second I supervise the Major Case Squad, and I'm working a case. In the course of my investigation, I found reason to question Detective Taylor. At no time prior to going to his house did I consider him a suspect in a murder investigation. Detective Rios and I drove to his house, and while there, we found evidence pertinent to our murder investigation in plain sight. We called in a warrant, and we called the local police. We did everything right. It's not my fault you look incompetent."

I almost thought she'd punch me, but Captain Bowers stepped between us before she could.

"Let's tone this down. Everyone in the conference room can see you two right now."

I looked to the conference room. Neither Sylvia nor Bowers had elected to close the blinds as they left, so the two Professional Standards detectives watched with rapt attention, while Taylor and his lawyer conferenced on the far side of the room. Despite their disinterested appearance, I doubted my conversation with Sylvia had escaped anyone's notice. Sylvia left our group and then pointedly walked into the conference room, closed the black shutters, and then pulled the door shut behind her as she exited once more.

"I need you to think about this," she said, upon returning to us. She took a deep breath and forced a fake, angry smile to her lips, ignoring Emilia and Captain Bowers entirely. "If word got out that we are investigating one of our own for the murder and torture of four young

221

men, the public will go ballistic. They'll come after us—they'll come after me—with goddamn pitchforks. It doesn't matter if Taylor did it or not. I can only put out so many fires at a time, and this is a big goddamn fire."

For her, everything came down to that: the appearance of justice. If I had called her office and updated her the moment I suspected Taylor of something, she would have ordered an investigation, one the results of which would likely never make it to the paper or open court.

If she discovered Taylor and his partner killed our victims, she'd pressure the prosecutor's office to offer them both a deal they couldn't resist to keep quiet and avoid damaging IMPD's—and more importantly, her—reputation.

"I did my job. I followed the evidence and brought in supervisory officers where appropriate. And by the way, that fire with the reporters, there's a good chance Taylor caused that, too. I think he and his old partner killed Kristen Tanaka because she started investigating their prior bad acts."

Her face went flat, and her eyes turned cold and almost black. "I've given you a lot of leeway over the years, but that's over. You've shown yourself incapable of working within procedure on this case. You've forced my hand. As of this moment, you and your partner are suspended. You are to report to Captain Michaels at the Professional Standards division and brief him on your findings. He will assign detectives as appropriate."

"That's bull-" I started to say.

"No," said Bowers, his voice low but seemingly louder than both me and Sylvia. "You don't have the authority to do that, Ms. Lombardo."

She cocked her head at Bowers. "Excuse me?"

"You oversee the Department of Public Safety, which oversees IMPD," he said. "You gave up the right to make command decisions within our department when you resigned your position within IMPD. If you have a complaint about Lieutenant Rashid, you can bring it up with Chief Collins. He will then contact Deputy Chief Reddington, who will contact me. We will deal with our employees internally and in accordance with our guidelines."

Sylvia'a mouth popped open. "You're backing Rashid here?"

"I'm stating facts. I'm not backing anyone. Lieutenant Rashid is a pain in the ass, but he's a valuable member of our department. As such, he deserves our department's protections."

She blinked several times. "Think about what you're doing. Is this really how you want to play it?"

He didn't so much as crack a smile or grimace or change expression in any way. "I'm not playing anything or anyone. I'm doing what my job requires of me."

"This is very disappointing, Mike."

"You don't like the rules, rewrite them. You've done it before, and I'm sure you'll do it again," said Bowers. "Now if you'll excuse us, I have to talk to my subordinate."

She stormed off toward the elevator. Nobody spoke until the elevator doors closed behind her.

"This goes for both of you," said Bowers, still watching the elevator. "Do not antagonize Sylvia Lombardo. She can make your lives miserable with very little effort and for very little reason. Do you actually have anything tying Taylor to our reporters' deaths?"

I softened my voice. "It's a theory I'm working. If we keep looking, I'm sure something will shake loose."

"Until you do, keep it to yourself," said Bowers, looking toward the conference room. "Meantime, interview Bill Taylor and see what you can get out of him. I'll deal with Sylvia Lombardo."

Before I could thank him or acknowledge what he said in anyway, Bowers headed toward the elevators, his head held low. Once he was out of earshot, I looked at Emilia.

"Sorry for getting you in the middle of this. Life sometimes gets a little chaotic around me."

She smiled, her eyes wide. "Are you kidding me? That was awesome. You called your boss's boss's boss incompetent. I've never seen anything like it. I mean, you're probably going to be fired, but you'll go out guns blazing."

"People tell me that a lot," I said, walking to the conference room door. "Let's go talk to some assholes."

I held the door for Emilia, allowing her to walk inside first. Nobody stood to greet us, which didn't surprise me terribly. I looked at each of the four men in turn. All wore suits of varying quality, and all had the tired, bored look of men who wished to be anywhere but in that room.

"Evening, everybody," I said. "For those who don't know me, I'm Lieutenant Ashraf Rashid." I nodded to Emilia. "This is my partner, Detective Emilia Rios. I think you've spoken to her already."

Taylor scoffed and then crossed beefy arms across his chest.

"I didn't realize I had a choice in the matter."

Randy put a hand on his client's forearm to prevent him from speaking further. "We've already answered every question asked of us. We were about to leave."

I looked at the IA detectives. "That right?"

One, the man nearest to the door, nodded. "Detective Taylor has cooperated fully. He's been out of town, Ash. Got home just in time to see his colleagues traipsing all over his house."

"You could have just asked to search the place," said Taylor, throwing up his hands. "What did you even want,

Lieutenant?"

I looked at Emilia and then gestured toward the seats opposite Taylor and his lawyer at the table. She pulled the nearest one out and sat down. I sat beside her and felt the supple black leather beneath my hands and the padding in all the appropriate places. They had lumbar support; my office chair had two broken wheels, a vinyl seat patched with duck tape and padding more beaten in than the heavy bag at a professional boxer's gym. I wondered what the officer manning the front desk would do if I tried to sneak one to the elevator on my way out.

I, very briefly, filled him in on the day's events, including the search of his house and the evidence we found therein.

"Detective Rios and I are here to ask a few questions. This is an information gathering interview, and you're a detective. You know what that means. You can leave any time you want, but if you decide to stay, I can use whatever you tell me in court. You've already got an attorney, and it's your right to keep him with you during questioning. If you've got legal questions, I'm sure he can answer them. Given that, you mind talking to me?"

Taylor opened his mouth to say something, but Randy put his hand on the detective's forearm, stopping him.

"We will answer certain questions, but we've already been here for at least an hour. We'd like to cooperate, but we're reaching the end of our patience."

Meaning, he wanted to hear our questions to gauge what kind of shit his client had stepped into while also giving himself an excuse to leave at any time. I could work with that.

I looked at Taylor. "You have anything to say before we start?"

"You trespassed on my property. Fuck you, fuck your questions, and fuck your pretty little partner."

Emilia didn't even blink. I suspected she received a lot

of that sort of attention in interrogation booths. I pulled my notepad out of my jacket pocket and laid it on the table.

"Now that we've got that out of the way, let's start at the beginning. Do you know Chris Buchanan?"

Taylor looked at his lawyer. Randy nodded.

"Yeah, I know him. We worked cases together."

"He was your partner," said Emilia, nodding. Taylor looked at her and winked.

"In a manner of speaking," he said, leering at her chest and then licking his lips as he looked at her face. "If you had asked, I would have dropped him in a moment, though. How about you come over to this side of the table and sit on my lap, sugar?"

Evidently Taylor no longer felt encumbered by our department's rules against sexual harassment.

"How about Mark and Cesar Cruz, Joseph Gomez, or Jeremy Estrada?" she asked.

Taylor looked at his lawyer, and Randy leaned forward. "To the best of my client's recollection, he does not know them."

I should have expected that answer from a lawyer. Even if we proved Detective Taylor and the victims had regular contact, he could simply say he had forgotten them momentarily. We couldn't use the answer against him in court or in a departmental complaint.

"Since you've never heard of them, I'll fill you in," I said. "Nine years ago, someone beat them, cut off their hands and feet, pulled their teeth, and then castrated them before dumping their bodies in a park. Before they died, my victims had regular contact with your partner. Today, we found their property at your house. I had hoped you would have an explanation for that."

Randy leaned forward. "My client doesn't have to explain anything. As we've already discussed with your colleagues, Detective Taylor has been out of the country on vacation for the past week. We have no theories for how your victims' property came to be in his home."

"Vacation," I said, nodding. "How nice. Were you alone?"

Taylor nodded. "Yeah."

"Did you make friends while on vacation?"

The detective leaned back and fixed me with a hard glare. "Yeah, and then I forgot their names."

"I see," I said, nodding. "Where'd you stay?"

"In a hotel," said Taylor. "I've got a receipt."

As if on cue, Randy leaned to his left and picked up a black, leather briefcase from which he pulled an envelope.

"Four nights at the Treasure Island Resort on Grand Cayman," said Randy, sliding a hand-written paper receipt across the counter. If I could believe it, Taylor paid two-hundred and seventeen dollars a night for a single room with a beach view.

"Your name's not on here," I said, sliding the receipt back to Randy and glancing at Detective Taylor. He held his up in front of him and shrugged.

"Paid in cash. What are you going to do?"

"No problem," I said. "Just show me your plane ticket, and we'll end this discussion forthwith."

"It's a funny thing," said Taylor, a smile spreading across his face. "I drove to Fort Lauderdale and then took a ferry to Grand Cayman. I like having my car with me."

"I can't blame you there," I said, nodding. "I'm guessing you paid cash for the ferry."

"And the gas," said Taylor. "I don't like to use credit cards if I don't have to. Too many identity thieves around. I've got receipts if you want them, though."

"I'm sure you do," I said, nodding and waiting for him to say something. He beamed at me. I looked at him directly in the eye, and then took out my cell phone and snapped a picture of his smiling face. His smile switched to a scowl.

"Just FYI," I said, "I've got you on video robbing the storage unit in Chicago, and I've got a witness who can ID you from this picture. If I were you, I'd reconsider the bullshit story you just shared with us."

Randy took the envelope of receipts off the table and stood. "Is my client under arrest, Lieutenant?"

"Not until I run a lineup by my witness," I said, looking at Taylor. "Once she identifies you, I don't know how much I can help you."

"Since my client isn't under arrest, we'll be leaving."

Randy started toward the door, but Detective Taylor stayed seated. He narrowed his eyes at me and then grinned.

"Not just yet," he said, glancing at the professional standards detectives on the other end of the table. "I'd like to file a harassment complaint against Lieutenant Rashid and the woman he's working with. They broke into my house and dumped their junk inside."

"I think it's best if we leave," said Randy.

"Then go on and leave," said Taylor, glancing at his lawyer and then looking at me. "I've still got business."

Randy hesitated and then sat beside his client. The Professional Standards detectives had looked disinterested and even a little bored for most of the meeting. Now they both sat straighter. The older one spoke first.

"That's your right, but as your colleague, I'd advise you to listen to your attorney."

"Aww, shucks," said Taylor, not taking his eyes from my own. "I appreciate everybody looking out for me, but I've got to do this. Somebody's got to stand up for the little guy, right, Lieutenant?"

Engaging him further wouldn't get me anywhere, so I stood. Emilia did likewise.

"Stand up for whoever or whatever you want," I said. "But I'd suggest you get your affairs in order quickly. You're going to be wearing handcuffs for our next conversation."

"I'm truly terrified," he said.

I shook my head and left the room. Emilia and I may not have our murderer in custody, but I felt much closer than I had so far. Still, something nagged me. If Taylor really had stolen evidence from Chicago—and I think he had—why wouldn't he have hidden it better? And if he had killed my victims nine years ago, why? I didn't have answers for either of those, but I was getting closer. Even still, I didn't feel like I actually knew anything. That was starting to worry me.

Chapter 23

Theoretically, IMPD could hold Detective Taylor for questioning for twenty-four hours, but doing that to a fellow officer without serious and tangible proof that he had committed a crime would piss off everyone in the city with a badge. Not only that, it would probably justify the harassment claim he made against me. I had made enough enemies for one day.

Emilia and I took the elevator to her floor, where she picked up a few things at her desk, before heading to my office in the Alabama Street building. I had overplayed my hand in the conference room. Mrs. Cruz could identify Detective Taylor as one of the men who robbed our storage unit, but whether she would, I couldn't say. Our last conversation hadn't gone very well, so I didn't even know if she'd take my calls now. Hopefully Emilia would have better luck then me.

Once we reached my office, Emilia took over my desk and made a few calls before putting together a ten-picture lineup, including pictures of Detective Taylor and his partner Detective Buchanan. If Mrs. Cruz cooperated, officers from her local police department in Essex Fells, New Jersey would then show her those pictures and ask her if she recognized any of the men who robbed her son's storage unit. Essex Fells officers would even drive to her house to minimize Mrs. Cruz's inconvenience. It should take five minutes of her life total, five minutes in which she very well might send her sons' murderers to prison. I didn't see any reason for her to refuse, but people didn't always act in reasonable ways.

While Emilia worked on that, I stepped out of my office and called the storage unit in Chicago. The woman who first answered the phone sounded chipper, but her voice became a little subdued after I introduced myself and asked to speak to a manager.

"I'll see if I can track her down," she said, right before putting me on hold. I kept the phone to my ear and walked to the break room. Since it was after regular work hours, Emilia and I had the floor to ourselves, which meant I didn't have to worry about keeping my voice down. It also meant I had to make my own coffee. I cleaned the glass carafe, but before I could actually start making coffee, a second woman's voice rung out from my phone.

"Lieutenant Rashid, thank you for your call."

She had a smoker's rasp and none of the cheeriness I heard in the first woman's voice.

"Thank you for talking to me. I don't think we've spoken before, but I was at your business a few days ago as part of a quadruple homicide investigation. One of your clients rented a storage unit-"

"I know the history," she said, interrupting me. Her voice had a sharper edge to it than I had heard a moment earlier. "What do you want?"

"On my last visit, the young man working the front desk showed us surveillance video of a robbery. I'd like a copy of that video if at all possible."

She didn't even pause to think. "The young man who showed you that video violated company policy and no longer works for us. If you'd like a copy of the video, we'll need a search warrant."

My shoulders and back slumped, but I tried to keep the crestfallen feeling out of my voice. "I can certainly get a warrant, but your company is in no trouble whatsoever. As far as we're concerned, you guys just did your job. If you're worried about negative publicity-"

"I'm worried about upholding company policy," she said, interrupting me again. "No warrant, no video. Good night, Lieutenant."

She hung up, and I sighed and leaned against the countertop by the sink. That complicated things more than I wanted. I looked at my phone, trying to think of an alternative, before dialing the number for the Chicago Police department's liaison. He sounded as excited to hear from me as I felt to contact him.

Once I explained what I needed, he requested that I send him a formal request on my department's letterhead. Once I faxed that to him, he would petition the prosecutor's office in Chicago to write a search warrant affidavit on my behalf. The process would take three to four weeks, and I should expect to receive the video once his own department's people finished reviewing it for any crimes committed in their jurisdiction. That should take another several weeks. At the end of his spiel, the asshole had the gall to ask if I really needed the video after all. I told him to expect my fax shortly and then hung up.

After that, I wanted something stronger than coffee, so I put the clean carafe back on the coffee maker and went to my office. Emilia breathed out of her nose heavily and stared at my computer screen, unmoving. Her cheeks looked flushed, and her jaw moved as she ground her teeth.

"I take it your phone call with Mrs. Cruz didn't go well."

She looked at me with cold, angry eyes that softened only a little when they met my own.

"It didn't go at all," she said. "As soon as I introduced myself, she hung up. I thought she had a problem with her phone, so I called her back. My call immediately went to voice mail, so I told her why I was calling and what I needed from her. Ten minutes later, I got a call from a lawyer telling me that he considered any further contact with his client harassment. I couldn't believe it. I'm working a homicide. What kind of a person does that?"

"I don't know," I said, shaking my head and then

glancing at my watch, "but it's late. We've done enough for one day."

She looked like she wanted to say something, but then she nodded and stood up.

"Maybe you're right," she said. She rubbed her eyes. "Tell Hannah hello for me."

I didn't intend to grimace, but I did anyway. Emilia stood straighter.

"That wasn't the reaction I expected," she said. "She okay?"

"She's fine," I said, reaching to turn off my monitor. "Everything's fine."

She waited for me to say something else, but I didn't have anything to say.

"I guess I'll see you later, then, partner," she said.

I nodded. "See you tomorrow."

We left the building at the same time, but we had parked in different lots and went in different directions outside. The evening air felt good. Normally, I loved that time of day because I knew I'd drive home soon and hug my kids, kiss my wife, and cast off the scales of the day. My home life made my work life tolerable. Now, I didn't know what I had to come home to, so I walked to my car and sat in the driver's seat, my legs dangling outside.

I started by calling Linda Baker, my family attorney. She answered quickly and started speaking before I could even say hello.

"Ashraf, here's what's going on. CPS took your children into custody immediately upon seeing the police officers in front of your home. The social worker did not investigate the situation thoroughly beyond discovering that your wife had been arrested for murder. A juvenile court judge I know issued an injunction against CPS barring them from placing your kids in a group home or foster home. Right now, they are with their Uncle Jack and Aunt Yasmine. They'll stay with them until we have a formal hearing at which point we'll hash things out."

Some of the tension left my shoulders. "Are they okay? Have you talked to them?"

"They're confused, but they're as good as they can be," she said. "They're well-adjusted children with loved ones. That's as good as the system gets."

I leaned back against the seat, breathing a little easier. "Can I see them?"

Linda cleared her throat. "Because of the seriousness of the charges against your wife, the presiding judge issued an order barring contact with your kids. I pushed and argued, but he wouldn't budge. The best he would allow is a one-hour supervised visit tomorrow at 3:00 in the afternoon, right after Megan comes home from school."

I felt waves of anger, embarrassment, and confusion wash over me. I wasn't going to kidnap my own children, and I certainly wouldn't hurt them. They were kids. They needed to know they were safe and loved. They needed to hear that from me, not just their aunt and uncle.

I felt powerless. I hated feeling like that. I drew a deep breath and thought through my answer so I wouldn't say something unintentionally rude to a woman who was only trying to help me.

"Thanks for your hard work on this, Linda. I appreciate it."

"You'll get through this. I know it's hard, but everything will work out."

I quickly thanked her again and then hung up so I wouldn't snap at her. She didn't deserve my rebuke. I sat there for a few minutes, working up the energy to call my wife's attorney. I didn't talk to him long, but he had already met with Hannah to tell her what would happen. She had an initial hearing tomorrow morning at which she would plead not guilty. Her legal team would fight for bail, but Hannah and I both had extended family who lived overseas, and we had money. Even though we had lived in the United States our entire lives, that made her look like a flight risk, especially when facing a murder charge. She wouldn't get out until the Hamilton County Prosecutor's office realized they had arrested the wrong person.

I thanked him for his hard work and set up a time to talk to the office's business manager tomorrow so we could set up a payment schedule. Hannah surely wouldn't go to trial. No one in his right mind would think my wife had killed someone. If she did go to trial, though, we were looking at a quarter-million dollar legal bill. Even with her latest book deal, I didn't know how we'd end up paying for that. But I'd worry about that eventuality if it came to pass. For now, every part of my body felt heavy.

I closed my door and drove to a grocery store near my house, where I purchased a case of cold beer and a large bag of ice. Normally, I wasn't a beer drinker, but Budweiser sounded nice on a warm, late summer night.

My faith forbade me from drinking alcohol, and for years, I had listened to those prohibitions. Now, though, for one night, I wanted to forget all that. My kids and wife were gone, and I didn't know when I'd see them again. I felt such an overwhelming dread that it encompassed my entire life. I didn't want to feel that anymore, so I filled my party cooler at home with beer and ice, and dragged it to the back deck, where I sat and watched the night sky fade to black. I didn't feel good out there, but somehow, seeing the expanse of stars above my head and knowing my kids and wife might see the same thing made me feel a bit better than I had before.

I opened a beer, took a sip and leaned back on the chair. About twenty minutes after I sat down, somebody knocked heavily on my fence's side gate. Before I could say anything, it opened, exposing a heavy-set man. The orange glow of a cigarette lit his face and then disappeared as he exhaled.

"Come on in, Paul," I said. "I'm just hanging out. Kind of thought you'd be busy with the serial killer task force."

"Bad guy hasn't taken anybody for a few days, so things have slowed down," he said, walking towards the deck. "I knocked on the front door, but you didn't answer. What are you drinking?"

I looked at the bottle in my hand. "Beer. You want one? I got a case."

"I never turn down a beer," he said, walking to my cooler and then pulling out a bottle. He twisted off the top, grabbed a wooden chair from our patio set, and set it beside mine. "You sure you want to drink that?"

I took a sip and felt the cold liquid travel down my chest. It didn't burn away my feelings like bourbon; this drowned them. That was good enough for me.

"Yep," I said, nodding.

Paul sat down heavily and drank his beer. We sat in silence for a few minutes. "Mike Bowers told me the police in Carmel picked up Hannah. You doing okay?"

I sat straighter and glanced at him. "He tell you anything else?"

Paul shook his head and then looked around the ground. "You got another beer bottle I can ash in?"

I drank the remaining quarter of my beer and passed him the still cold bottle.

"Knock yourself out," I said, reaching to my cooler for another bottle. I hadn't gone drinking in a long time, so even that first beer hit me hard. "They're charging her with murder. Child Protective Services already took my kids. I can't even see them."

Paul brought his hand to his head. "Jesus, Mary, and Joseph. I didn't know. I'm sorry, man."

I swallowed the lump in my throat. "Me, too."

Paul didn't say anything after that, probably because

there wasn't anything left to say. We sat there and drank under the stars for a while. Then, Emilia Rios knocked on my gate and stepped into the yard.

"Hey, boss," she said. "I called your cell, but you didn't answer. Then I knocked on the front door. I thought you might be back here on a nice night."

I sat straighter and waved her to the deck. She grabbed a deck chair and put it beside Paul's.

"I brought some coffee, but I guess you already have something to drink."

"Yeah. I've got beer if you want one," I said, nodding. "Bowers send you, too?"

"Nope," she said. "I came on my own. Where are Hannah and the kids?"

"It's a long story," I said, standing up. Paul could tell her the truth; I didn't want to go through it again. "I should get the phone, just in case somebody calls."

Emilia hesitated and then looked at Paul and then to me. "All right. Get the phone."

I could already hear them whispering as I went inside. Megan's drawings covered the fridge, my son's race cars lays strewn about the floor in the living room, and a purple and yellow silk hijab lay on the counter in the kitchen. Everywhere I looked, I saw my family.

I looked down to the beer in my hand. Maybe I should have just bought a bottle of bourbon. As I sat there in silence, the house's landline rang. I hadn't expected a call, but it could have been the lawyers, so I picked up the handset from the cradle and glanced at the dial.

Unknown caller.

I hit the cancel button, ending the call. Within ten seconds, the phone rang again. Somebody wanted to talk, evidently. I sighed and answered but didn't say anything, preferring to get a feel for my caller first.

"Is this Lieutenant Ash Rashid?"

The voice cracked halfway through and then became much deeper. It sounded like a teenage boy on the verge of adulthood, one who hadn't yet made his way through puberty. I tried to match that voice with a face or name but I couldn't come up with anything.

"Yeah. Who is this?"

"You're a piece of garbage-"

I hung up before he could say anything else and then added his number to our block list. Those kind of calls didn't happen often, but I passed out of a lot of business cards to a lot of people, and sometimes I later arrested those people. Usually, nasty phone calls were a sign that I had done my job well. I carried the phone back to the deck. Emilia stood up. She picked at her fingernails and shook her head.

"I'm so sorry, Ash," she said. "Paul told me. I can't believe it. You're going to get her back. Don't worry. And your kids, too. You're going to get them back."

"Let's just have a seat and talk about something else."

Emilia immediately sat down, but I didn't know if we had anything to say. Sometimes, those silent conversations were the best kind, though. Knowing I had friends who would leave their own comfortable lives to sit with me on the back deck felt comforting.

About five minutes after we sat down, my cell phone rang. As with the landline, the caller blocked the caller ID. When I answered, he didn't even bother waiting for me to introduce myself before screaming obscenities in a computer-modified voice. I hung up and, once again, blocked the number. Two nasty phone calls in one night usually meant one caller with two phones, but these two sounded different.

I put my cell phone on my deck railing and took a drink. Then the landline rang again. This time, a woman screamed that I was a racist before hanging up. I put the phone back on the railing.

"You always that well loved?" asked Paul.

"Started getting nasty phone calls about the time people started watching my house. I don't usually get this many in one night, though. Guess I'm special now that my wife was arrested for shooting a guy up the street."

Almost as soon as the words left my mouth, the landline rang again. I looked at the dial but didn't recognize the number, so I hit the cancel button. Then my cell phone rang. I wasn't in the mood to put up with harassment, so I turned off my cell and unplugged the landline's base in the kitchen. Then I went back outside and grabbed a fresh beer. Before I could even open it, something loud crashed in front of my house. Paul and Emilia bolted upright, but none of us moved until a car peeled out, its tires chirping against the blacktop. Emilia ran toward the side gate. Paul threw his cigarette into his beer bottle and lumbered to his feet.

"Check out your house," he said, already running after Emilia. I tossed my beer onto the cooler and ran inside. I sniffed the air, half expecting to catch a whiff of gasoline or smoke from a molotov cocktail. Instead, I smelled the outdoors. As I ran to the front room, I found glass on the floor and saw the tail lights of a car disappearing around a curve in the road. I flicked on the overhead lights as Emilia and Paul rounded the side of my house. My front bay window was broken. Broken glass covered my floor.

Emilia ran onto my porch and looked through the window.

"You okay?"

"Yeah," I said, bending down and picking up a red brick. A rubber band held a torn, handwritten note to its face.

Go home, camel jockey.

Like most Muslims, my family and I had experienced our share of discrimination. Usually it peaked after a terrorist attack. Never before, though, had people come to my house. It made me feel sick. Paul joined Emilia on the porch and looked in at me.

"Careful. You don't want to cut yourself."

"I'm not going to cut myself," I said, holding up the brick to show them. "It's just a prank."

Paul grunted. "That's more than just a prank."

"No," I said, shaking my head. "If they really wanted to make a point, they would have used a gun."

I tossed the brick down and stood up. If there was one good thing about this situation, at least my kids hadn't seen this. They deserved to hold on to whatever childhood they had left.

"I've got a sheet of plywood in the garage," I said, rubbing my eyes. "I'll tack it up and cover the window. Thank you guys for coming out, but I'm going to go to bed after that."

"You want to call the police?" asked Emilia.

I shook my head. "It was probably kids."

I think we all knew no kids had thrown that brick, but they didn't try to argue with me. The plywood weighed about eighty pounds, so Paul helped me hold it in place while Emilia screwed it to the two-by-sixes that framed my house. It didn't look pretty, but it would keep the bugs out. Afterwards, Paul clapped me on the shoulder. Emilia gave me a hug and whispered that things would be okay. I wish I could say I believed her.

"I've got a pretty decent couch," said Emilia. "You're more than welcome to stay with me."

"And if you don't want to start rumors by staying at your attractive partner's house, you can stay with me," said Paul. "Becky and I have an empty bedroom."

"I appreciate the offers, but I should stay here," I said, taking a step back, "in case they come back with torches."

Emilia gave me another hug and then she and Paul left. I grabbed some work gloves from my garage and started cleaning up. The large shards of glass I wrapped in paper grocery sacks, while the small pieces I sucked up with my Shop-Vac. I went over the carpet with the regular vacuum after that and heard it pick up a few small pieces. I couldn't guarantee that I got everything, but it felt clean and I couldn't see anything glinting from the carpet. That was good enough for now.

After that, I turned the lights low, grabbed a book, and settled on the couch in the front room. A couple of people drove by and honked their horns, which probably didn't endear me to my neighbors, but nobody threw anything else at the house, and nobody tried to firebomb us.

Growing up, I hated reading, mostly because my mother dictated my entire reading list. Though she grew up in Egypt, she had a PhD in literature with an emphasis on ancient Greek playwrights. She thought human beings understood the world best through books, so she made me read the works of Sophocles, Aristophanes, Euripides, and other playwrights more obscure. After that, we read Milton, Dante, Shakespeare, Thorough, Whitman, and Melville. I resented her for it at the time, but looking back, I saw why she made me do it now. Those books shaped western civilization, a culture she never truly understood. She wanted me to fit in, and she wanted me to read those books because she loved me. I never thanked her for that, and I wish I had.

Sometime after eleven, I fell asleep with *Sanctuary* by William Faulkner on my chest. My rest, unfortunately, ended at two in the morning when someone pounded on my front door. I wanted to ignore it, but it was loud and insistent. Plywood covered the front window, but through the frosted glass beside my door, I could see that blue and white police lights lit my neighborhood. That didn't relax me, but at least I wouldn't have to worry about someone shooting me the moment I stepped outside.

Captain Bowers stood on my front porch. He wore a pair of jeans and a navy polo shirt. By his tousled hair and the tired expression on his face, I'd say someone had gotten him out of bed, too. As soon as he saw me, he looked behind him and made a slashing move with his hand across his throat. Someone in his awaiting car killed the police lights. The last time Bowers came to my house like this, someone I cared about had died. I almost felt my knees go a little weak.

"Who's dead?" I asked.

"We'll talk about that. I need you to get dressed, get in your car, and follow us downtown. And turn on your phone. I tried your home number, your cell phone, and I even sent you an email."

He turned to go back to his car, but I reached forward and put a hand on his shoulder to stop him.

"Who's dead, Mike?"

He stopped moving and then looked at me. "If I tell you, you'll hurry up?"

I nodded. "Yeah."

"Bill Taylor. This doesn't look good for you."

Chapter 24

Bowers stayed in the living room while I ran upstairs and changed into some jeans and a polo shirt. It wasn't the most presentable look, but I didn't plan on going on television anytime soon. When I got back downstairs, the captain was on one knee, picking up a shard of glass from near the front door. I should have probably swept over there, too. He looked up at me and then to the plywood covering my front window.

"Something you want to tell me?"

"Somebody threw a brick through the window. I've been getting nasty phone calls all night. That's why my phone was off."

Bowers nodded and then handed me the glass. I wrapped it inside a paper grocery bag in the kitchen and then threw it away. Captain Bowers was on his phone when I returned, but he didn't stay on long.

"I have a uniformed officer on the way. He'll sit in your driveway. Since Taylor just filed a harassment complaint against you, detectives from Professional Standards need to talk to you. Is that going to be a problem?"

"No," I said. "I've been home all night. Emilia and Paul were here."

"Good," said Bowers, taking a breath. "That will help."

"How'd Taylor die?"

"We'll talk once you're cleared," said Bowers, nodding toward the door. "Let's get going."

I grabbed my keys and followed Bowers' patrol vehicle in my VW. I didn't know where we were going, so I stayed close to his tail. It was late, and the streets were almost empty. We took I465 south around the city and then 170 west. Had it been daytime, we would have been better sticking to surface roads, but with the interstates empty, we practically flew across the pavement. Taylor had evidently died outside a jazz bar on Massachusetts Avenue, a funky little road that ran diagonally through the city. Around us, there were sandwich shops, ice cream stores, even a bakery that made treats for dogs. All were empty at this time of night.

I parked behind Captain Bowers about a block away from a line of police cruisers. Beside the bar, there was a pie-shaped parking lot bounded by Massachusetts Avenue on one side and New Jersey Street on the other. Officers had erected a perimeter maybe two-hundred feet square by the building. Despite being such a busy commercial district, very few lights lit the area. I had worked a lot of homicides in areas like that, and usually, they turned out to be continuations of arguments started in the bar or muggings that had gone bad.

Of course, none of those cases had involved a police officer I suspected of involvement with a murder. Even if he hadn't talked to us yet, Taylor was the only real lead we had in this case. Without him, I didn't know how we'd go forward.

I stepped onto the sidewalk and felt the warm night air hit me flush in the face. Though most of the area bars had already closed for the evening, I could hear the faint sounds of the city around me. Car engines, distant conversation, footsteps, laughter, the occasional honking of a horn. This was a good location. Stable, safe. I had no doubt that this part of Massachusetts Avenue had its fair share of property crime, but we didn't find too many bodies around there. And if the city had too many aggravated assaults—muggings and the like—we would have stationed more patrol units around the area. Already, things didn't feel right to me.

Bowers and I walked toward the crime scene's

perimeter and signed in with a uniformed officer. Detective Nancy Wharton had caught the case. I didn't trust or like Taylor, but he didn't deserve whatever happened to him. Nancy would do right by him. She joined Bowers and me near the crime scene tape.

"Lieutenant, Captain," she said, nodding to me and then Bowers respectively. "Didn't expect to see you two here."

"What have you got?" I asked.

She looked over her shoulder and then started walking without saying anything. The coroner hadn't yet arrived, so Taylor lay where he died, face down on the concrete. One arm was pinned beneath his chest, while the other, his right, stretched perpendicular to his body. Someone had turned out the pockets on his pants. Blood pooled beneath him. A crime scene technician squatted near the body, photographing shell casings on the ground. Nancy read from a notepad.

"The shooting, according to the bar's staff, happened shortly after 12:30, right after they had closed. Last call was at 12:00. Bill Taylor ordered a vodka on the rocks. He finished and left by 12:25. His server remembered because he was the last customer in the bar and because he gave her a twenty-dollar tip and then tried to grab her rear end.

"Within moments of Detective Taylor's departure, the staff heard the shots. They hid inside and called 911. Eventually, the bartender peeked out and saw Taylor prone on the sidewalk. Nobody saw the shooting, and nobody saw anyone running from the scene. As best as the staff can remember, Detective Taylor kept to himself while in the bar. He didn't get into any arguments and seemed to have a good time."

She looked up from her notepad and then started pointing to shell casings on the ground.

"So far, we've found six shell casings. They're all .45-

caliber rounds, but we've got four different brands of ammunition."

She didn't say it, but that told us something important. A law-abiding citizen who kept a gun for protection usually chose a particular type and brand of ammunition and stuck to it. In my duty weapon, I used the same 165-grain .40 caliber rounds every single time. It was a high-velocity, high-energy round with superb stopping power. The average homeowner with some money to burn would chose something similar, but the average gangbanger didn't have the kind of access to safe and legal firearms that law abiding citizens did. He used whatever rounds he could find that happened to fit the gun he carried. I had pulled a gun off a kid and found rounds from seven different manufacturers inside. The guy I arrested didn't know the difference; he just knew, or at least hoped, that when he pulled the trigger, something would go boom.

"We go through his pockets, or did someone else?" I asked.

"That was our killer. Took his cell phone, wallet, and keys. All signs point to robbery."

On the surface they did, but a robbery gone bad on the same night I brought him in for questioning felt like a big coincidence. I looked around the parking lot. It had room for probably thirty cars, but only five remained. "Who's cars are these?"

Nancy pointed toward a group of people standing beyond the crime scene tape. "Probably the staff at the bar."

"There are only four staff members and five cars," I said. "We know what Taylor drove?"

Nancy crossed her arms and cocked her head to the side. "What are you thinking?"

"I'm thinking it's weird to shoot a guy, steal his keys, and then leave his car," I said. "They have a busy night in the bar?"

"I haven't asked yet," said Nancy, looking to Captain Bowers. "Why?"

"Bill Taylor was potentially involved in a quadruple homicide Ash is working," said Bowers. "We brought him in for questioning this afternoon."

Nancy's eyes widened. "You're serious?"

"Yeah," I said. "My shooting happened nine years ago. We tied Taylor's old partner to my victims. When Emilia Rios and I went to visit Taylor this afternoon, we found evidence from my case burning in his backyard fire pit."

"You think this is payback?" she asked, furrowing her brow.

"It's a possibility you need to consider," I said. "You also need to know that Taylor filed a formal complaint against me this afternoon alleging harassment. I've been home all night, but Paul Murphy and Emilia Rios were with me for most of it. In addition, there's an asshole doing surveillance of my house who keeps a log of my comings and goings."

"Why is someone watching your house?" she asked.

"Because they're assholes," I said. "Aside from that, it's a long story."

Thankfully, she raised her eyebrows and wrote it down but didn't ask me to elaborate. I stayed at the crime scene for the next few hours, acting as Detective Wharton's second. I started simply by telling her about my own investigation and the various twists and turns in that. Then, I started knocking on doors.

It wasn't a heavily residential area, but there were still a few apartments on top of commercial buildings. Bowers could have assigned another detective, but the night felt nice and I didn't mind being outside for a while. Plus, it kept my mind away from my house and personal life.

The Coroner's office took Taylor's body away at about

four in the morning, and then the crime scene technicians left. After that, Wharton went into the City-County building to see if she could locate Detective Taylor's next-of-kin. That left me alone in the dark. Every muscle in my body felt exhausted, but the thought of going home to an empty house sounded even more depressing than hanging out on a street corner in which someone was just gunned down. I let my feet do the thinking and started walking.

I had worked a lot of cases that took an emotional toll on me but few that left me feeling like I did at that moment. Four young men died nine years ago. As bad as that sounded, the real tragedy was how they lived their lives. They blackmailed and exploited young women to make money. And now, I had a dead police officer who in all likelihood covered up their crimes.

For years, I had let my job eat away at me. I had missed more of my daughter's soccer games than I had seen, I had no idea who her teachers at school were, I didn't even know what she liked to do when she came home from a day at school. Likewise with my son. I loved Kaden, I loved playing with him and sitting beside him, but I barely even knew him beyond what I saw in a two-hour window when I came home from work. And for what? To investigate four moral retards and their idiot police sidekicks? It didn't seem worth it.

This wasn't the first time I've thought that, but it might have been the first time I felt it this deeply. Even my big successes now were always tinged with tragedy. About six months ago, I brought down a cult that kidnapped and brainwashed prostitutes, but a lot of people died to make that happen. They even came after my wife. She had to shoot somebody. Before that, I disrupted a sociopath's attempt to usurp her husband's criminal empire, but that sociopath and her crew still murdered almost eighty people they helped smuggle across the border from Mexico. Emilia Rios almost died on that case. I didn't know how I would have handled that.

When I started this job, I felt good every time I put on my badge. I felt like I was making a difference in the world. Maybe I was just delusional, but I was proud of myself and the work I did. I was proud of my badge. Now it seemed that every time I turned on the news, I saw videos of police officers shooting unarmed civilians, harassing the people they were supposed to serve, and generally making the job a lot harder for those of us who actually gave a shit about helping people.

I was tired of it. I was tired of the dirty looks people gave me when they heard what I did for a living, I was tired of officers like Bill Taylor who used their position to help criminals, and I was tired of playing vicious office politics just so I could get the things I needed to do my job.

Worse than any of that, I didn't care that Bill Taylor was dead. Ten years ago, the victim I investigated wouldn't have mattered. Drug dealer, pimp, mugger, I would have worked tirelessly until I found the man who killed him. I used to like myself back then. I was a little naive, maybe, but I was good. I did my best for people the rest of the world didn't care about.

My job had taken a lot from me over the years. It had made me cynical, even mean at times, but now, I had come to realize it had just taken something else from me, something that mattered. I wasn't that good man anymore. Knowing that hurt.

Chapter 25

I drove home a few hours before sunup. As Captain Bowers had said, a uniformed patrol officer waited for me in the driveway. I thanked him for watching the place while I was gone. He said a couple of people had driven by, but nobody stopped. That was something, at least.

I checked my voicemail and found I had almost four dozen messages. I didn't recognize any of the numbers, so I deleted everything and crashed on the couch in the living room.

My cell phone woke me up the next morning when John Meyers business manager called to ask about a fee schedule. I made an appointment to meet him in person and then tried to go back to sleep. No matter what I did, sleep wouldn't come. The house was too quiet. I should have heard my kids laughing or fighting or playing, and I should have heard my wife typing away at her keyboard in the office. Instead, I heard only the echo of my memories.

Nobody at work expected me, so I showered, dressed, and then got in my car. I had a destination in mind, but I found myself making a detour to my sister-in-law's house first. A judge had ordered me to stay away, but I couldn't. I needed to see my kids, even if just through a window as they passed by on their way to the breakfast room.

I pulled onto Jack and Yasmine's street and then slowed as I passed their house. More than anything in the world, I wanted to park, knock on the door, and pull my kids into a hug that wouldn't end until we were at home again. I didn't, though; instead, I sat outside in my car, watching and hoping. A dark shape, a short figure, passed one of the front windows. I couldn't tell if it was Kaden or Megan, but I knew it was one of them.

And then the figure was gone. I swallowed a lump that threatened to grow in my throat and pulled away from the curb, heading once again to my destination, the Hamilton County Jail in Noblesville. I had only been there a couple of times on prison transfers, but it was a reasonably nice facility for a jail. They housed both men and women and had room for a couple hundred inmates. Hannah would be safe there. She had an arraignment at eight that morning, so she should be back by then.

When I arrived, I took out my Indiana Bar Association card and showed it to the receptionist. She reserved a room for me to meet with my "client." I didn't like lying and saying I was on Hannah's legal team, but that was the only way I could see her without guards or other inmates staring over my shoulder.

Within half an hour of arriving at the jail, Hannah and I were alone in a cold room with metal furniture and no windows. Hannah wore a short-sleeved orange jumpsuit with a tighter, long-sleeve thermal shirt beneath and a simple blue cloth over her head. It didn't cover her as well as her own hijab would have, but it was better than nothing. She looked tired.

As soon as the guard closed the door, she stood and held her arms out for me. I wanted to pull her close and whisper that everything would be all right, but I shook my head.

"You wouldn't hug your lawyer," I said. "The guards see that, they'll know I'm not here to give counsel."

She closed her eyes and took a deep breath and then sat down on a metal stool built into the floor. "I understand. The judge denied bail at my initial hearing. He said I was a flight risk, and the totality of evidence against me demanded that I be held until trial."

"We're going to get you out," I said. "The kids are with Yasmine and Jack."

"How are they?"

I wanted to tell her they were fine, happy even, like they had gone on vacation. I couldn't lie to my wife, though.

"I don't know. The judge who placed them ordered me not to contact them."

She put her hands on her head. "This is a nightmare. I just keep praying and hoping that I'll wake up soon, but I don't."

"Are they treating you okay?"

She waved away my concern. "I'm fine. The guards in my section are all women. They don't have a *halal* meal, but they're giving me the kosher one. Most of the female inmates are here for drug offenses, so they're not all bad." She sighed. "I don't want to talk about this with you. I want to talk about anything else. How are you?"

"I'm fine."

She smiled at me, and I felt something loosen in my gut. Her smiles always had a way of doing that.

"You don't sound fine," she said, reaching across the metal table to touch my hand. She squeezed my fingers and then drew her arms back, glancing at the door. I hadn't gone in there to talk about me, but I told her everything—about my case, about my doubts, about how I felt at the end of the day. She nodded when I finished speaking. "You haven't changed, honey. I know you better than that. That good man I love is still in there. You don't even need to look for him. He'll find you."

"It's as easy as that?" I asked. Hannah nodded.

"Yeah. Just be yourself. Everything else will work out. I'll get out of here, the kids will come home, and we'll be together again. I believe in you, and I believe in the system. It's not perfect, but it's the best we've got. It works because of men like you. If good people stop caring, the whole thing breaks down."

I didn't know if I believed her, but I said I'd think about it. I stayed for another fifteen minutes, making it a half-hour visit. As a guard led my wife back to the women's section of the jail, she looked better than she had when I first got there, but I still felt disgusted she was there at all. This whole situation was wrong. I drove to the lawyer's office after that for a conference with the business department. The initial retainer for pre-trial work was fifty-thousand dollars. Hannah had recently signed a contract licensing her first two books in the UK, so we had the money in our bank account, thankfully. I cut them a check on the spot. If we went to trial, it'd be at least another two hundred and fifty thousand plus the cost of any expert witnesses. All total, they warned me that it might cost us upwards of four-hundred thousand dollars to defend. We didn't have that kind of cash lying around, but we could find it somewhere.

Four hundred thousand dollars to defend a woman accused of a crime she didn't do. If that's what justice cost in America, something had gone very wrong.

While I was in the office, I met Hannah's legal team and heard about her case. As I expected, the police in Carmel had swabbed Hannah's hands and clothes yesterday for gunshot reside and did find some. They were waiting for a particle count to see the concentration.

If the count was two-thousand or more on Hannah's hands, face or clothes, that would have indicated that she had fired a gun recently. Much less than that, she could get through casual contact with me. No matter what the count turned out to be, the lawyers had a private lab on retainer to double check the evidence. That would be the state's Achille's heel. Hannah hadn't fired a gun recently. One way or another, I'd get my wife back, hopefully soon.

After that meeting, I drove to work and went to my office. It looked just as I had left it. With Bill Taylor dead, I needed to find his old partner, Chris Buchanan. Emilia had already done a thorough search for him, but she had played by the rules. I didn't plan to do the same.

Our union kept a number of attorneys on retainer for those occasions when officers got into trouble. At one time or another over the course of his career, Buchanan surely would have retained the services of one.

I called the list up on the union's website and started calling the offices one-by-one. The first couple didn't get me anywhere—either the office staff had never heard of Buchanan, or they didn't have any interest at all in talking to me. The fourth, though, went a little better. The office had three attorneys, all of whom specialized in cases defending police officers and the city from suits, both civil and criminal. Once I introduced myself, the receptionist immediately transferred me to her boss, an attorney named Gary Stoddard. Once he answered, I cleared my throat.

"Afternoon, I'm not sure what your receptionist told you, but I'm Lieutenant Ashraf Rashid with IMPD, and I'm calling about a retired officer who may or may not have been a client of yours. I know it's a little unusual, but I'm having a hard time tracking him down."

"Nice to meet you, Lieutenant. I saw a piece you wrote for the Indianapolis Criminal Bar Association's newsletter a couple of months back. It was good to see. Not too many cops would step into the lion's den like that."

Very few of my colleagues knew it, but I had written an article arguing that alternative punishments to prison for non-violent drug offenders actually enhanced public safety rather than diminished it. I hadn't written it to get on anyone's good side, but I had found criminal defense attorneys much more amenable to my requests and suggestions after publishing it.

"Rehab and job training for drug addicts seems like a much better solution to a rampant drug problem than merely locking drug addicts up together in a place where they can get as many drugs as they want."

"It's a refreshing attitude," said Stoddard. "What retired officer are you looking for?"

"Detective Chris Buchanan," I said. "Like I said, I have no idea if he was a client of yours or not, but I'm getting desperate to find him."

Stoddard clucked his tongue a few times. Then, I heard the rapid-fire clicking of keys at a computer.

"He's not one of my clients, but my firm has represented him in the past. What do you need?"

I don't say anything, but I found myself relaxing and smiling.

"I'm just trying to track him down," I said, trying to keep my elation out of my voice. "A detective in my unit just closed a case of interest to him. About five years ago, patrol found the body of a prostitute near the Fairgrounds. Detective Buchanan had run her as a confidential informant for years. Anyway, last night, we got DNA results back from a guy who raped two young girls in the same area. In addition to matching those girls, his DNA matched a sample found on Detective Buchanan's CI. We made an arrest for her murder this morning. I wanted to let Buchanan know we finally got the guy."

Stoddard blew out a long breath. "That's good news. What do you need from us?"

"An address or phone number would be great. He didn't leave his contact information with HR, and nobody else around here seems to have it."

Stoddard sighed. "I don't know if I feel comfortable giving out a client's personal information without permission—even for something like this."

I allowed disappointment to edge into my voice even as I found myself hoping he'd give in.

"I understand. I just thought this was something he should hear. He's waited for years for it already. Word will probably trickle down to him eventually. Thanks for your time, counselor."

I kept the phone to ear but didn't say anything, hoping he'd take the bait.

"Hold on just a second," he said. He hemmed and hawed. "Look, if I give this to you, you can't give it to anybody, okay? If the guy wants his privacy, he deserves privacy."

"Detective Buchanan's information will not go beyond me. It's not going to make it into any report, email, or briefing."

Stoddard typed again for a moment. "I don't have a phone number for him, but I've got an address in French Lick. Would that work for you?"

My chest felt lighter. "That'd be perfect. I'll send him a letter."

He recited the address, which I wrote down. Afterwards I thanked him and hung up. I felt dirty for lying, but if this panned out, Stoddard's firm might end up with a whole lot more work defending Buchanan in court. That wouldn't make what I did right, but at least Stoddard wouldn't go away empty handed. With the address in front of me, I called Emilia Rios. She answered on the second ring.

"You busy?" I asked.

"At the moment, I'm transcribing some interview notes. What do you need?"

"I've got Chris Buchanan's address. He lives in French Lick."

She paused for a few seconds. "How'd you track him down?"

"Sometimes the master needs to keep a few secrets," I said. "It was a little dirty. You up for paying him a visit in about two hours?"

"Yeah. Paul's around here somewhere, too, and I doubt he'd mind going. Aleda Tovar kicked him off the serial killer task force for agreeing with the FBI's analysis that we don't actually have a serial killer. She thinks you put him up to it to make her look bad."

I stopped myself from rolling my eyes. As much as I respected Lieutenant Tovar for her work in public relations, she had no business leading a complex investigation. I only hoped no one else died for her inability.

"That's typical," I said. "I'll give you and Paul a call in another hour or two. Meantime, I've got to take care of something at home. Finish your paperwork, and I'll see you in a while."

"Sounds good, boss."

She wished me luck with whatever I had to do and then hung up. I pushed back from my desk. I had both looked forward to and dreaded this moment all day. I grabbed my keys, my suit jacket, and my coffee and left. As much as I resented the presence of a chaperone, I had a supervised visit with my kids, and I wouldn't miss that for anything in the world.

Chapter 26

The visit wasn't nearly as bad as I expected. The social worker met me at Yasmine and Jack's house. She looked as if she had just graduated college, but her business card said she had a Master's Degree in Social Work. She was there to make sure I didn't hurt the kids and to to teach me how to be a better parent. How she thought she could do that without knowing me, my children, or even having children of her own, I didn't know. After signing her paper when I showed up, I ignored her.

Since Kaden didn't go to school yet, he was already at the house when I arrived. The moment he saw me, he ran to me and threw his arms around my neck. I couldn't think of a better way to greet him. Megan came about ten minutes later, and for the next hour, the world disappeared. They told me about their days and what they had done. Both of them had questions about Hannah, but I didn't have a lot of answers except to say that things would turn out fine. Kaden probably believed that, but Megan was old enough to know I had no idea what would happen. They seemed okay staying at their aunt and uncle's house, at least. Yasmine and Jack didn't have kids of their own, but they had bought a four-bedroom house in anticipation of having their own children one day. In the meantime, that meant both Megan and Kaden had their own comfortable bedrooms. It wasn't quite like being at home, but it was as close as they were likely to get.

And then, at the one hour mark, the social worker politely interrupted us and said the visit was over. No arguing, no warning, just business. Both kids begged me to stay. I wanted to stay with them more than anything in the world, but I couldn't. Leaving them made me feel as if I had just put my guts through a wood chipper. I hugged them tightly. Megan let go afterwards, but Yasmine had to pry Kaden from around my neck. I had a wonderful sister-in-law, and I had never thought ill of her in my life, but in that moment as she pulled my son from me, I hated her and I hated myself for feeling that. I just wanted a few more minutes with my kids. That didn't seem like too much.

I hated the social worker and CPS most of all. She looked almost smug, as if she were doing me a favor by letting me see them at all. I understood how the system worked, and I understood the necessity of people like her, but CPS had only blunt instruments to solve problems that truly required scalpels. From the outside, my home probably did look dangerous. My wife was sitting in a jail cell, my front window was broken, and a police car sat in my driveway. Maybe my kids should have stayed at their aunt and uncle's for a while. Maybe they were better off there for a while, but that should have been my choice. They were all I had.

I left my heart in that house and walked to my car with my kids standing in the doorway, watching me go. I wanted to go to a bar and drink until I felt better—or at least until I didn't feel like punching out the world—but I had work to do.

I waved to Megan and Kaden one final time and then drove back to work. On the way, I called both Paul and Emilia and asked them to meet me in front of the City-County building. Since the sun didn't set until late this time of year, we had four to five hours of daylight left. I planned to use it well.

French Lick, Chris Buchanan's adopted hometown, was a small resort town about a hundred miles south of the city. I didn't know a lot about the place except that basketball great Larry Bird came from there. That made it all right in my book.

If we left immediately, we could hit Buchanan's house by five, pick him up, and return to Indianapolis by nine or ten. We'd then spend the rest of the night sweating him in an interrogation room. I didn't expect a former detective, a crooked one at that, to talk to us, but I had a plan for him anyway.

When I neared the City-County building, I found Paul and Emilia already standing outside the east entrance on Alabama Street. I pulled to a stop near the curb. Once my team was in my car, I pulled away. Paul sat in the front seat beside me, while Emilia sat in the back.

"Thanks for coming, both of you," I said, glancing in the rear view mirror and then to Paul. "Emilia tell you what's going on?"

"Mostly," he said, nodding. "You think you've got a lead on a dirty cop who helped your victims cover up a nasty blackmail scheme. You think he killed your victims nine years ago, too?"

"Possibly," I said, "but I don't know. Buchanan's got to know something, so we're going to bring him in."

"What about Bill Taylor, Buchanan's old partner?" asked Emilia, glancing from me to Paul. "We think Buchanan killed him?"

I tilted my head to the side. "I doubt it, but I don't think we have any evidence one way or the other. If nothing else, I'm hoping Buchanan could shed some light on it. As long as we lock up a bad guy at the end of the day, I'll sleep fine. Questions?"

"Think we're going to have time to go by the casino in French Lick?" asked Paul. "Because they've got a casino down there, you know. We can just tie Buchanan up, gag him, and leave him in the trunk, can't we? I'm pretty sure that's still allowed if you're going to the casino."

I waited a few seconds to give Paul his moment and then looked to both of them. "Either of you have serious questions?"

Nobody did, so I drove on. No major highway connected Indianapolis with French Lick, so we took a state road south. Soon enough, the trees, fields, and rolling hills of southern Indiana surrounded us. Emilia slept while Paul and I discussed his serial killer task force.

Neither of us was convinced that the city actually had a serial killer, especially after that serial killer mysteriously stopped killing and threatening after three murders. I didn't know what to make of it, but I hoped they got the guy soon. Anybody who could light a house on fire with a family inside had no business being on the streets.

We hit French Lick in a little over two hours. The town looked like many other small, rural communities spread across the midwest. It had a JayC grocery store, a couple of gas stations, a CVS pharmacy and a winery somewhere nearby. Red, white and blue garland hung off the sagging brown porch of an insurance salesman's office.

The houses, by and large, had expansive lawns, gravel driveways and pickup trucks parked out front. Everything about the town—from the people sitting on their front porches, to the sagging rooflines of the buildings—had a tired look to it. It was probably a nice place to visit, and maybe even a nice place in which to grow old, but I doubted the town had much for those between.

It passed in an instant, and we were once again in the country. According to my GPS, Buchanan's cabin was about four miles from town on a winding road through the woods. Normally, I might have let Paul or Emilia off a couple hundred yards from the cabin so they could circle around in case Buchanan tried to run, but he had retired a couple of years ago in his mid-fifties. Now, he was nearing sixty, and while I had met a lot of healthy men at sixty, none were sprightly. If Buchanan ran, he'd have a bad day whether or not we had someone back there.

I pulled off onto the gravel shoulder in front of the house. The woods to the left, right, and rear of the home had a thick, lush canopy but little undergrowth or scrub brush. Virgin forest. If needed, we could sprint through that almost as easily as if we were running through a field. A white ford Focus sedan, very likely the same one that tailed us from Chicago, sat in the open, detached garage. I looked to the backseat and pointed it out to Emilia.

"Looks like we're at the right place."

She nodded. "So what's the plan?"

"We've all arrested violent felons before. Paul and I will knock on the door, ask him to come peaceably and let him know that we'll shoot if he gets twitchy. Emilia, I need you near the side of the house in case he runs out back. Keep your gun out, but hopefully you won't have to use it."

Paul cleared his throat. "We want to bring the locals in on this?"

I shook my head. "Buchanan's retired IMPD. We'll clean up our own mess. Sound good with you guys?"

They both nodded, so we stepped out of the car. The late evening sunlight filtered through the leaves overhead, dappling the ground with light and shadow that swayed in a sweet smelling, late-summer breeze. Birds sang in the trees. A plane rumbled somewhere far over head but then disappeared. It felt peaceful. I pulled my firearm from my shoulder holster, checked the magazine, and then chambered a round. Beside me, Emilia and Paul did the same.

I would have liked to go in with a vest, but Buchanan hadn't shown himself to be a direct threat to us. If we went in visibly prepared for a fight, Buchanan might just give us one. If we went in with our guns holstered and our voices calm, we were much more likely to come home without extra holes in our guts.

All three of us walked down the gravel driveway toward the house. Buchanan's cabin had a big, covered front porch, large picture windows, and a red, metal roof. The builder had constructed it from roughly-hewn logs that had aged to a dark reddish brown. If they were as thick as they looked, they'd easily stop a round from penetrating, giving him genuine cover as well as concealment in a firefight. Hopefully, this wouldn't come to that.

Once we reached the front porch, Emilia split off from our group and walked to the right of the house, giving her a view of both the back yard and the front. She removed her firearm from the holster at her hip and nodded once she reached her position.

Paul and I walked on the porch. The wood creaked beneath my feet, announcing our arrival. I paused and listened, half expecting to hear someone coming. Nothing, though. I knocked on the door hard.

"Chris Buchanan, it's the police. We'd like to talk to you. Please open the door."

I waited another moment and then pounded on the door again.

"This is Lieutenant Ashraf Rashid with IMPD. I need to talk to you about your old partner. If you're in there, please open the door. I'm coming in, either way."

I waited for about thirty seconds before a shaky voice called out.

"Who's your Commanding Officer?"

I glanced at Paul. He shrugged.

"Captain Mike Bowers," I said. "We're working a homicide. Open the door, detective."

"I don't know him. Give me another name I do know."

I gritted my teeth before speaking. "My badge will vouch for me. If you need more, you're on your own. Open the door. You don't want to do that, I'll kick it down, and we'll both have a bad day. Your choice, but you've got ten seconds."

I pulled out my firearm and motioned for Paul to stand away from the door just in case Buchanan decided to answer us with a shotgun.

"One... two... three..."

A deadbolt slid back and the door swung open.

"I've got a rifle beside the door, but I'm unarmed."

"Good," I said. "Now step outside so we don't have to shoot you."

"How do I know you guys are really cops?"

I closed my eyes and started to retort, but Paul spoke before I could.

"How else would we know you got drunk and puked shrimp cocktail on some poor intern from the crime lab during our holiday party in, what was that, 1994?"

"You know about that?" asked Buchanan, genuine surprise in his voice.

"Everybody knows about that," said Paul. "You were one of the biggest assholes in the department for twenty years. That verify us, or is Lieutenant Rashid just going to shoot you? Believe me, he will, too. This is not a man you want to piss off."

A moment later, the door opened wider and a man a couple of years north of sixty stepped out. He had several days worth of growth on his chin and bags beneath his eyes. Wrinkles covered his white, cotton shirt, while several dark stains covered his jeans. Even from several feet away, he reeked of body odor. He looked different than he had on the surveillance video from the storage place in Chicago, but we had our man. He had a nice house with white walls, lightly colored hardwood floors and pine baseboards. Past all that, though, I saw a familiar shape in the front hallway.

"Chris Buchanan?" I asked. He nodded. "You're a hard man to find."

"Someone tries to kill you enough times, you learn how to stay lost."

"For the moment, you'll have a reprieve. We're not here to kill you," I said. I nodded past him to the old wooden chest in his front entryway. "But just FYI, next time you see a chest full of porn in a storage locker, you probably shouldn't steal it and then keep it in your front hallway. You're under arrest for obstruction of justice, but I have the feeling we'll be adding to those charges soon."

Chapter 27

We didn't have a search warrant for Buchanan's house, but his arrest allowed us to do a couple of things in order to protect ourselves. First, because I suspected Buchanan was capable of violence, I could search those areas under his immediate control. Mostly, that meant I could search anywhere within lunging distance in which he might have stashed a weapon. Because I didn't know if Buchanan had accomplices, I could also perform a protective sweep and go through his entire house looking for spaces in which someone might hide. During that sweep, I could confiscate anything in my plain view that told me he was involved in criminal activity.

Defense attorneys hated the rule, and I could understand why. At the same time, it kept me, my team, and everyone else in the house safe. Things moved fast when we made an arrest. If a stranger walked out of a dark room while a suspect was resisting arrest, accidents could happen. An officer very easily could interpret rapid hand motion as an attempt to pull a weapon. I didn't want to hurt anyone, but I was more than willing to protect myself and my team if a threat arose. That rule allowed us to defuse a lot of potentially nasty situations without bloodshed. In my mind, that made it a winner.

We secured Buchanan's wrists behind him with zip ties, after which Paul led him to my car. Emilia and I took the house room by room after that. Buchanan had three bedrooms, one of which he had converted to an office. We didn't find anyone lurking in a dark corner, but we did find four aging laptop computers and chargers in the kitchen. Neither Emilia nor I were computer experts, so we probably wouldn't have been able to confiscate those laptops but for one thing: each of them had a plaque glued onto the cover that said they were the property of TNT Enterprises. This was really not Chris Buchanan's day.

In addition to the laptops, we found four firearms, several hundred rounds of ammunition, and what seemed like hundreds of cans of soup in the basement. Buchanan had prepared for something, but what, we couldn't say.

At about seven in the evening, we grabbed dinner at a Denny's—even taking Buchanan in with us and buying him a breakfast sandwich—before beginning the two hour drive back to Indianapolis. We arrived in the City-County building at a little after nine, and put Buchanan in an interrogation booth, where he promptly told us to eat shit.

Emilia took him down to booking. The prosecutor's office would arraign him on felony obstruction of justice charges in the morning, but they'd be sure to let the judge know that we planned to add significantly more serious charges later on and that Buchanan had a proclivity for hiding. Hopefully, the judge would either deny him bail or make it so high he couldn't afford to pay it.

In the meantime, Paul and I took over the homicide unit's conference room and went to work on the laptops. Neither of us knew much about computers, but the boys didn't try to hide anything. The two laptops I looked at had the usual things I'd expect from a laptop owned by a guy in his early twenties: papers from college, a massive collection of music, digital pictures, and porno. Lots and lots of porno organized by the name of the female performer in folders.

In addition to the videos, each folder also contained a PDF with private emails, job applications, graduate school applications and other private information stolen and used to blackmail the girls into performing sex acts on film. Jean Whitfield had a folder there and six videos. I didn't watch those, preferring to respect her privacy.

The information on those laptops turned my stomach, but they laid out the case against the boys in detail. After an hour of cataloging files and then copying them over to the department's cloud server, I glanced up at Paul.

"I've got porno and personal information on mine," I said. "You have anything interesting on yours?"

"I have hit pay dirt, my friend," he said. "Give me a little bit. I've got to put this together, but we're going to up the charges on Chris Buchanan earlier than I expected."

"Take your time," I said, standing. "I'm going to get some coffee. You want anything?"

He looked up and shook his head. "Nah. Gives me heartburn this time of night."

I left him there, poured a cup of coffee into a styrofoam cup in the break room, and then took the elevator down to the ground floor so I could go for a walk. Standing in the middle of a major city, I couldn't see the stars, but the sky looked clear and a breeze blew through the buildings around me pleasantly.

Unless Paul had overestimated the worth of what he found on those laptops, we would very shortly make a major arrest and take a bad cop off the streets. I should have felt happy, but after looking at those laptops and thinking about what their former owners did for a living, I felt pissed off.

I walked and sipped my drink before finding a bench beside Market Street. Emilia and I had sat on benches not too dissimilar just a few days ago while interviewing Jean Whitfield in Chicago. When she walked up to us, I saw a strong, confident woman who had everything she wanted at her fingertips, but as she told us what Jeremy, Joseph, Cesar and Mark had done to her, I saw that confidence and strength disappear, and I saw a broken, scared woman appear. I hated to think it, but that was the real

Jean, the one who probably hid herself behind a dozen locks on her apartment door, who buried herself in work rather than facing the world. My victims didn't just violate her for that one day; they hurt her for life. And it never should have happened.

More than anything, that burned me up. That my victims could hurt perfectly innocent people the way they did and get away with it for so long…it made me think they got off light.

I sat on that bench and watched the traffic go by and drank my coffee until it became as cold and bitter as I felt. I tossed the last half into a storm drain and went back to my building, where I found Paul Murphy and Emilia Rios in the conference room, stacks of printed emails in front of them. Both of them nodded to me and then returned to the papers. I pulled out a chair and sat down.

"Okay," I said, pulling out a notepad from the inner pocket of my jacket. "What have we got?"

"A lot," said Paul. "For starters, we've got enough to charge Buchanan with murder."

I cocked my head to the side. Looked like my four victims really did have something worth stealing in their storage unit.

"Let's go from the beginning, then."

"Okay," said Paul, exhaling a long, slow breath. "Here's what we've got. This laptop was owned by Joseph Gomez, and it seems that he was a computer hacker. Somehow—and don't ask me to tell you how—he intercepted the emails sent by everyone at TNT Enterprises. He organized everything by day, recipient, and by sender in a database. The emails themselves he saved by day as PDF files. I printed off a bunch of them. They're on the table."

These guys really were something else. Not only did they assault women, they spied on their partners. Every day, they seemed to give someone in the world a new reason to want them dead. Probably not the best way to live one's life.

"I found something similar on the laptops I examined," I said. "They had porn on them, but they also had personal emails and other documents which they used to blackmail the girls involved."

"Like I said, I don't know how they did it," said Paul, "but they were watching their partners at TNT. Apparently, they were watching other people, too. And let me tell you what: these guys at TNT are bad dudes. Our two main actors there are named Evan Kelly and James Conner. From what I can see, they founded TNT together in 2001 as a single website distributing porn developed by other people. Given time, they started producing their own stuff. They even bought some of their competitors. In a couple of emails, they allude to partners, but these partners are never mentioned by name. Both Kelly and Conner show them a certain amount of deference, though. Whoever they are, they mean business."

I started jotting some notes down.

"Did you ever see anything mentioning a woman named Jessica?"

His eyes took a distant cast for a second, and then he slowly nodded. "Yeah. She shot some videos for them. One of them had a sexual relationship with her."

"Probably not the woman I'm thinking of. She's a lawyer. She's their current general counsel."

"Okay," said Paul, nodding. "That makes sense now. In a couple of emails, they talked about taking her to school once she finished filming a set. I thought it was some kind of euphemism."

It still might be, but I nodded. "Let's fast forward a bit. Tell me why we can charge Buchanan with murder."

Paul turned through his notepad. "That's where this

gets interesting. From what I can piece together, Conner and Kelly kept a number of girls on salary. They brought in new male talent all the time, but they shot the same girls over and over again because that's what the fans wanted. Jeremy Gomez intercepted these girls' emails, too. Most of them were seeing Johns on the side."

I glanced up from my notepad. "You mean they were prostitutes?"

Paul nodded. "That's what I gather."

"Did Evan Kelly or James Conner act as their pimp?"

He shook his head. "Best I can tell, Conner and Kelly knew about the hooking, but they didn't care as long as it didn't interfere with the pornography production schedule. I don't have any information about who handled their booking."

At least that was one crime I couldn't pin on them. I wrote it down and then nodded. "Go on."

"In addition to selling themselves, some of the girls sold drugs. James Conner provided heroin, cocaine and marijuana. By his emails, he didn't want his girls on meth because that made them ugly. Best I can tell, Evan Kelly didn't know about that arrangement. What happens next is fuzzy. A couple of the girls they had on salary started getting reckless. One of them contracted gonorrhea, which put her out of commission for a while. Another girl was arrested for soliciting and possession. Kelly and Conner decided to reign them in. In March of 2006, Kelly and Conner started emailing Detective Buchanan. I don't know how that came about.

"After some back and forth, Buchanan emailed on April third to say he and Taylor had taken care of Nikki Lust, real name Crystal Hicks."

Paul looked at Emilia.

"Once I got up here and Paul told me what he had found, I looked up Crystal Hicks," she said. "Patrol officers found her body in an apartment on the east side of Indianapolis on April seventh, 2006. She had been dead for somewhere between three and four days and still had the tourniquet on her arm and a syringe in her vein. I haven't been able to get in touch with the primary detective on the case, but the coroner called her death an accidental overdose. She had track marks between her toes and inside her lip, so she looked like a habitual user. I don't think the case got anywhere, but it's not hard to put two and two together. They killed her and dumped her."

She was probably right, but we still had some work to do to prove that. I sat back a moment to think about how I wanted to approach this. My victims nine years ago spied on their business partners and discovered those business partners ordered a murder. That murder was carried out by Chris Buchanan and Bill Taylor. Now, Taylor was dead, and his old partner had been hiding out in a cabin in the woods. That gave us more than enough to arrest Buchanan, but it didn't tell me shit about my original case.

"Okay," I said, looking to Emilia. "I know you just walked him through booking, but see if you can get Buchanan in an interrogation room before the sheriff's department transfers him to the jail. Let him know we plan to up the charges to murder with aggravating circumstances. Paul," I said, panning my gaze to him, "keep working these emails. See if we can tie Buchanan to anything else or if we have anything else we can use against him. I'm going to see if I can get in touch with somebody from the Prosecutor's Office. We're going to need some guidance on this."

"Murder with aggravating circumstances," said Paul. "You're really going all the way with this."

"Oh, yeah. He put a needle in a woman's arm and killed her. We're going to return the favor."

Chapter 28

Even after Emilia told Buchanan that we planned to up the charges against him, actually getting him into an interrogation booth took more work than any of us expected. As soon as we had him in the booth, he asked for a soda, a sandwich, and a cigarette. They didn't seem like such outlandish requests, so Emilia went to a sandwich shop for a ham sandwich and a drink, and Paul gave him a cigarette. Once he ate his sandwich, smoked his cigarette, and drank his soda, he said he had to go to the bathroom. We acquiesced, of course, and let him go to the men's room. After that, he asked for another cigarette. We cut him off at that point, and he demanded to see his lawyer.

That's when things really went to shit. He used my phone to call the emergency line at Stoddard & Maclin. Unfortunately, Gary Stoddard had the pager that night and came into the station within half an hour. I hadn't seen Stoddard in person before, but I had just spoken to him on the phone a few hours earlier. He wore a sleek gray suit with light blue pinstripes, a cream-colored shirt, and light blue tie. He looked younger than I expected, maybe thirty-five. Not a single gray hair graced his head. When he saw me, his entire body went red.

"You're Lieutenant Rashid?" he asked.

"You must be Gary Stoddard," I said. "I'm sorry for deceiving you on the phone earlier. I don't like doing that, but we needed to get Detective Buchanan downtown for his own safety."

"His own safety," said Stoddard, his head bouncing as he nodded. "I did you a favor. That's never going to happen again."

"Kind of figured. Just so you know, I plan to play it

straight from here on out."

He scoffed. "Just direct me to my client so I can speak to him in private. I don't want any cameras on."

I stepped back and pointed to the interrogation booth. "He's all yours. Knock on the door if you need anything."

Stoddard was in the room for about three minutes before he pounded on the door for us to let him out. As soon as Paul opened the door, Stoddard burst through, his face as red as it had been when he first saw me. He pointed at me and then at the ground, practically salivating he was so mad.

"The only thing you've given my client to eat tonight are ham sandwiches and a soda."

Paul and Emilia both glanced at me. I lowered my chin. "Yeah. That sounds right."

"He's Jewish. You forced a devout Jewish man to eat ham. What the hell is wrong with you?"

Emilia stepped forward. "He asked for a ham sandwich. I bought him a ham sandwich and a Dr. Pepper. What do you want?"

Stoddard glared at her. "What about at Denny's in French Lick?"

That was Paul's turn to answer. He sighed. "He ordered two pancakes and Moons Over My Hammy. It's a ham and egg sandwich with hash browns. Ham is in the title."

"He said you refused to give him anything else."

"We let him order whatever he wanted under ten bucks," said Paul, shrugging. "Not my fault if he orders something he can't eat."

I looked past Stoddard and into he interrogation room. Buchanan formed both his hands into pistols, pretended to shoot me, and then blew over the tips of his fingers as if he were blowing smoke. I sighed.

"Your client's an asshole. I'm pretty sure he's just

messing with you."

Stoddard scratched his forehead and then turned around to go back into the room. Paul shut the door again and looked at me.

"Guy's kind of wound up tight, isn't he?"

"He's had a long day," I said. "Let's just give him a few minutes."

Our few minutes stretched into almost half an hour. In that time, Susan Mercer, the Deputy Prosecutor, arrived and asked for a briefing, so Emilia went over the evidence with her in the conference room. At a few minutes to eleven, Stoddard knocked on the door again. This time, he seemed in much better control of himself when he looked at me.

"My client's willing to deal, but not with you. He wants someone from the US Attorney's office as well as the Prosecutor's Office."

"We have Susan Mercer from the prosecutor's office nearby, but I don't know about the US Attorney's Office. And just to let you know, I'm not sure how much we're going to be willing to deal on this. We've got him dead to right on at least one murder."

I might have over exaggerated our evidence for the moment, but we could shore up the case quickly enough.

Stoddard shook his head and muttered something. "Fine. Can Ms. Mercer make me a deal on behalf of the entire office?"

"She's the Deputy Prosecutor, so I certainly hope so."

"Take me to her, then."

Paul shut the interrogation booth's door, and I led Stoddard to the homicide unit's conference room. Emilia hastily stacked up the emails Paul had printed and then gave the lawyers the room. They argued for a while, and then Susan left to make some phone calls. After an hour, an Assistant US Attorney showed up, and then Stoddard argued with him.

Emilia had been awake most of the previous night, so she went down to Pamela's—a storage room in the sub basement in which we had put a few cots for officers who couldn't make it home for a while—to take a nap. Paul and I stayed up and read emails from Joseph Gomez's laptop. I had hoped to find something connecting Buchanan to my four original victims, but I couldn't find anything there.

At a few minutes before midnight, a strained-looking Susan Mercer emerged from the conference room. She waved me toward her.

"He's pleading guilty to Crystal Hick's murder in exchange for a reduced sentence and transactional immunity for anything about which he testifies at court."

Transactional immunity meant we'd never be able to prosecute him for any crimes to which he admitted beyond Crystal Hick's murder. Prosecutor's didn't give it out without very good reason. Evidently, he did know something worthwhile.

"What kind of reduced sentence?" I asked.

"His attorney wanted two years. I wanted forty to life. We settled on twenty. He's sixty-two now, so he'll be eligible for parole when he's seventy-two. He will be entered into the system under an assumed name and kept in protective custody the entire time. He's not going down easy street here. This is real prison time."

The minimum sentence for murder in Indiana was forty-five years in prison. Twenty years didn't seem like much—especially if he received parole after ten years—but even that much time in such a harsh environment could do a lot of damage to a man already in his retirement years. The fact that Susan agreed to enter him into prison under an assumed name caught me by surprise as well.

"Who's he going to snitch on?"

Susan looked toward the conference room. "Some

guy the FBI's been looking at for a couple of years. He's apparently got fingers in all sorts of places. As soon as we get the papers drawn up, Buchanan will answer whatever you ask."

"Let's just hope he knows something worth all the trouble."

Susan tilted her head to the side. "I don't think that's going to be a problem."

We waited another half hour for the paperwork to clear, so I made a fresh pot of coffee. Finally, at a little after one in the morning, Buchanan and I sat across from each other at a steel table. His lawyer sat to his left while Susan Mercer sat to my right. I opened my notebook and put it on the table.

"Okay, Detective," I said, reaching into my inner jacket pocket for a pen. "As your lawyer has explained, we're recording everything you say. I assume you understand the deal you signed this evening?"

"Yep," he said. "I get protective custody, and you get everything I know. I think I'm going to catch up on my reading."

"Just so you're clear, you'll catch up on your reading in prison," I said, opening my notepad to a clean page. "So let's start with the obvious: did you kill Bill Taylor at the bar on Massachusetts Avenue?"

Buchanan scoffed and then shook his head. "You really don't know anything, do you?"

"I knew enough to find and arrest you," I said, glancing at Stoddard. He glared at me. "Sorry again about that." I turned to Buchanan. "We gave you a deal for information. I expect you to answer my questions. Did you kill your former partner?"

"No."

I blinked. "Do you know who did?"

"Probably the Wolf."

I raised my eyebrows. "And who is that?"

"The power behind the porn. He owns TNT Enterprises."

Stoddard leaned forward. "We're straying a little out of your area, Lieutenant. The Wolf is for the FBI."

I didn't bother looking up from my notepad. "With all due respect, counselor, I get to determine the parameters of my own investigation. If you don't like that, maybe you should choose a new profession."

"Ash..." said Susan, a warning growl implicit in her voice. I looked up and found Stoddard staring at me with black, angry eyes. As much as I respected Susan, she didn't know how to interrogate someone with an attorney present. Buchanan had a deal in front of him, and nothing he said at this point would hurt him. His lawyer only got in the way, so I ignored Stoddard and looked to his client.

"Let's back up a little bit. What's your relationship with TNT? How did it start, what did you do for them, and how did it end?"

"How'd it start?" asked Buchanan, raising his eyebrows. I nodded, and he shrugged. "Ten years ago, some little shit called me up and said he heard my partner and I liked to help people. He wanted to know if he could hire us."

"Was this little shit Evan Kelly or James Conner?"

"It was Cesar Cruz," said Buchanan. There was my connection. Buchanan knew my victims. "He and his friends ran a porno site for TNT. I didn't know James or Evan at that time."

I wrote it down and then glanced at him. "So Cesar wanted to hire you. What kind of help did he want?"

Buchanan leaned back and crossed his arms. "He and his friends found out their bosses at TNT were selling heroin to the actresses they cast in their porno. Cesar wanted us to help them blackmail their partners with the information. He thought we could get ten grand a month.

We'd split it fifty-fifty."

I shook my head in disbelief before writing it down. If nothing else, Jeremy, Joseph, Mark and Cesar were consistent: they screwed everyone.

"Did you do it?"

"Nah," said Buchanan, shaking his head. "Bill Taylor and I drove up to Chicago and talked to Evan Kelly at TNT. He made us a better offer. We help them manage Cesar and his friends, and in exchange, we get a cut of their website profits. That was a whole lot easier. From time to time, we did special favors, too."

I wrote it down. "So you turned the tables on Cesar and his friends. We'll get back to them in a moment. What kind of favors did you do for TNT?"

"Crystal Hicks for starters," said Buchanan. "She was out of control. James called us and said they needed her and the other girls reigned in. Bill Taylor and I made an example out of Crystal. The other girls fell in line, from what we heard. We did a couple of other girls, too, but I don't remember their names."

Susan drew in a breath. A couple other girls. I understood Susan Mercer's rationale in cooperating with his attorney, but I couldn't help but feel he got the better end of the bargain.

"We'll talk about the other murders you committed later," I said. "Maybe some time in jail will jog your memory and help you remember the other innocent women you murdered."

He smiled and shook his head. "If you think these bitches were innocent, you've never seen what they did for a living."

I wanted to reach across the table and smack some sense into him, but Susan put a hand on my forearm and squeezed hard, stopping me. I could take the hint; we needed this guy and the information he possessed. No one would win if I alienated him now.

"Okay, let's focus on something else. Jeremy Estrada, Joseph Gomez, Mark and Cesar Cruz. You remember them?"

"Hard to forget those idiots."

I nodded. "Good. Did you kill them?"

"Nah," said Buchanan. "They were shit heads, so we would have if someone had asked. You wouldn't have found the bodies, though."

I couldn't fault him for a lack of candor, at least.

"Do you know who did kill them?"

Buchanan shook his head. "Nope, but probably the Wolf. "

"And that's the guy who secretly owns TNT?"

"Yes, the very dangerous man who secretly owns TNT."

I wrote the nickname down and underlined it. Now we were getting somewhere, and the pieces had started to fit together. Nine years ago, my victims called Bill Taylor and Chris Buchanan because they needed help blackmailing their partners in their porno business. Unknown to them, the men at TNT were connected to a very powerful gangster. Bill Taylor and Chris Buchanan turned on my original victims for more money. Then, the gangster who ran the entire organization decided to have them killed anyway. We didn't have a great case, but we had enough to build on.

"So you think the Wolf killed Cesar, Mark, Joseph and Jeremy," I said. Buchanan nodded. "Have you ever heard The Wolf order anybody's execution?"

"No. I've never actually met him."

I looked up and glanced at him and then Susan Mercer. Her facial expression didn't change, but I had known her for a long time. I saw the panic in her eyes.

"You gave us the impression that you knew him," she said. "That's why we offered you a deal."

Buchanan started to say something, but Stoddard

cleared his throat, stopping him. All eyes turned to the lawyer.

"My client told you he had information pertinent to a major investigation into a very dangerous crime figure. The information he possesses will be instrumental in a successful prosecution. That's why you offered him a deal."

Susan muttered something and then glanced up to the video camera hanging in the corner behind Stoddard. Her expression did not look amused. I wondered what the US Attorney in the observation looked like right about now.

"Just to reiterate," I said, "you murdered Crystal Hicks and several other girls, but you have no direct knowledge about the murders of Jeremy Gomez, Joseph Estrada or Mark and Cesar Cruz."

"Not direct knowledge," said Buchanan. "I didn't hear anybody order their murder, but these little shits ripped off a guy you don't want to rip off. I wouldn't be surprised if he killed them personally."

"But you'll testify that Evan Kelly and James Conner, both of whom are employees at TNT Enterprises," said Susan, "paid you to murder Crystal Hicks?"

"I will," said Buchanan. "Ten-thousand cash, and both me and Bill got to screw a model. Not a bad job."

With Buchanan's testimony, Evan Kelly and James Conner would never see the sun rise as free persons again. Jurisdictional issues might get a little tough considering they made the order in Chicago, but between the emails and Buchanan's testimony, we had them dead to rights. If I were the US Attorney, I'd probably take them both in custody, put them in a room, and offer them a deal: the first one to flip on his partner and the Wolf would get preferential treatment at sentencing. The other would get life in a Supermax prison.

I looked at my notebook, trying to piece things together.

"So, let's assume The Wolf killed Cesar, Mark, Jeremy and Joseph," I said. "Do you think he would have killed a journalist investigating their case?"

Buchanan shrugged. "Of course he would. Who wouldn't?"

I could think of entire classes of people, but I didn't think Buchanan wanted to hear that. Even having never met the man, I knew a few things about The Wolf now that I hadn't known before. He was ruthless, obviously, but more than that, he had a tactical mind. He planned things. If our assumptions were right, he murdered my original victims and removed their identifying marks before dumping their bodies in a park. It sent a message: anyone who stole from him would regret it.

After Kristen Tanaka started investigating nine years later, The Wolf murdered her and those she had associated with and made their deaths look like the result of a serial murderer. To plug any further leaks, he then tracked down Bill Taylor, followed him to a bar, and then hid so he could gun him down after last call. He then made that murder look like a robbery. The Wolf liked to hide in the shadows until the correct moment to strike arose. I could use that.

The basics of my plan came to mind quickly, but it would take some work to set up. I had even done something similar before. It sort of worked. Even once we got things in place, I had to be right about our killer if I expected to have any chance of success, but somehow, in my gut I knew I was.

"How do you feel about sleeping in a hotel tonight?" I asked, looking at Buchanan. "We'll call it one last hurrah."

Susan Mercer and Stoddard both furrowed their brows at me, but Buchanan simply nodded.

"I'd say it sounds better than sleeping in jail."

"Good," I said. "I'll make some calls."

Chapter 29

Neither Susan Mercer nor the attorney from the US Attorney's office approved of my plan, but Buchanan and his attorney did. That was really all that mattered. If we got lucky, we'd get a murderer off the streets before he could kill anyone else. If we failed, I'd waste some time and a little money, but no one would get hurt. That seemed like an acceptable risk for the reward.

After the lawyers left, I locked Buchanan into the interrogation room and met Paul and Emilia in the homicide unit's conference room to get them up to speed.

"How much of my conversation with Buchanan and the lawyers did you see?" I asked.

"You want to use him as bait to draw out The Wolf," said Emilia. "I'm a little confused about why you think this would work, though."

"Because he's watching the building right now. He's probably with the reporters out front."

Paul furrowed his brow. "Why would you think that?"

"Because it's what I would do," I said. "Think about it. You need to kill a guy, but you know he's in hiding. You don't have the tools to find him on your own. What do you do?"

"By your thinking, you would apparently let the police find him for you," said Emilia. "That's sneaky."

"It is. I think it's also what happened to Bill Taylor. We arrested him, released him, and then he was executed outside a bar within hours. Nobody knew Taylor was there—nobody even knew he was in the country—and, yet, our killer still got him. The Wolf was watching us, and we did exactly what he wanted. If I had to guess, he probably followed Taylor from our station to his lawyer's office to the bar, where he hid so he could execute him without witnesses around."

"And you think he'll go after Buchanan if we release him," said Paul. "You're taking a pretty big risk dangling him out there."

"The risk we can control," I said. "We'll put an ankle monitor on him so he can't run, and we'll stash officers around the hotel in case The Wolf takes the bait. If we set everything up before he arrives, our killer won't suspect a thing. We can use the Violent Crime Unit. We'll put three or four officers in the room and a sniper across the street. The moment Buchanan arrives, the officers already in his room will take him to a secure location in the bathroom and wait. If The Wolf comes during the night, he'll meet four heavily armed police officers in the room and a couple dozen outside. If he pulls a gun, we've got one less bad guy in the world."

Emilia lowered her chin. "Buchanan agreed to this?"

"Yeah," I said. "Say what you will about the guy, he's loyal to his friends. He wants to catch his partner's murderer as badly as we do."

Neither Emilia nor Paul said anything for a few minutes. Eventually, though, Paul shrugged.

"I'd like more lead time to set things up, but it sounds doable."

"We'll need to check out the hotel first," said Emilia, "so we know where to put people. And we're going to have to find a hotel willing to let us do this. I don't know how many are going to be open to having a police sting in their parking lot."

"I've got a place in mind," I said. "It's a dump on the east side of town. I've put witnesses there before. We'll have to kick the hookers out of the parking lot, but it should work just fine. If we do this, I need you two to get down there and direct our team. You'll tell them where to set up and what to expect. I'll work logistics here."

Emilia looked at Paul. Both of them nodded before

she looked to me.

"We're on it, boss," she said. "We'll make you proud."

"Just bear something in mind: I'm giving you tactical lead on this because you're both very good officers, but the guy you're going after is a professional shooter. He's already killed one police officer at least. Use your judgment and let the Violent Crime Unit do their jobs. They've got a lot more training for these sorts of situations than we do."

Paul winked. "You saying you'd miss us if we took a dirt nap?"

"I'm saying I don't have many friends, and I'd rather not find new ones. Okay?" I said. "For my sake, stay out of the line of fire."

They both promised to do their best, so I gave them the name of the hotel. Once they left, I got to work. First, I called the hotel I had just sent Paul and Emilia to. The night manager was on probation and usually cooperated with whatever we needed. It wasn't out of the kindness of his heart. At any time, we could have gone in there, found three or four prostitutes working his parking lot, and arrested him for a parole violation. That gave us leverage over him.

The hotel had fifty-two rooms, but only nine had occupants. That left an entire wing to us. That would work just fine. He gave us two adjoining exterior rooms on the first floor. If I remembered the place correctly, there was a Mexican restaurant just across the parking lot. It'd be a good spot for an officer with a rifle. With the accommodations set up, I called the Lieutenant in charge of the Violent Crime Unit and filled him in on the situation. Where it would take our SWAT team a good hour or two to assemble, VCU could be out there with vests and tactical rifles in twenty minutes. I couldn't argue with that.

That just left me to deal with Buchanan. I met him in

the interrogation booth. He smirked at me.

"Tell me, Lieutenant," he said, leaning forward. "Do the lawyers give you your balls back when they leave, or do they keep them?"

"Cute. Have you been sitting on that one for a while?"

Buchanan shrugged. "Didn't give me much else to do in here but think."

"Get used to it. Pretty sure the prison you're going to won't have a intramural softball league."

"We'll see about that," he said, winking. "You get this shindig set up?"

"I did," I said, reaching into my pocket for my keys. I flipped through them until I found the small key for handcuffs. "Before I unlock you, I wanted to tell you how we're going to do this. You're going to get into a cab and take it directly to the hotel. I'll follow you in my car. When you arrive, you will go directly into your room, and you will listen to the officers stationed inside. You'll be wearing an ankle monitor. If you disable that ankle monitor or try to run, I will hunt you down. If I can't find you, The Wolf probably will. Either way, you'll have a bad day. Your best shot for staying alive long enough to reach parole in ten years is to cooperate with me. Understood?"

"I'm not an idiot. I made the deal for a reason."

"Not an answer to my question, but good enough," I said, reaching forward to unlock his wrist. He rubbed his skin were the metal had chafed.

"Can I get something to eat before we go?"

I shook my head and then reached into my pocket for my phone. "No. You're going to sit here and shut up."

He gave me the finger, but I ignored him and called a local cab company. Their dispatcher said they'd have somebody outside our front door within ten minutes, so I gestured for Buchanan to stand.

"Come on. We're going to take a walk outside. If this is going to work, we need to be seen."

He stood up and then looked around the room. "You going to give me cab money?"

"We'll take care of you," I said, putting a hand on his elbow to escort him out of the room. We took the elevator to the basement, where I stopped by the equipment room for an ankle monitor and a forward-looking infrared video system that would allow me to see body heat even through walls. With it, I should be able to watch everything that was going on in the hotel room even as I sat in the parking lot. I put the ankle monitor on Buchanan's left ankle and then put his jeans over top. We left the building like that.

It was a sleepy night outside, and very few people in the reporter's encampment seemed to move. Only a dozen or so tents remained on the lawn, but there were still a lot of cars parked along the streets nearby. Our murderer—assuming he was watching—could have been just about anywhere.

Buchanan and I walked through the crowd of families toward Washington Street. The air smelled faintly of sewage and diesel exhaust. Somewhere distant, a heavy truck rumbled. No one seemed to watch us, but I hoped I was wrong about that. Right on time, a yellow minivan taxi pulled to a stop in front of us on Washington Street, and the window rolled down.

"I'm looking for Ash Rashid. You him?"

"Yeah," I said, stepping forward. I told the driver where to take Buchanan and then handed him thirty bucks. "No matter what he tells you, don't take him anywhere else. In fact, if you can, lock the doors."

The driver leaned forward and then eyed Buchanan up and down. "He a prisoner or something? Nobody told me I'd be transporting a prisoner."

"He's not a prisoner," I said, lying as smoothly as I

once told the truth. "He's an IMPD detective we've put in witness protection. Unfortunately, he's also an idiot who doesn't know what's good for him. I'm tired of driving him around."

"I'm not in any danger driving him, am I?"

I shook my head and then pointed toward the lot in which I had parked. "No. I'm going to be following a couple hundred yards behind you. You may not see me, but nothing will happen." The driver looked as if he would balk, so I drew in a breath. "Would you do it for fifty bucks extra?"

"Make it a hundred."

I reached for my wallet, fanned through my cash, withdrew everything and held it toward him. "Here's eighty-three dollars. It's what I've got. Enough?"

He looked at Buchanan again and then nodded as he snatched the money. "Fine. That'll do. He sits in the back, though."

"Fine," I said, opening the rear sliding door and gesturing for Buchanan to go inside. Once he sat down and buckled in, I looked at him. "Remember what I said. You run, you're going to have a bad day, Detective Buchanan."

He nodded and then saluted. "Got it, chief."

I slammed the door without saying anything. Within moments, the cab pulled away from the curb. I pretend to watch it leave, but mostly, I watched the surroundings, hoping to see brake lights light up or hear an engine turn over. As before, nothing seemed to move and no one seemed to follow. I walked into the City-County Building as calmly as I could force myself to walk, but once I was sure the civilians outside couldn't see me anymore, I ran toward the exit on Alabama Street. By the time I reached the lot in which I had parked, I knew the cab would be long gone, but I also knew where they were going. I could catch up. I didn't think the cab driver would give us problems, but I didn't trust Buchanan. I wanted eyes on him as soon as I could.

I didn't spin the tires as I pulled out of the parking lot, but I didn't dawdle, either. The hotel was almost seven miles straight east, but the multitude of one-way streets downtown made things a little difficult. I headed south on Alabama Street—the only direction I could travel—before hanging a right onto Washington Street and then another right onto Delaware Street before finally pulling a third right onto New York Street. From there, I had a mostly straight drive through an economically depressed part of town. Occasionally I saw people on porches, but mostly the neighborhood looked dead at this late hour.

Once, I saw a group of probably four or five young boys hanging out on a corner. I wouldn't have thought anything of it, but they had a lookout—a kid who couldn't have been more than twelve—who approached my car as I pulled to a stop at a light. I flashed him my badge, and he immediately backed off, his hands in the hour. His compatriots scattered. Just a crew working a corner. Maybe we could have narcotics do some buy-busts later, but the dealers were gone for the night.

I caught up to the cab about two blocks later and breathed easier. There were three cars between us, so I reached into my jacket for a notepad and pen and wrote down the license plate of the car in front of me. I couldn't get the plate numbers of the other cars, but I jotted down descriptions in case one of them held our murderer. The rest of the drive to the hotel was uneventful. All three cars in front of us disappeared, one just a couple of blocks from the hotel. The others left considerably further away. In this neighborhood, though, with the streets laid out in a tight grid, anyone could have followed us on parallel roads just a block away. Their disappearances didn't mean anything.

The taxi pulled into the motel's parking lot and then stopped beneath the awning adjoining the office. I slowed as Buchanan exited the vehicle, but I didn't stop driving until I reached the parking lot of the Mexican restaurant nearby. The lot was empty, and I couldn't hear any other cars. It was as good a spot as any to watch what went down.

I took out my infrared scope and carried it to the side of the restaurant and scanned the surrounding area. The engines of three cars in the lot glowed orange, indicating that they hadn't sat for very long. Probably Emilia, Paul, and the rest of their team. I scanned the building as well. The camera only let me see heat, but it clearly outlined every human being in the building. Our team had the entire wing of the hotel to themselves save a room on the end. At first, I thought it had one person in it, but then I noticed that person's hips rising and falling rhythmically on the bed and a second pair of legs sticking up in the air. I looked away quickly.

Buchanan left the front office a few minutes later, twirling a key on a ring around his finger as if he had just rented a room. Thankfully, he followed my instructions and walked to a suite we had already rented on his behalf. The moment he opened the door, an officer inside the suite led him to the bathroom in back while three additional officers remained in guarded postures in near the front door.

For almost half an hour, nothing happened.

Then everything went wrong at once.

Chapter 30

I noticed the car the moment it turned into the parking lot. It had rust over the wheel wells and azure blue paint. A brightly lit triangular sign on the roof announced it as a pizza delivery vehicle. A lot of people ordered pizza while staying in hotels, so I didn't think anything of it until he pulled to a stop outside Buchanan's suite. I swore under my breath as a lanky kid stepped out of the car with an insulated delivery box in hand.

"What are you doing, kid?"

He looked at a cell phone and then walked toward the hotel. Buchanan might have asked to order a pizza—it sounded like something he'd do—but the team with him wouldn't have allowed it. Something else was going on here. I panned my infrared camera around the parking lot. The cars were empty, no one stood on the roof, and no one was waiting for us in the parking lot. Then, I looked at the surrounding buildings and felt my heart skip a beat.

Ten years ago, a small strip mall occupied the space next to the hotel. I didn't know what had happened to the buildings, but all that remained now was a broken foundation and a parking lot full of weeds. Along the edge of that parking lot, a dozen cars sat facing the interstate. It was a popular location for people trying to sell a car. I had flashed those cars with my infrared camera upon driving up, but they were all cold and empty then. Now, an orange glow emanated from the hood of one. It was a red Chevy on the end, one whose license plate I had written down not half an hour ago. The driver must have slipped onto the lot while I was watching the hotel.

I zoomed my camera in. A man crouched behind the vehicle's engine block with a rifle in hand.

"Shit."

I sprinted back toward my car for cover and then pulled out my handgun. The pizza delivery guy hadn't knocked on the door yet, but he would at any moment. The instant my team opened the door, the shooter would fire and gun down a cop, someone I knew. I didn't have time warn them. I took a deep breath and hid behind my open car door.

At ten yards, I could unload my pistol's entire magazine into a man's center of mass without problem. At thirty yards, a couple of shots might go wide, but the target would still go down without issue. At two-hundred yards, though, I might as well have flung rocks at him. My handgun wasn't made to shoot that far.

Unfortunately, it was all I had.

The pizza delivery guy knocked on the door. The rifleman prepared himself by laying the rifle on the hood of the car to act as a stabilizer. I didn't have time to think of a better plan. I had to act.

I fired six shots. The sound echoed against the hotel and surrounding buildings. Two of the side windows on my target's car shattered, and he dove to the ground. I risked a glance to the hotel in time to see the pizza man dive down behind a car as well. And then my target popped up to grab his rifle. I fired twice more, driving him back down but not before he reached his weapon. Long term, I didn't have a winning strategy, but at least he hadn't shot a team member.

I glanced at the hotel. The front door hadn't opened, but I could imagine the panic going on inside. Sirens had come to life in the distance. Then, my window exploded and a bullet whizzed so close by my head that it sounded like a bumble bee had just passed. Shards of glass hit me in the face, but I had so much adrenaline in me that I could barely feel them.

I hugged my door and then fired in the direction of

the shooter until my magazine ran dry, hoping that would give me a moment to get to better cover. The moments my shots ended, he fired at me again. This time, the round passed through the door about six inches from me.

I dove inside my car, hoping the engine block would give me some protection. A round slammed into the front of my car, sounding as if I had just hit something on the highway.

I replaced my spent magazine with a full one, considering my options. If I stayed still in that car, I'd eventually get shot. If I tried to run to the hotel and the relative safety there, I'd get shot in the back. If I returned fire, I'd give the shooter an easy target. At this distance, he had every advantage. My only chance was to take that away.

I slid so that my feet touched the pedals and then hit my car's start button. The engine came to life. This was either a really bad idea, or a really great one. I didn't know which yet. I peered over the top of the dashboard. A round hit the front window. The safety glass didn't shatter, but it splintered in a radiating pattern from the point of impact. I couldn't see through it at all, but that didn't matter. I only needed to drive straight. I dropped the car into first gear and floored the accelerator. My car took off. I kept my head as low as I could, peering through the bottom inch of the window to steer.

At the edge of my parking lot, my car rammed the curb hard, and my head bounced against the steering wheel. For a split second, my vision doubled. Before I could recover, my car hit the grass and then I went airborne as I crashed into the second parking lot's curb. My car shuddered and then accelerated hard as its tires bit into asphalt.

I rammed the shooter's Chevy going close to thirty. My airbags didn't deploy, but I flew forward into the steering wheel and then back. I had stars in my eyes, but I didn't have time to do much more than blink them away.

I kicked my door open and crawled out. The man with the rifle looked momentarily stunned by the impact of our two vehicles. His eyes were wide. I had looked into those same eyes once before. This was the guy who lit Charles Holden's house on fire.

"Hands where I can see them," I shouted, holding my weapon aloft and trying to focus on the man in front of me. "You reach for that rifle, I will shoot you."

He didn't reach for the gun. Instead, he vaulted over the hood of his car and took off. All around me, sirens closed in on my position. People shouted from the hotel. None of that mattered. I acted on instinct and sprinted. If I lost sight of him in the decaying houses surrounding the hotel, he could disappear.

He hit the end of the parking lot and spun. I didn't have time to raise my weapon before he pulled out a pistol and fired. Each shot buzzed around me. I dove to minimize his target. The pavement tore through the fabric over my knees and elbows. As I pushed off from the ground, pea gravel bit into the palms of my hands.

My target ran again, this time into the backyard of a two-story home behind the hotel. I followed, but by the time I hit the edge of the parking lot, my target was twenty yards away. The sirens were closing, but my backup couldn't help if they didn't know who to follow.

I hit the grass at a dead run. The soft ground gave good purchase compared to the hardscrabble of the parking lot, and I vaulted forward. The home directly in front of me had a sandbox in the backyard and a pair of children's bicycles leaning against the house. If this guy opened fire again, we could very easily have rounds going through a kid's bedroom.

The shooter looked over his shoulder at me, and then darted to the left, sprinting along property lines before turning into an alleyway. Metal trash cans crashed to the ground as he passed, but then he disappeared around a tall privacy fence along someone's backyard. I couldn't hear footsteps anymore, so I skidded to a stop, knowing he was very likely trying to ambush me. I took a breath and stuck my head around the side of the fence, peering into the alley. Two shots rang out. Both rounds thudded into the siding of a nearby home, and I found myself hoping and praying they hadn't hit one of the inhabitants. The shooter sprinted again, and I gave chase.

We ran up the alley and across a street to another alley. The sirens were just a block or two away by that point. If I could force him north somehow, I could flush him out near a major road. I might be able to get some help there.

As he ran, he risked a glance over his shoulder at me. Then he turned into a yard. The homes here sat on tiny lots with so little room between them my shoulders sometimes brushed against their brick or siding exteriors. By that time, the shooter was maybe twenty feet ahead of me. If I had carried a taser, I could have shot him in the back.

He looked behind at me and raised his weapon to fire. Even the best shooter in the world would have had a tough time hitting a target while running, but I could die from a lucky shot just as easily as I could die from a well placed one. I ducked and hid against the side of the house, expecting him to start firing. He didn't, so I took off running once more. He had gained maybe fifteen or twenty feet by then.

I dug down and grunted and sprinted once more, closing the gap. And then, his momentum stopped immediately, and he fell backwards as if he had run into an invisible wall. I slowed so I wouldn't topple into him. The sound of a chain link fence striking its posts reverberated around us. We stood on a crumbling concrete driveway between two brick homes. Lights around popped on at the noise.

"Throw down your weapon and lay on the ground."

He looked around him, considering his options.

"Throw down your weapon. Now."

He took a deep breath but kept his hands at his side. "Shoot me."

He slowly lifted his arm. He had a gun in hand. In that moment, I had to make a choice, one I had made all too often in my career.

Him or me.

I fired twice, hitting him in the chest with both shots. He fell backwards against the fence but stayed upright. His gun clattered to the ground. I ran toward him and kicked his firearm out of reach and then pulled out my phone to call 911.

I didn't know exactly where we were, but dozens of officers around me had heard the shots. They came running. A couple of them had paramedics training, so they started working on the guy I had shot the moment they arrived. Whether he'd survive, I didn't know. I hoped he would. He had too many questions to answer.

Things sort of blurred after that for a while. I stayed at the scene of the shooting until an ambulance took our shooter away. And then, I answered questions and talked to a few of the neighbors to let them know what was going on. After about half an hour, I walked back to the parking lot in which I had left my car.

Uniformed officers had cordoned the entire area with yellow police tape. My car had a bullet hole in the front window almost directly over the steering wheel and another two bullet holes in the radiator. The bumper hung on the ground, while the front end looked as if an entire professional football team had beaten it with sledgehammers for a few hours.

After a few minutes, I felt a light hand touch me on the small of my back as Emilia Rios walked toward my wrecked vehicle. When she saw it a few days ago, she had walked her hand up the hood and gave it an almost lustful look. Now, her shoulders drooped and she moved with a slow, pained gait.

"I really loved this car," she said, sighing.

"I'm fine by the way," I said, glancing to my right as Paul Murphy walked towards us. I looked at Emilia again. "I appreciate your concern."

Before she could say anything else, Paul whistled and stood beside me. "Is this the fourth car you've totaled in the last six months?"

"Lieutenant Rashid is fine, by the way," said Emilia. "I'm sure he appreciates your concern."

"Of course he's fine. Otherwise, he'd be on the ground bleeding," said Paul. "You are fine, aren't you, Ash?"

"Yeah," I said. "And it's the third car I've totaled."

"I hear they took the shooter down to the hospital," said Emilia. "If you want, I can drive you there."

"No," I said.

"What do you want to do, then?" asked Paul.

I looked at the big man and then to Emilia. They were good people, good friends, but for the moment, I didn't want to see them. I didn't want to see anybody. I had seen enough people for the night.

"I want to go home."

Chapter 31

Despite my wish to go home, I couldn't leave the scene after an officer-involved shooting. A patrol officer brought me some coffee, and I sat down with detectives from our professional standards division for the next hour telling them what I had done, what the man I shot had done, and why I had reacted the way I did. It was a righteous shooting and everyone knew it, but we still had to go through the procedures.

To an outside observer that probably didn't make a lot of sense, but it was one of the most important things we did that night. I had just shot a man—maybe even killed him. I needed to prove to my community that I had acted to save my life and the lives of others, that I didn't shoot because I wanted to or because it was easier than taking him into custody.

I didn't get a free pass because I carried a badge. There were a lot of bad cops in the world, men and women who bullied their way through life and harassed the people they took an oath to protect. I didn't aim to become one of them.

I finally left the crime scene at about four in the morning. Until Professional Standards cleared me, the department put me on administrative leave. I'd have to go in for a psych evaluation, too. Both were standard procedure. With my wife in jail and my kids in the custody of CPS, I probably could have used a few sessions with a psychiatrist. A patrol officer drove me from the crime scene to the City-County building, where I signed an unmarked cruiser out of the motor pool until I had my own car fixed. Then, I drove home, crashed into bed, and slept until about eleven the next morning. I could have stayed home, but I still had paperwork to do and a few loose ends to tie up at work.

Upon reaching my office, I checked my messages. I had a couple dozen voicemails from reporters. I ignored them all. I also had one from Susan Mercer, the deputy prosecutor, asking for a call back. That one, I returned right away.

"Susan, it's Ash Rashid. I got your message."

"Ash, good," she said, clearing her throat. "Mike Bowers briefed me on what happened last night. I'm confident you'll be cleared in the shooting. You don't need to hear it from me, but you did good work. You brought the guy in alive."

"I appreciate that," I said. "I'm sure you didn't call me for just that, though. What can I do for you?"

"Your shooter last night is awake. His name is Aleksander Petrovic. He's from the former Yugoslavia, but he and his wife currently own a rug importing business in Brooklyn. He's quite successful, from what I gather."

I leaned back in my chair. "Why's he killing people in Indianapolis, then?"

"That sounds like the kind of thing you should ask him. If you leave now, you might be able to beat the FBI. If they beat you there, he's going to disappear into witness protection somewhere. Bill Taylor may have been a prick, but he was IMPD, and this guy very likely killed him."

I rubbed sleep out of my eyes, not sure that I wanted to bother. "Even if I get him to admit to something, can we charge him or are the feds going to take over?"

"If we move before they do, we can charge him before they even know we've talked to him," she said. "So get out to Methodist hospital and interrogate him. I'm going to hold off the US Attorney's office as much as I can."

It felt like a waste to me if we were just going to lose

the case, but I nodded anyway. "All right. I'm on it. I don't know where my partners are, so I might be on my own."

"Then record everything."

"Okay. I'll do it," I said. I thanked her for the call, hung up, and then rubbed my eyes. I grabbed a fresh notepad from my desk and a cup of coffee from the break room before going to my car.

Methodist Hospital was about two miles northwest of the City-County building, so the drive didn't take too long. I checked in with the information desk, showed them my badge, and they directed me to Mr. Petrovic's room on the fifth floor. Two uniformed officers stood outside the room. Susan Mercer had told them to expect me, but I showed them my badge anyway and signed their log sheet before going in.

Inside, Petrovic reclined on clean white sheets. Handcuffs secured his wrists to guard rails on either side of the hospital bed, while an IV on a stand beside his bed pumped fluid into his veins. Someone, a nurse probably, had drawn the blinds shut, blocking most of the noon sun. I walked to the foot of his bed and pulled out his chart. I didn't understand much of the medical jargon, but I read through the triage report completed in the ER.

I had shot him twice the night before. One round hit his left clavicle and then ricocheted out his back, passing cleanly through his body without hitting any major organs. The second round hit his left shoulder, shattering it. He'd feel that for the rest of his life. After a two-hour surgery, physicians retrieved the remnants of the bullet and repaired what damage they could. He'd need further surgeries eventually, but he'd live for now.

I returned the clipboard and chart to the receptacle at the end of his bed and then threw open the window, allowing natural light to enter the room and fall on Petrovic's face. He stirred but didn't open his eyes. I cleared my throat and then jostled his foot. His eyes slowly opened.

"Hey," I said. "Good of you to wake up."

He closed his eyes and nodded. "Lieutenant Rashid."

"Oh, good, you know my name," I said, forcing a smile to my lips. "You can probably guess why I'm here then. I assume someone's read you your rights by now. If not, you probably know them."

"You should have killed me last night."

I tilted my head to the side. "That was the plan when I shot you in the chest. Congratulations on your continued existence."

He turned his head to look out the window but didn't say anything.

"You come to the midwest to kill people often?" I asked.

He didn't even bother looking at me that time, which was about what I expected. The kind of men who murdered and ambushed police officers tended to be the silent type.

"Speaking hypothetically," I said, "can you think of any reason why a successful businessman from New York would come to Indianapolis to kill a police officer?"

I waited for about ten seconds, but he acted as if he hadn't heard me.

"Okay. You don't want to talk. I get it. I'll leave you to the FBI, then."

I started walking out of the room, and then he cleared his throat.

"I need a favor."

I stopped near the doorway and then turned. "I don't often grant favors to people who try to kill me."

"I need you to call my wife and tell her that I'm okay. If you promise to do that, I'll answer your questions."

I crossed my arms. "Did you kill Bill Taylor?"

He lifted his head, winced, and then immediately lay back on the pillow. His throat bobbed as he swallowed.

"Will you call my wife?"

"If you answer my question."

He nodded. "Yes. I killed Bill Taylor. I followed him to a bar, hid in the parking lot, and shot him when he came out."

I looked at him directly in the eyes. His gaze didn't waver from my own.

"You could have read that in the paper. I'm going to need details."

He blinked and then looked toward the window. "I used a 1911 with .45-caliber ACP rounds from Magtech, Remington, Federal, and Winchester. I wanted it to look like a street crime."

We hadn't given those details out. I reached into my pocket for my cell phone. I turned on a recording app and asked him to repeat what he just said. He did. Whether he knew it or not, that admission sealed his fate. Not only had he just admitted to murder, he had admitted to ambushing the victim. That made him eligible for the death penalty.

"Why did you kill him? Help me understand."

"Call my wife and tell her I love her and that I tried my best."

As he said the last, a tear fell down his cheek. I had met a lot of men and women capable of gunning down a police officer, but rarely did I see them cry except at a sentencing hearing. I took a breath, considering how I wanted to approach this. He could shut down at any moment, or he could keep talking. It didn't matter to him, either way. I had him dead to rights, but he still had something I wanted: answers. That meant he had the leverage for the moment. I stopped the recording app on my phone and held it toward him.

"You call her."

He slowly reached out and took the phone from my hands. With his wrists secured by handcuffs, he couldn't put the phone to his ear, so I put it on speaker and dialed for him. A woman with an accent slightly thicker than Petrovic's answered. He cleared his throat.

"It's Aleksander. I'm borrowing someone's phone."

"What's wrong with your phone?" she asked. Before Petrovic could answer, she continued in the light, conversational tones of a loving wife chiding her husband. I felt like an intruder listening in. "I swear, you're worse than your daughter, the way you lose your things. Sophia leaves her phone here, she leaves her phone there. And when she's not leaving it somewhere-"

"Vesna, please," said Petrovic, his voice stronger than it had been. "We have to talk."

For the next five minutes, he told his wife that he loved her, but that he wouldn't come home again. He said the sins of his past had caught up to him. His wife grew silent. I could hear tears in her voice when she said that she understood and that she loved him and always would. She told him goodbye, and somehow, I knew it was the last time they would ever speak. I had violated a number of procedural rules allowing Petrovic access to my phone, but he hadn't used that phone to order a hit or plan an escape from prison. I almost felt sorry for the man.

Then, I closed my eyes and saw him holding a lighter in Charles Holden's house. My sympathy evaporated, and I pushed the record button on my app to start a conversation.

"For the record, this is Lieutenant Ashraf Rashid of the Indianapolis Metropolitan Police Department. I'm in Methodist Hospital speaking to Aleksander Petrovic. Do you agree to speak to me of your own free will, Mr. Petrovic?"

"Yes."

"Good," I said, drawing in a breath. "Why'd you kill Bill Taylor?"

"Because I wanted to," he said, his voice calm and

measured.

"Did you kill Kristen Tanaka?"

He nodded. "Yes."

"Why?"

He sighed. "This is going to take a while if you keep asking questions like this. Just ask me who I killed in Indianapolis, and I'll answer."

I nodded and shrugged. "All right, then. Go right ahead. Who have you killed in Indianapolis?"

"Jeremy Estrada, Joseph Gomez, Mark Cruz, Cesar Cruz, Kristen Tanaka, Charles Holden, David Parker, and Bill Taylor. I would have killed Chris Buchanan as well, but that didn't work out. I also killed another woman, but I don't know her name. Shooting at you last night was nothing personal. I hope you understand."

I closed my eyes. "Let's back up for a minute. You killed and dumped Mark, Cesar, Joseph and Jeremy in the Franklin Young Park nine years ago?"

"Yes," he said. His voice didn't even warble. "I ruptured two of their eardrums with pencils, beat them with baseball bats, cut off their genitals with a reciprocating saw, pulled their teeth, and then cut off their hands and feet. I thought about cutting off their heads, but I didn't know if my reciprocating saw could do it. I had a hand saw, but that seemed like too much work. Instead, I beat their faces so you couldn't recognize them. The appendages I removed, I threw in the dumpsters behind fast food restaurants across town. Most of them smelled so bad a rotting foot or two would be barely noticeable."

Some of that information we had released, but the details—particularly the ruptured eardrums—we hadn't. To hear him say it so bluntly felt unnerving.

"Why?"

"You don't need to know why," he said, shaking his head. "I admit doing it. I chose that park because I knew you would assume they were involved in the drug trade and focus your investigation there."

I took a deep breath. "And you killed Kristen Tanaka because she identified them."

He nodded. "Yes."

"How did you know she ID'd them?"

He blinked but his expression remained cold and impassive. "She posted it on Facebook. She said she and Charles Holden were working on a book."

"No," I said, shaking my head. "I don't think so. She was a journalist in a very competitive field. She wouldn't have preempted her own story by putting it anywhere for others to see. She would have wanted a splash. You'll forgive me for saying so, but I also find it hard to believe that the two of you happen to be Facebook friends."

He blinked again but said nothing. Then he shrugged. "Believe what you want."

"If you killed Holden and Tanaka to prevent their investigation, why'd you kill David Parker? He was just a reporter. He didn't do anything to you."

Petrovich shrugged. "I needed a distraction. You could have made a career bringing down a religious serial killer. Instead, you continued investigating four pieces of shit who died nine years ago. Why?"

"I like shit."

Petrovich smiled and then laughed until he started coughing.

"You ever heard of a man named The Wolf?" I asked.

Petrovich drew in a breath. "Heard of him, yes. Work for him, no."

"Who do you work for?"

"I own a business," he said. "I suppose I work for myself."

"Does the Wolf scare you so much that you'd lie to me protect him?"

"Very little scares me anymore, so no."

He looked sincere, although I didn't know how much stock I could put in the words of a man who had admitted to killing nine people. I didn't know how the prosecutors would approach this, but I had hoped for something more, some bit of understanding. Instead, I was left with nothing. More and more, that's all this job left me with.

"Thank you for your time, Mr. Petrovich. A lot of people will be in to talk to you today. I'd appreciate it if you didn't mention that I let you call your wife."

"Of course," he said, nodding deeply. "Thank you for that. There is one murder you haven't asked me about, though."

"Which one is that?"

He looked at me in the eye, not saying anything for at least ten seconds. "I don't know her name, but I think you know the woman. She was watching your house."

My heart began to thud. "Gloria Johnson. My wife was charged with her murder."

Petrovich held my gaze. "It was never personal. I needed you distracted so I could complete my work."

I lowered my voice. "You killed her and framed my wife?"

"Yes," he said. "I watched your house and stole a van similar to the one your wife drove. I covered the license plate with mud, shot the woman in front of your house, put a red scarf over my head and drove off as quickly as I could. The witnesses saw the scarf and made their own inferences. Outside your neighborhood, I ran the light and caused an accident so there would be photographic evidence."

My hands trembled, and my breath caught in my throat. "My wife is in jail because of you. Child Protective Services took my children because of you."

"I'm sorry. That was never my intent."

Almost more than anything in the world, I wanted to wrap my fingers around his throat and squeeze.

"Where's the van and the gun?"

"The long term parking lot at the airport. It should still be there."

I turned off the recording. I felt a lot of things at that moment—confusion, frustration, hope—more than anything else, though, I felt rage pouring through me. My vision tunneled on him. Heat rose to my skin. It took everything I had not to cross the room and punch him.

"You had better hope that van's still there because if it's not, I'm going to finish the job I started last night."

"For both of our sakes, then, I hope you find it."

I turned and left, already on the phone to Captain Bowers. He answered quickly.

"Mike, it's Ash. I need you to clear an hour for me. We've got a lot to discuss."

Chapter 32

On my way downtown, I called Susan Mercer to request that she meet me in Captain Bowers' office for a debriefing. Things moved quickly once I got there. I played Bowers and Susan the recording of my interview, and they went to work.

Susan called the US Attorney's office to let them know she planned to amend the charges against Petrovich, and Bowers called the Indianapolis Airport Police Department to ask them to search their long-term parking lot for a red minivan matching Petrovich's description.

My legs practically itched. I wanted to go out and search for the van myself, but with my wife in jail for that murder, this had to be airtight. That meant I needed to stay far away from it to limit even the presumption of bias in the investigators. Bowers said he'd call me when they had news, so I took my cell phone and rode the elevator down to the ground level. Already, the sun beat down on the sidewalk outside, turning the concrete and buildings around me into a great heat well. I didn't care. I needed to move.

I walked all the way around the building once and then hung a left on Market Street to walk toward Monument Circle in the center of town. Even in summer, school groups surrounded the Soldiers and Sailors monument as their teachers lectured about the importance of the common soldier in the civil war. Cars slowly traversed the brick street around the monument.

I went to a sandwich shop and bought a bottle of water to settle my stomach and then walked to a bench in front of Chase Tower. As much as I tried, I couldn't stop my feet from bouncing. The woman beside me got up and left, probably thinking I looked like a meth addict. After half an hour of nervous waiting, my phone rang. It was Mike Bowers.

"Tell me we've got good news," I said, not giving Bowers time to say anything.

"We got good news," he said. "Airport police found the van. We're waiting on a search warrant now, but there's a bright red shawl on the front seat and mud covering the license plate in back."

That was it, then. I felt as if I could breathe for the first time in several days. I'd have my wife back.

"Thank you, Mike."

He cleared his throat. "Hang in there. I'll keep you updated."

I thanked him again and then hung up. I walked back to my office. Though I tried to focus on work, I couldn't think about anything but Hannah.

An hour after his original call, Bowers called me again to let me know they had gotten into the car and found a firearm stashed under the front seat. Once they matched it to the rounds found in Gloria Johnson's body, we'd have everything we needed for a very, very strong case against Petrovich.

I called Hannah's lawyers and told them what had happened. They would contact the Hamilton County Prosecutor's office about having the charges dropped. It might take a day, but at least that part of our nightmare was over. I wished them luck and thanked them.

After that, I called the law firm representing Anita Cruz, the mother of Joseph and Cesar Cruz, to let them know we had made an arrest in her sons' murders and that we would begin exhuming their bodies from the city-owned cemetery so she could give them a more appropriate burial at home. Given everything that had transpired between us, I didn't expect her to call me back, and she didn't.

I closed a case, but it didn't leave me feeling very good. Most of the time, I had a cathartic moment at the end when things made sense. I didn't have that here. My original victims—the four boys in the park—died because they preyed upon those they considered weak. They cheated, they lied, they hurt everyone they came across. I didn't know how I felt about the death penalty, but the world was a better place without them. I felt the same about Bill Taylor. He and his partner hurt those people they took oaths to protect. Kristen Tanaka and Charles Holden died because they did their jobs well. David Parker and Gloria Johnson died to prop up an illusion. It was all pointless.

My job had always taken a lot out on me, but it also gave me so much in return. Now, though, I felt empty.

It took three hours and the threat of a major civil lawsuit to get my wife out of the Hamilton County jail, but once we walked outside, I held her in the parking lot for almost ten minutes as she cried against me. Immediately after that, we drove to her sister's house so she could see the kids.

That violated the protective order issued on behalf of the Hamilton County Child Protective Services, but I didn't care. Nothing in the world could have kept my wife from hugging her children. We stayed there until night fell and then afterwards. Hannah tucked the kids into bed, and then we drove home, knowing we'd have them back soon.

Over the next few days, Hannah spent more time at her sister's house with the kids than she did at home. Unfortunately, the family court system moved slower than the criminal court system. When our lawyers contacted CPS, they claimed they still needed to conduct their own independent investigation into the events, after which we would have a formal hearing before a judge.

I welcomed that day; as much as I appreciated and

respected the work CPS performed, they had leapt to conclusions here that didn't match the facts. Hannah and I weren't bad parents, we didn't abuse our children, and we never knowingly exposed them to anything dangerous. The whole situation sucked.

At work, things returned to some degree of normalcy. Detectives from our professional standards division conducted a two-day investigation into my shooting of Petrovich, ultimately calling it a righteous shoot. I got my gun and badge back. I also met with a psychiatrist, but mostly that meant filling out paperwork. Aside from that, I went to meetings, talked to other detectives, and filled out paperwork, doing the kind of work that helped a major bureaucracy run efficiently and well.

My break ended five days after my interrogation of Petrovich. It was a Monday when I got the call, and I was sitting in my office, having just left a morning briefing with the department's other division heads. Before answering, I glanced at the caller ID.

Rodriguez, H.

I hadn't expected a call from the Coroner's office, so I was a little surprised.

"Dr. Rodriguez," I said, upon picking up the phone. "What can I do for you?"

"Like you asked, I had four bodies exhumed a couple of days ago. I need to talk to you about them."

"Okay, sure," I said, taking a breath. "Their case is closed, though. We've got a confession. Guy knew details of their murder we didn't make public."

"I understand," said Rodriguez. "But there's something you need to see. Can you meet me in my office?"

I leaned forward to call up my schedule on my computer. I had some free time for the next hour. I had planned to spend that going over some memos from our gang intel unit, but I guess that could wait.

"Sure. I'll be over soon."

He thanked me and then hung up. The Coroner's office was about a mile and a half away. Realistically, I could have walked there without much issue, but it wouldn't have been a pleasant walk in this late summer heat. I took the elevator to the ground floor and drove to the Coroner's building in an unmarked cruiser I had signed out of the motor pool. Dr. Rodriguez waited for me beside the receptionist's desk and led me back to his office. He looked agitated and shifty. That wasn't like him. Inside his office, he handed me a pair of manila file folders.

"These are the autopsy reports from the young men whose bodies you had me exhume. I went through them to confirm that we had exhumed the correct bodies. These reports don't make us look good."

"Okay," I said, taking a deep breath and then sitting on one of the chairs in front of Hector's desk. "What's wrong with the reports?"

"They were half-assed for one thing," he said. "Coroner was a guy named Sam Garner, and he clearly didn't think too much of these victims. He didn't even bother taking a complete set of x-rays."

I cocked my head to the side. "Garner wasn't the best Coroner the city's ever had. Thankfully, he's gone now."

"Thankfully is right," he said, reaching into his desk once more. This time, he came out with an oversized envelop containing x-rays. He crossed the room and then hung two of them on the x-ray illuminator. "I took extensive x-rays of all four exhumed bodies. These are the tibia, the long bone beneath the knee, from Cesar Cruz. The other victims have similar features. Do you know the background of these four young men?"

"They're Hispanic, and they grew up in New Jersey. They're pretty well off, from what I gather," I said, tilting my head to the side. "Beyond that, I'm not sure what you're asking."

Hector nodded and drew in a deep breath before turning on the illuminator.

"That's what I thought. See those opaque transverse lines in the metaphyses of the bone?" he asked, tapping the x-ray near some white lines running from one side of the bone to the other. To me, they looked like scratches.

"I don't know what half those words you used mean," I said, "but I see the lines."

Hector nodded emphatically. "Okay, the metaphyses is part of the long bone that contains the growth plate. When a kid gets everything he needs growing up, the long bones will keep growing continually until their ends fuse. If he's malnourished or if he gets a serious infection or experiences major trauma, he's going to stop growing. If that infection clears up or if his diet improves, he'll start growing again, but there's going to be a line on his bones that indicates an increased mineral density. They're called Harris lines, and all four of the bodies I exhumed have them."

I started to get a sinking feeling in my gut. "I assume that's important. What are you saying? Bottom line it for me."

He turned off the illuminator and waited for me to look him in the eye. "I'm saying that I have no idea who these four bodies are, but they are not four wealthy kids from New Jersey."

Chapter 33

I gave myself a moment to process what he had just said before opening my mouth again.

"Anita Cruz gave us personal items owned by her sons and the other alleged victims. I know you haven't had a lot of time, but did you run the DNA on them?"

Hector nodded and closed his eyes. "I put a rush on it when you called and asked me to exhume the victims. The samples you provided, the items Mrs. Cruz gave you, matched their bodies. You should also know that none of them are biological siblings."

"If these guys aren't from New Jersey, what do we know about them?"

Hector exhaled and then shrugged. "They're probably not American or western European. Our safety net isn't bullet proof, but we've at least got a safety net. At the very least, they would have received a school lunch growing up. Beyond that, I don't have a lot. None of them have seemed to have any surgeries, but all of them have had broken bones. If I had to make a guess—and this is only a guess based on their skin tone and tattoos— I'd say they're very likely Central American. Beyond that, I don't know that I can tell you anything."

Something was wrong here. If we didn't have the DNA from Mrs. Cruz, I would think we had merely misidentified the bodies. She wanted us to think these were her sons, though. She and the other families could have adopted these boys from homes in Central America, but surely they would have said something by now. Beyond that, I didn't know what to think.

"Thanks," I said. "I don't know what this means yet, but you did good work on this."

"I feel like I just gave you a lot of work."

"You did, but it's good. I don't know what the hell's going on yet, but I will."

He wished me luck, and I stepped out of his office, already dialing Emilia's number on my phone. She answered on the third or fourth ring.

"Ash," she said. "How you doing?"

"Good," I said. "You on assignment right now?"

"Sort of. Homicide picked up a body last night. Stabbing at some kind of neighborhood party. We're still gathering details and interviewing witnesses. I'm assisting."

"Who's the primary on it?"

She paused for just a second. "Andy Wells."

I knew Andy, so I nodded. "Good. I'm going to give him a call and see if he can spare you. If he can't, I'll have another detective assigned to his team. I need you right now."

She paused, and when she spoke, I could hear the smile in her face. "I'm pretty sure telling me you need me right now constitutes sexual harassment, but I appreciate your interest."

"Very funny. I need you to start looking through adoption records in New Jersey for four names. Mark and Cesar Cruz, Jeremy Estrada, and Joseph Gomez."

She hesitated for just a second. "Aren't those the four assholes we just arrested Petrovich for murdering?"

"That's a more difficult question to answer than you probably realize," I said. "I need to find out if these guys were adopted. If not, we've got a situation."

"Couldn't you ask their families?"

"No. I'll brief you when I see you. This just got a little complicated."

I called Captain Bowers next and told him what Hector had discovered. He took it in and then told me to get down to his office to talk things through in person.

For the next three days, we worked almost around the

clock with officers from almost a dozen local and federal government agencies. Emilia couldn't find any documentation about an adoption in New Jersey or anywhere for the four boys. That gave us probable cause to investigate Anita Cruz as well as the parents of Jeremy Estrada and Joseph Gomez. It didn't take long for us to find that Dr. Rodriguez's discovery was a whole lot bigger than we realized.

Working with our federal law enforcement partners, it took us four days to get the pieces together. I called Anita Cruz on a Thursday afternoon from the homicide squad's conference room. A voice recorder captured the conversation in case we had to play it back in court later, but Captain Bowers, Paul and Emilia listened in on handsets anyway.

"So nice to hear from you, Lieutenant Rashid," said Mrs. Cruz.

"I understand your frustration," I said. "I apologize for how long this has taken us, but the process takes a lot of time and work. We've finally cleared all the bureaucratic hurdles preventing us from releasing your sons to you. To ensure that everything goes smoothly, I'll be on the same plane as your sons. You don't need to do anything but show up and fill out some paperwork at the airport. Our Coroner's office has your funeral home's information on file. They're already working with the mortuary staff to ensure that your sons are given respectful treatment."

She didn't say anything, but I could hear her breathe. "You people have been so awful to us this entire time. Do you have any idea what you've put me through? I wanted to bury my boys. That's all. Do you have any idea how hurtful it is to drag us through all this?"

I drew in a breath, pretending to be penitent. "I cannot express how sorry I am for your loss. I am deeply sorry for the difficulties you've faced. Our office just isn't accustomed to the interstate transfer of remains."

"For the next family, I hope you have learned."

I apologized again and then gave her the flight information. She and the other parents would meet me in the airport, at which point they could take custody of their sons' remains. She questioned whether I was the most appropriate choice to send, but I assured her that my department had already purchased the plane tickets.

"You're a real son of a bitch, Lieutenant Rashid," she said. "I hope you know that."

She slammed the phone down. I cocked my head to the side and hung up and then looked at Captain Bowers and Paul and Emilia. They hung up their own phones. Only Emilia smiled.

"She thinks you're a son of a bitch now," said Emilia, "just wait until she sees you in person."

Paul snorted and then tried to cover it up by coughing.

"Thanks, Emilia," I said. "I appreciate the encouragement."

"I meant that in the best possible way," she said, still grinning.

"Can we just get going?" asked Bowers. "I've got a lot of work to do today."

I turned my attention back to the phones and called the parents of Jeremy Estrada and Joseph Gomez. Both conversations went about as well as they had with Anita Cruz.

Things settled after that. Paul and Emilia went back to their regular assignments while Bowers and I confirmed arrangements in New Jersey. That night, I went home to be with my wife. The kids were still at their aunt and uncle's, but we had a hearing coming up on Monday. Four more days, and we'd get them back and put this entire nightmare behind us. When we went to bed, I held her all night. It felt good to have her back.

The next morning, I left the house at six to make my early morning flight. Since I didn't plan to stay overnight in New Jersey, I carried only a briefcase with a book, a laptop and documents necessary for the job ahead of me. Surprisingly, I didn't feel nervous for this. Instead, I felt excited. Maybe it made me an asshole, but I looked forward to seeing Anita Cruz's face as her entire world came crashing down on her.

Upon landing at the Newark airport after an uneventful, two-hour flight, a plainclothes airport police officer met me at the gate and led me to a conference room, where I met five middle-aged men and women. All had passed through a metal detector, so I knew none had a firearm. Anita Cruz stood up immediately upon seeing me. She tried to slap me, but I caught her wrist and shook my head. Her eyes smoldered, but she dropped her hand to her waist. Then I looked to the other parents to make sure they weren't converging on us.

"Mrs. Anita Cruz, Mr. And Mrs. Gomez, Mr. And Mrs. Estrada," I said, nodding to each of them in kind before settling my gaze on Cruz. "You are under arrest for the murder of John Does 1, 2, 3, and 4. You have the right to remain silent, but if you chose to speak, I can use whatever you tell me in court. You have the right to an attorney anytime I question you. If you can't afford an attorney, one will be provided for you. That clear?"

Mrs. Cruz took a step back. Mrs. Gomez brought her hands to her face and began crying. Both Mr. And Mrs. Estrada plopped down on the conference table chairs.

"In two hours, we will fly back to Indianapolis. Two air marshals will accompany us the entire time, so please don't do anything stupid," I said. I reached into my briefcase for a paper Susan Mercer had given me the day before. "This is an offer from our prosecutor's office that one of you will get to sign. When we get back to Indianapolis, we will talk to you individually. The first person to tell us the truth about what you've done and can identify our victims will be charged with four counts of manslaughter. We'll recommend fifteen years for each charge, but the sentences will be served concurrently. With good behavior, this lucky citizen will walk out of prison in eight to ten years. The rest of you will each be charged with four counts of felony murder. The minimum sentence for each count is 45 years, and we will push for consecutive sentences. You will never walk freely again. That's something to think about on the plane."

Almost before I finished speaking, Anita Cruz spoke up.

"I'll sign it now. Katherine and David Gomez spoke Spanish better than everyone else, so they hired the guys from the parking lot of a Home Depot in Indianapolis. Jacob and Missy Estrada provided the money. They talked me into everything. I didn't do anything wrong."

"You bitch," said Katherine Gomez. They all started shouting at each other and pointing fingers after that. I had the feeling we'd have a long flight back to Indianapolis. I let them go for a minute, but then I whistled to get their attention. They looked at me with expectant, pleading eyes.

"I probably should have mentioned that Anita Cruz is ineligible for the deal," I said, looking at her. "We tracked your ex-husband, Alonzo, down in prison. You didn't tell us you were once married to a money launderer. He already rolled on you, by the way. A hundred bucks in his commissary account, and he talked to us for almost two hours. He did not have nice things to say about you."

She opened her mouth to say something, but I ignored her and continued speaking.

"Before you guys all start speaking at once, here's what I already know: nine years ago, your four idiot sons signed a business deal with a company called TNT Enterprises. Unknown to them, TNT Enterprises was owned by a very temperamental, very powerful gangster from Chicago named the Wolf. When your idiot sons found out their partners at TNT sold drugs, they hired two police officers for protection and to help them blackmail their partners. Unfortunately, the Wolf and his employees at TNT gave the officers a better deal. As you can imagine, The Wolf was not pleased that his business partners would try to blackmail him. Given the opportunity, he would kill each of them.

"According to Alonzo Cruz, when Anita found out what happened, she came up with a plan to protect your sons. She would kill four people who looked like your boys and then tell the Wolf someone beat him to it. You with me so far?"

Anita glowered, but the rest of them gave me appropriately defeated looks.

"Anita then convinced Alonzo, her ex-husband, to hire a man named Aleksander Petrovich to torture and murder four young men who looked somewhat like your boys. Apparently Alonzo had washed some of Petrovich's money in the past. Petrovich cut off their hands and feet, ripped out their teeth, and beat their faces so badly we couldn't identify them. He then dumped their bodies in a park in Indianapolis. For nine years, we had no idea who they were, but then we matched them to missing person's reports you four filed in Chicago. You then gave us their personal items, so we could identify the victims by their DNA.

"At this point, I'm confident in my case against you. My interest is in discovering the identify of my victims. That's it. The first person to tell me gets the deal."

Anita looked behind her at the other parents and then back to me.

"If I'm going to prison, so is everyone else. They were just four Mexicans we found. They were probably illegals. Nobody knows who they are. That's why we hired them. Nobody would miss four Mexicans."

Mrs. Estrada started sobbing. Her husband held her. Mr. Gomez, though, cleared his throat.

"Tell them, honey," he said.

Mrs. Gomez looked at her husband, her eyebrows arched. "Are you sure?"

He nodded. "Yeah. Take the deal. I'll be fine."

She looked at me and then drew in a breath. "My husband and I saved their wallets. They're in a safety deposit box in a bank in Trenton."

I looked at Mrs. Gomez and then to her husband, nodding. "Congratulations. You two are the least horrible people in the room. Once we get back to Indianapolis, I'll call the police in Trenton and have them get started on the safety deposit box. If you told me the truth, we'll get the paperwork going at that time."

Mrs. Gomez slumped against her husband. Both of them started crying.

"I'm not going to jail," said Anita. "What would you give me for our sons?"

"Shut up, Anita," said Mr. Estrada, taking a step forward. I looked at him and shook my head. He held up his hands and then took a step back.

"Our sons are alive. I'll tell you where they are," she said, this time more fervently. "That's got to be worth something, right?"

"Now that you bring your sons up, I feel like I should have led with this: we've been investigating each of you and your finances for the past several days. Our partners at the FBI tracked money from each of your accounts to a bank in Bankok, Thailand. At the request of the FBI, the State Department exerted pressure on that bank to tell us where the deposits were being withdrawn. Thai authorities picked up your sons in Phuket. After their extradition hearings, a Federal Marshall will escort them from Thailand to the United States, where they will face trial for dozens of sexual assaults, four murders, and several counts of conspiracy. They're alive, but they'll never leave prison."

Anita covered her mouth. "What do you want, Lieutenant? What can I give you to make this go away?"

"From you?" I asked. She nodded. "You hired a murderer to torture four innocent men. I can't imagine the kind of pain they went through before they died. It makes me sick to my stomach to think about what you people did to them. And you did it because you thought you could get away with it. You thought nobody would care about four Mexican boys, four illegals as you put it. You're one of the most vile persons I've ever met. Few things in my professional life have given me as much satisfaction as knowing that you'll spend the rest of your life in a maximum security prison. So sorry. You've already given me everything I could ever want from you."

She broke down in tears. Apparently I was wrong about her already having given me everything I wanted because I found that vaguely satisfying, too.

Chapter 34

True to her word, Katherine Gomez's safety deposit box contained four wallets from four young men. My real victims came to the United States from Honduras. They didn't have green cards or Visas, they didn't come on a plane, and they didn't have money to hire expensive lawyers. They came in the night. They came illegally. They broke the law, but they didn't do it with malice; they wanted a better life for themselves and their families back home. Nothing they did earned them the deaths dealt to them.

Once the plane touched down in Indianapolis, and I transferred my arrestees to deputies from the Sheriff's department, I had only one task left, one I usually dreaded. Now, it felt right to do it. Emilia Rios and I spent the next two days on the phone. Since she had grown up in a Spanish-speaking household, Emilia took charge. We must have interviewed a hundred people, trying to track down our victims' families. Eventually, we got lucky. A parish priest in Chicago called a priest in Mexico City, who called a priest in San Salvador, El Salvador, who called a priest in a tiny village in a mountain range in the west of Honduras.

I didn't know the village's name, but Emilia showed me pictures. It was beautiful and sad. Lush vegetation crawled up the sides of the nearby hills, while a dirt road meandered beside rickety wooden homes with grass and reed roofs. Morning mist draped over the valleys and lowlands. Chickens pecked at the dirt beside one of the homes.

None of the houses had satellite dishes or television antennas. I couldn't see a telephone poll or utility line anywhere. It looked like something from a movie, like some impossible place that couldn't exist in our modern world. Our victims had grown up there. They should have died there as old men, surrounded by those they most loved. Instead, they came to the United States, where they were never given a chance.

Emilia and the local priest set up the call. I preferred doing next-of-kin notifications in person, but this was a special circumstance. Since the village didn't have electricity or phone lines, we'd communicate via an app on the priest's cell phone and Emilia's tablet. For the entire hour prior to our call, I could barely sit still. I fixed my tie at least eight times, and I straightened my shirt even more.

When the time came, Emilia and I sat at my desk with her iPad propped up in front of us. For a few moments, the FaceTime app was blank as it called the priest in Honduras, but then a grainy picture appeared as Father Damien answered.

Emilia and Father Damien did most of the talking. I could speak Spanish reasonably well, but the two of them spoke with native fluency and speed, so I had a hard time keeping up. After a moment, Emilia leaned back on her chair and looked at me.

"The floor's yours, boss," she said. I leaned closer to the iPad so they could see me. Unfortunately, I couldn't see a lot of them, so I asked the priest to pan the camera around. He did. The people to whom I spoke were in a small chapel with white walls. It looked as if half the village had turned out. A frail looking elderly couple sat in the front pew, holding hands. Beside them sat a man and woman who looked as if they were in their early sixties. The row behind them looked similar, as did the one behind that. A dozen children sat on the hardwood floor, while the adults stuck to the pews. I looked at Emilia and lowered my voice.

"Who are all these people?"

"Parents, siblings, wives, and children. Our victims left behind a lot. They've been waiting a long time for this call."

I had done a lot of next-of-kin notifications, but never one quite like this. After nine years, they had to know their loved one had died, but now it would become real. I didn't know how they'd react. I gulped air and jumped in, then.

"*Buenos días*," I said. "*Yo soy* Ash Rashid. *Soy un oficial de policía…*"

I spoke for almost twenty minutes with Emilia and the priest translating where needed. Despite the children in the room, I didn't hold back. I told them the truth as delicately and kindly as I could. Nearly everyone in the room cried when I finished. A couple of them, older women mostly, started talking to me at once. I recognized a few words, but I couldn't understand them through the tears.

"I'm sorry," I said. "*Lo siento. Lo siento mucho.*"

Emilia a hand on my elbow and leaned toward me. "They're not sad. They're thanking you. They're saying you brought their sons home."

For just a moment, I held my breath. Something I had been holding inside me for a long time broke. The anger, the cynicism, the sense of righteousness I felt upon arresting Anita Cruz and her co-conspirators melted away.

In that moment, I knew that I didn't do this job for them. I didn't do it to lock people up. I did it for the people on that video screen, those men and women the rest of the world forgot.

In the scheme of things, I didn't make a whole lot of difference to the world. If I died tomorrow, people around me would notice, some would even grieve, but then they'd go on with their lives. I wasn't important. I didn't matter to the world. Even my job didn't matter. Every time I arrested a drug dealer, a murderer, or a predator who would hurt those around him, another would rise to take his place. No matter what I did, I couldn't stop that. For so long, I had felt like Sisyphus, pushing a rock up a hill only to have it fall back again. I felt like I was wasting my time.

Those crying mothers, sisters, wives, children, brothers, and fathers, told me otherwise. Maybe I couldn't change the world, but I could make it better for some of the people in it. For me and for now, that was enough.

Emilia and I stayed in the office for a few minutes after that phone call, mostly to catch up, but she had other work to do. Hannah and I had a hearing that afternoon with a juvenile court judge, but it felt like a formality at this point. Hannah's arrest served as the sole reason and justification for taking our kids into the custody of child services. Without it, they had no reason to keep our kids from us. We'd get them back and soon. I missed them.

I thought for a moment and then called our human resources office. I had almost nine weeks of vacation stored up. Hannah would probably get sick of me if I took all the time off at once, but a couple of weeks alone with my family sounded nice. I took two and then called my wife. She answered before the phone even finished ringing once.

"Hey sweetheart," I said. "Care to guess who you're going to see a lot more of very soon?"

She paused, but when she spoke, I could hear the smile in her voice. "You're not naked beneath a trench coat on the front porch are you? Because I just got out of the shower and haven't put any clothes on yet. That'd be amazing timing."

"I'm sorry I'm not there to see that," I said. "But no, I'm not naked on the front porch. I just did something good today, something I'm proud of. I want to celebrate. I want to take you and the kids somewhere."

It almost sounded as if she sighed contentedly. I couldn't tell, though, because my phone beeped, signaling an incoming call. I didn't bother to look at it to see who it came from.

"I'm glad. You deserve to feel good," she said. "Plus, you've kind of been a cranky asshole lately. We all need a break from that guy sometimes."

"That stings," I said, allowing a smile to form on my lips. "I don't think you've ever called me a cranky asshole before."

"Prison changes a woman. Apparently, it makes me swear more often. If you come home soon, I might still be naked. If so, I'm pretty sure I can smooth over your hurt feelings. Maybe I'll even say a few other dirty words to you if you'd like."

My phone buzzed again. I pulled it from my ear to look at the caller ID. Unfortunately, it came from Captain Bowers, which meant I needed to call him back.

"Give me about half an hour. I've got to talk to somebody. After that, I'll see if I can find a trench coat so I can fulfill your naked-guy-on-the-porch fantasy."

"You truly know how to speak to my heart," she said. "I love you. I'll see you soon."

"I love you, too," I said, smiling. "See you at home."

I hung up, feeling pretty damn close to giddy. I hoped I didn't have to talk to him long, but I returned Captain Bowers' phone call. He told me he needed to see me in his office immediately and didn't make it seem as if I had any choice in the matter.

I jogged to his building and then rode up their elevator to the executive-level floor. Rich wood paneling covered the walls. The wood, glass, and steel furniture in the waiting room looked several steps above the utility grade stuff found in most city office buildings. I flashed my badge to the uniformed officer manning the receptionist's desk and then walked down a long hallway to Bowers' office.

Inside, I found Captain Bowers and Special Agent Kevin Havelock, the agent-in-charge of the local FBI field office. Havelock had at least a day's worth of hair on his chin, and the wrinkles on his shirt made him look as if he had rolled around on the ground before coming in. As I walked inside the room, he stood up and stretched his hand toward me. I shook it.

"Rough night, Agent Havelock?"

"Yeah," he said. "We need to talk. I have a job for you. Your department's already signed off on it if you agree."

I glanced at Bowers. He nodded, so I cocked my head to the side. "I'll listen to whatever you ask, but I just took the next ten days off. My family's been through a lot lately. I need the vacation."

"You'd have to start immediately, but it's important," said Havelock, closing his eyes. "I think you'll see why."

Bowers gestured to a pair of chairs in front of his desk. I sat and listened to Havelock's proposition. As much as it would hurt my family, within seconds, I knew I'd agree to the assignment. Havelock didn't give me a lot of details yet, but I had a necessary job ahead of me, one only I could do. When Havelock finished speaking, I told him I had a couple of things to do that day, but then I'd come into the FBI's field office for a full briefing.

As I drove home from that short meeting, a thousand and one questions bounced through my head. Unfortunately, I didn't have an answer for a single one. At the house, I parked my police cruiser in the garage and went inside.

"Honey?" asked Hannah from somewhere upstairs.

"Yeah, it's me," I said, walking into the kitchen.

"Are you alone?"

"Yeah, I'm alone," I said again.

"We've got less than an hour before we meet the

lawyers and have our hearing, so drop your pants and come upstairs for a quickie. We'll worry about the romance later."

She probably expected me to jokingly sprint up the stairs, but I couldn't. Agent Havelock had just taken the joy out of the day. I kept my pants on and climbed the stairs to our bedroom on the second floor. Hannah lay under the comforter. She smiled and bit her lower lip when she saw me.

"You're a little overdressed," she said, leaning forward and motioning me toward her, "but I can work with that."

"Something just came up," I said, staying near the door. She winked and then looked toward my waist. I laughed just a little, grateful for the comic relief. "I love you dearly. You're the most beautiful woman in the world, and I'd love to spend some time with you, but we need to talk."

The mischievous glint left her eyes and her smile disappeared. She sat straighter, nodding and holding the blanket over her chest.

"Are you all right?"

"I'm fine," I said. "I just had a meeting with an FBI agent. One of their agents infiltrated a suspected Islamic terror cell in Indianapolis approximately four months ago. His body washed up on the shores of the Ohio River near Madison, Indiana this morning."

She covered her mouth. "Oh."

"Yeah. They want me to go undercover and infiltrate the same group and see what I can find."

For a moment, Hannah kept her hand on her mouth. Her eyes blinked rapidly as she shook her head. "No. They killed somebody already. I don't care what they're doing. You're not getting involved. The FBI will just have to find somebody else, somebody trained for this sort of thing. Besides, it would take months to infiltrate a group like that. You can't just walk up to them and say 'death to

America!' and hope they accept you. I'm not letting this happen."

I looked at the carpet and then drew in a breath. "I already agreed. I'm sorry."

"Then you're going to tell them that you changed your mind," she said. "And that's final. Your career has always been your thing. I've never asked you to consider my feelings, but I need you to consider them now. I can't do this without you. I don't want you getting hurt."

I looked at her. She had beautiful brown eyes. When I saw those eyes on a normal morning, they looked kind. Now, they had a hardness about them I rarely saw.

"The group is led by Nassir Haddad. That's why they think I can get in."

"Oh, crap," said Hannah. The color left her face. The back of her skull hit the headboard behind her. "Did you tell your sister yet?"

"No," I said, shaking my head and taking a step forward. "And you can't, either. Nothing I've said in this room can leave this room."

"Rana's my friend. She's your sister. She deserves to know the FBI thinks her husband is a terrorist."

"Maybe she does, but we can't tell her. I'm going to work this case and see what's going on. The FBI thinks Nassir became radicalized after Rachel overdosed. That's how it happens sometimes. You lose a child and…"

I let my voice trail to nothing. Hannah ran her hands through her hair. The comforter fell from her chest, and she absentmindedly covered herself with a sheet. "This is a nightmare. Our family is going through a nightmare. Nassir's nuts, maybe, but he's a good man."

She was right. That was what bothered me the most. Nassir said crazy things sometimes—he sent me pictures of young single Islamic women because he thought I should take a second wife, he asked me to arrest a product tester at his grocery store for asking if he'd like to sample bacon—but he was fundamentally a good man. He wouldn't hurt anyone, and yet we had a dead FBI agent who infiltrated a group Nassir allegedly ran.

"If I don't look into this, the FBI will come after him in some other way. People will get hurt, maybe even people we know."

Hannah nodded, her eyes distant. When she focused on me, that distance evaporated, replaced by an intense clarity.

"But if you look into this, you've got to understand something: you're not going to be looking into random drug dealers or thieves. You're going to be investigating members of our community, our friends, our family. There's no going back after that."

I drew in a breath and nodded. "I know."

"I hope so," she said, holding the blanket to her chest as she leaned forward. "I'm going to get dressed. We've got to pick up the kids."

She climbed out of bed, and I watched her put on clothes. I had made it my goal to act so my kids could be proud of me, even if they couldn't understand everything I did. I wondered what they'd think if they knew I planned to investigate their kooky Uncle Nassir as a suspected terrorist. It didn't matter anyway, though, because I wouldn't find anything. Nassir wouldn't hurt anybody.

But then, if I really believed that, I wondered why I felt so damn scared all of a sudden.

Enjoy this book? You can make a big difference in my career

Reviews are the lifeblood of an author's career. I'm not exaggerating when I say they're the single best way I can get attention for my books. I'm not famous, I don't have the money for extravagant advertising campaigns, and I no longer have a major publisher behind me.

I do have something major publishers don't have, something they would kill to get:

Committed, loyal readers.

With millions of books in the world, your honest reviews and recommendations help other readers find me.

If you enjoyed the book you just read, I would be extraordinarily grateful if you could spend five minutes to leave a review on Amazon, Barnes and Noble, Goodreads, or anywhere else you review books. A review can be as long or as short as you'd like it to be, so please don't feel that you have to write something long.

Thank you so much!

If you liked *No Room for Good Men*, you'll love *Sleeper Cell*, the next thrilling novel in the Ash Rashid series!

Nothing is more dangerous than family

Police find the body find in the Ohio River. The victim's wrists and feet are bound, and he has a single gunshot wound to the forehead. The locals are baffled until they get an ID.

Lieutenant Ash Rashid doesn't want the assignment, but he knows he has to take it. Because it's a family matter. The dead man was an FBI agent who had infiltrated a suspected terror cell run by Ash's brother-in-law.

Ash investigates and dives into a world in which the most familiar faces are the most dangerous. Every new clue and every new insight he makes leads him closer to his murderer. They also lead him closer to home.

But even as Ash searches, long-laid plans are coming to fruition. Something deadly is coming, and Ash is the only person who can stop it. With the clock ticking, Ash will have to use every skill he possesses to find a mastermind intent on killing as many innocent people as he can. If he doesn't, those he loves most will pay the biggest price.

Available now at major booksellers!

Stay in touch with Chris

As much as I enjoy writing, I like hearing from readers even more. If you want to keep up with my world, there are a couple of ways you can do that.

First and easiest, I've got a mailing list. If you join, you'll receive an email whenever I have a new novel out or when I run sales. You can join that by going to this address:

http://www.indiecrime.com/mailinglist.html

If my mailing list doesn't appeal to you, you can also connect with me on Facebook here:

http://www.facebook.com/ChrisCulverbooks

And you can always email me at chris@indiecrime.com. I love receiving email!

About the Author

Chris Culver is the *New York Times* bestselling author of the Ash Rashid series and other novels. After graduate school, Chris taught courses in ethics and comparative religion at a small liberal arts university in southern Arkansas. While there and when he really should have been grading exams, he wrote *The Abbey*, which spent sixteen weeks on the *New York Times* bestsellers list and introduced the world to Detective Ash Rashid.

Chris has been a storyteller since he was a kid, but he decided to write crime fiction after picking up a dog-eared, coffee-stained paperback copy of Mickey Spillane's *I, the Jury* in a library book sale. Many years later, his wife, despite considerable effort, still can't stop him from bringing more orphan books home. He lives with his family near St. Louis.